"Patricia Rice's historicals are deliciously witty, sexy, and fun. . . . Never has the battle of the sexes been more charming than when the irresistible force of a Malcolm woman slams into the immovable object of a stubborn duke!"　　　　　　　—Mary Jo Putney

Praise for the novels of Patricia Rice

The Trouble with Magic

"Rice is a marvelously talented author who skillfully combines pathos with humor in a stirring, sensual romance that shows the power of love is the most wondrous gift of all. Think of this memorable story as a present you can open again and again."
　　　　　　　—*Romantic Times* (Top Pick)

"Rice's third enchanting book about the Malcolm sisters is truly spellbinding."　　　　　　　—*Booklist*

continued . . .

This Magic
Moment

❦

Patricia Rice

A SIGNET BOOK

SIGNET
Published by New American Library, a division of
Penguin Group (USA) Inc., 375 Hudson Street,
New York, New York 10014, U.S.A.
Penguin Books Ltd, 80 Strand,
London WC2R 0RL, England
Penguin Books Australia Ltd, 250 Camberwell Road,
Camberwell, Victoria 3124, Australia
Penguin Books Canada Ltd, 10 Alcorn Avenue,
Toronto, Ontario, Canada M4V 3B2
Penguin Books (NZ), cnr Airborne and Rosedale Roads,
Albany, Auckland 1310, New Zealand

Penguin Books Ltd, Registered Offices:
80 Strand, London WC2R 0RL, England

First published by Signet, an imprint of New American Library,
a division of Penguin Group (USA) Inc.

First Printing, August 2004
10 9 8 7 6 5 4 3 2 1

ACKNOWLEDGMENTS

As always, to my brainstorming partners, who know when I've gone too far or not far enough: Thanks for the creative pushes when I need them most.

And thanks to Katherine Bernardi, whose devious mind has again created the magical titles that elude me. Finish a book!

To my wonderful husband: Thanks for enduring my madness with such loving patience. Without you, I'd have no heroes.

Prologue

"Beware of the deep hole under the boards, Christina! It's cold and dark."

Christina Malcolm Childe, nine-year-old daughter of the Marquess of Hampton, hesitated on the verge of leaping to the top of a stack of old bricks and boards. She could hear her sisters and cousins running through the woods near her grandmother's home in a game of hide-and-seek—a game she fully intended to win by climbing into the oak tree above the old boards.

Seeking the source of the warning cry, she located an aura forming over the stack of bricks. Though she'd seen them often enough, auras had never spoken to her before. "Who are you?" she called in fascination, then felt a trifle foolish talking to an indistinct rainbow of color.

To her utter amazement, the aura did what no other had ever done—brightened into visibility. She stared at the simply dressed little girl sitting upon the old boards. She could see the outline of trees through the girl's transparent clothing.

"Who are you?" Christina repeated softly, more

afraid she'd scare the apparition away than fearing her manifestation.

"Beware!" the girl cried anxiously before fading away.

Stunned, Christina stood there a while longer, watching as the colors faded more slowly than the form.

When even the aura was gone, she raced back down the wooded path with a shriek of exhilaration, shouting "Mama!" at the top of her lungs.

Hermione, Marchioness of Hampton, appeared immediately. Plump from the birth of her latest daughter, she still glided with speed across the grass at any call from her children, trailing scarves and hat ribbons in her wake.

Her straw hat flew off her head and tumbled into the bushes as Christina ran into her arms. "There now, child, what's the matter? Have you skinned your knee again?"

"I saw a ghost, Mama!" Christina shouted excitedly. "Come see. Maybe she'll return. She says there is a big hole in the woods!"

Unquestioning, Hermione shouted at the bevy of nursemaids attempting to keep up with the running, laughing children. Ordering them to gather the girls out of harm's way, she took Christina's hand. "Show me where, dear."

Several of the girls escaped the maids to run after Christina, but Hermione shooed them off.

Worried by that action from her usually laughing mother, who always had time to hug a child, Christina clung to her hand. "It's just a ghost, Mama," she tried to reassure her. "I know they're there. I see their auras all the time. I've just never seen a whole ghost before. Or *talked* to one," she added with the irrepressible excitement of discovery.

"Spirits appear for a reason, dear. Show me where you saw her."

Puzzled that her mother seemed afraid when she'd always taught them that spirits were harmless, Christina tried to remember the path she'd taken. Old rabbit paths weren't easy to follow, but she'd crashed through the shrubbery just recently, so she could find the broken twigs. She liked playing in the woods and never got lost.

"In here, Mama. See, that's where I wiggled between the tree trunks." She slipped between the two slender trees and past the thicket of briars to stand in the overgrown clearing she'd roamed earlier. The bricks and boards really were the only place where a tree wasn't. She hadn't explored her grandmother's woods since she was a little girl. She hated to reveal her new hiding place and hoped the others hadn't followed.

Christina turned expectantly to her mother, then realized the marchioness couldn't fit between tree trunks and briars as she could. "It's all right, Mama. The ghost isn't here anymore."

"That's an old well, Christina," Hermione called worriedly from behind the thicket of brush. "The boards could fall in, and we would never see you again. Come along out of there. I'll have someone fill it up before you get hurt."

"I want to stay and see if the ghost returns, Mama.

May I, please? She's just about my age, and she knew my name. I've never seen a ghost before. Maybe she wants to play."

Hermione set her plump mouth in a grim line that Christina recognized far too well since her antics tended to bring such lines to her mother's lips more often than any of her sisters' did.

"Come along out of there, dear. That was most likely your great-great-great-aunt Iona. She's given her warning, so you won't be seeing her again. You may read about her in the library, if you wish."

Christina didn't wish. She'd rather talk to a ghost than read about one. "Why can't I see her again?" she asked, digging in her heels. She was dying to know about an Aunt Iona who appeared as a ghost, but more than that, she wanted to talk to an apparition again.

"She was the last Malcolm to see spirits," Hermione answered. "And she was lost in these woods when she was about your age. It's quite possible that old well is where she died. If so, she has stayed here to warn you, and now that she's completed her task, she'll return to where she belongs. It's up to you to act on her warning. Come away now."

Eyes widening as she comprehended that ghosts were *real* dead people, Christina followed her mother out of the woods, casting glances over her shoulder in hopes of seeing her aunt Iona again. Poor little girl, dying here all alone.

Christina wanted to weep at the thought that Iona had no one to play with while waiting so carefully to warn others. She hoped the little girl had gone home to her mother now that she'd done her duty, but Christina really wished she could have talked to her longer.

Just think of all the fascinating things a ghost could tell her! Her imagination could scarcely take in all the possibilities. Had it hurt to fall down the well? Had Iona been scared? Wouldn't she like to hear about her family? Did she have other secret hiding places as Christina did?

"Why can't I see more ghosts, Mama?" she asked, desperate to know how she could speak to the other auras she often saw about their home.

Hermione hesitated, threw a glance back at the woods, then shook her head. "I don't know, dear. Perhaps they come out only when you need them. Study the auras you see and heed their warnings when they speak."

Christina didn't see any danger in a bunch of old bricks and boards. But talking to ghosts would be exciting. She would always have friends then, and that would be a lovely gift indeed.

One

"It's all written 'ere in the mortgage, Your Grace, signed by your late father—may his soul rest in peace—in his own hand." Heavily bewigged, garbed in an opulent blue satin coat with gold braiding and a waistcoat that could not button over his big belly, Aloysius Carthage waved a thick document as if it were a sword.

The document was more dangerous than a sword if the merchant did not lie. Harrison Winston Somerset Beaufort Winchester, Duke of Sommersville, until recently styled Lord Harry, gripped his elegant walking stick behind the tails of his London-tailored coat and gritted his teeth as Carthage continued his speech.

"Yer father said I'm to take the estate in trade for the money 'e owes if 'e don't come up with the blunt by Michaelmas next," Carthage proclaimed.

Aristocratically handsome in the English manner of fair coloring, square jaw, and sturdy though not excessive height, the new duke gazed out at the soot-covered stones of the town house across the square, impatiently listening to the spiel of a man he scarcely knew. To all present the duke looked a man of leisure, a city gentleman of taste and refinement without a care in the world.

Inside, he boiled with fury, like Vesuvius prepared to erupt.

"Sommersville is *entailed*," he said coldly, not bothering to engage the eye of the merchant rattling his faradiddle. He knew Carthage owned an estate in the neighborhood of Sommersville. He could not imagine why the man thought to take advantage of the newness of Harry's role as duke to perpetrate this obvious fraud. "The estate cannot be sold. You have no legal right to make this claim."

In truth, he knew nothing about law or rights. He simply knew that his father's estate had passed through generations of Winchesters dating back to the Conqueror's time, growing from an inconsequential barony to fifteen thousand acres of imposing ducal estates. He might not be the son who'd been raised to estate duties, but by Jove, he would not be the son who lost the whole damned property his ancestors had spent generations accumulating.

Could a duke keep his title if he had no estate? he wondered irrelevantly. He'd never possessed any inclination for the title, given that it would mean losing his father, older brother, and his brother's progeny to gain it.

But that was exactly what had happened. At least, his brother had no progeny to lose. Harry almost wished Edward had an infant son to inherit. He would fare far better as legal executor than as owner of fifteen thousand prime acres of Sussex. Mortgaged acres, evidently.

The late duke might have been eccentric, but Harry had loved his father and knew he wasn't a wastrel who would gamble away his livelihood. Or hadn't been, last he'd seen of him. Maybe he should have visited Sussex more often. His father had refused to come to London, and Harry kept promising to visit, yet seldom did. They had their differences, as any family had, but he refused to believe his father had gone completely mad.

He stifled a gaping pit of regret beneath anger.

He wished the old man could be here now to explain this tomfoolery. And if his older brother could just walk in and punch Carthage in the beak for his presumptuousness, he'd never taunt Edward again for his mulish preference for rural life.

As it was, he'd never taunt his brother again, unless he talked to his grave. Given the family predilections, he might be reduced to that soon. Losing brother and father in the same fatal accident was enough to drive a man to seeking lost souls.

But Harry had an image to uphold if he meant to keep his position in politics, so he wouldn't be talking to graves anytime soon.

"Your Grace."

Harry ignored the unctuous voice of the solicitor whom Carthage had brought with him, in favor of gazing at the house across the square.

He was finally rewarded with the familiar sight of a golden-haired sylph dashing down the front steps, lifting her full skirt to reveal slim legs garbed in men's boots and what looked suspiciously like the glitter of a buckle on a pair of knee breeches. Knowing the wretch, he supposed she did it apurpose to mock him. Instead of waving at his window, she checked over her shoulder to be certain no one followed—as someone certainly should have—then danced down the street to where a cart and horse waited.

His betrothed, Lady Christina Malcolm Childe—beautiful and cheerful as a sunny day, undisciplined as the worst-mannered street urchin. He couldn't help smiling every time he looked at her.

He allowed the smile to play on his face as he turned to face Carthage, the solicitor, and Jack—his estate steward, distant cousin, and the closest thing he had to a father now. "I have other business to see to, gentlemen. Jack, have the family attorney look into this, will you? I'm certain he'll be able to straighten out these good fellows."

As the younger son raised for politics, Harry was very good at polished diplomacy. He simply wasn't familiar with his father's holdings. He didn't even know the names of the family attorneys, unless they were the fellows who sent his allowance.

Despite his unparalleled ignorance, Harry quirked his eyebrows imperiously and waited for the men to depart.

Instead of leaving, Carthage crossed his arms, and his black-clad solicitor dared to approach the desk. Jack nervously crushed his battered leather tricorne, not speaking a word to gainsay them. Of middling height, wiry build, and balding pate, Jack was a veritable encyclopedia of all things rural, but he was out of his element in the city.

"Your Grace," the solicitor continued, "if you will but hear us out, we can make this matter plain. Your brother never signed the entailment."

What? Harry wanted to shout, but of course, he couldn't. Dukes didn't shout. They didn't have temper tantrums either. They raised cool eyebrows, nodded regally at those below them—which was almost everyone—and went about their business. As he should go about his. Not that he had a clue how to do so, since he'd never had any business to go about.

"I beg your pardon," Harry said with the aristocratic hauteur of his betters. "The estates have been entailed since the twelfth century. I doubt that my brother had much to do with it."

"That's just it, my . . . Your Grace," the solicitor said eagerly. "Each heir accepts the entailment with his signature upon attaining his majority. Your brother didn't sign the papers."

Cold sweat slid down Harry's spine, but he smiled negligently and swung his walking stick with the cool aplomb of a man without a worry in the world. Politics taught a fellow that. "Edward would have done nothing to endanger Sommersville," he insisted. "If you will only consult with my attorneys, you will see that all is in proper order."

"It ain't, Your Grace," Carthage intruded. "Me and your brother talked it over. He didn't sign the papers apurpose. He knew the old man was bankruptin' the place and that he'd need the blunt to live on. We had an agreement, me and him. We would build homes for toffs like me. It's an ideal situation . . ."

"Jack!" Harry roared, finally losing his patience at the enormous folly and presumption of the man. "Show these gentlemen out at once, and don't dare to let them in my presence again."

Striding across the study, Harry threw open the door, prepared to call for his butler and footmen if necessary.

Apologetically, Jack bowed and gestured for their guests to depart. A footman magically appeared to escort them. Harry knew the servants had been listening at the door again, but he could scarce blame them. Since his father never used the family's London town house, he had always occupied it. The place had been hell and chaos since the news of the double deaths of the duke and the marquess.

Jack closed the door behind their uninvited guests. Despite his kinship to one of the great families of the kingdom, Harry's cousin wore his thinning gray hair clubbed in a black ribbon and sported the coarse cloth of country clothes. With a solemn expression, he forced Harry into staying instead of running off to follow Christina. "It's time you face facts, lad."

Jack had called him "lad" since he'd been in shortcoats. Harry couldn't pull rank on him now. In truth, he was desperate for Jack's sage advice. His cousin had handled the family estates since before Edward's birth. Jack would never have come up to London if it hadn't been a matter of dire emergency.

With a sigh, Harry sank into his desk chair and swiveled back and forth. "Can't you face them for me,

Jack? I know nothing of tenant rent or pence per acre or what crop we should seed this spring. Tell me what agricultural bill would most likely help us, and I'll stand up before all Parliament and argue them into it, but don't make me count sheep."

"You're bankrupt, Harry. You won't have sheep to count if something isn't done soon. Carthage has it right. If you can't pay off that piece of paper of his, you'll lose everything."

The bleakness that had come over Harry ever since the first creditor had appeared on his doorstep replaced the moment of hope he'd experienced at the sight of Christina. He'd never owed a farthing he couldn't pay the next day. He didn't know how matters had come to this point.

"My father had an income of more than fifty thousand pounds per annum, Jack," he protested. "He could have built Rome and London and had blunt left to spend. Where did it all go?"

Jack held out his palms in a helpless gesture. "He frittered it away building that monstrosity he called a home. He didn't care much about the land after your mother died. You know that."

"But Edward did! He lived for counting sheep. Couldn't he have taken things in hand?"

"Lately, he caught the building bug just like your father. He wanted to build fancy new cottages and move the village out of sight. He spent more time talking to architects and landscapers than to his own tenants. Money has to be managed to grow, and no one's managed yours in many a year. We haven't seen fifty thousand in a long time."

To Harry, even half of fifty thousand was a sum so enormous that he couldn't imagine spending it in a lifetime, much less a year. Even living in the expensive town house, he'd carefully managed his two-thousand-pound allowance to cover his living expenses with sufficient left over to invest. His parliamentary duties for his father's pocket borough were light but offered opportunities for investment and earning a little extra. He lived quite comfortably on his income.

He didn't see how his father and brother could have spent fifty thousand in the entire course of their lives. They didn't come up to London or have wives or daughters to eat up the income with gowns and new furniture and entertaining. Harry couldn't remember the last time his father had entertained.

"I'll go to Sommersville and take a look at the books," Harry conceded wearily. "They must have snugged the money away somewhere."

"I keep the books, Harry," Jack reminded him. "There's nothing to hide away and debts higher than a mountain waiting to be paid. We need cash just to buy seed and plant the fields this spring. No one will lend us a tuppence until your father's debts have been paid."

"I'll talk to our creditors," Harry said desperately. "Maybe they can be made to wait another year. Surely, once the rents are paid in the fall—"

Jack shook his head. "We need to show them cash up front. The dowry your betrothed will bring will hold them off until the fall. You need to set a date and marry."

Marry! The new duke swung around to gaze out the

floor-length window. Christina was nowhere in sight: happy Christina, blithe Christina, addlepated, mischievous witch Christina.

A duchess?

April 1755

"Lord Harry has made an appointment to see your father this afternoon," cousin Lucinda announced excitedly, entering Christina's bedchamber without knocking.

"The Most Noble Duke of Sommersville, you mean." Christina plopped down on the edge of the bed and began to pry off her boots. "Or His Grace, the Duke of Sommersville." She dropped the boot on the faded carpet and pried off the other. Then she shimmied out of her half brother's breeches and stockings. "I expect he's come to cry off."

"Christina!" Shocked—not by her cousin's breeches but by her assertion—Lucinda tucked the outlandish clothes into their usual place in the bottom of the armoire. "He cannot do that. You have been betrothed for *ages.*"

With the ease of expertise, Christina untied the old skirt that hid her breeches. She'd spent these past weeks exploring inside London's city walls, looking for the ghost of Hans Holbein, the artist Lucinda most admired. It was much easier—and less conspicuous— to skulk about disguised in boy's clothing.

"Sinda, my dear, do you remember when all London whispered in astonishment after you painted the portrait of the earl's daughter in her casket—before the child died?"

Lucinda clasped her fingers and looked nervous. "I thought they'd ride me out of town on a rail. I want my work to be recognized, but not in such a fashion. I don't mean to do these things," she murmured, "but if anyone notices this latest painting . . ."

"You really should quit doing portraits and work anonymously," Christina chided her. "One of these days, there will be no one about to rescue you from your muddles. I'm sure I can get you out of this one if I could only speak with Holbein's ghost. He persuaded society that his artistic fantasies were fashionable and not dangerous."

"I'm not *dangerous*," Sinda insisted. "I didn't even know Lord Pelham. I couldn't know he would die. I just painted what I saw in my head."

"You see people dead before they are. That's dangerous. I found Holbein's grave in St. Andrew's, but his ghost doesn't haunt it," Christina offered. "If I knew which house he died in, it might help. If he could draw all those macabre pictures of people dying and be celebrated for it, I don't know why you can't."

"Because he was a man and not a Malcolm," Lucinda said with a touch of acid. "Besides, even if you found Holbein's ghost, he'd speak German. You have too much imagination for your own good. I thank you for your efforts, but what has any of this to do with Harry?"

"The reason you weren't run out of town last time was because Harry laughed at the gossips," Christina said matter-of-factly, unhooking her too-large bodice to slip out of the man's shirt she'd worn under it. "Harry told everyone he met that Malcolms were always good for a little amusement, and he poked fun at their 'superstition.' He is such a popular fellow that everyone was too embarrassed to condemn you after he belittled their fears."

"Oh, how thoughtful of him! I had no idea." Sinda watched Christina with curiosity. "But that means he's perfect for you."

"Sinda, you aren't *listening*. He doesn't believe in our Malcolm gifts. He takes nothing seriously. When I tell him about my ghost hunts, he calls me his 'imaginative little creature.' I vow, he asked for my hand because it kept us both from having to seriously engage anyone else. He never intended to marry me."

"But he's a *duke* now," Lucinda protested. "He must marry and raise heirs, and he's betrothed to you. He must take that seriously."

Christina dropped a lacy chemise over her head and reached for a white silk stomacher, ignoring the corset Lucinda held out. "And raise *heirs,* Sinda. Just listen to yourself and think for a change, will you?"

"Oh." Lucinda dropped to a tapestried chair seat and looked pained. "Malcolm women don't marry dukes who don't already have heirs."

"Right. Malcolms always have daughters, never sons. That's why there are dozens of girls and no little boys running around."

"Ninian had a boy," Lucinda pointed out.

"To an Ives, who are a race of demons. Harry isn't an Ives. If both your mama and my mama had nothing but girls, what are the chances I'll be any different?"

Christina stepped into her rose silk skirt and pulled the bodice sleeves over her arms.

Lucinda leaped up to fasten the hooks in back. "But he can't call off a betrothal," she wailed. "It just isn't done."

"He's a duke worth thousands of pounds a year. He can pay my father off and buy any woman who catches his fancy. Can you imagine me as a duchess? His ancestors would fall out of their noble picture frames."

Although she did her best to sound pragmatic, Christina's romantic nature wished it could be otherwise. She probably didn't love Harry, but he was the only man she'd ever met who didn't scold her for her antics. Since her favorite pastime was chasing ghosts and other creatures invisible to the normal eye, this required a certain degree of open-mindedness that the rest of mankind did not seem to possess.

She and Harry didn't spend much time in each other's pockets, but they saw each other regularly at London's entertainments. One of her favorite memories was of the night at the Grosvenor's ball when she'd grown weary of the overheated, smelly ballroom and had wandered out to the garden, certain she'd seen a brownie under a tulip leaf. She didn't know if Harry had been conducting a liaison or if he'd followed her, but he'd found her sitting on a tree branch in her ball gown, waiting for the brownie to reappear.

He'd looked quite refined in his embroidered vest and plain ruffled cravat, when all others wore lace frothing from neck and cuff. Harry had a knack for dressing simply and looking richer than any other man in the vicinity. He'd leaned his elegant shoulders against the tree trunk, propped one polished shoe against the bark to display a splendidly sculpted leg in evening breeches, and twirled a rose in his fingers while he located her amid the leaves.

"I hadn't realized nightingales wore silk plumage," he said, as if he came across maidens in ball gowns sitting in trees all the time. "The yellow suits you."

"Thank you," she answered a trifle crossly. "If you came out here just to tell me that, your mission has been accomplished. You may leave now."

"And return to that noxious ballroom? Do you despise me that much to banish me there?"

She could never be cross with Harry for long. Kicking her feet so that her petticoats bobbed, she gave up her pursuit of brownies in favor of dallying with a charming man. Just looking at Harry gave her pleasure. Out of respect for the occasion, he'd powdered his hair and tied it in black silk to accent the white lawn of his jabot. Since he normally wore his thick blond hair in the same manner, it did not seem pretentious to see him so now. But it was his laughing eyes that always held her captivated.

"I cannot despise you," she replied saucily, "but you have chased off all the brownies in the garden for the evening. They know they cannot compare to your magnificence."

His deep rich laugh warmed her, because she knew he wasn't laughing at her but at her description of him. Harry did not suffer from an ounce of vanity.

"I apologize, my faery lady. I did not know I surpassed brownies in elegance. Shall I attempt to be more shabby next time we meet?"

Enchanted by his romantic gallantry, she forgot brownies and auras and any of the other things with which she entertained herself. Instead, when he stepped up on the bench to help her down, she held out her arms to him and allowed him to swing her from her perch.

Standing there on the bench beside him, she probably whispered something unutterably foolish in reply, but Harry wasn't listening any more than she was. He kept his hands on her waist, and she kept her hands on his shoulders, and it had seemed the most natural thing in the world for her to lift her face and for him to tilt his head down and for their mouths to come together.

It had been bliss, pure bliss. His lips had been soft and warm and respectful, but she'd opened her eyes and seen the red aura of his passion heating when she returned his kiss with all the fervency she possessed. He'd stepped away then, just at the moment when she thought to learn more. Always cautious was Harry.

She'd spent many a night reliving that kiss, wondering where it might have taken them had they been anyone else but two people who preferred independence to the marital state.

"Christina! You haven't heard a word I said."

Jolted back from her lovely daydream, Christina ran her hands over her face and into her hair, spinning to find the looking glass. Her lamentably light hair flew every which way, and she hastened to pin it into a respectable coiffure.

"If you'd wear a corset, you'd have a smaller waist than any lady in town," Lucinda observed with her critical artist's eye.

"In other words, I'm skinny and you'd have me skin-nier. Isn't it enough that I'm tall enough to be a boy?"

"A short boy," her cousin scoffed. "What will you do if Harry calls off the betrothal?"

"Congratulate him on his intelligence, of course." Having spent the better part of her life stumbling into one adventure after another, Christina had learned how to put on a brave face for all occasions. She just didn't think she'd ever faced such a sudden and crush-ing pain in her heart before.

Harry was hers. He'd always been hers. Even as youngsters, he used to take her on pony rides in the park. She'd thought when they grew old and tired of playing, they'd eventually marry and settle down into old age together. She couldn't imagine doing the same with anyone else. She was twenty-two years old and well beyond looking for another mate. Her rosy pic-ture of the future had been knocked cock-a-hoop, and insecurity crushed her usual optimism. What would become of her?

Putting on a brave face, she dismissed her foolish fears with a smile. "I shall tell him I'll dance at his wedding and ask who the lucky duchess might be."

Christina's father was a marquess, and Lucinda's fa-ther was a duke—both men having taken Malcolm women as their second wives after their first wives gave them heirs. She and Lucinda and their sisters and cousins traveled in noble circles and were not mightily impressed by titles.

But they were expected to marry well and wisely. As a respectable second son of a duke, Harry had not been a grand match, but a sensible one as far as everyone was concerned. Christina's boyishness didn't "take" with most gentlemen, no matter how her would-be suitors had pretended otherwise. She could see it in their auras that they thought her foolish or sought her dowry out of avarice. Harry was the only man who adored her for herself.

And for his own sake, she would have to let him go.

Defiantly fighting the hot moisture of tears, she powdered her nose and faced the looking glass. She might be tall and on the thin side, but the rose silk over pocket panniers gave her confidence that she didn't come off too badly. She teased a little curl down her neck from her hairpins and pronounced herself satisfied.

"I think if I painted you now, it would be in full battle regalia," Lucinda whispered. "Would you prefer broadsword or longbow?"

Christina had no need for a reply. A knock on the door warned she had been summoned. She hugged Lucinda for courage. "Don't paint anything dangerous until I return."

Back straight, chin up, she sailed out of her chamber before the footman could even ask for her presence.

The servant raced down the stairs ahead of her and opened the door to her father's study, announcing her to the occupants as if this were a grand ball and she the lady of the hour. Christina winked at him as she swept past.

Inside the shadowed study, two men waited. Her father sat at his desk, his fingertips pressed together in a steeple across his lips, disguising his expression.

Christina read an odd uncertainty in his aura. Her father was never uncertain.

Her wayward gaze flew to Harry.

He stood silhouetted against the partially opened drapery. Until that stolen kiss, she'd been more aware of Harry's laughter and voice and eyes than the hard body beneath his elegant clothes. Now she was conscious of his long, muscular legs, and the wide-shouldered strength of him. He wasn't overly tall or bulky, but in her eyes he was the epitome of an elegant, idle gentleman. A perfect match for her. Until now.

"Christina, the duke would like a word with you. Since you've been betrothed these last five years and have behaved with all due respect, I'll trust the two of you alone."

She hardly saw her father depart. A ray of sun slipping past the heavy drapery revealed a Harry she had never seen before. His normally amiable features seemed etched in harshness today. His laughing lips pressed together in a thin line. She'd never noticed the squareness of his jaw or the determination in the lift of his chin. His eyes no longer danced but appeared shadowed and cold.

"It's time we marry, Christina."

She blinked. That wasn't Harry's voice. That was some stranger's. Harry's voice was chocolatey warm or laughingly charming. This man sounded cold and distant and—commanding?

She searched his aura, finding the familiar hues of passion and sincerity, but it was grayer somehow than she remembered. She couldn't always identify the patterns, but given the sound of his voice, she'd say his aura was currently colored with icy resolve. Definitely not a Harry color.

"We must do no such thing, Harry," she scoffed, speaking to him as she had always done. "You are a wealthy duke now, and you'll need a regal duchess to bear you heirs. I was sorry to hear about your father and brother. Such a dreadful accident!"

She had longed to go to him when she'd heard the news, but his family had been safely interred and his door wreathed in black before she'd known of the deaths. She'd been given no opportunity to offer condolences beyond sending a formal note of sympathy.

"That damned monstrosity of a house my father worked on ought to be pulled down," Harry growled. "It isn't safe."

"Walking on parapets is seldom safe," Christina said. "It is unfortunate that they were together when the stones gave way."

The black of his mourning flickered darker, but Harry dismissed her comment with a wave of his gloved hand. "We cannot undo what's done. We're betrothed, Christina, and I find I need a wife. I've obtained the license. It can be done on the morrow."

Blinking, not certain she had heard him right, Christina dropped abruptly to the wing chair beside the door. "Tomorrow? That's not possible." Her startled heart beat against her chest like a trapped bird. She had been prepared for anything but this.

"Of course it is," he said angrily. "It's just a matter of standing before an altar and repeating our vows. All the rest was done years ago."

She didn't like the sound of his voice or the dark colors ruling his aura. Had some demon possessed him? The Harry she knew would have gone down on bended knee and pressed kisses to her hand and said sweet words just to tease her.

This one was ordering her about as if she were his horse, treating the marriage vows as if they were an agreement to buy a new coat. "We agreed," she whispered. "We did not wish to wed until we were old and gray. What has changed, Harry?"

"That's rather obvious, isn't it?" he asked with an edge of desperation. "I'm the last of my father's line. I need an heir to carry on the title and to inherit the estates."

"But I can't give you that." She hated the wretched sound of her voice, but she wasn't accustomed to this pain eating up her insides. She had never thought to be married as if she were a brood mare. She'd hoped for romance and love and happiness. Or at least a good friend.

This Harry wasn't even the friend she knew. At her refusal, he looked almost dangerous, a golden blade prepared to strike, although she wasn't certain of the direction he would take.

"It's not impossible." He dismissed her objection with scorn. "Your cousin had a son. We'll simply keep trying until it happens, that's all. We've wasted too much time as it is."

Oh, no, this wasn't right. This wasn't right at all. Panic fluttered about in her chest, replacing the pain. She wasn't fond of babies. She'd never thought much about having them because she'd expected they'd wait until they were very old to marry. How naïve of her. Even then, there were ways of preventing too many babies—

But this stranger who inhabited Harry's body didn't seem to care if she wanted babies or not. Without his cooperation—

Oh, dear. That could be ugly. She might be a maiden, but she knew all about lovemaking and babies. She had married sisters and cousins after all. And an entire Malcolm library to peruse when she was curious. And she was always curious.

There was lovemaking, and there was animal mating. She wanted a husband who respected her and made glorious love to her. She didn't want a husband who rutted to make screaming infants whether she wanted them or not. Her soul was filled with horror at the thought.

"I think we need time to consider," she said placatingly. "It is very sudden."

"We've been betrothed for years, Christina," he said impatiently. "That's time enough. Your father has agreed to a ceremony in the morning. I know your mother will want her frills and whatnot, but I've been assured that can be accomplished easily. All you need do is show up."

Her romantic vision of wearing a trailing medieval wedding gown, walking up a grassy aisle with doves fluttering beneath a canopy of trees, shattered into crumbling bits. She blinked away a tear and sought for some way out.

Except she didn't want out. She wanted her old Harry back.

"I won't show up," she said defiantly, standing again. "You know that if I decide to disappear, I can."

"Damn it, Christina, grow up! This is neither the time nor place to play games." Pushing back his long coat, he shoved his hands into his pockets and glared at her. "I'll have you locked in your room and post a guard outside your window if I must, but we will be married on the morrow. I'm holding you to your promise."

Only that flicker of uncertainty in his grim aura gave her courage to stand up to him. "Then we will marry tomorrow and you can court me after."

"What?"

Hurriedly, before he could come forward and throttle her, Christina continued, "I want a husband who loves me. You've spent these last years dabbling with politics, making the rounds of clubs and gaming halls, dancing with every beautiful female in the kingdom. You've never courted *me*. How can you expect me to be a wife when I'm not even certain you know my heart? You don't even believe in ghosts," she added for good measure. "Or that I can see them. A man who loved me would believe in me."

"That is the most ridiculous . . ." Harry paced in front of the window, his heels smacking loudly against the parquet floor. He drove his hand into his thick hair as if he'd grab his head to be certain it stayed on. He halted and swung to face her. "What blackmail is this?"

"It isn't blackmail. It's common sense," she said indignantly. "I want you to make love to me, not make babies. Until you can do that, I suggest we forget about marriage."

"Make love . . ." His voice trailed off as he stepped closer. "One can't do one without the other."

His greater breadth loomed menacingly, and Christina knew it was now or never. She had to be very persuasive or he'd ignore her wishes and ruin everything. "One can, actually, but I'll not ask that you prevent babies if you'll only give me time to make you love me."

She thought it must be shock that held him silent for a full minute. He stood half a head taller than her, and she was intimately aware of his strength to her weakness. He was a duke. She was promised to him. He could do anything he liked.

"What makes you think I don't love you?" he finally asked in a voice somewhat less than a low roar.

"Instead of yellow and purple, your aura is all brown and blue right now. I don't see one iota of love in it." She crossed her hands in front of her and waited.

He growled. He walked away. He pounded the desk. She didn't flinch.

He swung around, glared, and radiated outrage and frustration. "Two weeks," he said. "I give you two weeks to make me love you, and then you'll be my wife in all the ways a wife should be."

He strode for the door. "I'll see you in church tomorrow."

Christina expelled her pent-up breath as the door slammed. She had two weeks to find the real Harry—the only man she could ever love. What would happen if he were truly lost?

Could she call the marriage off once the vows had been said?

Would she want to?

28

Two

Harry opened the door to his wall safe and removed the leather-bound volume of velvet pages holding his coin collection. He carried the heavy leather volume to his desk, then opened it, stroking with fondness the Roman nose on a gold coin he'd first found when he was but seven. Basil, the local squire's son, had found another soon after, and the competition had been heated between them until Harry had gone off to Oxford. He hadn't seen Basil in years, and who had the best collection was no longer important.

"They refuse to leave, Your Grace. We can't have those dreadful persons in the foyer when you bring your duchess home tomorrow."

Harry grimaced at his manservant's words. Settling back in his desk chair, he glanced around at his favorite room—the study. The town house belonged to the estate, of course, but he'd used it since attaining his majority and taking the election for one of his father's pocket boroughs. He loved the intellectual stimulation of London and had many fond memories of all-night discussions in this room.

Besides this house and the one in Sussex, the Sommersville estate included barren wastelands in Wales and Scotland. Only the Sussex acres produced any income. He'd have to send Jack off to Scotland to see if they could sell the land and hunting box there, but it might take years to sell acres of rocks. The idea of raising cash by selling the London town house was repellant. He just needed a little more time until he could straighten out this mess, then he and Christina would return here so he could take his new place in the House of Lords.

Turning a velvet page to reveal another row of Roman coins, Harry clenched his jaw but acknowledged the servant with a nod. The meeting with Christina had been unpleasant, but he'd set his path. Now he must follow it. "Luke, carry these to Lord Scarsdale. He's offered five hundred pounds for the lot. You may say they're worth a thousand. You know what to do from there."

Luke had been his manservant since childhood. He could haggle a Bedouin out of his robe. Having dressed Harry in his first coattails, he could also be as stubborn as any family.

"That is your Roman coin collection, Your Grace," Luke protested. "You have spent a lifetime collecting those. There isn't a more splendid collection in all the kingdom."

"I know. That's why I want at least seven hundred pounds for it. It will pay off the fools below so my lady need not be bothered with their ilk."

Luke gaped but took the book of coins. "Your Grace, surely . . ."

Apparently seeing something in Harry's face that

brooked no argument, Luke compressed his lips, bowed, and walked out.

Harry felt horrendously guilty for pressing Christina into marriage. She'd had every right to protest his crude behavior. Sheltered by her wealthy family, she'd been pampered and spoiled all her life. He'd never meant to change that. He enjoyed her unfettered spirit and fanciful nature.

The thought of taking her to the abomination that was his estate raised all his protective hackles. He'd fought Jack's advice for weeks, pooling his available cash and selling some of his more viable investments to pay the first installment on Carthage's damned mortgage. But he still owed a king's ransom.

He'd haunted the estate solicitor's office while the firm had pored over their records, looking for loopholes, searching for signed entails. The solicitors could not find Edward's signature on an entailment anywhere, although they swore the document had been prepared and delivered to Sommersville a dozen years ago.

Harry had slipped bribes to judges, spoken privately with half the Lords in their clubs, but he had yet to discover a means of preventing Carthage from foreclosing on Sommersville if he didn't meet the payments or find signed entailment papers. From what Carthage had said, the latter seemed unlikely. If Edward had signed the entailment, he would have returned the papers to the solicitors.

The visit to Christina's father today had been a last act of desperation.

As a younger son, he'd never been responsible for

anyone or anything except himself. Suddenly, he was responsible for fifteen thousand acres, an entire village, a rambling mansion, and every relative that ever crawled in off the family tree. He'd no idea he had great-great-aunts still living in Northumberland or third cousins in Cornwall relying on the estate's allowance.

Creditors had been lined up at his doors for weeks. He couldn't order a pair of boot soles without a bootmaker producing a bill from the estate and demanding its payment.

And because he'd felt guilty as hell asking for Christina's hand for her dowry, he'd agreed to her father's monstrous suggestion—that if he could not keep his wife in the manner to which she was accustomed, he had to return Christina to her family.

If he couldn't pay off the mortgage, he could lose his wife as well as his estate. He'd been more angry and ashamed at the marquess's demand than Christina's, if truth be told.

Slamming his hat on his head, Harry grabbed his walking stick to beat off the rabble at his door and strode out to set about his next unpleasant task— doubly unpleasant given Christina's ultimatum.

He'd had every intention of paying off his mistress before he married. He took wedding vows seriously, and under the circumstances, he damned well couldn't afford Melissa any longer.

When he'd gone to the marquess to claim his betrothed's dowry, he'd had some thought that at least Christina would be an enchanting bride who would soothe his physical needs and comfort his aching soul in his time of trouble.

Instead, he'd confronted a romantic child demanding that he *love* her before she'd act as his wife. He had to assume that meant she refused to share his bed. Well, he'd see about that. He'd known Christina a long time. She was a capricious little thing. All the rest of the world might be out of his control, but Christina would come around soon enough.

Meanwhile, he'd have to give up the woman who had taught him all he knew about sex. He couldn't imagine it would be a pleasant parting.

He couldn't imagine anything pleasant happening ever again. The rest of his life stretched out before him in a long hard road of duty.

Wincing as another valuable vase smashed against the door he'd just closed behind him, Harry decided he needed a few more stiff drinks and the company of sympathetic comrades to ease his last lonely night of bachelorhood. Staggering from the quantity of brandy he had consumed while listening to his mistress's wails, he directed his steps down the familiar path to his club.

Maybe he should have accepted Melissa's pleas for him to spend the night, but it had seemed disloyal to Christina. Remembering his betrothed's look of shock this morning, he figured he'd been a little hard on her. He hadn't expected her refusal. He'd had some strange idea that Christina was different from the common run of women and would be sympathetic to his needs.

Of course, he hadn't explained his needs. He couldn't begin to admit the humiliation of bankruptcy.

The instant Harry walked through the door of his club, he regretted it. He could swear they'd all been waiting for him. Cheers rang out and glasses were raised as he entered the lounge, and someone pressed a drink into his hand.

Freddie, Viscount Sinclair, shouted for a toast. "To the next sacrifice to family and title, may his freedom pass on to us for many more years!"

"You want me to drink to that?" Harry muttered, but he needed the brandy and lifted the glass to his lips for a good gulp.

"Aren't you afraid she'll cosh you over the head with a broomstick if you stray, Harry?" some wit in the back of the room called.

He didn't even question how word of his impending marriage had traveled around London so swiftly. Servants tattled, and it wasn't as if one could hide wedding preparations. He simply wasn't in a humor to hear jests about Christina or her family of eccentrics, not so soon after being hit with the results of his father's peculiarities.

He'd been taught that image was everything, and as a younger son, he'd worked hard to uphold his. Christina's family had enough wealth and power that he wouldn't worry about theirs. He had more important things on his mind—like how he'd feed a household while bankrupt.

"My betrothed is one of a kind," he declared boldly. He meant it as a compliment, but his comrades hooted in derision.

"I saw her skulking around the crypts of St. Andrew's just last week," shouted someone from another corner of the room. "Does Sommersville have any graveyards for her to haunt?"

So that's what she'd been about lately. Sighing, Harry figured he'd have to cure her of that propensity. The mother of future dukes did not generally go about exploring crypts, especially in cemeteries behind the old city walls in an area frequented by men, not all of them gentlemen.

"Lady Christina may explore Sommersville's graveyard all she likes," he said, although in his ill humor he preferred to ring her unconventional neck, "but I daresay she won't have as much time for it once we're wedded."

"And bedded!" Freddie shouted.

Harry gulped the rest of his brandy and took another. Bedding Christina would certainly curtail her activities, but bedding her was the problem, wasn't it?

"Don't you fear she'll have witchy daughters who will be as crazy as your old man and will haunt that mausoleum you call a home?"

Harry flushed and looked for the source of those fighting words, locating a man in rural broadcloth lounging against the fireplace, apparently as foxed as he was. "Basil? What the devil are you doing here?"

"What, you think I'm not good enough to belong to the same club?"

"Don't be an ass, Chumley. You rarely come to London."

Basil Chumley normally resided in Sussex where their estates ran together. The Chumleys hadn't the

wherewithal to send their son to university or keep
him in London, so he and Harry had seen each other
only briefly over the past decade or more. The differences in their circumstances had always created an
element of competition between them, but Basil had
never derided Harry's family in public. Of course,
Harry had never been a duke before. Had time and
distance or straitened circumstances provoked Basil's
hostility?

Only neighbors such as the Chumleys knew of the
late duke's deterioration into senility these past years.
It wasn't precisely sporting to bring it up. Had his
head not been spinning, Harry might have called his
old chum on it, but he hadn't the impetus left to question Basil's spite.

"The family came up yesterday for my sister's presentation," Basil answered. "Seems we arrived just in
time to see you tie the knot. I trust the lady's dowry
is large enough to pay for her eccentricities as well as
what's needed back home," he added with a sneer.

"My lady will help me right the place," Harry said
stiffly, deciding there wasn't enough brandy in the
world to drown his sorrow. Knowing he had to take
his bride to the absurdity that was his rural home instead of showering her in pleasures tore at his pride.
Basil could go to the devil.

"I wish you well of the witch, then. Even if she
brings you a fortune, I'll wager she tumbles the castle
on your head," Chumley rejoined.

Considering how Harry's father and brother had
died, this produced an instant's silence among the

drunken crowd. Even Basil flinched when he realized how his words sounded.

Finishing off the brandy, Harry flung the glass at the fireplace. It smashed with a satisfying flare of flame from the dregs of the alcohol. Politely, he bowed to the man he now considered his ex-friend. "Thank you for your kind wishes. I am well aware of the spirit that prompts them, and I heartily return the sentiment."

His audience erupted in nervous laughter as he wished Chumley the same fate Basil had expressed for him.

"I've heard you're a gambling man, Harry. A thousand pounds and my Roman coins against yours that she'll make you the laughingstock of all London by this time next year," Chumley shouted over the laughter.

Chumley's collection was nearly as good as the one Harry no longer possessed, but by the same token, he no longer had a thousand pounds. He wasn't about to admit either in the face of his friends.

He'd worked hard to uphold his image as a gentleman of leisure. It suited him better than the dull one of dedicated politician. Now he had to take on the role and burden of duke as well. He might as well learn to stand tall and take blows to the chin without flinching.

With a shrug, Harry accepted Basil's challenge. "My betrothed will be a duchess who will grace the halls with more wisdom and refinement than you are like to see in a lifetime." With that absurdly defiant prediction about an imp who chased brownies, Harry swung on his heel and marched unsteadily for the door.

All would be right once he had a little cash and time to uncover the source of the estate's problems.

It would be even better once he had the delicious, capricious Lady Christina in his bed. To hell with Basil and his odd behavior.

"I wish Felicity could be here," Christina murmured half to herself as her mother adjusted the white cape over the bodice of her yellow silk gown. They stood in the wings of the cathedral's nave. She could hear guests murmuring as the church filled, and she kept glancing over her mother's shoulder in hopes of seeing Harry.

A gold chain fastened the cape around Christina's throat. The cape partially covered the low neckline and lace of her gown, but that wasn't its purpose. Its purpose was steeped in Malcolm tradition and lost to the ages.

"You know your sister cannot travel so close to her time," Hermione, Lady Hampton said. "Although if she knew you were finally marrying Harry, she'd probably have the baby on the road trying to get here."

"Ninian had a girl this time, didn't she?" Heart racing as she searched the shadows of the church, Christina tried to appear nonchalant.

She didn't fool her mother. Hermione pinned the circlet of rowan more firmly to Christina's flowing hair.

"Your cousin has already provided the earl with his heir. It is only right that Ninian have a girl next to carry on our traditions. If Harry is not concerned, then you needn't be either."

But she was. She couldn't imagine enduring Harry's hatred if time after time she bore him girls.

She couldn't imagine having a litter of babies. Or even one.

She was terrified. She'd never risked quite so much on her previous adventures. This adventure would endure a lifetime and likely affect generations to come. Gulping, she looked over the whispering crowd.

"Why are so many people here?" she asked. Malcolm weddings tended to be untraditional by society's standards. Generally, only family attended.

"Harry is a duke and your father is a marquess, dear. It is the uniting of two great families. People are curious."

People might be curious, but Christina didn't think they had come to see two families united. She saw a preponderance of unmarried gentlemen gathering on one side of the church, and a very odd assortment of what appeared to be merchants in the back.

All her female sisters, aunts, and cousins filled the other side. She even recognized some of her Ives brothers-in-law with her half brothers. The sight of her family reassured her and gave her courage. No matter what happened, she would always have family to rely on. That steadied some of her jitters.

Light poured down the aisle as the cathedral doors opened. Heads turned and whispered murmurs rose to a noisy wave of sound. Christina followed their stares to the entrance.

Standing in the doorway, the Duke of Sommersville threw a long shadow down the aisle. Sunlight burnished his thick, gold-brown hair. Christina wondered if he'd disdained the formality of powder for a reason, but she dismissed the question to admire his formidable presence. A crisp jabot of expensive lace spilled over his elegant silver velvet coat and black vest. He wore silver breeches tailored to his trim, athletic figure, and Christina could hear a whisper of female sighs fill the air as he strode forward, his hat flattened under his arm.

She narrowed her eyes at his stiff gait. She had seen Harry dance with grace, climb trees with ease, and lounge carelessly at card tables. She had seen him both sober and foxed. She had never seen him walk as if he had a poker up his rump. If he was practicing to be the stiffest, grandest duke in the kingdom, he was succeeding.

Her sister Leila and her aunt Stella were lying in wait for him. Before his eyes could adjust to the cathedral's dim interior, they had spirited him over to Christina and hurriedly begun to adorn him with the black cape and rowan crown as befitted a Malcolm wedding.

Harry looked so very noble in his severe garb that Christina was half afraid to say a word. His eyes didn't dance when they met hers but looked stern as he conceded to her family's ministrations. He'd been fairly warned by her father, so he could not complain of the odd goings-on. By wearing the black vest, he'd even come prepared for it. The cape looked like a natural part of his ensemble.

He was still a stranger, a man instead of the laughing boy she remembered. Was he biding his time until she was fully his, to do with as he would? Was that a line of dull blue in his aura? It was too blurred by brown to tell. Brown was a very bad sign, or maybe it simply meant he was confused. She could accept that, although she much preferred his usual shades of vibrant yellow and purple.

He was expecting her to be his duchess. She'd been brought up to believe she could be anything she liked, but duchess had not been on her list of interests. She was woefully inadequate for the role.

"Half of London is waiting," he said, as if he could read her thoughts. He offered his arm once her mother had fastened his cloak with its gold pin. "You cannot cry off now."

"I'm not a coward." Straightening her shoulders, she took his arm, noticing that Harry made the unusual cape look regal. He only needed a scepter to complete the image.

"Only a child lacks fear," he murmured without looking at her. "Grow up and admit that the future is terrifying."

She didn't want to grow up. She liked her life just as it was—with nothing to fear on the horizon.

At some unseen signal, the organ bellowed a loud note. Harry grimaced as if in great pain, then stiffened his spine even straighter.

The moment had arrived. She could either run away or refuse to believe that her life would change once they married. Setting her chin, she chose the latter and clung to Harry's arm when he started down the aisle.

"You're foxed," she whispered as he dragged her with him.

Leading her in a stately procession around the room

according to Malcolm tradition, Harry did not cast her a glance. "Not now," he gritted out between clenched teeth.

Christina pondered that response as her youngest sisters and cousins scattered flower petals before them. Did he mean "not now" as in "now is not the time, so shut the hell up"? Or did he mean he was no longer foxed, just suffering from the aftereffects? And why would he feel the need to overindulge anyway? Did he dread this marriage as much as she?

Before she could follow the path of her inquiries to their logical conclusion, Harry halted her before the altar where the bishop waited.

It was early spring and there had been no time to fetch hothouse trees to provide the forest background preferred by Malcolm tradition. Instead, the bishop stood before a table of palms and orchids carried from town conservatories. Sporting its first spring leaves, a rowan tree in a pot represented the forest.

Christina watched Harry with curiosity as the titters and talk carried on behind them, but he appeared to listen intently to the solemn words the bishop spoke, oblivious to the mockery of their peers. Despite the harshness of his demeanor, Harry seemed earnest in accepting the Malcolm oath to "love, honor, and take this woman in equality."

Christina swallowed a gulp of relief and hoped that she was right in believing that beneath the mask of stern and proper duke lurked the intelligent, understanding Harry she knew.

She simply had to keep remembering that through the wedding breakfast to follow and the night to come.

At the bishop's command, Harry produced a diamond and pearl ring in an antique setting that must have belonged to his mother. The light filtering through the rose window caught the facets of the gems, sending dancing rainbows across her hand.

His grasp was as warm and strong as his voice. A thrill of anticipation filled her, giving her the courage to repeat her oath firmly. She held Harry's gaze even though his changing hues frightened her. He was hers, for now and forever. She smiled in delight at that thought.

A flock of white doves flew into the air the instant the last syllable fell from her tongue. Laughter and curses followed, but Christina clung to the power of Harry's unwavering gaze.

In anticipation of Harry's kiss, she didn't hear the bishop pronounce them man and wife. She only knew the moment Harry dipped his head so the heat of his mouth seared hers, sealing their vows into eternity.

Another explosion of doves toppled candles and palms and sent guests shrieking into the aisles.

In the confusion, Harry pulled her closer and parted her lips with his tongue.

Three

Christina's kiss not only stole Harry's breath away, it drove his hangover headache out of his skull. Had it not been for the escalating confusion behind them and the bishop's peremptory cough in front, he would have idled longer, exploring her eager sweetness, basking in the one bright promise in his future.

He tasted enthusiasm and awe on her lips. It had been a long time since a woman had kissed him like that. Wooing Christina into his bed suddenly took precedence over all his woes.

With reluctance, he released her to face the congregation and the chaos caused by the frightened doves. Splendidly coiffed matrons ducked and shrieked. Gentlemen still half foxed from last night's celebrations stumbled about in ragged attempts to capture the offending birds, doing more harm than good. Harry sighed. At least this would be the last of the Malcolm madness. Now they could get on with their lives together.

Christina watched him warily, as if waiting for him to pitch a fit. She'd have a long wait before she caught him losing his temper or his dignity. This was her wedding, and if this was what she wanted, he would not sour it for her. She was his wife and helpmeet, future mother of his children, and for this, he owed her a great deal of respect. By marrying him, she put herself completely in his care, and he took his responsibility seriously.

He prayed she wouldn't be the final burden that broke his back.

Offering his arm, he led her through the crowd rushing into the aisle in their haste to escape the usual result of a flight of outraged birds.

"Has your family considered holding these ceremonies in the park?" he inquired politely, dodging an opportunistic merchant who thought to make the best of Harry's public appearance. "The birds would have a wider territory for their depredations."

"We prefer the park, but the law now requires a church. Civilization is much of the reason our traditions and abilities fall by the wayside."

Christina stopped to kiss the cheek of a handsome lad who handed her a wedding gift. The boy had the look of an Ives about him, so Harry assumed it was one of her brothers-in-law, apparently one of the bastard younger ones.

"An odd time for a wedding gift," he murmured, shoving his way through the milling crowd, praying she didn't realize half of them were his creditors and not just idle bystanders.

"David does things in his own time."

To Harry's relief, Christina did no more than glance at the gift as he assisted her into the waiting carriage outside the church.

He'd heard rumors that Christina and one of the

younger Ives were sweet on each other, but until now, he hadn't concerned himself with the gossip. The appearance of the Ives brothers at their wedding warned that it wouldn't just be Christina's family she could fall back on should he fail her. Her sisters had married into a family as formidable as her own. Ives men would all be down his throat if he did not make his new wife happy.

Harry tugged at his uncomfortable cravat before climbing into the carriage and signaling the driver to move on.

He'd borrowed the rig from the marquess since he owned none of his own. A sedan chair hadn't seemed appropriate for his bride. He hoped the estate still possessed a carriage or two so he would not shame Christina by forcing her to walk everywhere. He'd done what he'd thought best, but he was still uncomfortable with the obligations of keeping a wife.

Perhaps that would change once they shared a bed and got to know each other better.

Now that he had the right, Harry contemplated removing the cape that hid Christina's delectable form. Previously unwilling to be caught in the trap of marriage, he'd avoided lustful thoughts about his intended, but now seemed an appropriate moment to engage in them. The gap between her cape and her bodice offered a teasing glimpse of bare breasts and the shadow between. He knew she was slender. How much of their fullness was enhanced by stays?

"Has a fancy for you, does he?" he asked, following his earlier concern rather than behave like a sex-starved schoolboy.

Christina looked startled. "David? A fancy for me?

I cannot imagine it. He is only a few years older than I."

"You know how gossip is," Harry said offhandedly, although that particular bit of gossip had gnawed his insides. "Your sisters and cousin married Ives. They all looked for you to do the same."

His wife tilted her lovely head in that curious manner of hers, studied him for a moment, then smiled. "Why, Harry, I believe you are the tiniest bit jealous. Did you think me so faithless as to run off with someone else?"

"Of course not," he said, oddly reassured by her words despite his attempt to be blasé. "I did not think you meant to marry at all."

"Malcolms always marry," she said carelessly. "It's probably a family curse." She glanced out the window as the carriage rolled past his home on the first leg of the square. "Why are all those shopkeepers hanging about your house these days? Have your father's duties already descended upon you?"

His creditors were watching the carriage pull up across the park at the home of Lord and Lady Hampton. With the money from the sale of his coin collection, he'd paid off all those who had hung about yesterday. Apparently the word had gone round and another set wished to try their luck today. He hoped Luke would find some way to lure them back to the kitchens where they belonged. Or drive them away entirely. He didn't want to have to explain his embarrassing predicament to Christina.

"The estate is a very complicated affair." Brushing off her question, Harry stepped from the carriage and offered his hand to assist her out.

Inside the dim church, Harry had scarcely had time to appreciate his bride's beauty. Out here on one of London's sunnier days, she glowed brighter than daylight in her yellow gown. She threw back her cape to reveal enough lace to pay his meals for a year, but the cascade of white had the desired effect of drawing his gaze to her breasts.

She belonged outdoors. Her flawless skin possessed a creamy sheen that ripened like sweet apricots in the sun. Gold glinted in her unbound hair, and her eyes reflected the blue skies above when she raised her head to look at him. She was tall enough in her heeled shoes to meet his eyes. Her waist was as slender and supple as any willow reed.

Harry had the inexplicable urge to dance her through the street, swing her about in joy, and cavort like a boy to show how happy she made him.

But dukes didn't dance in the streets like madmen.

Or attract the attention of creditors.

He hustled her up the stairs into her parents' home, through the lines of servants waiting to welcome the guests for the wedding breakfast. The day ahead stretched long before they'd be allowed to make their escape.

Normally, Harry enjoyed company. He liked flirting with the ladies, discussing the latest political situation with his peers, exchanging jests with his friends.

But his entire world had turned inside out with the deaths of his father and brother. He missed their presence at what should be a celebratory occasion.

He had to be the Duke of Sommersville and speak intelligently with Christina's father and his wealthy cronies in case he had need of their assistance, while he watched from afar as Christina flitted from guest to guest, laughing and teasing.

Instead of arguing with his host as he might once have done, Harry remained noncommittal on the Tory views that the marquess and his peers thought he would adopt now that he'd become a landowner.

Leaving the others to argue affairs of state, Lord Hampton took him aside to complete the business that constituted an aristocratic marriage. "I've arranged for Christina's dowry to be deposited with your banker this morning," the marquess assured Harry. "If you wish, I can have the arranged amount sent to this Carthage person."

Harry bowed his head to hide his shame. "Thank you, sir. I'd like to keep my communication with the man to a minimum."

"You're certain you'll have no trouble paying the balance?" Hampton demanded. "Should you lose both dowry and estate, I won't leave my daughter destitute. I'll bring her home at once."

Harry had no certainty of anything at all. He simply knew he could not lose the estate and shame the family name by not paying his debts. He had to believe the land would keep them once matters were in order. If he were fool enough to lose his inheritance, then he deserved to lose Christina as well. "There should be no difficulty, sir. It's prime acreage. You have not married your daughter to a beggar."

The marquess nodded approval and returned to the political argument, leaving Harry to fend for himself.

He set himself to learning the names of all of Christina's sisters and cousins and her notorious Ives in-laws. He gritted his teeth at the ease with which all the big, dark, handsome men teased his duchess. Dunstan Ives attempted to draw him into a discussion of farming, but Harry knew as much about agriculture as Dunstan knew about Roman ruins.

His own friends had toddled off to bed after observing the ceremony. He had a vague recollection of having made a preposterous wager with Chumley. He couldn't remember the last time Basil had left Sussex. What the devil had got into Basil to challenge him in such a manner?

"My mother says we may leave once we've greeted all the guests," Christina murmured, coming up to take his arm. "I'm sure we've spoken with half of London. Might we leave now? I had an appointment I would keep this afternoon."

Startled, Harry glanced down at his flushed and glowing new wife. She'd changed from her pale yellow morning gown to a modest blue traveling gown that concealed every delectable bit of her from head to toe. They both recognized their marriage as one of convenience, a uniting of two powerful families. He shouldn't expect her to look at him with joy and expectation of the night and the life to come.

But he did, confound it. He wanted her to be eagerly asking him to take her to his home and to his bed. She'd all but stolen his breath from his lungs with that kiss this morning. She was the inexperienced one. Shouldn't she show some shyness or curiosity instead of treating this day as any other? She looked as if she were ready to run off to explore a new gravesite and leave him to his own devices.

He didn't want to be left to his own devices, he realized. He wanted her by his side as he braved the disaster that was his new future. He would like to have *one* delight to look forward to in the days ahead.

Of course, once his new duchess discovered he was bankrupt and could lose everything he owned in less than six months' time, she might not be quite the delight he anticipated. And what would she make of the monstrous home to which he must take her?

Glancing out the window at the square crowded with carriages and sedan chairs and gawking passersby, Harry tried to discern if his doorstep was clear of creditors. From this angle, a tree blocked his view, and there were too many people about to be certain.

"At some point, we must leave for Sommersville," he told Christina. He couldn't ignore the dire state of his father's affairs much longer, and he had no intention of leaving her behind in London.

"To Sommersville? Honestly? You'll take me to the country?" Looking excited, Christina glanced about the crowded room, apparently searching for her family. She practically bounced beside him as she found her mother.

Surprised that he'd stirred her interest, Harry studied her eager expression. "Of course. Did you think I'd lock you in an attic?"

"No, but you never go to the country. You and my father are much alike, always talking politics, and the session will be starting soon. I thought you would wish to attend now that you're a Lord."

He would like nothing better than to stay and take his place in government, but he wouldn't have lands left if he didn't return to the country. He didn't think there were any landless dukes in the kingdom, and he had no desire to be the first.

"And you don't wish to stay and attend the parties as a duchess?" he inquired, knowing as soon as the words left his mouth what her answer would be. He was a great gallumping fool. He'd married a *Malcolm*. They did not think like the rest of the world, and Christina in particular had a taste for the idiosyncratic. She watched for *brownies* while attending state balls.

"I have been to parties," she said with a moue of distaste. "I have been every year for these last six years. I would much rather be somewhere new, doing something adventurous. Does Sommersville have ghosts? Might I bring my horse? I haven't been riding in ever so long."

"I suppose I might arrange for a carriage in the morning," Harry said. "The stables are large, so you may bring as many horses as you like."

Waiting for her mother to disengage from her conversation, Christina glanced out the window Harry had been staring out of earlier. His town house awaited just across the square. He'd want to take her there, to a place just like her father's, turn her into a proper wife just like her mother. She didn't know how to reconcile herself to the life he expected of her now that he was a duke.

"Why wait until morning?" she exclaimed, caught up in the appeal of escaping town before Harry remembered his tedious duties here. "Let us take our horses and be gone now!"

She didn't know if she could trust Harry not to expect a marriage night, but if they rode all the way to Sussex . . . surely he would not expect anything of her after so exhausting a journey. And perhaps she'd find some sign of her old Harry once he left society.

"I can't let you ride that distance," he said, horrified.

The old Harry would have chortled and agreed. The new, responsible Harry rightly asserted his ducal dismay at so unseemly a journey.

"We can stop at an inn along the way." She knew the suggestion would catch his very male attention, and it did. The gleam in his eye gave him away even if the brightening hues of his aura hadn't. She wouldn't disabuse him of his lustful notions just yet. If he thought her the kind of silly gudgeon who would fall for his male charm, then more fool he.

She was aware that a husband had a legal right to demand anything he wished of his wife. That Harry had agreed not to exercise those rights immediately didn't mean he wouldn't try. In fact, she rather liked the fantasy of him trying.

He glanced again at the throng beyond the window. His aura darkened, but she noted an intriguing spike of white that could mean any of a number of things. Given Harry's character, she thought it might be a protective streak. But who was he protecting, and from what?

He studied the full skirt of her travel gown. "Can you ride in that?"

"I can," she replied in delight, although she didn't mention she happened to be wearing breeches under it. The love of adventure swelled her heart as she read capitulation in Harry's eyes. No other man she knew of would agree to her scheme. There was hope for him yet.

"Side saddle," he conceded. "Your mother was to send your wardrobe to my house today. Is there a portmanteau we can tie to a saddle?"

"Of course." He didn't need to know that it was the one containing her bridal nightclothes and her mother's candles scented for seduction. There was bound to be something suitable in it that she could wear until the rest of her luggage caught up with them.

"I'll send a footman over and have my manservant pack a bag and order the groom to saddle up," Harry said.

He looked very solemn and concerned, and Christina could not resist. Standing on her toes, she kissed his cheek, then eluded his arm when he reached for her. "I must say farewell to my sisters, if you'll speak to my mother. Harry, you are a gem among men."

She was almost regretting that she'd asked for a postponement of their wedding night. She was eager to know all that the marriage bed held, and with the old Harry back, she'd have nothing to fear.

She just hoped there was enough of the old Harry remaining to appreciate the fun that lay ahead of them.

Running up the stairs to where she'd left her sisters and most of her cousins, she glanced over her shoulder. Harry was bending over to hear something her mother was attempting to tell him in her breathless, rambling manner. His broad shoulders nearly hid Hermione from view. He radiated patience, but tension held him stiff.

Her father came to stand beside her new husband, and she could see they were very much alike: both tall and strong and of formidable countenance when they spoke on serious subjects.

She didn't know what they were talking about and didn't want to know. Turning, she raced up the stairs, hoping Leila and Lucinda were still there. She had last-minute instructions to give as well.

Four

"Let us arrive incognito," Christina suggested as she and Harry approached the lights of the inn ahead. They had left in early afternoon, but it was spring, and dusk was upon them.

Harry's aura had grown darker the farther they rode. Despite her jests and excitement, a morose pall had turned him into a wooden soldier.

"We can tell the innkeeper we are brother and sister on our way to Dover and thence to France." She offered the story she'd concocted during his silences to remind him that this was not a normal wedding night.

"We are nearly on the verge of war with France over the colonies." With an irritated wave of his hand, Harry dismissed her playacting. "Let's at least find some use for my title and claim the best rooms available. You must be exhausted."

"Have you ever seen me exhausted? And what need have I of title and recognition? I've had that all my life. What I crave is freedom." With that, she kicked her horse into one last burst of speed, striking out ahead of him.

Burdened by their baggage, Harry could not follow as swiftly, but he was hot on her heels by the time she reached the stable yard and had leaped down without aid of a groom. She didn't think she'd exposed a great deal of stocking-clad leg or revealed her unorthodox undergarments, but Harry looked like a black thundercloud by the time he reached her.

She didn't give him time for a scold. She'd had quite enough of that from her family. She meant to set out on her new life as she meant to live it—as her own woman. She smiled triumphantly at Harry and strode off for the inn while he gave instructions to the groom.

"Two rooms, please," she called to the innkeeper, who hurried forward upon her arrival. "We'll have a fire and a bath. And if you'd have supper carried up, that would be excellent." She adored giving her own orders instead of waiting for someone else to speak for her. She waited proudly for the innkeeper to send servants scurrying.

Instead, he stared at her, nervously looking over her shoulder as if waiting for someone else's arrival. Must she wave coins at him to catch his attention?

"You do have rooms, don't you?" she inquired, tapping her foot.

"Yes, of course. Be ye traveling with your maid?" Short and thin, he looked anxious as he turned his attention to her.

"My brother will be in shortly. He's seeing to the horses. It's been a long journey. I'd like to be shown a room now." Since the odd man didn't move, Christina lifted her skirt and started for the stairway on her own.

Her statement seemed to relieve his anxiety, but now the innkeeper adopted a mulish expression. "I'll be waiting for the master, miss. This here's a gentleman's establishment."

"It's an inn, isn't it?" Christina glared at him. "You have rooms? I won't insist on a fire and bath, if that is your difficulty."

Ducking to avoid the low lintel, Harry entered the inn carrying her portmanteau. He glanced from innkeeper to Christina and raised inquiring eyebrows. "No rooms?" he guessed.

The innkeeper looked enormously relieved. "We have a gentleman's common room, good sir, but my wife is visiting her mother this week. The lady says she has no maid, and I have no one to assist her, and only the one private room available. I did not wish to insult your sister with the lack of accommodation—"

"She's not my sister. She's my wife. Send our things up to the room along with a bath and supper, if you would. We'll make do without a maid." Carrying her bag, Harry pushed past the innkeeper and on toward the stairs as if he owned the place.

Hands on hips, Christina watched in astonishment as the recalcitrant landlord hastened to do her husband's bidding, leaving her standing alone.

Well, bother it. Catching up her skirts, she ran after them. Harry had some nerve accepting the one room for both of them. How was she to learn to do things on her own if he always came barging along, taking matters into his own hands? She didn't want a caretaker.

She supposed that was one of those things they'd have to work out together. Her sisters had told her all about being married to demanding men. She would simply have to learn how Harry's mind worked and teach him to understand her. Learning to live together no doubt required a certain education and training of both parties.

"I'll have your bath sent up directly, my lady," the innkeeper promised, brushing past her on the narrow stairs.

My lady. Well, so much for incognito, although Harry must not have mentioned his true title or she'd be *Your Grace'd* to death. Dukes were a rare breed, and she'd wager the innkeeper had never laid eyes on one. He'd no doubt have failure of the heart did he know he must provide services for a duke. It would be akin to entertaining a king. Everyone from the kitchen help to the guests would be peering around doors for a glimpse of them. Incognito would be her preferred means of travel if she meant to keep her freedom.

Entering the bedchamber, she watched Harry fling his greatcoat over the bed, start to peel off his dress coat, then think better of it.

"We're not sharing this bed." She threw her gloves down to join his greatcoat, then shed her cloak and stood beside the fire to warm her toes. "You promised."

"I promised to give you two weeks to make me love you. We could accomplish it much faster in bed. Am I unpleasant to look on?" Apparently deciding dishabille wouldn't shock her, he threw his dress coat on the bed to join the other outer garments. "Do you fear the marriage bed? I find it hard to believe you fear anything."

"I don't." Except maybe her reaction to his decidedly masculine presence in vest and shirtsleeves. Harry was quite a diverting sight to see. Dropping into a chair, Christina stuck her booted feet closer to the fire. "But I'm not the kind of woman who flings herself upon any man who beckons. I'm my own woman. And you've given me no reason to be anything else."

"You're *my* woman." Harry stretched his chin up to unfasten his jabot.

The open linen revealed a fascinatingly soft curl of brown hair, and Christina had to turn away from the intimate sight. She wasn't the missish sort, but she wasn't ready to be seduced either, even if Harry's unperturbed attitude sadly rattled her. "That's ridiculous and old-fashioned. You can't own another person. That is slavery."

"Perfectly legal," Harry said with a shrug, doffing his vest next, leaving only his linen to hide his naked chest. He took the chair across from her and tugged at his riding boots. "I own you, fair and square. I can lock you in a tower and feed you swill, and the law can't touch me."

The way he said that with such indifference sent cold shivers down her spine. Had she been unable to read his aura, she might be planning her escape now. But she'd spent nearly a lifetime studying Harry's aura. He was tired and angry and looking for trouble. She just happened to be the target at hand. Well, perhaps she'd also given him some reason.

"If I believed for a minute that you were capable of such a thing, you would never see me again." She bent over and began removing her ankle boots. The adventure of undressing in the same room as a gentleman added spice to the evening.

Before she even saw him rise, Harry had her by the waist and was lifting her from the chair with unanticipated strength. She squealed in surprise, then gave an unladylike yelp when he dropped her amid the garments littering the bed. Before she could scurry out of his way, he fell down beside her, pinning her in place with an arm across her breasts and a leg across her hips.

"Don't press me, Christina. I'm capable of almost anything right now. I do not know myself, and you certainly cannot know me. I want you in my bed. I have every right to demand it. I'm having some difficulty grasping why I shouldn't."

She wanted to give a snappy answer, but she could scarcely breathe. She stared into the clouded brown of his eyes, saw the pain there, and had no moment to react before he leaned over and placed his mouth on hers.

She closed her eyes to absorb the heady sensation of his kiss. The pressure of Harry's heavy weight and closeness was far more intimate than the kiss they'd shared at the altar. She could feel the strength he used to keep from crushing her and knew it would be akin to breaking iron bars to move him.

His lips pressured hers to part, and she really couldn't resist. His breath intermingled with hers, tasting of the honeyed hard candy he'd offered her earlier. His tongue . . . she really shouldn't allow his tongue . . . She squirmed at the intimacies he stole, but she opened her mouth wider to let him plunder. His hand clasped her arm tighter, and his tongue . . .

Oh, it was wonderful and tingly, and she felt the power of it all the way to parts best left unmentioned. And then he began nibbling her lips, pressing sweet kisses where he nibbled, and she didn't know what he would do next—

A knock and an embarrassed cough intruded.

Harry kissed her—hard—then pushed away. Too embarrassed to look him in the face, Christina hastily sat up and brushed the hair from her eyes. A young lad carrying their supper dishes hesitated in the doorway.

"Cook said as you would want your supper first while he heats the bath water," the boy said hastily, dropping the tray on the table. "I'll be back to pick this up."

He all but ran from the room, slamming the door after him. Behind her, Harry chortled.

"You've given him fancies now," he said.

He reached for her again, but Christina leaped up from the bed to examine their supper dishes. She could feel the flush in her cheeks, and her breasts still tingled with the need to be touched. Her lips felt swollen and not her own. That wouldn't do at all. She desperately wanted what her sisters had in marriage, but Harry didn't *love* her.

"You're the one who is shameless enough to do that in the broad light of day," she said. Satisfied that the food looked tasty, she set the plates out on the table, arranged her skirts, and took a seat. "If you thought to frighten me, you didn't."

"I didn't seek to frighten you." Pouring ale into the tankard provided, Harry grabbed a drumstick off the plate and paced up and down the limited floor space. "A man has needs, and a woman is made to satisfy them. That's what marriage is about."

With firelight flickering off the gold strands of his hair, his linen shirt billowing above his tight breeches, Harry looked all male animal with little of the civilized duke about him. She'd never quite seen him in that light before, and if she glanced to where his shirt met his breeches . . .

Christina concentrated on her food, but the hunger she felt had little to do with the plump pigeon or the beef pie. "Marriage is about money and land and titles and lots of other things, when it ought to be about *love.*"

Harry swigged from his tankard. She was very aware of the heat of him hovering near her shoulder. She was learning marriage was also about intimacy. There didn't seem to be a modest or retiring bone in Harry's body—his amazingly *athletic* body.

"Love is a foolish romanticism dreamed of by women," he replied. "Men may admire a woman's looks or respect her intelligence or appreciate her talents, but to expect more is to whistle down the wind."

"I had a grandmother who was said to do that. They say she created a cyclone once." Christina poked at the early spring peas. With Malcolms, everything was possible, so Harry's protests didn't sway her much.

He finally sat down across from her to dig into his pie. Christina noted that, unlike many men, he used his polite manners in private as well as public, but he ate like a starving man. An astonishing quantity of food disappeared in a short time. Her own meal went neglected as she watched him in fascination.

He caught her looking, dabbed his mouth with his napkin, and leaned back in his chair. "I won't pounce on you. I'll give you the time I promised if you need it. I just don't want you to think there's anything lacking in either of us if the results aren't the sort you fancy."

"I used to see affection when you looked at me," she said quietly.

In Harry's experience, Christina was many things, but quiet wasn't one of them. He lifted an inquiring eyebrow.

"Now, all I see is confusion and anger and maybe a touch of despair. Is marrying me so very dreadful?"

Stunned by her insight into the turmoil within him, Harry shook his head vigorously. "Marrying you is"— he didn't know how to express the perplexity of being torn two ways—"is what I need right now. I dislike disrupting your life this way, but we both have duties, and we might as well be about them."

She made a moue of distaste and poked at her food some more. Even disheveled from their long ride, she couldn't be anything less than glorious in his eyes— perhaps because he saw the joy and courage in her and craved it for himself.

"I want love, like my sisters have, not duty." She stabbed a bit of meat with her fork and shredded it with her knife. "Will you tell me what is bothering you?"

Not likely. He wasn't in the habit of confiding

doubts, much less his deepest nightmares. He waved his fork dismissively. "The usual things. The loss of my family. I never expected to inherit. I know nothing of estate duties. I hate being unprepared."

She nodded in understanding. "I'm not prepared either, so we'll learn together. Is your house very large?"

Harry tried not to snort ale out his nose at this ingenuous question. "You'll see on the morrow. You needn't worry about the staff. My father and brother lived bachelor lives, and the staff serves well without instruction."

They would both do better if he could find the source of the estate's financial problems and escape back to London and the lives they knew, but he didn't know how quickly that could be accomplished.

Watching his bride of a few hours pick at her food, remembering the eagerness of her response to his kiss, he felt his spirits lift. Her dowry had forced Carthage to slink back into his hole for another few months. Perhaps that's all it would take once Harry halted the flow of cash into the Abomination. Then he could spend the next few years producing heirs.

He was looking forward to that part of his duties. He had the feeling Christina would be an imaginative lover. She certainly brought a great deal of imagination to the rest of her life.

Auras, indeed! He smiled fondly and shoved back from the table. He'd best leave her to bathe alone or he wouldn't get a wink of sleep tonight.

"Your bath should be ready shortly," he said. "I'll wait downstairs until you're in bed."

She tilted her head to study him in that manner he recognized.

"Your lust is showing, Harry. I'll unbar the door *after* I'm done."

Maidens shouldn't notice such things, but knowing she did aroused him even more. With a muttered imprecation, he adjusted his breeches, grabbed his coat, and went down the stairs, shouting at the innkeeper to bring up the bath.

Five

Harry's black mood returned the next day as they rode into Sussex. As a boy, he'd loved growing up in the countryside, rambling through the Roman ruins that were scattered across the landscape.

The death of his mother when he was sixteen had sent him straight down the old Roman road into London in a desperate bid to escape his father's grief. Rather than recall the pain of those days and his father's subsequent mental deterioration, Harry watched Christina.

When he'd returned to their bed the previous night, she had been slumbering as if exhausted. Beyond an indecipherable murmur, she hadn't noticed his arrival. He'd almost laughed at the man's shirt she'd donned as nightshift. Only Christina would wear so outrageous a honeymoon garment. Her true nature might be utterly hopeless for a duchess, but Harry found her lack of pretension refreshing in an otherwise uncertain world.

Given the state of his arousal, he'd thought never to find sleep after he climbed in beside her. But these past weeks must have taken their toll on him. He'd slept the sleep of a babe with his wife snuggled against him.

This morning, she had been awake and dressed and ordering breakfast before he was ready to greet the light of day.

She was avoiding him like a skittish mare, sending him flirtatious looks, then skipping away. He wasn't at all displeased with their courtship so far. It wouldn't have been fair to bed her last night and then expect her to ride a full day's journey today. But he'd set a pattern he meant to keep. She would sleep in his bed until she was his wife in more than name. He was determined to have some pleasure of this life of duty he'd inherited.

Seeing the familiar stand of oaks at a bend in the road, dreading what lay ahead, Harry dallied, letting the sway of Christina's hips on the horse distract him. He was torn between opposing desires to wallow in lust or strike out across the field to relieve his tension in a good gallop.

Since clouds were forming out at sea, and he didn't want Christina caught in a squall alone, he spurred his horse to ride beside her.

"The churchyard is in dire need of work," she said, reining in as they passed the parish church.

Harry frowned at the overgrown graveyard and walkway. "Perhaps the village is no longer using it."

He'd been visiting in Oxford when word had finally reached him of the tragic deaths of his father and brother. The winter roads had been impassable. By the time he'd ridden as far as London, his family had already been buried in Sussex. Perhaps the vicar had used the estate chapel for the funeral.

He wished he could have attended. Some part of

him still couldn't believe he wouldn't see stout Edward riding down the road to greet him, or that his father wouldn't be leaning against the gatehouse when he rode up.

"The roof looks rotted on that rear corner," he noted, striving for unconcern. "I've not been this way in some years, and my father seldom wrote of village affairs."

"It seems a shame. That's a fine stand of rowans in the yard. I'd wager there's been a church of some sort here since the beginning of time."

"I believe they found traces of a Roman mosaic in the cellar. Maybe the villagers decided they didn't wish to worship in a pagan place." Harry didn't believe his own words but rode on. Coming home incognito was an excellent idea, he decided. He'd sent word ahead that he'd be arriving, but everyone would be expecting a caravan of carriages. He could study the situation more closely arriving quietly on horseback.

"That must be the village." Christina eagerly leaned forward in her seat to gaze upon the buildings at the bottom of the hill. "Will it have a stationery? As a Malcolm, it's my duty to keep a journal of events."

"The mercantile used to sell books and papers. It's a far cry from London, though," he warned her.

She gave him one of those looks he was coming to think of as her "seer-look." Anyone who believed in witches would certainly think himself hexed by now. Or bewitched. He thought that look enchanting.

"I love living simply. London is all artifice and not for me."

Harry didn't think she'd lived in the country long

enough if that was her opinion, but he politely refrained from saying so.

Sheep gamboled in a nearby field, and Harry could see newly plowed furrows in the distance. The hedgerow could use some work. Perhaps the field hands were too busy with spring planting to clean up the roadside. It wasn't as if he knew anything about the seasonal chores required.

Christina examined the village unfolding in front of them as they rode down the hill. "How far is your home?"

"A mile or so by road. It can't be seen until one comes upon it." Harry frowned as the blacksmith's cottage came into view. He remembered it as a bustling place where men gathered to discuss the weather and local gossip while Abraham mended their wagon wheels and shod their horses. The yard was empty and silent today.

The only reason he could think of for this oddly inactive street was a funeral. But if there was a funeral, everyone should be gathered at the church.

"Do you have no carpenters or thatch menders?" Christina asked, slowing her horse to gaze around her.

"We employed several last I was here." The wind picked up with the approaching storm, and Harry watched a loose tile slide down the vicar's roof. The colorful flowers he remembered filling the vicarage yard had been replaced by the new green leaves of spring vegetables.

Shouldn't there be some sign of the townspeople preparing a welcome for a returning duke? Or had it been so long since any duke had gone away that they'd forgotten the traditions he remembered from childhood?

"Is that a tavern?" Christina indicated a half-timbered Elizabethan cottage that had once housed a family of weavers.

A crudely painted sign bearing a red lion swung over the door now. The wattle and daub paneling between the timbers had cracked, and gaping holes revealed the lathes inside. In the prosperous villages they had passed, failing wattle had been replaced by brick nogging or weatherboarding. Why hadn't Sommersville prospered as those other villages had?

He could almost feel disapproval radiating off his new wife as they rode through a dirt street empty of all but a few dogs. Christina fell silent, but her head veered back and forth, taking in the deplorable state of the mercantile and grocer's establishments, the tumbledown remnants of houses, the lone sheep tethered and grazing in someone's front yard.

Behind the hedgerows and fenced-in backyards, women looked up from hanging their wash, but no one recognized him, Harry realized with relief.

Why hadn't Jack told him that the village had come to this pass?

His steward was still in Scotland, looking for buyers for the hunting box. He'd have to have a word or two with him when he returned. Jack had told him the estate was in debt, but that was no reason for the village not to prosper. Unless the crops had failed, the tenants should have cash to spend.

He caught up with Christina after examining the dilapidated condition of a cottage. "I have distant cousins living on the estate property. I think you'll enjoy their company. We all grew up together. My grandfather left them the use of the dower house. Margaret is perhaps a year or two older than you, and Peter is a year or two younger than me, so we should make an amiable group."

"Your cousins have never married?"

"Not that anyone has told me, but it seems no one has told me much in some time. They came up to London several years ago so Margaret could be presented. They may have a small trust fund in addition to their father's salary, but I don't believe Grandfather left her a large dowry. I assume Peter must earn his living if he wishes to have his own household. They live simply. I think they prefer the rural society of Brighton to London."

She nodded without comment.

She was beginning to make him feel uneasy. Shouldn't a woman chatter incessantly, or comment upon the countryside, or ply him with questions about the home that would be hers? What was happening inside that whirling dervish mind of hers?

"This is the drive." After riding a mile or so from the village, Harry stopped to pull the bar to open a gate. The gatehouse appeared to be in good repair, and the gate swung readily.

Oaks lined the drive, blocking the view of the stately home ahead. The *once* stately home, he revised. In his youth, it had been a rambling structure of crumbling old castle harmoniously merged with a brick manor house of the 1500s. He remembered playing among the stone parapets of the castle and leaping to the slate roof to hide among the brick chimneys of the manor.

His mother had overseen the construction of a new wing and begun restoration of the old parts before she died of ague. His father had obsessively continued building and restoring after her death. Harry had left for Oxford the day his father hired workmen to dig a tunnel from the new wing to the stable so the duke could come and go unnoticed—although why he wished to do so had never been explained.

Every holiday that Harry had returned home, there had been some new and more grotesque "improvement." He'd left for good when his father began constructing stairs to towers that no longer existed and windows overlooking a courtyard that had long since been built over. The towers that remained had doors opening onto thin air, and interior walls sported windows looking into the next room—sometimes through the ceiling.

He hadn't been able to bear watching the deterioration of his once hearty, jovial father into the haunted architect of a nightmare.

Spring leaves whispered on the trees above them. The lush lawn spread down to the fields just as he remembered. He knew that the copse of woods on the next hill hid the remains of a Roman villa where he'd spent many a happy day hunting treasure. He'd always loved Sommersville.

He fell silent as the mansion rose into view above the trees.

Christina gasped in delight at the sight of pennants flying from a distant tower and row upon row of brick chimneys extending across a . . . She looked closer. A parapet? Castles had parapets. Houses had chimneys. Sommersville apparently had a lot of both.

She pondered the oddity of the brick dome over the stone portion that ought to be a castle, and the stone parapet that fronted the brick portion of the house that ought to be a Tudor mansion. She wasn't an architect, but she'd seen many beautiful stately homes. This wasn't one of them.

A new brick wing jutted out to the front with the symmetrical windows and centered door in the current mode. The builder had used a tile roof to match that of the Elizabethan section, and the two parts might have blended harmoniously had the new wing not possessed an elegant portico entrance while the manor entrance was stripped to a single granite step.

Curious, she turned to Harry, but her question died on her tongue. His aura was streaked through with black. His face was a shuttered mask. He held his jaw so tautly that a muscle ticked near his eye. He rode with shoulders stiff and back straight, and nothing of his usual careless seat in the saddle was evident. He looked every inch the formidable duke.

Harry did not want to go home, she concluded. From the looks of it, he ought to turn around and gallop back to London as quickly as his horse could take him. Biting her lip, looking longingly at the fascinating structure ahead, Christina halted her mount.

"If you did not wish to bring me here, you should have said so." She tried to keep the hurt out of her voice, but she wanted honesty in their marriage. She thought Harry had always been honest with her, but he wasn't being so now.

"I know you're used to better," he said stiffly. "I'll do whatever is necessary to make you comfortable here until we can return to London."

She blinked and tried to analyze the white spike of light through his dark aura. Sometimes reading auras was even more difficult than reading expressions or tones. Perhaps she ought to just stick to words until she had a better understanding of her new husband.

"I'm comfortable in the woods." She gestured at the copse of trees now dipping to the rush of an oncoming storm. "If it's me you're concerned about, you may smile now."

That, at least, relaxed his thunderous expression. His golden-brown eyebrows shot up, and he wore that "what now" expression he sometimes adopted when she said something particularly odd.

She didn't want Harry to think of her as an oddity, or as an "imaginative little creature." She wanted him to see her as a woman worth loving. Uncertain how to go about that, she kicked her horse into a gallop and raced ahead of him.

To her satisfaction, he galloped his big black gelding alongside her, not pulling ahead as he could easily do but guarding her flank as if he were an old-fashioned courtier. Delighted, she brought her mount to a dancing halt at the granite step and bestowed her best smile on him.

"I can't believe this is my home and you're a duke, Harry. This is like some magnificent fairy tale come true."

He swung off his horse and stood ready to help her down. "Then let's hope this isn't the palace cursed by the wicked witch where the princess comes to grief. Come along, Rapunzel, let's see what spell you can cast."

Thrilled that he hadn't called her foolish, Christina placed her hands on his shoulders and let him swing her down, even though she was perfectly capable of dismounting on her own. Harry's hands tightened around her waist, and he brought her so close she could see the whiskers on his jaw and smell the very male odor of perspiration from their long ride. She inhaled deeply, wanting to know more of his masculinity after being surrounded all her life by females. His heat felt good against the cool wind plastering her clothes to her body.

His hands lingered, and from the way he gazed into her eyes, she thought perhaps he'd kiss her again. She longed to explore the sensations he had introduced her to earlier, but just as he lowered his head, the front doors of the Tudor manor swung open.

"Harry! Where's your carriage? We had no word of your arrival."

Reluctantly pulling back from Harry's embrace, Christina watched as a beautiful woman swept toward them in a froth of lace, black silk, swinging panniers, and perfume. Behind her followed a gentleman in equally expensive mourning attire, although he wore an expression of amusement and interest instead of the sorrow of his companion. She immediately liked the looks of his reddish-blond hair and the shades of blue in his aura. She thought she could trust him.

The woman she wasn't so certain about. There was a little too much dull gold in her aura that could indicate jealousy and selfishness, but she was radiant in black. Defensively, Christina clung to Harry's arm.

"Christina, my cousins, Margaret and Peter Winchester." Harry pulled her to his side as Peter bowed low. "Meg and Pete are cousins, thrice removed, I believe we decided. Their father, Jack, runs this place." In introduction, Harry gestured proudly. "My bride, Christina."

"Your Grace." Margaret made a sweeping curtsy, her neatly coiffed blond head dipping low.

Disconcerted to be so addressed by someone older and more elegant than herself, Christina tried not to grimace. She hated starting out on the wrong foot.

A rainbow glimmer hovering in the dark of the open doorway just behind the pair caught Christina's eye, and her dismay dissipated. "Oh, do you have ghosts?" she cried, hurrying forward, ignoring Margaret's elegant display of manners. "Harry, if you have given me a haunted house, I shall adore you for the rest of my days."

Leaving behind a trail of dismay and male laughter, she dashed up the front step in pursuit of the faint rainbow floating in the interior. A house as old as this one might possess dozens of spirits. She might finally learn to converse with them. What if this apparition was the old duke or Harry's brother come to inspect her?

Halting abruptly at that appalling thought, Christina turned to call for Harry.

In that moment of hesitation, a limestone lintel

smashed to the ground where she would have stepped next, missing her by inches.

Overhead, thunder cracked, lightning flashed, and the first drops of rain began to fall.

Six

Peter reached Christina before Harry could, protecting her from the cloud of dust raised by the crashing stone and catching her arm to keep her from falling backward down the entry step.

Harry contemplated punching his handsome cousin's eyes out but decided that would be an undukely reaction, especially since his duchess shook herself free to crouch beside the crumbled lintel, showing no sign of demurely fainting away.

For a brief moment, he'd had a devastating image of Christina lying crushed and lifeless on his doorstep, and his heart had stopped beating. He never wanted to experience that terror again. The house had claimed far too many lives already. To have it harm Christina in any way was a disaster to be prevented at all cost.

"How extraordinary," Christina cried, setting Harry's heart back in motion. "I think the ghost was warning me to stay back."

Ignoring Peter's upraised eyebrow at the duchess's interesting viewpoint, Harry crouched beside her to be certain she hadn't been hurt. His cousins would think Christina as eccentric as his father, but his concern right now was to remove her from harm.

Later, he'd worry about how his bride's predilection for ghost hunting would appear to both family and rural society.

"Why the devil hasn't this hovel been pulled down by now?" he roared at no one in particular as thunder rumbled in the background.

Instead of inspecting the shattered stone, he brushed the hair from Christina's face and ran his fingers along her jaw to be certain she hadn't been hit by flying debris. Startled by his action, she watched him through widened eyes. Ascertaining she hadn't received so much as a bruise, he pulled her to her feet and half carried her—protesting—away from the Tudor entrance. "You'd think with all the construction, someone would have fixed the crumbling bits," he growled.

Christina dug in her heels, but Harry had already had enough of this homecoming. Forcing his cousins to follow, he caught Christina's hand and dragged her through the raindrops toward the entrance of the new wing. "I want men out here on the morrow to either fix it or tear the deathtrap down."

"Oh, Harry, no, you can't do that!" Christina stopped in her tracks, halting his progress to lay a gloved hand against his chest while raindrops cascaded down her brow. "It's a perfectly splendid house, and I do so want to meet your ancestors."

"My ancestors are dead and in their graves, just as they should be!" He never yelled. He was known for his unshakable good humor. What the devil had come over him? Christina, most likely. He couldn't get rid of the bloody image of her lying crushed under a chunk of stone. "The place isn't haunted—the foundation is crumbling, and the walls should have been pulled down long ago. The house killed my family!"

She looked suitably shocked by his vehemence, and thoughtful. Good. Maybe now she would leave the moldering manor alone. Pulling her by the hand, he continued their progress toward the new wing.

"Actually, if the foundation was failing, the workmen would have noticed," Peter said, falling in beside them as if Harry wasn't having a howling fit on the front lawn.

"Parapets do not crumble and lintels do not fall without cause," Harry grumbled. "Who is the architect my father hired?"

"Oh, he didn't hire an architect." Coming up on his other side, Meg gestured vaguely. "He told the masons and carpenters what to do."

Harry tried to recall the last time he'd seen Meg, but all he could remember was a gangly adolescent with a painful fancy for Edward. He'd just gone up to Oxford when she'd had her come-out, and he could see she would fit into any London ballroom now.

"Harry, don't make any decisions until you have someone knowledgeable look it over," Christina urged as they dashed under cover of the portico entrance.

He didn't know if he could afford anyone knowledgeable. Even if there wasn't a sinkhole undermining the foundation, there might as well be for all the money that had been poured down it. Trying not to growl, Harry nodded his agreement.

Even so, Christina pulled back and looked at him oddly. He supposed his *aura* had turned pink and purple or some such.

"Where are the servants?" he demanded, finally noticing that no orderly parade waited to be introduced to the new duchess. They'd had plenty of time—and a noisy warning—to realize he'd arrived.

With its Corinthian columns, the new entrance should have provided ample excuse for an ostentatious display of household staff. "Where's Dalrymple? And Mrs. Hoskins?"

Peter cleared his throat. A frown of concern marred Meg's white brow. Harry threw them both black looks for not answering, but he had other concerns at the moment.

"Stay here. I'll not have any more beams falling on your head." He left Christina on the outside steps and opened the front door.

The grandiose foyer stood empty and smelled of mold. He glanced upward to be certain the skylight wouldn't come crashing down, checked the doorways and stairs for signs of habitation, then held out his arm for Christina. "Looks as if you'll have the pleasure of hiring your own people." At the thought of the cost of staff, Harry could feel the cash being sucked from his pocket, but he'd counted on trained staff to ease his bride's transition into duchess. He'd rather not imagine what Christina considered to be her duties in the role.

At the lack of welcome, Christina glanced at the three of them as if they might be up to mischief. She'd been raised in the household of a marquess and would recognize the lack of consequence represented by an unstaffed household. Harry froze when she cautiously stepped inside to the inlaid tiles of the Sommersville coat of arms on the foyer floor. He watched in relief as she whirled around to take in her new home with the excitement of a child at Christmas.

She sighed in delight at the high, arched plaster ceiling adorned with gilded moldings and a mural of clouds and gods, examined the elaborately carved columns and statuary guarding the interior doorways and staircase, then turned back to face her waiting audience.

"There's a door in the ceiling. How does one go through it?"

Naturally, she'd spot the one oddity. "One doesn't," Harry replied, catching her hand again so she didn't explore deeper. "One falls through it if one trespasses on the roof."

Harry was afraid to see what undiscovered abominations might lurk in the shadows. His mother had ordered the murals and statues, so he knew they posed no danger. As far as he was aware, the door in the ceiling was his father's only addition to the foyer since the duchess had died.

"This wing is superb," Christina offered, looking up at him with a smile, "but there are no ghosts in it. What happened to the servants?"

Leave it to Christina not to mince words. Since his own query on the matter hadn't been answered, Harry crossed his arms and awaited an explanation from his cousins.

Peter shrugged. "Your father apparently let them

go. He and Edward lived simply. They shared a valet and hired someone from the village to come in and cook in the evenings. I suppose they saw no reason to keep the place up since they never entertained."

"Why didn't they entertain?" Christina whispered near Harry's ear, apparently not wishing to draw attention to his family's oddity.

Harry liked having her close. He didn't know how she managed to smell like a pine forest after a long hot ride, but he'd always thought her scent refreshing. "My father lost interest after my mother died. I don't know Edward's excuse."

"He was too busy," Meg answered for him. "He had to act as magistrate in your father's absence, watch over the estate since your father would not, and he had business in Brighton and Dover that kept him away a great deal. Since he had no duchess to act as hostess, he preferred to entertain his friends elsewhere."

Edward had been considerably older than Harry, and they'd never been close. Looking around at the empty mansion, Harry regretted that. His brother couldn't have had much of a life living in their father's shadow.

He couldn't afford to waste time regretting the past. There was too much yet to do. "We'll need a cook and a housekeeper at the very least. Christina, you can send down to the village tomorrow and see who's available." He'd turned his back on her for only a second, and she had already wandered off to examine a statue of a Roman god.

At his suggestion, she looked surprised. "I have never hired servants. How does one go about it?"

Harry had hoped to start immediately on the estate books, leaving the household to Christina's care. It was just dawning on him that there might be some disadvantage to marrying a female who hadn't been trained to the role of duchess. They would have fared well in his small London household, but running an estate of this size required an army of hired help and the organizational skills of a general.

"We'll wait until Luke and your maid arrive tomorrow. They can inquire in the village." No point in starting out by criticizing her inadequacies.

Harry crossed the enormous foyer for the wide staircase opposite the door. He had no idea how he would pay for anything, but there had to be some money here in the house or in a bank somewhere. The estate earned an income far beyond what the king could spend. In his senility, his father must have found reason to hide sums from Jack. "Are the two of you still living in the dower house?" he asked his cousins.

"It's warmer there," Peter explained.

"It wouldn't have been proper otherwise," Meg murmured.

"To hell with proper. If you have servants, we can use them here for now. Find rooms, start fires," he ordered. "I refuse to live in a mausoleum."

From her place in the shadows, Christina thought Meg's face lit with delight, but the other woman quickly hid it behind a demure expression. Peter grimaced in a manner akin to Harry's, but he took the order well.

Christina didn't wish her ignorance to be a burden upon anyone. "You might ask your cousins if they would *like* to live here," she reminded her husband, joining him on the imposing staircase. "Just because you are now a duke doesn't mean you have the right to rule other people's lives."

"Actually, it does give me the right, not that it matters." He started up the stairway with the air of a king come to claim his kingdom, scanning the columns, the artwork, the dirty marble stairs. "Everybody does what they want around here anyway. It's not as if they'll pay attention to me."

"You're the duke, old man," Peter called up to him. "If we don't obey, you can cut off our allowance."

Looking startled, Harry glanced over the balustrade at them. "I thought you had your own trust funds."

"It's hardly enough to keep us in style," Peter replied. "*We* appreciate servants and sound roofs over our heads as much as anyone."

"Right. If I'm already paying for your servants, you can move them up here." He loped back down the stairs and grabbed Christina's hand. "Let's find something to eat first."

Considering the desire she felt and the magnetism Harry exuded, Christina thought the kitchen was infinitely preferable to a bedroom right now. She started to ask Meg and Peter to join them, but the pair had already melted into the shadows of the old house, apparently choosing to leave the newlyweds alone.

With fascination, Christina followed Harry through an enormous dining room into a back hall to a servants' staircase and down into the kitchen. The only time she had spent in kitchens involved stealing victuals for her forays into the woods—or graveyards. But even in her limited experience, she knew this was a grand example of one.

"Your family dreams big, doesn't it?" she said, admiring the ceiling-tall fireplace lined with neatly blackened iron grates and boxes whose purpose she could not begin to fathom.

"A damned nuisance, given how small the family is," Harry replied. Grabbing kindling from a stack on the hearth, he heaved it into one of the smaller grates.

While Harry started the fire and put a kettle on for tea, Christina explored the pantries. "There's some salted ham and jars of preserves," she called. "I don't suppose there are chickens and eggs anywhere about?"

Swinging around to leave the dark pantry, she walked into the solid wall of Harry's chest.

He caught her before she could fall back. His grip on her upper arms was painful, but the look in his eyes robbed her of breath. Before she could speak, he crushed her mouth beneath his.

It wasn't a romantic kiss, not the pleasant kind she'd dreamed of, but a force well beyond her inexperienced imagination.

Harry consumed her, drank greedily of her mouth, parted her lips, and took his pleasure with her tongue. Caught unprepared, Christina liquefied like butter placed too close to the stove. She clung to his vest to stay upright, tilted her head to kiss him back, and learned the age-old terror and pleasure of desire.

As Harry hauled her into his arms, she slid her hands into his hair, and their bodies collided and caught fire. Christina finally understood what it was that drew her sophisticated sister to a farmer and her country cousin to an earl. It wasn't logic. It was magic.

And a man whose aura screamed "Be wary!" possessed the power to unleash that magic on her.

Terrified of her own reaction more than the force of Harry's, Christina pushed away, falling back against the pantry shelves and trying to catch her breath while she stared at this new Harry she had never known. He bunched his fingers into fists and stepped back, as visibly shaken as she was. She'd completely undone his hair, and it spilled half over his shoulder like some drunken sailor's. The lust in his aura wasn't far removed from that of a sailor. Or a pirate.

Without a word of explanation or apology, he walked away.

Christina had the decided notion that Harry's home unsettled him in ways she could not understand, and unless she lost herself in the corridors tonight, her husband had every intention of making her his bride.

And she wasn't at all certain that she wanted to stop him.

Seven

"Why are we in such a hurry?" Christina asked as Harry tugged her hand to lead her from the kitchen after their meal.

He nearly dragged her up the enormous front stairs and down a corridor covered in plaster dust. After retreating from that kiss in the pantry, Harry had eventually returned, only to watch her over their meal as if she were a luscious fruit ripe for picking, so she had a fairly good idea why he was in such a rush.

Considering that her mouth practically watered while returning his heated gaze, she thought Harry might be quite correct about the "ripe" part. She could easily be a juicy plum ready to burst. But she resisted his tug and dawdled in order to look around. Or to delay the inevitable.

Judging by the amount of dust on the mourning cloths over the statuary in the hall, they hadn't been swept free of cobwebs since the death of the Prince of Wales some years back. She sneezed and ran to keep up.

"I want to see what kind of disaster we must live in," Harry said. "The next inn is miles away, and I don't want to have to go out in the storm." He flung open several doors. "This is the new wing my mother had built. I'm hoping one of the bedchambers has been finished."

Peering over Harry's shoulder, seeing only small salons without carpet, walls without plaster, and linen-draped furniture stacked erratically, Christina didn't comment on their decidedly unfinished state. Harry slammed the doors and stalked onward.

"Is this still the new wing?" she asked as they seemed to traverse a mile of corridor, past a gallery of framed ancestors and a wall of windows overlooking . . . Christina glanced down. A dirt pit?

"The last I was here, the new wing housed the public rooms. Mother wanted a modern salon and dining parlor on the main floor, with the ballroom on the top floor. My parents designed suites in between the two floors, but as you see, they weren't completed after my mother died. We continued using the bedchambers in the old manor."

"Oh, the pretty brick part with all the chimneys!" Delighted that they'd be using the older part of the house where ghosts were more likely to linger, Christina decided to ignore the black spikes in Harry's aura. Maybe mourning for the loss of his family was causing them.

"The rooms have fireplaces, at least, although I can't promise there aren't bird nests in them," he said gloomily, flinging open a set of double doors. "We should have traveled with the coach so your maid would be here to air out the linens."

He stood back so Christina could enter first. Thinking it might have been nice if Harry had made some romantic gesture of carrying her over the threshold, but willing to give him credit for thinking of linens, she entered what appeared to be a study.

An aging secretary desk spilled over with dusty books and papers. A stack of cracked leather trunks teetered in a corner beside heavy blue draperies. Her quick inventory included a cricket bat, a net with a long handle, a box of crumbling stones, a globe of the world, and a wing chair buried beneath more books.

"It appears all is as you left it, Harry," she said dryly. "I trust your favorite hound isn't mummified beneath that monument by the window." She studied the gray hunk of stone with odd characters carved into it.

"No, we buried him by the Roman villa," he said, apparently as taken aback by the room's condition as she. "I found the 'monument' in the dirt dredged up from my father's tunnel."

"Tunnel?"

He ignored the question to cross the moth-eaten carpet, apparently inspecting the premises for falling ceilings or rotten floors. She'd seen her brother-in-law examine a crumbling castle in just such a manner. She didn't think Harry knew a great deal about construction, but if there were any rodents hiding in the heaps of dirty clothes, she'd prefer that he find them first.

She admired his courage in the face of . . . what did one call it? Devastation? He'd obviously left the room like this when he was but a boy, so that wasn't quite the word. Negligence? This went well beyond mere negligence. The placed looked as if had been torn apart and not put back together again.

"How old were you when you last lived here?"

"I left for Oxford at sixteen." Kicking aside a battered saddle, he opened a connecting door. "I came back for holidays, though. The maids always kept the place dusted and didn't disturb my personal possessions. The last few times I was here, I stayed in a guest room because the housekeeper said the family rooms needed repair."

Christina watched the powerful muscle over his square jaw tighten as he stared into the adjoining chamber, and her stomach did a little jig. In that moment, he was nearly a stranger to her—a mature man with pressing responsibilities, a dangerous look in his eyes, and a sexual attractiveness she had difficulty resisting. And he was looking into the bedchamber she suspected he meant for them to share.

"I don't suppose I can expect your mother's rooms to be kept as she left them?" she asked brightly.

He turned back to her, and the dangerous light in his eyes flared brighter. She gulped and held her ground. This was Harry. She refused to be afraid just because it looked as if he was struggling with invisible demons.

"My mother's room has been bolted shut since her death."

So much for that escape. She tried to think of a witty rejoinder to make him laugh, but all she could think about was the immense task of restoring this old house to a condition that would make Harry happy again.

She didn't even know how often one changed linens or how meals appeared upon the table. She'd always expected to live in a household full of servants who knew these things.

She was woefully ignorant of the tasks ahead of her.

And not terribly interested in learning. She wanted to find the ghosts and hear the story of what had happened here.

Declaring his old room unfit for habitation, Harry stalked down the corridor in search of a better one. Lifting her skirt to follow her husband, Christina sought some means of defusing his growing temper. She wasn't at all certain she approved of the more forceful Harry, but she couldn't deny he excited her in new and dangerous ways. He was like a thundercloud racing through the musty corridor, sweeping it clean with his energy.

She glanced longingly at all the closed doors they passed in pursuit of better accommodations, but Harry evidently had a particular room in mind and didn't indulge her curiosity. By now, she was so twisted and turned around, she figured it would take a week to find her way outside.

Harry hurried her down a staircase she hadn't noticed earlier. "I should have inspected the premises before bringing you here," he said.

"And left me at home without you?" Not really paying attention to his protestations, Christina stopped on the landing to gaze out a pretty leaded-glass window. To her puzzlement, it looked over a narrow shaft between this part of the building and the old castle. If she opened the window, she could reach out and touch the stone of the old walls.

"*That's* why I didn't inspect the place first," he

called back to her from farther down the winding stairs.

"You thought I was better off here than in London?" Laughing at that, Christina raced after him, more excited than ever by her new home.

"I thought *I* would be better off with you here." Harry rattled a locked door at the bottom of the stairs, felt around for a key along the frame, and apparently finding none, slammed the old latch with his boot heel.

Nearly bowled over by his admission as much as by his action, Christina gaped for a full minute after the door sprang open.

"I'm tired of locked doors," Harry said, as if that explained his behavior. Apparently unaware of her astonishment, he caught her hand and dragged her down still another gallery, this one with normal windows overlooking a perfectly normal pastoral scene of fields and trees.

In the fading afternoon light, shadows hollowed Harry's jaw. His restored hair ribbon had loosened again, and a strand of hair had escaped, giving him a disheveled appearance. After watching his display of strength on the door, Christina was prepared for him to wave a cutlass and order the mains'l set.

"Of course," she murmured. "One does become so bored with the tedium of keys."

He shot her innocent expression a disgruntled look but made no comment as they proceeded onward.

Nervously, Christina paced the bedchamber where Harry had finally left her. The pleasant room had the unused look of a showpiece, lacking the riot of life in

Harry's boyhood study. The bed seemed relatively new and the covers not moth-eaten. There weren't any personal items strewn about. Harry had lit a fire in the grate, and the room hadn't filled with smoke. She could not object to the accommodations at all.

She *could* object to Harry's evident intention of returning here to join her. She could hear him rattling doors up and down the hall in search of candles. She didn't think he would linger long on the search.

She hated acting like a nervous maiden. She was the adventurous Malcolm, the one who was willing to jump in where angels feared to tread. Mating was a perfectly natural act, and nothing she should fear.

She just didn't want her first time to happen this way. She wanted Harry to look at her with love, not lust. She wanted his complete attention, not the distracted air of a man determined to do his duty.

But she could hardly condemn him to sleeping in the kitchen after all his solicitous efforts on her behalf.

He'd carried in her satchel with its seductive shifts and perfumed candles, and her usual decisiveness had fled at the sight of the contents. She'd certainly give him the wrong impression if she used them.

Harry wasn't waiting for impressions. If she didn't don her lacy nightshift, he'd take her in her boy's old shirt, without the enhancements of her mother's charmed scents.

She *hated* dithering. Casting off the traveling gown she'd worn these last two days, she washed in the warm water Harry had carried all the way from the kitchen. She was having difficulty enough adjusting to the role of wife without picturing her laughing, charming Harry as a stern duke who shouldn't have to haul water.

She'd donned a normal shift this morning instead of her boy's attire, hoping to appear more like a duchess. The shift wasn't a romantic confection of lace and ribbons but a sturdy linen meant for traveling. The room was too cool to dally long in without a robe, but she didn't have one with her.

She pulled the rose damask coverlet off the bed, shook it out, and sneezed from the dust. Wrapping its length around her, she sat on the bed to remove her ankle boots and stockings.

Harry returned, triumphant, having scavenged a handful of candles from other chambers. With his hair more mussed than ever and dirt smudging his usually immaculate jabot, he looked very manly. Christina bit back a sigh of appreciation when he loosened his jabot to reveal the strong column of his throat.

"I thought you'd be in bed by now." After one quick glance at her, Harry systematically began setting candles in brackets and lamps.

Christina thought it best not to tell him she had a satchel full of the most expensive candles money could buy and could have saved him a search.

She needed all the willpower she could summon to keep her from reaching for him. She could scarcely tear her gaze from his long, powerful legs concealed only by his tight doeskin breeches as he poured water into the basin and scrubbed his face. What would it feel like to have his bare legs next to hers?

She shut down that thought and forced herself to

say, "I'm not sleeping with you, Harry. The house is littered with beds—choose another."

Grabbing a linen towel, Harry turned to look at her. "We slept together last night. What's the difference?"

She could only glimpse the muscled chest beneath his untied shirt, and she really wanted to see all of it. The image of Harry half naked rose in her mind, and she had to stare at her boot toe rather than reveal her longing. "You're not thinking about sleep tonight," she said. "That's the difference."

"How can you know what I'm thinking?"

She heard his annoyance, listened to him moving restlessly around the room, but she refused to change her mind. Harry had interrupted her before she'd removed her shoes. She could walk out if necessary. "I'm not ignorant, Harry. That kiss wasn't one of courtship."

"If you know that much, then you may as well learn the rest."

Christina winced as Harry's shirt landed on the floor not far from her feet. She didn't dare look up.

"Once we get past this first time, you'll have nothing to fear."

He sat down beside her to pull off his boots, and Christina leaped up as if scalded, then fled across the room. "Just listen to yourself, Harry! 'Get past the first time,' indeed. Is that all this night means to you?"

He froze with his boot over his knee, his splendidly naked torso shadowed in the candlelight. He had his arm across his chest in the act of removing his boot, so she could only admire the bulge of his shoulder, but that was enough to give her visions for a week.

"Christina, I have a lot of things on my mind right now. Love and romance come with time. They'll come much faster if we share a bed."

"It's not the bed sharing I object to," she pointed out. "Did you think your name and title bought my body? Did you listen to the vows we said yesterday?"

Dropping his foot back to the floor, Harry stood, and Christina could enjoy the full glory of his muscled chest. He was broad in the shoulders and narrow at the waist without an ounce of softness on him. A trickle of smooth dark hairs ran between the ridges of his upper chest into a narrow band that drew her gaze downward to his breeches.

She gulped at the bulge pressing at his breeches placket and hastily raised her gaze to his face. She liked it better when Harry was laughing at her. She didn't know the cold duke walking toward her now.

"I meant those vows," he said. "Didn't you? You promised to be my wife. A wife shares her husband's bed. Legally and morally, you have no right to deny me, Christina."

He reached for her, and Christina backed against the wall. She didn't want to succumb to temptation, but she didn't want him to force her either. She simply wished for a little . . .

An aura of peaceful blues walked through a connecting door to shimmer in the far corner she could see past Harry's shoulder. Eyes widening, she watched in awe as the aura formed a silhouette resembling a plump, rather stooped old lady. Auras didn't look like people, she tried to tell herself, but the impression was very distinct—as it had been the day Aunt Iona had warned her.

"Christina?" Harry glanced from her frozen expression to the corner where she stared.

"A ghost just entered, Harry," she whispered. Without thinking, she pressed her hand to his chest to push him out of her way.

The heat of his flesh shocked her. She jerked her hand back and dodged around him. She hadn't seen a ghost so clearly since childhood. It was quite amazing. When would she ever have another chance?

Harry gripped her arm to prevent her from examining the apparition any closer. "Don't use that nonsense to put me off. Come to bed, and I'll show you there's nothing to fear."

She looked at him blankly, then back to the aura pacing in front of the bed as if to prevent them from using it. "Harry, don't you see her? How can we go to bed with a ghost in the room?"

With an expression of disgust, Harry flung aside her arm and swept his shirt from the floor. "Fine then. Play games. The ghost can keep you company. By Jove, I don't need any more eccentrics playing havoc with my life right now."

With that, he slammed out of the room, leaving Christina alone with her shock and dismay.

Eight

A bright ray of light split Harry's head in two. Cursing, covering his eyes, he tried to remember where the devil he was and why.

"I found you!" a cheerful voice called, shattering his splitting head.

Oh, right. He'd just spent his second wedding night drinking himself into a stupor in one of the Abomination's many moldy rooms because of the woman to whom that cheery voice belonged.

"Go away," he grumbled uncharitably. He'd swilled several brandies in an effort to sort out his outrage and dismay, and he wasn't any closer to deciding what he ought to do than he'd been before.

"I can't. I'll get lost again. Breakfast was ready an hour ago."

His head hurt too much to consider the plight of his stomach. He tried squinting into the sunlight to see beyond the voice, but pincers grabbed his brain and dug in. "Have your friendly ghost lead you back."

"She went away when you did. I've looked everywhere and can't find her. Do you suppose it was your mother? There was a lot of love in her aura, but I think she was quiet and a bit shy. I could be wrong, of course," Christina added, opening the draperies to let the sun pour in.

"Shut the damned things!" Harry roared. Or thought he roared. Anything louder than a whisper pounded like thunder.

"I didn't think to bring you coffee. I'm sorry." She didn't sound apologetic. And she didn't close the draperies. "I haven't learned this wifely business yet. My sister Felicity is a natural at it, but I'm more comfortable outdoors than in."

Harry wondered what the punishment was for murdering a duchess. He rather thought even old Henry Fielding would consider it justifiable homicide when he heard the circumstances, but the wise magistrate had died last year. Besides, Harry was the magistrate out here. Dukes probably could get away with murder.

A perfumed hand cooled his overheated brow. "I know the recipe for a hangover. Mother taught us a few useful things. Come along to the kitchen with me and you might live."

"I'm not sure *you* will," he replied testily. But the fresh scent of pine and her cool hand soothed some of the pain. Eyes closed, he took stock: He'd found a long divan to lie on at least. He was still dressed. A blanket of some sort covered him, although he couldn't remember putting it there. His mouth felt like cotton lint. And the ache in his groin hadn't abated.

"I have learned my lesson," she said cheerfully, removing her hand. "Never offer to feed a hungover duke. But I fear you can't be rid of me until you show me the way back. Did you know this room is nearly identical to the priest's study next to the chapel in St.

Andrew's Cathedral in London? Right down to the narrow cot in the windowless cell next to it. Why didn't you sleep on the cot?"

He didn't want to know how she'd seen a priest's study. He didn't want to know why the smoking room had become a priest's cell. Groping for the back of the divan, he sat up and held his head in place with his free hand.

"Oh, good—that's progress. Meg and Peter have probably given up on us. Would another sip of brandy help? I think there's a swallow left."

The strong aroma of fine French brandy drifted under his nose, and scowling, Harry opened his eyes to grab the goblet offered. He drank in haste, feeling the brandy burn through the cotton lint in his throat, waiting for the wallop that would give him strength to stand and strangle her, although his reason for doing so had begun to fade.

"I've talked with Meg's cook and maid, but they want to be paid first. Isn't that odd?"

Balancing his aching head on his palm and propping his elbow on his knee so he didn't topple over, Harry let the alcohol wake him fully. Christina had no inkling of the financial trouble they were in. He couldn't blame her for simply being herself, especially since she was little more than a child accustomed to having everything handed to her.

"I'll show you the garden door. You can go around to the kitchen from there." He stood, and Christina's arm slid around to steady him. He was starting to remember why he'd thought she would make a charming wife. She never complained or nagged or wheedled. She accepted his behavior for what it was and merrily went her own way.

Which was why he was in this state. He wanted her way to be his. Stupid of him. He shook off her helping arm and stood on his own.

She slid her warm hand into his, and he clutched it tight. The physical contact with another human being was inexplicably comforting.

"A garden door? Excellent," she said cheerfully. "I feared I would step out into that fearful pit or risk being crowned by stones again."

Harry shuddered in memory. "On second thought, I'll escort you."

"That really isn't necessary," she chided, leading him from the sun-filled study into the darkened hall. "I must learn to get about on my own. I don't wish to interfere or be a burden to you. We shall carry on as we've always done."

That sounded good until he remembered how Christina normally went on. "You're my wife now," he muttered, steering her down a side hall toward the back of the manor. "I'll look after you."

"Don't be foolish. Peter is already waiting to talk with you, and I'm sure you have a steward who requires your attention. My mother seldom sees my father from sunup to sundown."

That's rather how he'd expected to go on, but not just yet. He'd spent years watching Christina flit about the city without the right to insist he accompany her. Now he needed her company—her support and her help as well. Putting Sommersville to rights would not be the work of one man or one day.

"If you'll notice," he said dryly, "we did *not* spend time together after sundown. Unless you wish to reverse that course, humor me."

That—thankfully—shut her up.

"There you are," Meg cried. "Peter, I told you we shouldn't intrude upon newlyweds. My goodness, Your Grace, you look as if you've slept in those clothes. It's a good thing your servants will be arriving shortly."

Christina sought for even the slightest flicker of spite in Meg's aura but found none. On the other hand, Harry's aura darkened.

"Exploring this abomination of a house is dirty business," he said, as if that explained his dishevelment. "The two of you needn't wait on us. And forget the formal address. When you call me Your Grace, I look around for my father."

Peter did look as if he had been about to leave the breakfast room, Christina decided, but Meg was serenely ensconced at the gleaming table with its silver coffee and tea sets and delicate china. The room hadn't appeared quite so elegant when Christina had left it earlier. It hadn't occurred to her to order Meg's maid to find the china service.

"We might talk of one or two things after breakfast," Peter said. "Father left me some instructions in his absence."

"Excellent. I need to look at the books." After a proprietary kiss to Christina's forehead, Harry grabbed the cup of coffee Meg poured for him and started for the door. "Christina, I'll put you in charge of hiring staff. Just enough for the four of us for now. We'll try to live in the new wing until I've found someone to assure me of the safety of the rest of the place."

"I thought the bedrooms weren't finished in this part of the house?" Christina protested, not letting him escape so easily. She supposed hiring staff couldn't be too terribly difficult, but housing them might be a problem if she wasn't allowed the use of anything except public rooms.

"For all I know, my father turned the ballroom into attics by now. Take a look around, see what we require, make lists." Looking authoritative despite his rumpled shirt and mussed hair, Harry paced, sipping his coffee.

Not quite understanding why Harry must personally do the work when a duke ought to have an office and staff to handle it, Christina wished she could wave a magic wand and put everything right so she could have her jolly Harry back. She'd been imagining playing in the Roman ruins with him, not hiring staff. "Is it the custom here to pay servants before they begin work? If so, I shall need coins."

Harry's back stiffened as she repeated the question he hadn't answered earlier. Christina glanced from his darkening aura to Peter and Meg, but she saw only their surprise.

"I'll see that you have pocket money for immediate expenses," Harry said. "Once we work out what is needed, I'll set up a household account."

That didn't answer her question, but it would have

to suffice. Harry and Peter departed, leaving Christina with Meg. She rather missed Harry's attentiveness now that he'd set his mind to estate duties.

She helped herself to some eggs and toast and tea, trying to think of something she could talk about with the elegant stranger who was far more at home here than she. Odd, to have a home that belonged more to others than oneself. She missed her family already.

"It is very strange to have a house like this with no one to take care of it," she ventured to say, pushing cold eggs around on the plate with her fork.

"The old duke's mind did not operate on earthly planes," Meg replied dryly. "He did not notice food unless someone put it before him."

"Then shouldn't Edward or someone else have seen to it that the place was properly maintained and the duke fed?"

"Edward generally ate with us in the dower house," Meg explained. "He had his horses and his dogs and didn't seem to care much about the mansion. That was the duke's passion." Meg shrugged and poured another cup of tea. "The deterioration of the household was a gradual process. No one thought it peculiar."

"Or no more peculiar than the duke himself." Christina might be untrained in the household arts, but she knew people well. One had to, after all, when all society considered one's family peculiar—or rather, *eccentric,* since they had wealth and position. "I suppose I shall have to talk to Cook and ask her who she recommends for the kitchen," Christina added.

"Would your maid know anything of household servants?"

"I know the village folk. I'd be happy to help," Meg offered.

Christina wanted to leap with joy and accept, but she supposed she shouldn't shirk her duty. "That is extremely generous of you. Shall I go with you and meet them? I must learn more about Harry's home."

"They would be terrified to personally meet a duchess," Meg assured her. "I grew up here. Why don't you explore and see how you wish to house them?"

Christina beamed at her. "I would love that. For some reason, Harry dislikes the house. I wish to make him happier here."

"The house killed his brother and father," Meg said sympathetically. "Your task is not an easy one."

That sobered Christina's joy. "Harry likes old things." She called up her memories of the laughing conversations she and Harry had shared over the years. "He collects Roman coins and likes exploring ruins. I should think he would be proud of his ancestral home. He cannot blame the house for an accident."

"Perhaps once the ghosts are replaced with life, he'll be happier here," Meg suggested.

Christina hid her wince behind her teacup. *Life* meant babies. She'd rather find ghosts. Perhaps she could make Harry understand the house wasn't at fault for the death of his father and brother.

"I believe I'd like to sketch a diagram of the rooms so I have a better idea of what might be safely changed to house everyone. If you would excuse me, I can see there is much to be done." Rising from the table, Christina practically danced out in excitement. She could look for ghosts and make Harry happy at the same time. She would dearly love to have Harry looking at her the way her sisters' husbands looked at them.

Deciding a duchess really shouldn't wear breeches, Christina refrained from donning her favorite ghost-hunting clothes. Once the carriage arrived with her trunks, she could change into one of her older gowns, but for now, she would wear her one good gown and stick to sketching diagrams in the newer rooms that weren't quite so dusty.

She started at the foyer they'd entered yesterday and used that as her base. It seemed to be in the center of the new wing. To the right of the front door was a formal salon, and beyond that a small ladies' sitting room with a Queen Anne secretary Christina thought surely must have belonged to Harry's mother. She glanced through the drawers but other than discerning that the duchess had lovely stationery that someone had rummaged through and left disorderly, she found nothing of interest.

Located behind the sitting room and salon, on the stable side of the house, were a man's study and a billiard room. Eminently practical. Exceedingly boring.

On the back side of the sweeping foyer staircase was a small hall leading to a covered back door overlooking the stables. Carriages could pull around here and footmen could unload trunks without getting wet. Christina liked the way the duchess had designed this floor. She saw no evidence of any of the remodeling that Harry seemed to fret over.

On the left side of the front foyer was the grand dining room with a massive table that could easily sit thirty, she calculated, no doubt with extensions for twenty more. Her head ached at just the thought of emptying the towering china cabinets of their porcelain and crystal to set such a table. She checked the silverware drawers but they seemed oddly sparse. Guests would have to share forks if they tried to seat too many. Odd. Had the servants walked off with the silverware, unbeknownst to the old duke? Or perhaps the butler had locked away the silver service.

Making a note to ask Harry, she added the room to her diagram. Behind the formal dining room was a butler's pantry and the breakfast chamber she'd shared with Meg that morning. The table had already been cleared and Meg was nowhere to be seen, so she located the servants' stairs and descended into the kitchen.

Compared to last night, the room was a bustle of activity. Cook, a sturdy woman who wore a white cap and wielded a wooden spoon, shouted orders at two young girls who were scrubbing pots and chopping vegetables. Meg sat at the large trestle table speaking with several women Christina assumed were potential servants. Surprised that she'd found help so quickly, Christina started to check the time on the big wall clock, but Cook had seen her entrance and barked a command.

Everyone instantly stopped what they were doing and dropped curtsies.

This was the reason duchesses didn't appear in kitchens, Christina noted wryly. "Please, go on about your duties. I'm just passing through. Where does that door lead?" She hastened toward a door she'd seen last night but hadn't opened.

"That's the archive room," Meg explained. "All the old journals and family documents are kept there. My father has an office behind it."

"Journals!" Christina was familiar with journals. Her family was notorious for keeping stacks of them. She wasn't much for pen and paper, but her sister Felicity loved them. Perhaps this summer they could have a good visit and dig through the old volumes. "Would your father mind if I poked around a bit?"

"Of course not. The estate belongs to you, not to us. My father is just the steward here and seldom spends much time in his office."

"Where is he now?" Christina crossed the kitchen, and spurred by Cook, the servants returned to their chores.

Meg stopped interviewing to accompany her. "He's in Scotland. Harry wanted to sell some family lands and a hunting lodge up there, and my father is looking into it."

"They're not entailed?" Hand on the doorknob and itching to explore, Christina halted just long enough to question this oddity. She hadn't thought Harry the kind of man who would sell off family holdings except in a dire emergency.

"No. Apparently none of it is," Meg whispered. "But do not say I told you. There is apparently some legal uproar over the matter."

Christina gazed longingly at the partially open door to the archives. She dearly wished to continue her exploration, but a dukedom—*not entailed?* "How can that be?" she murmured so she couldn't be overheard.

"Peter says Edward never signed the legal documents. He had some plan to parcel out the land into smaller estates. But I am not privy to these matters and cannot say for certain that this is true."

Christina stared blankly over the lovely kitchen designed by Harry's mother, thought of the wonderful old manor and castle probably brimming with Harry's ancestors and heirlooms, and couldn't comprehend selling such riches.

"Harry could sell the house?" she whispered in horror, grasping the full extent of the situation.

"Quite possibly," Meg replied. "Especially since he dislikes it so."

Nine

"Christina! What are you doing over here? Didn't I tell you to stay in the new wing?" Harry's roar carried down the corridor Christina was currently traversing after a day of exploration.

She turned to wait for him to catch up. Now that their trunks had arrived, he was dressed respectably in a dark blue coat and gold vest that nicely set off his tawny hair, but his expression wasn't any less frazzled.

"What the devil is going on here?" he demanded as footmen and maids skittered to and fro, carrying furniture and linens up and down the hall from one room to the next.

"I put my maid and your manservant in charge of choosing suitable chambers."

"You left *Luke* in charge of choosing our chambers?"

He sounded so horrified that she didn't waste time explaining that their choices were limited given the destruction by field mice and squirrels. "He seems a perfectly pleasant man. He and Matilda were snarling and circling like caged cats, so I left them to work it out. I'm sure they'll find something suitable."

"Caged cats," Harry muttered, "do not choose their

cages for a reason. I don't want anyone over here until I know it's safe."

Entering the chamber her maid had chosen for her, Christina set her sketch down on the dresser. "I cannot house servants in a ballroom, a card room, or a library. Unless you care to finish the bedchambers in the new wing, we must all sleep over here. I don't know what you're fretting about. Your father has opened the old manor to the new wing on every level. It's perfectly accessible."

"I will not lose a wife because she is too headstrong to take care of herself," he growled. "I've sent to London for someone to check the safety of these old buildings. Until they've passed inspection, stay out of any areas I haven't had tested."

Harry succeeded in looking exceedingly formidable. His eyebrows drew down in a frown that would suit any duke in the kingdom. His jaw clenched, and a muscle over his sculpted cheekbone jerked. She thought even his queue quivered.

Christina studied the dark flecks in his brown eyes, then patted his bristly cheek. "All my life people have been telling me what to do, Harry Winchester. I'm willing to listen, but not to nonsense. Do you see any floors collapsing?"

Longing to turn her touch into something much more fierce, Harry stifled his frustration. Instead, he changed the topic, unwilling to argue before the parade of footmen trailing in and out with furniture. "How did you find so many servants so quickly?"

"Meg did," she said. "But they insisted on being paid before they would work, and you didn't leave enough coins. That's an odd custom. Do they pay you back if they quit after a day or two?"

Harry had a hunch that the pay was for work that had gone unpaid during his father's time. He kept hoping he'd figure out where his father had hidden his wealth—he prayed it was in a bank account and not converted into a cellar full of expensive French wine and artwork. Despite a day's search, he'd found no bank drafts or receipts or letters giving evidence of any hidden wealth.

"I'll give you more funds," he said. "Don't worry about the servants quitting. We offer the best employment in the area. How did you persuade them to stay if you couldn't pay them?"

"I used my pin money. It didn't cost much, so I also told Meg to order fresh linens. We've put together enough furniture in the attic rooms to house everyone. We'll need new feather beds if we hire more people. The shopkeepers demanded payment in advance as well. Perhaps you should arrange to set up accounts with them so I needn't bother you excessively."

"I'll do that." He tried not to sound too grim, but he was clenching his back teeth. He needed Jack here to explain why the village merchants hadn't been paid. That was beyond negligent. The village depended on the estate for their livelihood. If this had gone on for long, it was no wonder Sommersville looked as if it had slid into a slough of despond.

Sweeping through the room, Christina emptied her pocket bag onto the freshly made bed and began sorting through a strange array of artifacts. "Matilda, tell

Luke that His Grace would like to wash and dress for dinner."

At Christina's casual dismissal, the servants scattered, leaving them alone. Harry noticed the chamber chosen for their use had a distinctly feminine air. The delicate bed didn't suit his taste, nor did the rose comforter and flowered draperies, but who was he to complain? The place smelled of fresh air, no rodents ran about, and he could actually see himself in the mirror.

He wanted to see himself on the tester bed with Christina. "What are you looking for?" He began removing his jabot so he could shave, but his wife's activity held him intrigued.

"When I was exploring, these things dropped out of the air," Christina said, holding one of the objects up to the sun. "I was trying to see if there was any connection between them. Your ghosts appear to be rather shy."

At her nonsensical answer, Harry considered pounding his head against the wall, but he feared he'd bring the roof down. "Out of the air?" he asked in trepidation, hoping he'd misunderstood.

"Yes, I suppose. I never actually saw them fall. I'd hear a noise and turn around and there they'd be. Look, this one is a very worn ring. And here's an old coin. Did they have coins like this in King Hal's time?"

Harry took the copper coin. "King Hal?" He studied the image imprinted on the metal and understood her reference before she answered.

"Doesn't it look like Henry the Eighth? Could the coin be that old?" she asked.

"This section was under construction during Elizabeth's reign, so I suppose it's possible the coin could have fallen into the rafters during that period. I should think coppers like this would be in circulation for decades." He turned the penny over to inspect the other side, relieved to hold a real coin and find a reasonable explanation for its existence. "I've not studied currency from the period, but it looks genuine."

Curious despite himself, he began poking through her trove of treasures to see what else she'd found. "No diamonds or pearls, I see." A pity. If they were to have ghosts, they ought to be useful ones showing him the way to a treasure trove of jewels.

He caught himself before he uttered that undukely remark . . . or before asking if she'd seen any more ghostly auras. No point in encouraging her, or giving anyone an excuse for calling him an eccentric as well, although out of unseemly curiosity, he really wanted to know more.

"If the objects all come from the same spirit," Christina said, "I could assume she was a married woman from the sixteenth century, and that she has secrets to be unlocked." She displayed a tarnished brass key in her palm.

"That's going too far, Christina." He glanced at the key. Old houses like this had more keys floating about than the sea had shells. "All your running around has no doubt jarred loose some old rafter. I told you it's not safe over here. Now let's get dressed. I'm starved."

He looked for his shaving gear on the washstand and, not finding it, searched for his valise. Assuming

Luke had carried it off, he opened the wardrobe for his clean shirts.

The wardrobe was crammed with silks and laces, without a coat or shirt in sight.

"Christina, what is the meaning of this?" He gestured at the colorful array.

She glanced up with a slight frown. "Meaning of clothes? Meaning of wardrobe? Meaning . . . ?" She lifted her eyebrows expressively.

"Where are my things? I need a fresh shirt."

"Oh, that." She began gathering up her oddities. "Luke has put your things in your wardrobe. He complained excessively about not having cedar something-or-other and wanting papers to line the drawers. I gave him some of my mother's aromatic pomanders. I hope you don't mind their scent."

Harry ignored all her perambulations except the relevant one. "*My* wardrobe? And where would that be?"

"Across the hall. The rooms on either side of this one had leaky windows and water stains, I assume from the storm yesterday. But the one across the hall is quite lovely. It overlooks the front lawns, and you can literally count sheep."

"I don't *want* to count sheep," he said in a voice any sensible woman would have recognized as belonging to a man on a dangerous brink. "I want to sleep in a bed with you. Tell Luke to get my things over here, now. Haul over the whole damned wardrobe if he must!"

"Don't be ridiculous, Harry. Dukes don't sleep with

duchesses. No one expects it." She began lining up her treasures on the dresser as if he wasn't a level short of roaring like an angry lion. "We can take this time to know each other while you're waiting for your London inspectors to approve of the larger suites."

Deciding there was no more point in arguing with Christina than there had been with his addled father, Harry stalked to the hall door and shouted. "Luke, bring my shaving gear over here immediately! And then start hauling in my clothes and a wardrobe."

He was the duke here now. People had to listen.

For the first time since the deaths of his father and brother, Harry was almost glad he was a duke. He watched smugly as servants leaped to his command, bustling like ants to haul his belongings, a larger washstand, more pillows, and a dresser into the already crowded room.

Matilda and Luke started arguing over the bedding to be used. Two burly footmen held the dresser aloft, waiting for the duke to name its position. Several round-eyed maids with their arms full of clothing stared at him as if he might snap off their heads.

Turning around to demand that Christina take charge, he watched her eyes widen at something in a back corner. Before he could say a word, she lifted her skirt and petticoat and dashed out of the room through a doorway he hadn't noticed earlier.

"Luke, get this place in order," he commanded. Before his startled manservant could protest, Harry ran out the main door and glanced down the hall in the direction Christina had gone.

She didn't emerge from the next room, so he

opened the door a crack and peered in. Empty drawers hung open, cobwebs covered the bedposts, and a musty odor struck his nose, but he still didn't see Christina.

That didn't make sense. The door she'd gone through had been on the other side of the wall to this chamber. He could swear the rooms up here only connected in the family suites, not in guest rooms like the one she'd appropriated. Although, what his father had done since his last visit was unknowable.

Slamming the door open so hard that it hit the wall, Harry cursed at his lack of a candle. The servants had apparently washed the windows in the other room so sunlight still illuminated it. In here, ragged draperies hung over filthy glass and the barest of light entered. He stubbed his toe on a blanket chest and barked his shin on a chair when he staggered forward. "Christina!" he bellowed.

He thought he heard a muffled reply, and his gut clenched in sudden fear. What if she'd fallen through a rotten floorboard? Instantly more concerned than angry, he shoved aside the clutter of old furniture that had accumulated in the room, attempting to locate the sound of her voice.

"A solar, Harry" drifted down from somewhere above his head. "Look, look at this!"

He recognized her excitement. She wasn't in pain. Relief flooded him. He bent his head backward to scan the ceiling, turning in circles to figure out where she could be. He was tired, angry, and confused, and now she had him spinning in circles! "Christina, where the devil are you?"

"Up here. The key unlocked the cupboard and there are steps inside."

Steps. In the cupboard. His father had been at it again.

With exasperation, Harry sought anything resembling a cupboard. Finding a door built into the wall, he pulled it fully open to find the narrow ladder inside.

"Damn it, Christina! You could kill yourself on this thing. Come down here at once." Which was an insensible thing to say since he was already climbing up to get her. Christina had that effect on him.

He didn't want her to have that effect on him. He wanted her to stay where he put her and act as he needed. Be a proper duchess. A soothing, calming, sensible woman who would make order out of the chaos into which he'd plummeted.

He might as well ask the sun to curtsy and perform a minuet in the heavens.

Light poured through a mullioned window that had been built into the slanted ceiling. He'd explored every inch of this house when he was a youth, and he didn't think there had been a room up here originally.

Glancing around from the top of the ladder, he saw Christina investigating a spinning wheel. An old card of wool was still attached to the distaff, and he could swear thread was still wrapped around the spindle. "Don't touch that," he warned as Christina reached for it.

Her hair sparkled golden in the fading light as she looked up, laughing. "You have been reading fairy tales," she cried in delight. "Isn't this just like Sleeping Beauty's castle?"

"No, I don't think so. For one thing, this isn't the castle, it's the manor house." He hauled himself up the last step and climbed out onto the wooden floor, testing the planks with his heavy weight. They seemed sturdy enough.

"Look! Look at this. Isn't it cunning?" She dashed over to a tabletop attached to the wall, and before Harry could stop her, released the latch and pushed the table up. The top became a decorative wall panel, revealing a crudely carved, brilliantly painted gothic chest containing a washbasin and pitcher beneath. Vermilion and gold seemed to be the order of the day, Harry decided, appalled at the décor.

A medieval tapestry of a lady and a unicorn woven with glittering threads hung behind a bed frame sans mattress. A massive trunk—painted with red and gold medallions—sat in one corner topped with the crude writing instruments of an earlier time.

"I don't know my history well, but this looks as if it could be a lady's solar from the time this house was first built," Christina said. "Do you think it's been hidden here all these years and no one else has found it?"

"I sincerely doubt it," Harry said dryly, knowing history—and his father—a little better than that. "This looks like one of my father's fantasies. The paint from that period did not survive this long, and if the original structure had a solar, it's long gone. My father made this up."

She stared at him blankly. "Your father? Why?"

Harry shrugged, as uncomfortable with his father's eccentricities now as he had been when the duke lived.

"I have no idea. He never bothered to explain."
Wanting nothing more than to escape this insane
room, he gestured toward the ladder. "Come along.
We're supposed to be dressing for dinner. What on
earth made you come up here now?"

"The lady with the ring led me here. I think this is
her home."

Blithely, Christina hurried down the ladder, leaving
Harry rubbing his tired eyes and wishing he were in
London, where the city bustled with live people in-
stead of ghosts.

Ten

Lying in bed in the early morning dawn, Christina tried to absorb the oddity of Harry's broad back not inches from her fingertips. He had wide, solid shoulders, and she longed to observe the supple musculature she'd felt when he held her, but out of politeness, he'd worn a nightshirt to bed.

He'd been a wee bit stiff with her last night after dinner when they'd discussed the hidden room with the spinning wheel. Harry didn't like believing his father was eccentric or mad and preferred not to mention any evidence of it, it seemed.

If she shifted just a little bit, she could touch her toes to his long—bare—limbs.

She resisted. In repose, Harry's aura was calm and reassuring, but he'd worked himself into a rare state yesterday. She still didn't know him well enough to encourage advances that might be rough or hurtful.

Although once they'd settled their argument about following ghosts, his kiss last night had been more than gentle . . .

She wouldn't think about that. Harry was determined to seduce her. She was equally determined not to be seduced. Sort of. Intellectually speaking, that is. And she wasn't very intellectual.

But she was good at self-preservation, and not being seduced by Harry until she knew him was important. Except when she was lying beside him in bed, wishing he would turn over and kiss her again, or that she could run her hand through his thick golden hair.

It had been the most difficult thing she had ever done last night when she'd reminded him of his promise not to make love to her until he loved her. She still wasn't certain if she would have had the courage had the lovely blue lady not returned to haunt the corner of the room. Harry hadn't been happy when she'd stopped his kisses with her hand and made him vow it again. But the lady had shimmered as if she were pleased.

Christina could be in a great deal of trouble if she pleased ghosts instead of her husband. Something else she must think on.

Deciding that she'd vacillated long enough—and that if Harry happened to wake up when she was on the wrong side of the argument, she'd be in deep water—Christina flung back the covers and slipped out of bed.

Harry instantly woke. "It's too early to get up," he muttered. "Even the cock hasn't crowed."

He turned over on his back with the pillow propped behind him, and Christina could see silky brown hair behind his half-unbuttoned shirt. He'd shaved for dinner, but his jaw was bristly again. And his mouth— may the goddess preserve her, but she longed to taste his lips again. They held her captivated: not soft, but sensual and moist with expectation.

She was grateful the bulky covers prevented her from seeing anything below his waist. From the look Harry was giving her, she knew what was on his mind, and she hastily diverted him. "I haven't explored the grounds yet. I'd like to go riding. It looks to be a glorious day."

Harry slanted the sunshine a dark look and, grumbling, sat up and dropped his legs over the far side of the bed. "I'll go with you. The grooms your father sent with your horses are expecting to leave this morning. I need to persuade them to linger until I find someone to take their place."

"You have no grooms? Who takes care of the horses?" Horrified at the possibility that the stable had been as neglected as the house, Christina darted to the window to take a look. But the stable was on the far side of the new wing and the old manor merely overlooked a terraced garden and fields.

She turned back around in time to catch Harry struggling to button his breeches over his shirt. She blushed at the intimacy, but she supposed this was all part of getting to know him.

Catching her glance, he strode across the room half unbuttoned and pulled her into his arms. "Anytime you're ready, I am," he murmured his favorite refrain.

His kiss was as tender and wonderful as she remembered. Holding her by the waist, he snuggled her hips close to his, and she felt the stir of his rising manhood against her lower belly while his mouth ravished hers.

She wore only her nightshift, and his every touch inflamed her. His hand strayed lower, his kiss deepened, and she was in grave danger of melting into a puddle on the floor.

Images of falling back into bed with Harry on top of her, pushing up her shift, touching her where she ached to be touched, filled her mind. If only she could accept this was just Harry, the man she'd known half her life, she could—

She shivered in a sudden draft. Blue flickered at the corner of her eye. If her assumption was correct that the blue lady had led her to the spinning wheel, then it was possible she resided in the attic just above this room.

Christina almost recovered her senses enough to break their kiss, only Harry pressed his thigh between her legs, distracting her. Grabbing his shoulders, she lifted herself so he could intrude farther. He obliged, sliding her shift higher until his leg rubbed her in a most intimate place through the linen.

Her breasts were crushed against his chest with only their shirts to shield them. Her nipples puckered into aching points of need, and she moaned into Harry's mouth.

As if he read her mind, Harry slid his fingers into the space between them to cup her breast. His thumb sought and found the puckered crest, and Christina nearly expired of the pleasure and relief of his caress. Harry's tongue thrust boldly into her mouth, and she accepted it. He pushed her backward, toward the bed, and her knees were too weak to fight him.

A knock rapped at the door.

"Go away," Harry growled.

Pressed against the bed by Harry's weight, Christina mindlessly ignored the knock, but a scream of fright from across the hall returned her to her senses.

"Your Grace!" The knock grew more frantic. "There's something wrong with the Blue Room."

"There's something wrong with the whole damned house," Harry muttered, glaring at the door.

He didn't release her, but he shifted position enough to give Christina the strength to shove against his chest. Unyielding muscle prevented her action from being more than futile protest. Obviously torn, he glanced down at her.

"Blue Room?" he inquired.

"The room Luke chose for you across the hall. Harry, let me go. That's Matilda, and she sounds frightened."

If she looked half as mussed as Harry did, the entire household would know what they'd been doing. His half-lowered eyelids had a carnal look that sent shivers of delight up her spine as he studied her state of undress, but at a second scream, he straightened, freeing her.

She had no idea where her robe might be. Without further concern to her attire, she raced to the door. "What's happening?" she demanded of the terrified maid in the hall.

Matilda was a sensible country woman who had grown up in a marquess's household, earning her place above stairs with her quick wit and aptitude for learning. She did not frighten easily, but her face was pale and her eyes wide. " 'Tis a ghost!" she declared. "It's tearing about His Grace's room like a demon."

Hearing the crashes, Christina sprinted barefoot across the hall. Before she could open the door, Harry caught her by the waist and swept her off her feet. Her toes bumped his shins, and his nose practically pressed against hers.

"Keep back, Christina," he warned. "I'll take a look first."

She couldn't very well kick him without shoes, but she'd like to. It wasn't fair that he was so much stronger. Wrestling out of his arms, she clung to his side as he opened the door.

Christina caught the flicker of blue just as a vase full of fresh daffodils flew across the room and splattered against the far wall. With the opening of the door, the room fell deathly silent, and cold air blasted past them.

"She's gone now. Matilda, fetch my robe, will you? And some slippers?" Ducking beneath Harry's arm, Christina entered to survey the destruction of yesterday's hard work.

Harry grabbed her shift and tugged her back, attempting to shove her behind him. "I told you to wait. There could be a thief or a madman in here."

"Desist, Harry, do." Christina tugged at the fingers holding her back. "It's just the lady I saw yesterday. I wonder if we've angered her." Although given the timing of the lady's interruptions, Christina had other ideas she thought best not to mention to Harry. Why would a ghost be warning her not to go to bed with her husband? Or was the lady protecting something or someone?

"What lady?" Harry demanded in a roar.

So much for seduction. Christina sighed and quit fighting his grip. Instead, she surveyed the destruction from his arms. The broken vase seemed to be the worst of it. Accustomed to the nobility having separate dressing rooms, Matilda and Luke had evidently declined to carry all Harry's things to the bedchamber. His riding crop lay in the middle of the carpet, and his box of stickpins and watch fobs had been knocked off the dresser and overturned. The young scullery maid who had entered to light a fire in the grate had sunk to the floor in a fit of uncontrollable weeping.

Christina elbowed her husband, and apparently assured the situation was under control, he released her so she could go to the distraught girl.

"Come along, and we'll fix you a bit of tea," she said, taking the maid by the arm and assisting her to rise. "Were you doing anything unusual to raise the lady's ire?"

Apparently shocked into silence, the girl obediently stood up. Her dirty face was streaked with tears.

"I'll take her, Your Grace." Matilda entered in a rustle of starched petticoats. "No doubt she knocked the things about and scared herself."

"I did not!" the maid protested. "They flew through the air like birds. I didn't touch nuffin'."

"I'm sure you didn't." Christina sent Harry a glance, but he was absorbed in studying the vase they'd both seen flying across the room of its own volition. "Matilda, do not blame her. I saw the lady myself. I would just like to know what caused her to knock things about."

By this time, Luke and the other maids had appeared in the corridor and were murmuring among themselves. Only Harry's manservant stepped forward to begin righting the room, and he gave her an odd look at her statement.

Christina was quite accustomed to this reaction. She had learned at an early age to ignore the stares and go on about her business, mentioning her "sight" only to those she trusted. But she felt it imperative to learn more in this case. If this was to be her home, then she must have people about who believed in her.

"What lady, Your Grace?" the frightened maid asked.

"Well, it's obvious you didn't fling the vase," she said patiently. "We stood right here and watched it cross the room all of its own accord. I've seen the ghost of a lady up here, and until now, she's been quite well behaved. I thought perhaps she was distressed by some action of yours."

The murmurs in the doorway increased. One of the maids became hysterical and had to be led away. Luke had quit any pretense of cleaning up. Harry's manservant was of an age with Matilda, Christina guessed. In his forties, slender, dark-haired, and a bit rough about the jaw, but not unintelligent if Harry had kept him on all these years. She met his gaze boldly, staring him down until he returned to picking up the shattered vase.

By this time, Harry was poking a fireplace tong up the chimney and disturbing a cloud of dust and twigs.

"I just set the coals in the grate, mum," the scullery maid muttered, still sniffing. "I didn't want to bother you none whilst you was asleep. I just wanted to have this room warm when His Grace got up."

"Excellent thinking. Thank you very much." Distracted by Harry's actions, Christina half watched him while trying to question the maid. "Did you see anything unusual? Did you have time to light the fire?"

"I was using the flint when that stick flew at me. And then the things on the dresser started shaking, and I kind of screamed, and . . ." She gestured expressively at the resulting shambles.

A cloud of black dust exploded into the room, accompanied by Harry's violent curse. Shocked at his language, Christina pushed the maid toward the door and caught the brunt of the coal dust as it billowed across the newly cleaned room.

In the midst of screams and filth and cursing, Christina heard the distinct chirp of baby birds.

"Christina fixed a nest for them and has the maids feeding the things hourly. It had to be the mother bird charging about the room, protecting her young," Harry said dismissively to Peter's questioning as they rode toward the village later that day.

"Quite so. Glad to see you keep your head about you. Edward would go into a fury every time your father mentioned ghosts."

Harry sensed his cousin's doubting gaze and scowled. "My father was rightly disturbed by the death of my mother. I believe he hoped he could talk to her spirit or some such. Madness does *not* run in the family."

"No, of course not, or I'm likely to be crazed as well," Peter said cheerfully. "Although, I suppose we could claim it came from the distaff side of the family."

"My grandmother wasn't mad either. Nor anyone else on either side." For good measure, Harry added, "And neither is Christina or her family. They have odd habits and notions, but they're all perfectly lucid, intelligent, well-educated people."

"Glad to hear that. I understand the village is rife with rumors. I'm sure all will be well now that you're here to straighten things out."

"Someone should have told me how far out of hand things had gone." Halting on a hill overlooking the village, Harry studied the scene. Smoke drifted from several chimneys. A number of cottages boasted tile roofs. A few still had thatch, but despite the prosperous size of the buildings, the village had an air of abandonment. Too many chimneys stood unused.

Peter followed Harry's gaze. "I've been spending much of my time with friends in Brighton. We court the ladies, turn a few cards. Not much for a fellow to do here. My father tried to teach me about sheep and wheat, but I never saw much use for learning, what with him and your father and Edward to look after the place. Never really noticed how bad things had become."

Harry knew his younger cousin was personable and willing to help when asked, but Peter had never been a deep thinker. He could easily believe his cousin hadn't noticed the deterioration in the village, and if he never visited the manor, he probably hadn't noticed anything wrong there either. But Jack should have. Perhaps he should summon his steward home.

But he needed the cash from selling off that useless land in Scotland. Christina's dowry had paid a substantial portion of the mortgage, but the balance was due in a few months, and he apparently still had debts all over the kingdom, including some right here in Sommersville.

Taking a deep breath and girding himself for whatever lay ahead, he kneed his horse into a trot down the hill and into the village.

As Harry rode into the yard, the blacksmith spit on the ground, turned his back, and walked into the cottage, slamming his door behind him.

"Well, that was not an auspicious beginning." Harry debated stalking after the man, but he preferred an amicable solution, not a fiery argument. People liked him. Or they used to. He wasn't ready to accept that he'd become an object of hatred for no reason known to him, or that he must learn to rule with an iron fist.

"Maybe the missus set him off on a wrong foot this morning." Peter wheeled his horse out of the yard and toward the tavern.

"Shouldn't I stop and speak with the squire first?" Harry studied the disreputable tavern he didn't remember being there last time he'd visited. "I saw Basil in Town, and he didn't seem friendly. Perhaps I could go to his father and find out why."

"Chumley took his daughter into London for the season. The women were all atwitter about it last Christmas. That must be why Basil was there. He'd never go elsewhere. I heard he's fixed his interest on a lady hereabouts but her parents don't approve 'cause he hasn't the wherewithal to keep her. Makes the chap surly. I'd avoid him if I was you. How about the vicar?"

"Excellent thought." Harry made a mental note to see if the estate owed the Chumleys. That might explain some of Basil's attitude. "The Reverend Abbott's a bit stiff, but a good fellow." Harry nudged his horse past the tavern to the village green. On the right, set back from the shadow of the inn, stood the aging rectory with its Tudor framework.

"I'll leave you here, then," Peter called. "I ain't been to church in a month of Sundays and the vicar's likely to read me the riot act. I promised Meg I'd bring her back some thread."

Waving him away, Harry tied his horse to the hitching ring in the fence post and proceeded up the brick walkway between rows of lettuce.

A young woman with demurely downcast eyes and a cap covering her hair answered the door. Harry remembered the vicar's adopted daughter, but he struggled to recall her name. She had never been one for joining the parties of young people he'd enjoyed while growing up here. He knew her as quiet and bookish and devoted to her elderly parents.

"Miss Abbott?" he inquired, staying safely with the family name.

He thought he saw a hint of wariness in the way the corners of her eyes slanted, but she sounded perfectly pleasant.

"Yes, Your Grace. How may we help you?"

"Is your father home? I'd have a word with him, if I might."

"He's abed, Your Grace. He's not been well this winter. Mother is visiting the parish poor, of which there are a great many this year."

There was more than wariness in her voice. In fact, he'd say she was barely concealing biting sarcasm. "I am sorry to hear that." He hesitated, wondering how much he could safely say to this woman he barely knew. "I have noticed there isn't as much activity here as I remembered. I thought to ask your father's opinion on the problem."

Instead of studying his boots as she had been doing, she glanced up. Her eyes were a striking blue-green. If she'd been Christina, he would swear she was ready to bite his head off. To his relief, she spoke with firm precision.

"No opinion is necessary, Your Grace. It is obvious. If the duke cannot pay his debts, we cannot pay ours. I trust you've returned with a substantial sum to restore what's been stolen from us."

With that, she closed the door in his face.

Eleven

"Mora? You have a vicar's daughter named Mora?" Christina did not look up from the dusty journal she was studying but flipped a page, fascinated with the history of Sommersville as well as the village gossip Harry had brought with him.

She'd discovered this particular book open on a ledger desk in the archive room behind the kitchen. Several pages had been neatly marked with dried sprigs of thyme, and from its contents, she'd say one of Harry's ancestors had written this household history about the sixteenth century.

"What's wrong with her name?" He sipped his tea and tore at a piece of toast, apparently still annoyed at his ill treatment.

"It's one of the old names. Gaelic, at least. Maybe Celtic. It's a corruption of something else, I vow." Reading the passage of how Harry's ancestor—she thought it was the fourth earl—had cozened Queen Elizabeth into financing his grand architectural plans, Christina glanced up from the journal to see everyone at the table staring at her.

"Mora?" Meg asked in disbelief. "I thought it simply a fancy way of saying Mary. The vicar and his wife dote on her."

"She's quiet as any mouse and almost as invisible," Peter added. "The village thinks she walks on water. She should have been a nun."

"What's that to do with her name?" Harry asked grumpily. "And I don't see anything quiet or holy about a woman who slams a door in my face."

"She slammed the door in your face?" Amused, Christina studied her husband's irritated features. He grew more like a lion with every passing day. She missed her jolly companion, but she admired the strength and command of the duke equally well—when he wasn't shouting at her. "That's certainly nun-like behavior. Moral outrage and the courage to blast a duke."

"I'm glad you find it amusing. I barely even know the woman. If I've offended her, I'm not aware of it."

Christina could tell Harry was truly hurt. People generally liked him, and he had no notion of how to handle dislike. She could tell him that some people simply despised anyone with more power or money or beauty than them, but she thought he'd work that out on his own.

Instead, hoping to smooth the rocky path between them, she appealed to the Harry she knew. "Tell me how I can help. Meg is much more effective at dealing with the servants than I am. Give me something to do."

Still in a dudgeon, Harry scowled. "Stay out of the old parts of the house so I won't have to worry about finding your bones in the cellars. Choose menus, mend linens, whatever it is women do all day. I'll try to be home early. I need to ride out to a few of the tenant farms this afternoon."

"Why don't I come with you?" Desperate to find the connection between them again, Christina stood up, prepared to don her riding clothes. She'd cancelled their earlier plans to go riding to take care of the baby birds, but she was ready now to follow Harry into hell if need be. It certainly looked as if that's where he'd spent the morning. Whatever he'd been doing hadn't improved his aura.

"Some other time." Harry dismissed her offer with an impatient gesture. "I don't have time for family visits. I'll simply be talking business with the men."

Hurt and angered by his casual dismissal, Christina grabbed the journal and stalked out.

She didn't need Harry to make her life complete. If he didn't want her to be part of his life, then she would do fine on her own—which meant she didn't have to listen to his silly warnings about the old parts of the house. She knew how to test for rotten boards and carry spare candles and flints so she wasn't caught in the dark. She had lots of experience at exploring.

In her room—hers and Harry's—she glared at the bed they'd shared last night. If he continued to play the part of Duke Dunce, she wouldn't be responsible for her actions if he tried to make that a marital bed. A man who couldn't learn to love his wife would never love his children either. She wouldn't subject a child of hers to that heartlessness. Harry would have to remain without an heir.

Maybe that was what the blue lady was trying to tell her, although she thought it far more likely the ghost had merely meant to warn them that the scullery maid was about to set fire to the bird's nest. The chimney and the house could have easily gone up with it.

By the time Christina had stripped off her good clothes and donned her shabby boy's breeches, her ire had faded but her determination had not. She might not be a proper duchess, but Harry could hire people to run his household. He didn't need her for that. She had intelligence and gifts that placed her far above the common lot. She would simply have to prove her worth to him.

She should have known that a man who laughed at her ability to see ghosts didn't take her seriously. She'd thought he *understood*, but her adoration of Harry had got in the way of common sense. Well, she could correct that.

Finding the page of the journal that mentioned an enormous bed built especially for the visit of Queen Elizabeth upon the completion of the manor, Christina memorized the description of the room and set out to find it.

The state rooms were all on the first floor. Perhaps staying there would ease Harry's concern of her falling through rafters or ceilings. Although, she supposed, if the manor had cellars, that possibility still loomed.

She was tall, but light boned. She didn't think she would fall through anything easily. Locating the once elegant stairs to the Tudor manor's foyer, she tested each step on the way down. They seemed solid to her. Harry was just an old worrywart. This would be a perfectly lovely entrance once it was cleaned a little and the drafts were sealed up.

Someone had cleared the debris from the falling lintel and boarded the door. Jeweled colors danced on the parquet floor through the stained glass transom above the boards, so it took a moment before she noticed the purple and white aura flickering in the corner. Delighted that she'd located another ghost, she hurried across the foyer.

"Please, don't run away," she said when it moved toward a back hall. Her only strong example of a ghost had been Aunt Iona. She had no way of knowing if the other spirits she occasionally saw meant to warn her or frighten her, or if they simply existed without purpose. But this one seemed to have a specific goal in mind. "I want to help if I can," she called after it.

She couldn't tell if the ghost heard or responded, but it stayed within sight as she followed it into a drawing room draped in linen and cobwebs. At the far end of the room were double doors leading into a gallery and ballroom. Why did the new wing need a ballroom if the house already had one?

Filing away that question for later, Christina continued following the purple aura into a large, unfurnished gallery that led toward the rear of the house. Peeking in doors as she passed, she discovered the room Harry had slept in their first night here. Next to it, to her delight, was a beautifully refurbished chapel—except she could swear it was after a medieval style far older than the Elizabethan structure. Had she wandered into the castle part of the house already?

Even she recognized that old castles could be ex-

ceedingly dangerous—especially if they'd been neglected. Trying to place her location, she didn't enter
the chapel but remained in the relative safety of the
gallery. Hurrying onward, she glanced down a hall on
the end. It appeared to be a back entrance into the
ballroom, possibly for the servants to use from the
kitchen, which would have been outside the house in
earlier days.

Now that she studied it, she realized that the ballroom very well could have been the great hall of the
castle. It had soaring ceilings covered in heavy dark
wood and expensive oak paneling instead of the current fashion of ornate plaster. The massive fireplace
on this end could hold an entire haunch of venison.
She'd wager the third earl—or was it the fourth?—
had simply converted the hall of the castle keep into
a ballroom rather than build a new one in his elegant
Elizabethan manor.

So the chapel could very well be a medieval chapel.
Delighted, Christina wanted to linger, but the ghost's
aura was displaying a degree of agitation where it
waited at the end of the gallery. Against the dark
backdrop of wainscoting, she thought she saw the
shape of priestly robes.

She would come back and study the chapel later. She
wanted to see where this new ghost would lead her.

A bit of dust drifted down from the timber and
plaster ceiling of the gallery, but old houses were given
to crumbling. She hastened past a small cascade of dirt
and aimed for the doorway where the purple lingered.

She jumped in startlement at a loud crash behind
her. Ahead of her, the purple aura beckoned urgently.

Glancing over her shoulder and seeing only a fallen panel, she raced down the remainder of the corridor to catch up with the ghost.

Beneath her feet, uncanny laughter reverberated against the floorboards.

"Christina, what the devil are you doing?" Simmering after a disastrous tour of the estate, Harry found his humor did not improve when he entered their shared bedchamber to find his wife in breeches.

Once upon a time, he'd enjoyed seeing her splendid legs in breeches, but contemplating what she could have been up to in this moldering structure while wearing them would turn his hair prematurely gray. She had cobwebs in her hair, and her boy's shirt was smeared with dirt.

"I'm washing so I might dress for dinner."

Seemingly unself-conscious of her attire—or lack of it—she wiggled out of her shirt and dropped it to the floor, leaving Harry lusting after the lovely pale curves of her bare shoulders and arms. She wore no corset, and her shift scarcely concealed her breasts as she leaned over the washbasin.

"I am not a eunuch, Christina." Irritated that he had so little control over his physical response to her, Harry dropped down in a chair to pry off his boots. Maybe he shouldn't have insisted they share a room.

He took back that thought when she turned to stare at him. Her hair cascaded in golden waves to her waist. He definitely wanted to see her in any manner available. She added color to his dismal day.

"What's a eunuch?" she asked.

"At least your mother curtailed some of your reading material," he grumbled. "Never mind. I don't suppose you were wearing breeches because you were digging a vegetable garden, were you?"

"Whyever would I do that? Don't you have gardeners?"

He wished he did. Cook had complained to Meg, who had passed on the request for fresh vegetables to him. He'd had to tell her to buy them from local farmers, and then had to provide more coins for doing so.

What little money he had left would run out soon. A household the size of this one couldn't live cheaply, and the grain harvest was months away. He'd added the figures in the books until his head spun and hadn't found a hole in them yet, but it would take weeks to painstakingly comb through and total all the income and expense of an estate this large. He was operating on instinct alone when he believed his father couldn't possibly have spent as much as the land earned, no matter how much he'd tinkered with the house. The father he had known might have been losing his mind, but he was far more likely to have hidden funds for a rainy day than to have spent them all.

If his instinct was wrong or he couldn't figure out where his father had squirreled away his money, he would have to return Christina to her family. The possibility gave him cold shivers.

"No, I don't seem to have gardeners," he grumbled. "Or a garden. But I don't expect you to dig one either. I'd just like to know that you were doing something perfectly harmless while wearing those clothes." He eyed her shift with more than a degree of interest.

Christina had always been perceptive when she applied her mind to it, Harry reflected, as she grabbed a towel and darted behind her wardrobe door to dress. "I was searching for Queen Elizabeth's bed," she called from her hiding place.

Harry wasn't certain if he was relieved that she was out of sight so he didn't burst his breeches, or disappointed that he couldn't continue watching her dress. Shedding his own sweat-soaked shirt, he washed in the other basin Luke had carried in.

"It's downstairs, in the state rooms near the castle, and it's too heavy to carry. I don't want you over there!" He glared in the mirror, wondering if he had to shave for dinner in his own home. Then thinking of the bed he would share with Christina later that night, he reached for his shaving soap.

He couldn't ask his valet to shave him while Christina was dressing. He lathered his face and watched the mirror for a reflection of his wife emerging from the wardrobe.

"Too late to tell me now," she called from behind the door. "I don't think you need to worry about anyone wandering about over there. The ghosts have their own warning system."

"Do I want to know what that is?" Harry asked, scraping his jaw. Christina's lively imagination always caught him by surprise and made him smile, even when he knew he should give her a sharp scold for disobedience. He shivered at the thought of Christina in the castle where his father and brother had died, but he was more interested in her story than scolding.

"They laugh and drop paneling. Very effective. I need to see how they do it. Or why."

Harry squinted at the mirror, but she still hadn't stepped out. The reflective tone of her voice very much sounded like Christina on a brownie hunt. "Because it's dangerous, that's why. Stay out of the castle."

"If the bed is too heavy to carry, I don't suppose you would be interested in moving to the first floor?"

Christina emerged from the wardrobe wearing a blue silk gown unfastened in the back. Harry almost swallowed his teeth when her reflection revealed the generous cleavage produced by her corset.

"No, I don't suppose I would," he answered because that seemed to be the smartest reply to anything Christina asked. "Of course, if you're interested in sharing that bed as we were meant . . ." He raised an eyebrow to her.

She studied his half-lathered face with interest, then swung around and presented her back to him. "I'm interested, but *you* don't seem to be yet. Fasten me up, Harry. We're late."

"What makes you think I'm not interested?" he demanded, wiping off the rest of the soap before reaching for the hooks of her bodice, while debating the wisdom of fastening them. He pressed a kiss to her nape and was rewarded with her shiver.

"Because you're still treating me the same as your horse or the chair you sit in. Now stop that, Harry, or I'll have to call Matilda. She's had a trying day."

"And I haven't?" Outraged, but wanting to laugh

at her strange priorities, Harry gallantly resisted temptation and began fastening her bodice. He ought to earn gold stars in heaven for his forbearance.

"Matilda fell and twisted her ankle in the courtyard," Christina explained. "If the purple ghost hadn't led me through the gallery to find her, she might have languished there all day. From his robes, I think this one might be a priest. Were your ancestors Catholic, Harry?"

"My ancestors were whatever was politically expedient," he grumbled. "We're not a religious lot." He refused to ask why she thought a priest might haunt these halls. His family tree contained its fair share of rogues and scoundrels, as well as the usual number of younger sons given to the church. She could imagine a priest if she liked.

"I really do need to find out more about the spirits living here, Harry," Christina insisted. "It seems there is more than one, and some of them might be malevolent."

To hell with gold stars in heaven. He wanted reward for his patience here on earth. Not finishing her hooks, Harry slid his hands beneath her boned bodice, circling his arms around her shift and pulling her back against his chest. She gasped, but when he cupped her breasts in both hands, she melted against him. She engaged him on so many levels, he couldn't keep track, but the physical one was the least complicated.

"If you had been outside planning a garden or walking your horse or any of half a dozen normal activities, you wouldn't have needed a ghost to tell you that your maid needed help. You would have seen her," he murmured against her ear as he nibbled it. Her nipples puckered against his palms. He pressed his aching loins against her buttocks. Her skirt and petticoat prevented his feeling her supple curves.

"Harry, don't," she protested breathlessly. "I deserve a man who loves me, and you deserve the same."

"A man who loves me? No, thank you," he said wryly, although he knew what she meant. "Right now, I'd be content with a wife who gives me heirs. I never expected you to love me."

"You didn't?" Wide-eyed, she pulled from his grasp, holding up her bodice so she could turn and face him. "You didn't think I would love you?"

He shrugged and focused his gaze on the way her bosom rose and fell rather than on her enchantingly surprised expression. "Love is a romantic fantasy, like the Sleeping Beauty tale. Marriage is a legal, practical state for the protection of the woman and the children she bears. We suit each other very well, Christina. What more can you ask?"

At her silence, he looked up to catch tears in her eyes before she turned her back on him again. Reaching over her shoulder, she began fastening her own hooks. "If that is what you believe, we do not suit at all, Harry. I'm very sorry you don't believe you are lovable. I know I am difficult, but I still like to believe someone could love me."

He brushed away her hands and finished hooking her up. "You're adorable, Christina, and I want to take care of you. Isn't that enough?"

She held her hair out of his way, but as soon as her

bodice was fastened, he helped himself to her silky tresses, sliding his fingers through them to massage her scalp, not letting her go.

She didn't pull away, but she didn't fall into his arms either. "If you cannot believe in malevolent spirits, Harry, then you cannot protect me. I shall have to find out more on my own."

Harry squeezed his eyes shut and clenched his jaw to prevent roaring his wrath. Yelling at Christina would be akin to yelling at his horse. She would just skitter out of reach and run like hell in the opposite direction.

"I'll have the whole damned building pulled down before I'll let you endanger yourself. Wait until I've settled estate matters, and we'll explore together. In the meantime, do something about Cook's vegetable garden. That should be safe enough."

She drew away with that hurt look still in her eyes, but she nodded without argument, and Harry had to be satisfied with that.

Twelve

"Fish? You think I should put fish in the garden?" Standing in the courtyard behind the castle walls after Sunday services, Christina studied the ornamental fishpond, the long-abandoned vegetable garden, then a page of the journal.

She'd found this new book open on her bed this morning after they returned from church. Although it had a similar binding to the journals in the archive room, it wasn't the same one she'd been studying the other day. The handwriting was different, and this one wasn't extremely interesting, tending to describe such things as "the potatoe of Virginia being knobbie roots fastened into the stalkes with an infinite number of threddie strings." But it did seem to indicate that some early Winchester had used fish from the pond as a type of fertilizer.

"I wish Ninian were here. Or even Leila. They know far more about gardening than I do. Show me where the potatoes grow," she said to the blue aura who stayed near the castle wall where Christina could see her.

"Who are you talking to?" Meg stepped around the

yew in the corner and, finding only Christina, looked puzzled.

"As far as I can tell, Lady Anne Winchester. I haven't studied the family tree well enough to pin her on it, but I think she may have helped develop the courtyard and kitchen gardens when the manor was new."

Christina handed the old journal to Meg, knowing Harry's cousin would assume she referred to the journal. She didn't think Meg likely to understand that Lady Anne's ghost had just disappeared into the remains of the herbal knot garden behind the hedge.

She had only just come to the conclusion of the ghost's identity after learning the writer of the journal she'd read yesterday was a Lady Anne who was well-known for her spinning and gardening. Upon visiting the blue lady's room and seeing the blue aura at the spinning wheel, Christina had addressed her as Lady Anne, and the aura had shimmered in delight. That was sufficient acknowledgment for her.

Meg glanced at the ancient ledger she'd been handed, flipped a few pages of incomprehensible handwriting, and shrugged. "I'd be talking to myself, too, after reading this. Why don't you simply hire a gardener?"

"Because I don't know a gardener to hire, and Harry seemed to think this was something I ought to do. I know more about trees than vegetables." Christina wandered over to a gnarled fruit tree covered in flowers and small green fruits. "Look at this. The journal tells how cherry and peach branches were grafted onto an old hawthorn. There's a whole orchard of fruit beyond the wall, but I know nothing of how to care for them."

"You spoke of Leila and Ninian. Are they family?"

Feeling frumpy in the old skirt she'd changed into, her apron muddied from climbing the terraced mound in the back of the garden and digging about in the herbs, Christina regarded Meg's quiet elegance with suspicion. She didn't believe in perfection, although Meg did her best to convey it. Meg's aura seemed perfectly content, but there was an occasional hint of brown to show that all was not as well as she pretended. She supposed that could just be grief for the uncle and cousin whom Meg had known all her life.

"Ninian is my cousin, and Leila is my older sister," Christina explained. "Leila's husband is well-known in agricultural circles for his advanced thinking and scientific knowledge. Perhaps I could write to him for advice, although he's not much on letter writing."

"Why don't we fix up a few of the guest rooms and invite them to visit?" Meg asked, trying to hide her eagerness. "It's been ever so long since we entertained."

"Ninian just had a baby this past winter and may not be ready for travel. Besides, her husband is an earl who likes to dabble in government, and Parliament opens shortly. I wonder where Leila is right now." Thinking of actually entertaining family in her own home, Christina caught the contagion of Meg's excitement. "And Harry might like to talk with an agronomist. He seems worried about the estate."

"My father is experienced at farming," Meg reminded her, "and has not said anything that would give reason for concern, but men like to talk about new things. If it would make Harry happy, why don't you invite them?"

She'd much rather write an invitation to her family than struggle to figure out how to garden. Hugging the journal to her chest, Christina started briskly for the house with Meg on her heels. "I'll write today. Do you know of someone who can begin tilling the dirt? I'll read up on vegetables and herbs. Once the dirt is dug and I have seeds, it can't be too dreadfully difficult."

"I don't think anyone saved seeds," Meg said doubtfully. "You'll have to buy them."

Another thing she didn't know how to do. She hadn't realized how abysmally ignorant she was. Perhaps she could find a better means of communicating with Lady Anne. Or she could ride out and meet Harry's tenants by herself and ask them about seeds—except Meg had indicated that her title would intimidate them.

She dearly wished to explore the estate. She'd seen a ring of rowans on a nearby hill that almost certainly meant sacred ground. And she'd like to see if there were more standing stones like the one she'd seen at the edge of the garden. This could be a truly holy place. Perhaps that was why the ghosts lingered.

But she wanted to do it with Harry, who knew every inch of ground and much of its ancient history.

Of course, the ghosts would know the ancient history as well. Struck by a sudden thought, Christina halted and handed the old volume to Meg. "Would you take this back for me? I forgot to look at something. I'll be back in just a little while."

Without waiting for Meg to question, she dashed through the garden in the direction of the castle chapel. Leila would *adore* knowing there was a stone circle here, if she could verify it. And if the purple aura was a priest, wouldn't he know?

The tenant cottage door that had been open as Harry rode down the lane was closed tight by the time he entered the yard.

Sitting on his horse, studying the surrounding landscape, he debated whether to dismount. He was weary of confronting closed doors and cold expressions.

Perhaps he should have worn the attire of a wealthy duke instead of his everyday wool. Maybe he should take to wearing a wig so he looked like his father had. Why did his own people hate him so? He couldn't imagine either his father or brother doing anything so despicable as to generate such disrespect. And no one seemed inclined to tell him the problem.

Harry rode on, brooding over the unsatisfactory results of this day. They'd arrived fashionably late at church so there hadn't been time to talk with anyone beforehand. Afterward, the parishioners had melted away while he discussed the church roof with the vicar. Reverend Abbot had not been precisely forthcoming about the state of the local economy either.

If he didn't get to the bottom of the problem soon, he wouldn't have an estate to worry about.

While that might be desirable from the standpoint

of a man trained to maneuver through city aristocracy rather than rural society, losing the estate to a merchant such as Carthage would mean the tenant farmers would be out of their homes and relieved of their occupations.

Perhaps that was the problem. Carthage lived about here somewhere. Had the man promised the tenants something Harry couldn't deliver? Did they want him to fail?

He wished Peter hadn't had a prior social engagement in Brighton. His cousin was the only man in the area who was willing to speak with him. Not that Peter had anything sensible to say. He hadn't even noticed the church had a hole in its roof. Or if he had, he'd assumed someone else would take care of it. Perhaps Peter was better off wooing and marrying a wealthy woman.

Harry would have to call Jack back from Scotland. He hated admitting his ignorance, hated admitting he couldn't do everything himself. He'd thought he could ride in here, talk to a few people, solve the problem, and return to London and the life he and Christina had always lived. They'd go their separate ways as spouses in their class did, spend the late summer and autumn in Sommersville, and live a life of contentment, if naught else. He'd hoped for more than that, perhaps some adventure, some intellectual challenge, but right now, he'd settle for enough money to live on.

And an heir to inherit the estate he intended to save. If he was fortunate enough to have more than one son, he'd be certain they all knew how to manage the land.

But first, he needed a son.

He wasn't a rake, and seduction wasn't his hobby, but Harry thought he understood Christina well enough to overcome her refusals. He knew better than to woo her with jewelry, at least. She had a box full and never wore anything except the ring he'd placed on her left hand.

He wasn't about to encourage her dangerous obsession with imaginary creatures, but there were other means of courting her. His wife was a romantic, and he didn't think she was shy about the marital bed. So his task ought to be relatively simple. Once he had his marriage in hand, perhaps solutions to his other problems would present themselves.

He'd certainly feel a lot better. The vision of Christina flitting about their shared chamber wearing next to nothing had filled his mind's eye all morning, making it damned difficult to concentrate on hymns.

A dog dashed out of the hedgerow, barking and nipping at Caesar's heels, encouraging the gelding's restiveness. Clinging to thoughts of Christina in diaphanous gowns, Harry ignored the irritation.

He came to full awareness a few minutes later when he met Carthage in an obviously new phaeton. Harry had ordered the family attorney to find out more about the man after he'd been presented with the mortgage. As far as the attorney could determine, Carthage was a reasonably honest merchant who had invested the profits from his East India trade in land. He'd turned a small farm on the Surrey road out of London into rows of houses for middling sort of people like physicians and solicitors.

Apparently, Carthage had recently acquired a manor house outside of Sommersville, but wasn't interested in farming. Men like that seldom were. The challenge of turning a profit held more interest than soil.

Harry didn't bother reining Caesar to the side of the road, but without a nod or a tip of his hat, he raised his chin and, claiming aristocratic privilege, forced the carriage to slow to let him by. He was learning this duke business quickly. Plain old Lord Harry would have halted on the side of the road and doffed his hat in greeting.

"Your Grace," Carthage called from the open vehicle.

Scowling, Harry arched a questioning eyebrow as he came abreast of the phaeton.

"I'd like to wish you well on your new marriage," Carthage said in an unctuous tone that set all Harry's hackles on edge. "I understand Her Grace has already begun hiring and making changes to the manor. I trust she finds our fair county suited to her taste."

"The duchess is enchanted with the area," Harry responded stiffly. He knew this game well. Men such as Carthage who had grown up in trade, often sought weaknesses in others to twist to their advantage. Women were always a weakness, but he wouldn't let Christina be his.

"Excellent. I hear she shares some of your father's peculiarities. Will she be needing help with the construction? I've hired some of your father's workmen to improve my estate, but I'd be happy to share."

"I believe you've heard wrong. We are more likely

to tear down the manor than add to it." Harry refrained from gritting his teeth but acted as if Carthage were merely tying up his valuable time.

"If you sold me the acreage behind the Roman villa, I could put those men to good use developing houses for a better class of people. Then you'd have the cash to do as you saw fit with the rest of the land," Carthage suggested. "We would all benefit."

"The estate is entailed, sir. It will not be sold." Harry kicked Caesar into a canter, but Carthage's voice rang out behind him.

"You'd better do something about those crumbling towers before someone falls through them! I've heard complaints."

Harry spurred his mount, not acknowledging the insult. *Vulture,* he muttered, but the moment's peace he'd carved for himself had shattered with the warning that he needed to hire architects and contractors to prevent the damned house from killing anyone else.

He galloped the remainder of the distance home, determined to salvage a portion of the peace of mind he'd achieved earlier. He had a staff now. They'd have dinner waiting. He had a fascinating wife who could bring him joy with just a smile. He could even wonder what entertaining thing she'd done to turn their bedchamber inside out and anticipate the confusion with humor.

As long as he knew he'd have Christina in his bed tonight.

Leaving Caesar to the stable lads, he took the back stairs into the new wing, impatiently hitting his boots with his riding crop as he strode through the back hall, looking for a convenient place to drop his hat. They needed to find old Dalrymple and hire him back. He would have had a footman at the door as soon as Harry rode up.

Except that he couldn't afford Dalrymple or the footman.

He *could* seduce Christina. Concentrate on what you can accomplish, he told himself.

Shoving his crop in his boot, tucking his hat under his arm, he terrified the kitchen staff by running down the stairs and appearing without warning. "Cook, the duchess and I will dine in our chambers this evening. Do we still have wine in the cellars?"

At an affirmative nod, he ordered a rich burgundy and indulged in a sense of satisfaction. What else would he need?

Flowers. He needed flowers. It was still too early for roses, but he'd seen jonquils in the fields as he rode by. Ignoring the stares of the help, he strode through the kitchen and out the backdoor to the courtyard.

Perhaps he had time to scavenge the library for a pretty poem he could copy out for her. That should please her. Thank the heavens that Christina didn't require expensive gifts. He'd chosen his wife wisely.

Searching through the kitchen garden for the jonquils he knew used to grow in the knot garden, Harry was halted abruptly in the gravel path at the sight ahead of him.

Muddy and bedraggled, Christina leaned over the fishpond with his old butterfly net in one hand. With the other, she shoved waves of soaked golden hair over her shoulder and succeeded in smearing mud across her cheek in the process. Even as he watched, she dipped the net into the pond, dousing her cuff and splashing her bodice.

Before he could halt her, she reached farther to chase something in the bottom of the pond—and tumbled headfirst into the water.

Thirteen

Cursing the fish trapped by her billowing petticoats and floundering in the ooze at the bottom of the pond, Christina barely registered Harry's flying leap over the pond wall until he hauled her—dripping with mud and fish—into his arms.

Relieved, she grabbed his neck for balance and, without thinking, dripped green slime and muddy water down his coat. Harry cradled her marvelously closer, and she might have snuggled there forever if he hadn't begun bellowing protests. She emptied the water out of her ears but didn't listen until he stopped cursing.

"By all that's holy, Christina, have you no care for others?" he demanded, carrying her out of the pond as if she were made of air. "Don't you have any idea how *valuable* you are to me? How do you think I'd feel if you drowned in a damned *fishpond*!" The last was more a shout than a question.

"Valuable?" she inquired with interest, finally hearing something worth listening to. She loved the strength of Harry's powerful shoulders and muscled arms, and she held his neck a little tighter than was absolutely necessary. Through her wet clothing, she could feel his powerful stride in the movement of his flat belly beneath her hip. Even dripping in green slime, he looked princely to her. The dent in his chin deepened when he was angry, she noticed.

He shot her a scathing glance, and she dismissed the excitement that had stirred in her foolish heart. "Oh, *valuable* as in my dowry and the connections my father can provide. Although," she added thoughtfully, "if you're speaking about the shipping business my father wishes to share with all his daughters' husbands, he's merely looking to share his losses, so I'd be wary."

"Of course I was talking about shipping, you silly twit!" he yelled, carrying her across the kitchen floor to the stares of the entire staff. "I always talk about shipping when my wife nearly drowns in a filthy pond."

Christina punched his shoulder, wriggling to get down, but Harry proceeded undeterred.

"Hot water, blankets, tea," he commanded on his way past the gaping servants. "Build up the fire in our chamber before the duchess catches her death of cold."

"Harry, if you'd put me down, I could take off these wet things right here instead of tracking mud through—"

"How would I explain to your parents if you wasted away from a lung fever because I did not take care of you?" he demanded, hastening up the back stairs. "By Jove, if you can't be trusted in the damned *garden,* I'll have to lock you in a tower. What the devil were you doing in the fishpond?"

"Fishing, Harry. That's what one does in a pond, isn't it?" Deciding she enjoyed her position in Harry's arms well enough to quit fighting him, Christina set about studying his aura. He was quite furious, she could tell, but auras were fickle things. The white told her he was feeling protective, but of what? Her? The fish? Himself? The way he was yelling, she had difficulty deciding.

Although, his sarcasm had indicated he really *did* consider her valuable, so maybe he was a tad upset. Flushed with triumph at the possibility, she decided not to torment him too much.

"No, one sits nicely on the wall and admires the damned silly fish," he shouted. "One does not attack fish with butterfly nets."

"Oh, is that what the net was for? Why would you want to catch butterflies?" Christina winced as she imagined steam pouring from Harry's ears. Harry didn't like being distracted. She tried to mollify him before his roars brought down the rafters. "Lady Anne told me the best way to make potatoes grow was to put fish in the furrows. It sounded quite dreadful, but the pond was much too crowded and your fish were starving. Really, Harry, someone should have been catching the poor creatures or feeding them."

"Lady Anne?" he roared, carrying her into their chamber and dumping her before the fire.

Maids and a lone footman scurried in their path, setting up the bath and fire screen, pouring hot water, stirring the coals. Christina disliked creating scenes that would be gossiped about all over the county on the morrow, but Harry really did deserve some explanation. If only he would quit bellowing! He used to laugh at her escapades. She wished she could make him laugh again. He took things much too seriously since he'd become a duke.

She gasped as he began unfastening her gown as if he had every right to do so.

Well, she supposed he did have every right. She held up her soaking hair so he wouldn't get any wetter. "Lady Anne showed me where the potatoes used to grow, and there are still some trying to survive. And I read the journal—"

"Who the devil is Lady Anne?" he demanded, lowering his voice only an octave or two as his nimble fingers undressed her.

"The ghost who lives in the spinning room," she explained, quite reasonably, she thought. "Oh, and you must hear this, Harry. There is another ghost, Father Oswald. Lady Anne showed me his name on one of the pews in the chapel. He lives in the priest's study. He has a book on stone circles—"

"Out!" Harry shouted at the servants who were straining to hear every word. "All of you, get out!"

"Harry, a hot bath would be very nice," she murmured, clinging to her sodden bodice to prevent it from falling off now that Harry had unhooked it.

The servants looked a trifle confused. Defiantly, Christina's maid pointed at the tub. A footman hastened to continue carrying in buckets of water. Another maid followed in his footsteps. Matilda boldly limped in to open the wardrobe and find Christina's robe.

At the arrival of Luke carrying fresh clothing, Harry's patience snapped. *"If you do not all leave at once, I'll heave you out the windows."*

Releasing Christina, he grabbed the wooden chair at the vanity and held it up in front of him as if it were a knight's shield. Waving the riding crop he ripped from his boot, he backed the servants out of the room. "Fetch our dinner and leave it outside the door, but leave. Now!"

Her eyebrows no doubt getting acquainted with her hairline, Christina watched Harry's performance as gallant knight with more amusement than astonishment. He was frightfully angry. The Harry she used to know never became angry, so she assumed he wasn't dealing well with it now.

Matilda cast her an anxious glance, and Christina shrugged and held up her palms. She wasn't afraid of Harry, although he'd intimidated everyone else by now. Tall and distinguished despite the green slime dripping from his coat, wielding his aristocratic accent and bearing well, Harry could rout a field of armed soldiers with that chair. She supposed he had acquired that attitude to make the unruly occupants of the House of Commons listen to him.

She wondered how he would fare now that he would attend the Lords. Judging from his current performance, he merely needed a riding crop and a chair and they'd all grovel before him.

She applauded when he succeeded in emptying the room and barred the door. "Thank you, my knight. I'm sure the mud we've dripped all over the floor will clean itself while we bathe."

"Why aren't you in the bath by now?" Still roaring, he flung down his weapons and stripped off his coat.

Oh, my. She hadn't realized she'd soaked Harry's coat clear through to his vest and shirt. Wet, the linen molded nicely to his shoulders. Christina's stomach did a giddy dance of joy at the sight.

"Don't you want to dunk me yourself?" she taunted. Harry had always been great fun to tease, but she suspected she was waving a red flag in front of a bull right now.

"You'll catch your death standing there like that." Flinging off his wet shirt, he strode across the room bare chested.

Christina would have loved to admire all those lovely chest hairs some more, but she didn't think letting Harry get his hands on her would be conducive to her goals. She intended to have him laughing before she let him touch her again.

Dropping her sodden bodice, kicking off her ruined shoes, she shoved her skirt and petticoats down and raced up the bedstairs to a standing position on the bed, wearing just her soggy shift and stockings. "I'll be just as wet in the bath," she pointed out before leaping off the far side of the bed as Harry came after her.

He missed her by inches and fell across the mattress, muddy boots hanging away from the newly cleaned covers. Christina winced when she thought he would leap after her, but he wasn't too far gone to grasp the damage he could do. He stopped to yank off his boots. "If you're not in that tub by the time I get these off, I'll put you in there myself."

She'd like to see him try, but that would be playing with fire. She had enough sense to know where a combination of nakedness and Harry would lead.

Before he pulled off his second boot, she darted around the dressing screen. "Don't you want to hear about Father Oswald?" she called. "He's quite fascinating."

"Not if Father Oswald is *dead*. There is an entire graveyard of old bones out there and none of them are fascinating."

She could hear him rummaging around in the wardrobe drawers, slamming doors and stomping about in his bare feet. Not knowing how to interpret his tumultuous mood, she stripped off her corset, shift, and stockings and climbed into the bath. The water was quite hot, even if the level was lower than she liked. "His spirit is still alive. Shouldn't that count for something? He seems quite upset about a chalice in the chapel. It's rather ugly pewter. Do you think we could find—"

"The Holy Grail doesn't exist." His voice was a little lower than a shout, but not by much.

A nightshift, a robe, and a warm blanket sailed over the screen. The blanket caught on the screen, but the filmier garments drifted to the floor beside the tub. He'd found the wedding nightclothes her mother had packed. Trying not to read too much in his choice, Christina ducked her hair into the water and lathered it. "Surely you realize the castle isn't just a fortress. The towers were probably built in the thirteenth century, but your ancestors have lived here over the ages. Women don't like living in towers. The keep was added on to regularly, and the chapel was part of it.''

"I know all that," he grumbled. "Do you need help washing?''

She needed help rinsing her hair, but she wasn't about to tell Harry that in his current uncertain mood. "I'm not a child, Harry. If I told you I'd found a Roman centurion in the cellars, would you listen then? Is it only priests and old ladies to whom you object?''

"They're *dead,* Christina! They're figments of your imagination. If you need company to talk to, then invite your damned family.''

She could hear him pacing up and down on the other side of the screen and tried not to tease him too badly. "I did. I've invited Leila and Ninian to show me how to garden. But Father Oswald is not a figment. I found reference to him in the archive room. You really ought to read your family history, Harry.''

"I know my family history, and I can be fairly certain a damned *priest* isn't my ancestor. I'm sure there were dozens of Lady Annes since the name is popular. But there are none alive, and that's all that matters. You can't talk to ghosts.''

"Well, I admit, it isn't easy," Christina offered in hopes of placating him. Hastily washing off the remainder of the mud, she stood to dry off on the linen left to warm before the fire. "I can't quite tell what Father Oswald is telling me about the chalice. He toppled the old pewter one from the altar, so I assume he dislikes it. Overall, his aura is quite purple with a nice layer of white, so he's a good spirit, but whenever he touches the chalice, there's a sadness about him."

Silence. Worried, Christina toweled her hair and attempted to determine where Harry was. "Harry? Are you still there?"

"Are you done yet? I believe our dinner just arrived, and I'd like to wash so I can put on clean clothes."

He sounded suspiciously normal. She heard the door open and shut as Harry carried in their tray. Perhaps he was just hungry.

Wriggling into the diaphanous gown her mother thought brides ought to wear, Christina gazed at her seminakedness in dismay. If she stepped out there like this, Harry would turn into a raging bull again. Well, maybe not *raging,* but definitely a bull.

The robe hardly improved the situation. It was so light it clung to every curve when she tied it, and the top fell open to reveal a great deal more of her chest than she deemed wise. It would do very well when she thought Harry was ready for love, but telling her she was *valuable* wasn't quite the sentiment she was hoping for—although it did give her a nice tingle to know she wasn't a nonentity to him. She'd known men who wouldn't have dirtied their boots to help her out of the pond. Harry's reaction was very gratifying indeed.

She wrapped the blanket around her before stepping out from behind the screen. "Perhaps you ought to call for fresh water, Harry."

With a sigh of admiration, she froze where she was. Harry had removed his wet breeches and stockings and no doubt everything else, too, given the sodden lump of clothing on the floor. He'd donned a long quilted dressing gown of rich brown velvet, but no shirt ruffle hid the curls on his chest above the opening. He leaned one shoulder negligently against the wall while gazing out the wide window, his queue of hair falling over his collar.

At her silence, he turned back to the room, and his gaze slid approvingly over her damp hair. It had soaked the shoulders of her linen so that he could probably see her skin through the fabric. Christina raised the blanket to more thoroughly cover her breasts.

"Are you cold?" he asked with concern. "I'll add more coal to the fire. Have some tea while it's still hot."

Christina gazed with fascination at his bare, masculine toes and the glimpse of a muscled, hairy calf when the robe swung open as he walked toward her. She scarcely registered his question until he tilted her chin up.

"I'll hurry," he murmured before brushing a kiss across her lips.

Oh, my. Christina could hardly bear it when he walked behind the screen and threw his robe over the top. Perhaps she should offer to wash his back.

But he wouldn't listen to her about Father Oswald and Lady Anne, and his aura was still murky. She did not understand why he'd changed so. She realized he was grieving the loss of his family, but this change was caused by far more than that.

She poured some hot tea and noticed the servants

had brought several bottles of wine as well. She did not much like the complications of wine. It made her giddy, and she was already having difficulty keeping her head around Harry.

She heard him splashing in the bath, which made her even giddier than wine would have. Fanning herself with her hand, she set down the teacup. Her heart was racing, and her breasts were entirely too sensitive to the gauzy material caressing them.

She glanced around suspiciously for her mother's scented candles of seduction, but the ones burning on the table and dresser seemed to be perfectly innocuous beeswax.

"Here, let me draw the table closer to the fire for you."

Startled from her reverie, Christina almost leaped at the sound of Harry's voice.

He had bathed with amazing speed. His hair glistened from a good scrubbing, and she could see a dab of soap clinging to his unshaven jaw. She watched warily as he removed the screen from in front of the fire. Perhaps she should have handed him a nightshirt to wear under that loose robe. She would have felt remotely more respectable.

He carried a drop-leaf table over to the fire, set up the leaves, then carried the dinner tray over without spilling a drop of tea.

"We shouldn't leave Meg to dine alone," she murmured.

"I'm certain she has dined alone frequently. It is not our duty to entertain her." Harry took her arm to guide her to a chair he set before the table. "My responsibility is to take care of you and keep you well."

His solicitous concern was heartwarming, but she knew Harry too well. He wanted something, and she had a good idea what.

"Will you listen to me about Father Oswald?" she asked, refusing to accompany him to his cozily prepared dinner until she had the answer she wanted.

"You may chatter about him all you like in front of me, but not in front of the servants," he said sternly. "You will frighten them."

He'd brushed aside her blanket to hold her arm, and she could feel the heat of his palm through the delicate fabric of her nightclothes. Their bare toes practically touched. With interest, she inched forward so she could rub her toes against his. She tilted her head back to read his reaction to that intimacy.

Harry's gaze burned with desire, but he was clenching his jaw in an attempt to resist. He really did wish to take care of her. Perhaps he would even cherish her. She shouldn't ask more of him than he was capable of giving.

Surrendering to her fascination, Christina rubbed her fingertips over the silky hairs on Harry's chest. "You really must learn to believe me about your family ghosts, Harry," she warned, admiring the way his muscles swelled beneath her touch.

Boldly, he wrapped his arm around her waist and drew her forward, so that she understood the full extent of his desire and that she was about to be very roundly tupped if she did not cure her insatiable curiosity soon.

The observer fluttering nervously about the room kept her from losing her head entirely. Lady Anne had company this time. A purple aura waited patiently in the corner.

"The ghosts have never bothered me in all the years I lived here, Christina. I have no desire to meet them now."

Harry lowered his mouth to hers, but before she could succumb to such excellent temptation, she patted his shoulder.

"You might want to rethink that, Harry," she said, dodging his lips and pulling back to look past him.

Puzzled, he searched her face. "I don't wish to rethink anything, Christina. We have a marriage we need to get on with."

"And so we shall, but not with Lady Anne and Father Oswald watching. We ought to see what they want. I have learned it is not wise to ignore a ghost."

She pushed away, leaving Harry gaping while she put on her slippers. When she started for the door connecting to the next chamber, Harry roared and shoved the nearest chair in front of it.

Unperturbed, Christina picked up a candlestick from the dresser and departed through the hall door— hurrying after the ghosts who had been patiently awaiting her attention ever since Harry had carried their dinner into the room.

Fourteen

Grabbing clean breeches and hopping about to pull them on under his robe, Harry shouted, "Christina!" at the top of his lungs in a vague hope she'd stop for him. She didn't. The tail of her gown swung around the doorway and disappeared into the hall, elusive as the ghosts she claimed to see.

What did he need with resident spirits? He'd married one.

Sliding his feet into slippers, wishing he had time to don a shirt, Harry grabbed another candle and ran after her. He couldn't believe the little minx had so thoroughly hoodwinked him. Her announcement that ghosts were watching had doused much of his ardor, but his loins still ached abominably, denied the relief she'd promised with her winsome ways.

He'd been certain that had been desire in her eyes. He'd been so damned close . . .

The white lace of her robe trailed around an arch at the other end of the hall. Harry raced after it, not knowing whether he ought to throw her over his shoulder and haul her kicking and screaming back to the bedroom, or just protect her from herself by tying her up in the blanket and carrying her back as if she were the spoiled child she was behaving like. It was freezing in these old halls. She'd just been thoroughly chilled in the pond, and she was racing about with her hair still wet.

Their mutual bed would be far warmer and more pleasant.

"Christina!" he shouted in alarm when she disappeared down a far corridor and he realized where she was headed. He increased his pace, but his heavy tread upon the old floors must have vibrated the ancient timbers. The rusting suit of armor guarding the stairwell between the manor and the castle swayed. Before Harry could leap to catch it, it tumbled in his path. Catching his slipper on the hauberk, he tripped and almost fell with it.

With sheer frustration, he grabbed the battle-ax that could have cut off his toes and, clutching it in his hand, took the stairs at a reckless pace to catch up with Christina.

"Christina, these floors aren't stable! Come back here."

"These have recently been repaired," Christina called back. "Father Oswald wouldn't lead me anywhere dangerous."

"Your Father Oswald nearly decapitated me back there." Too furious to be reasonable, Harry was almost upon her when she seemingly walked through a wall at the bottom of the stairs. He stared blankly at the stones confronting him.

"That was probably General Rothbottom. Lady Anne has indicated that he hates being disturbed." Her reply floated from beyond the partition. "I suspect the general caused the dreadful laughter when I first entered this section. According to the journal Lady Anne showed me, your ancestor was a bit of a scoundrel."

General Rothbottom?

Perplexed, Harry studied the wall. Christina wasn't a ghost. She couldn't walk through walls. He slammed the heel of his hand on one stone after another until the one below a wooden shelf shifted. The wall groaned, and he shoved harder.

"Be careful," she warned, her voice echoing down the chilly stairwell he'd exposed. "It's been well oiled and slams quickly."

"Where the devil . . ." He didn't have to ask; he knew. She'd been exploring where he'd told her not to go—the old castle. And not just the castle, but one of the blamed rotting thirteenth-century towers.

Racing down narrow stone stairs hollowed by untold numbers of feet over the centuries, Harry managed to keep sight of Christina's trailing robe as they circled downward.

Fury warred with concern in an unpleasant combination that threatened to spin Harry's logic out his ears. His father had fallen off the bloody stone parapet on the roof of this place because the stones gave way. It couldn't be safe.

Heart in his throat as Christina disappeared beyond a bend, Harry almost tripped over the last shallow stair. Clutching the battle-ax tighter as if that would fight off any disaster looming ahead, he held his candle high to illuminate the damp passage. They had to be beneath the castle, in some corner of the dungeon.

"Christina!" he shouted.

"Over here." She sounded more puzzled than alarmed. "Father Oswald disappeared in here, but I cannot figure out how to enter." She stood in an arched niche in the stone wall, her candle held high as she examined what appeared to be a mortar wall where a door used to be.

"There are no such things as ghosts," Harry roared at her. "Nothing can go through that wall. The place is full of niches like that. We stick statues in them."

"If Father Oswald went in there, it's not just a niche, Harry," she answered sternly. "He's trying to tell us something."

The niche had no purpose that Harry could discern, but he was too furious to care. He'd had his wife in his arms, her lush lips against his, her eyes heated with desire—and he wanted her back where she belonged, not down here endangering her neck in a murderous castle that ought to be reduced to rubble.

Without another thought beyond slaying his enemy, he set down his candle and slammed the ax into the crumbling mortar.

A huge chunk of debris hit the stones of the dungeon floor.

Christina shrieked and leaped out of his way.

Relishing the release of tension, Harry smashed the ax into the wall again, letting his muscles do the work rather than reason with Christina. Dust rose in the air, coating the stones and him as the rotting wall fell in chunks beneath his blows.

Eager to see inside, Christina still had the sense to

stand back while Harry wielded his weapon. Amazed at the methodical power with which he shattered the solid wall, she almost forgot her reason for being down here. Never in all her years had she imagined that laughing Harry, her friendly dancing partner, could turn into a warrior on the rampage. He almost seemed to *enjoy* the destruction.

Watching Harry's robed shoulders and arms swinging rhythmically, she missed the moment he broke through the layers of wall into the room beyond. Only when he stopped swinging the ax and rested against it to peer inside with amazement did she wake to the moment.

After the earlier noise, the passage echoed with silence. A rank stench of moldering cold air poured from the concealed chamber while they stared into its darkness.

The *drip-drip* of water was the only sound as their candles illuminated the strange sight within. Crude rock walls and earth supported the tower above the chamber. Moss coated the stones from which a steady trickle oozed over an ancient carving of a man and a bull. A stone table grew out of the rocky floor.

On the table sat a tall goblet covered in cobwebs and filth. The gold of the cup and the filth-coated gems encrusting the stem still gleamed in the dim light despite centuries of neglect.

"Oh, my," Christina murmured in wonder, lifting her candle and daring to peer around Harry. "A chalice."

She thought Harry muttered something inappropriate like *holy shit,* but perhaps she'd misheard. She shifted to stand in front of him, but he caught her waist and hauled her behind him again.

"There could be rats or worse," he reminded her.

"What could be worse than rats?" Shivering, she stayed where he placed her. She might be intrepid, but she wasn't stupid.

"Spiders, snakes, mantraps, for all I know." Taking her question literally, Harry knocked out a few remaining splinters of timber and mortar to widen the passage. "I'm not sure my father was responsible for this wall. This seems to be an old chapel."

"Grotto, more like." Studying the green moss on the walls and the spring trickling over the stones, Christina was convinced this was once a holy place for those who worshipped forbidden gods. "Cromwell's army probably threw the Catholic artifacts in with the old Roman statues and sealed them all together because they were pagan."

Harry whispered another inappropriate comment and finished clearing the hole with a little more reverence than he'd shown earlier. "That looks like the Roman sun god, Mithras, on the wall. I wonder if they might have baths down here."

"In a grotto?" Growing braver, Christina edged beneath his arm. The stone altar in the center of the rocky cavern held a fascinating array of artifacts, but the golden chalice caught the light from their candles as if it weren't coated in the grime of ages. "I hate to tell you, but that could very well be a druidic altar," she said.

"That's possible if the castle was built over a

Roman ruin. The Romans tried to bury the local gods." Satisfied that nothing dangerous would slither through the opening, Harry held his candle high and entered.

He lifted the chalice in awe. "This has to be worth a fortune."

"Harry!" Assuming he jested, Christina elbowed him aside to examine the rest of the items on the altar. "Poor Father Oswald—these must be the remains of his vestments." She sifted through the rotted litter to produce visible threads of gold. "No wonder he haunts the place. Do you think they killed him?"

Harry surveyed the other objects on the high table. "The castle is so riddled with hiding holes that he'd have to be an idiot to be caught."

A stone basin flew off the altar of its own accord, crashing to the floor but not shattering.

Harry stared at the basin rocking quietly now that it had quit flying on its own. "I'd say the good priest wasn't an idiot." The basin settled. "Or the draft down here is a bit capricious," he added with dry sarcasm.

Absorbed in exploring the altar, Christina refrained from comment. Judging from his aura and his patience, Father Oswald was the most saintly ghost occupying Harry's halls, but even he had the right to communicate as he could when being called an idiot. Especially after he'd had the intelligence to communicate the whereabouts of this hiding place.

After warily examining the less valuable bits of silver and glass as if they might take flight at any time, Harry raised his candle to the walls. "That has to be a genuine Roman carved stone of Mithras killing the bull. I had no idea my ancestors built upon a Roman fortress."

"You may thank Father Oswald for the knowledge." Captivated by the astonishing array of ancient artifacts, Christina poked through the altar's contents, finding a pearl pin but nothing else she could easily name.

Before she knew that Harry was behind her, he swept her off the damp stone floor.

"Take the chalice. That's too valuable to leave in an open vault."

"Harry!" Wriggling in protest, Christina attempted to regain her feet, but Harry held her over the altar so she could reach for Father Oswald's most precious possession.

The priest's aura hovered into view the instant she reached for the chalice. She could swear she almost heard his sigh of relief as she wrapped the precious goblet in the blanket she'd thrown around her shoulders.

"Harry, put me down," she whispered, uncomfortable at having Harry's antics watched by a priest. "I'm perfectly capable of walking."

"The floor is wet, and your slippers are soaked. That blanket won't keep you warm much longer. I'll not have you becoming chilled."

"You can't carry me up all those stairs," she said in amazement as he seemed prepared to do just that.

She didn't want to add that if he hurt himself, they wouldn't be able to have a wedding night anytime soon. He'd fly up the stairs with her if she said any such thing. Instead, she did her best to think as he did. "The passage is too narrow, and I'll bruise my toes and elbows. Just take me out of the wet part, then put me down."

To her surprised delight, her husband actually listened, gently setting her on her own two feet when they reached a dry landing. As a reward, she handed him the chalice. "It is extremely heavy, Harry. Do you know someone who can polish and restore it? Judging from his colors, Father Oswald is in pure bliss right now."

"I might want to store it in the chapel, then," he said dryly, hefting the goblet beneath his arm so he could place a free hand at the small of her back and hurry her up the stairs. "Heaven forbid that the good man should hover in our chamber watching over it."

"Oh, excellent thought! Will it be safe there?"

"I'll lock the door. We may have to find other means of protecting it later, but I doubt a lock will keep Father Oswald out."

He still spoke of their ghostly company with skepticism—or sarcasm in this case—but he wasn't outright denying their existence. She supposed he was simply accepting that she believed in ghosts as he'd accepted her search for brownies, and that was more than any other man of her acquaintance would.

Christina nearly danced the rest of the way to the chapel, where Harry deposited the grime-encrusted chalice in its place on the medieval altar. Glancing over her shoulder as they left, Christina saw Father Oswald hovering over the precious goblet, rubbing it adoringly.

"You've done a marvelous thing, Harry," she murmured as they hurried through the cold corridors to their warm chamber. "That poor man must have spent centuries waiting for someone to restore the chalice to its rightful place."

Harry looked guilty as he opened their door and held it for her. "Do not read too much into this. That goblet could be the answer to more prayers than Father Oswald's."

Not liking the tone of his voice, Christina studied his aura. For the first time since he'd asked her to marry him, she saw the brighter colors she thought of as Harry's. Could finding a long-forgotten chalice make that much difference to him? Why?.

"Do you believe me about Father Oswald now?" she asked, trying not to load the question with too much importance.

In their absence, the servants had cleaned up the mess they'd created in their room and carried off the bath. Their uneaten dinner congealed on the plates before the fire. Dropping her damp blanket, Christina poured some tepid tea and sipped it while Harry reached for a bottle of wine.

She loved the way he looked at her right now. She was quite certain that was the color of desire dominating his aura, but she didn't need her gift to see the way his eyes closed halfway to focus on her and naught else. She stood in front of the firelight, knowing he could see straight through the frail fabric of her nightshift. "Harry?" she reminded him.

He jerked back to the moment and poured wine into a glass, sipping at it hastily. "I believe you see things others cannot," he admitted cautiously. "And I apologize for doubting you. I have not been myself lately."

"That is an understatement," she murmured wryly, hiding her inward dance of joy at his admission. How many other men would willingly agree that she might see beyond the material? She did so adore Harry. "So just who have you been?"

"A duke. Climb into bed. I'll add coals to the fire."

She thought his admission might be a sign that he actually loved her and took her seriously. Perhaps it was also a good time to give in to his desires.

She wanted him to kiss her again to ease her fears, but he seemed preoccupied. Perhaps he would remember where they were once they were between the sheets. She climbed into the enormous bed and pulled all the covers up around her while Harry stirred the fire.

"Can't you be Harry and a duke at the same time?" she asked.

"Harry had no responsibilities except to himself. Harry paid his debts and had money left to do with as he pleased." He jabbed harshly at the coals, tumbling ashes and sending a billow of smoke up the chimney.

Christina watched him with growing unease. The bad colors were returning, but there was a spike of honesty along with the anger, so she held her tongue, waiting for his explanation to continue. When he remained silent, she asked, "And the duke?"

"The duke is apparently a penniless bankrupt who

owes everyone in the entire kingdom and has mortgaged his estate away." Harry flung the poker back in
its rack and began to pace.

Christina blinked. She didn't know how else to
react. She came from a family of great wealth and
privilege. She'd never had to waste a precious moment
worrying about the roof over her head or the food on
her table. She had a family who had wrapped her so
thoroughly in cotton batting that she'd had to fight
her way out.

Was Harry telling her she had married a penniless
man? She stared at his broad back as he strode back
and forth, not looking at her. He didn't look penniless.
He looked like a prince, as he always had. His hair
might be disheveled, but it gleamed with health and
vigor. At this hour, he needed a shave, but his jaw
was as firm as she remembered. He carried himself
like a man who could command thousands with a
wave of his arm.

As he could actually. Dukes had that kind of power.

"Your father did all that?" she whispered in awe
and horror. She and her sisters had often made fun
of their father's money-grubbing ways, but she had a
sudden understanding of the marquess's motives. He
had sons who would inherit his estate. He had to provide ample dowries so his many daughters could live
comfortably with the men they chose to marry.

Harry's father had frittered away his inheritance
rather than leave it with his sons. Wide-eyed, Christina
carried that thought one step further.

"You paid your father's debts with my dowry?"

"I paid a *quarter* of his debts with your dowry," he

answered grimly. "Which leaves naught to earn more unless I uncover buried treasure."

"The chalice." Christina stared at Harry's broad back in horror. "You wouldn't sell the chalice?"

"I married you for your money," he stated flatly. "Of course I'd sell the chalice." Heaving a candlestick at the wall, Harry strode from the room.

Fifteen

Learning she was penniless was a shattering experience for Christina. She had always taken wealth for granted. Like the spoiled child Harry thought she was, she'd never considered how one earned money and achieved the security that she'd taken for granted. She needed time to ruminate.

Even though she'd just about decided to be the wife Harry wanted, she was almost glad Harry hadn't returned to their bed last night. Her incessant questions would have driven him mad. When she discovered he'd already ridden out before breakfast, she took her toast and sausage out to the grove of trees she'd admired from afar, climbed onto the branch that was easiest to reach, and meditated.

From her perch high on top of the hill, she realized she could see over much of Harry's estate. Farmers tended the fields. Sheep roamed the pastures. Although the village and house had been in sorry states, she didn't see evidence of penury on the lands. But what did she know of financial matters? Nothing.

What she *did* know was that Harry hadn't married her for her money. The Harry she knew had agreed to their betrothal because they got along well, were attracted to each other, and neither of them wished to be married until they were done adventuring. He'd married her sooner than he wished because of the money, perhaps, but Harry hadn't changed *that* much. He still wanted her. He might pretend it was her money that made her *valuable,* but that was Harry being proud. The knowledge that he valued her warmed her heart and forced her to concentrate on helping him instead of worrying about herself.

Being penniless bothered Harry enormously, she could tell. His nature was to provide and protect, and penury couldn't allow that. That was the reason for his dismal aura, not his marriage to her. Once she gave it proper thought, she realized that Harry was a very noble man, and she should never have been wary of his motives.

In the distance, she saw a rider who had to be her husband. Harry had always possessed an excellent seat. She'd love to gallop with him over the hills, explore the ruins he spoke about so often, picnic in the woods, teach him to laugh again.

And learn to be a wife.

She chewed her thumbnail at that thought. Learning to be a wife meant children. Children cost money. A dukedom, even a penniless one, required an heir. None of this added up to anything sensible.

Meditation wasn't really one of her strong points.

Harry halted his horse to speak with someone in the field. The worker kept hoeing his row. Christina thought that showed serious disrespect to Harry's title. Instead of shouting with anger or riding off, Harry climbed down from his horse, tied it to a post, and walked through the field on his own. The worker stopped hoeing to stare as Harry stooped to roll a large boulder out of the vegetable row and down the hill.

Admiring the strength of Harry's muscles, Christina didn't quite catch on that the farmer still hadn't said anything to him until Harry walked back to his horse without a word exchanged.

Why would anyone *not* speak with Harry? Harry was the kindest, most considerate . . . well, sometimes he was. He'd developed an obstinate streak lately. Still, all London knew Harry was a genial fellow. She couldn't think of a soul who would speak badly of him.

How had she been so blind to Harry's problems? She knew nothing of money and finances, but she knew a great deal about people.

Excited by the thought that she might be able to help Harry in some way, she climbed from the tree and ran down the hill back to the house. How difficult could it be to persuade tenants to converse with a duke?

Of what benefit was her gift if she didn't put it to good use? She should have known Harry hadn't lost his lovely aura because he didn't like being a duke or didn't like being married. She should have asked questions instead of blithely going her own way and expecting Harry to go his as they'd always done. They must learn to work *together*.

Finding Meg counting linen with the newly rehired housekeeper, Christina pulled her aside. "Are the tenants not talking to Harry?" she demanded in a whisper.

Meg looked startled. "He's only just got here. Why shouldn't they?"

Rounding on Mrs. Hoskins, Christina tried again. "Do you know anything of the tenants snubbing the duke?"

The housekeeper looked nervous, and Christina could see a spike of red anger in her aura that did not bode well.

"No, Your Grace," the older woman answered stiffly, folding a sheet into a tight square.

She was lying. Glaring at the housekeeper even though she understood the woman was merely protecting her position—as possibly all the tenants were— Christina gathered her skirts and hurried to her chamber. She'd been lollygagging around, reading old books and chasing ghosts like an indolent dreamer, when Harry needed her help. Not that the stubborn man would admit it.

She would visit the village first. If Harry was bankrupt, it stood to reason that the village wasn't faring well either. Perhaps she should start by learning the depth of their difficulties.

She donned a plain walking dress and, with directions from Meg, walked into the village. Locating the vicar's cottage, she strode up a brick walk between rows of a neatly tilled vegetable garden.

No one answered her knock. Watching the lace-trimmed windows, Christina caught a flicker of movement in one. Setting her lips, she pounded harder.

When still no one responded, she tested the latch. It was locked. Remembering Harry's unpleasant encounter with the vicar's daughter, Christina thought it was time to be equally rude. She marched around the cottage to the kitchen door and rapped on the windowpane. Without further warning, she shoved open the kitchen door.

A stout old woman with her hands buried in dough stared at her in dismay. A much younger woman countered Christina's entrance with a defiant glance that she quickly hid behind lowered lashes. With her dark red hair slicked back in tight braids and wrapped under a lace cap, she set her face without expression. Only a glance of her long-lashed eyes and the unbending stance of her slender frame offered a hint of her character. That and the flaring red spike of anger through the otherwise lovely purple and rose of her aura.

"I am Christina Winchester, Harry's wife," she announced without formality. Given her entrance, formality seemed foolish. "I am looking for the vicar or his wife. I assume you are the Mora Abbott of whom I have heard so much. It's a pleasure to meet you at last."

If she judged people at all well, Christina thought Mora's aura reflected shock followed by suspicion and a curiosity as great as her own.

"I suppose you have heard of me from Meg," Mora said stiffly, indicating a kitchen chair. "We are not accustomed to entertaining duchesses, much less ones who come in the back way. Would you like a seat?" With polite evasion, neither of them mentioned the reason Christina had not entered through the front.

"Thank you. I would like some tea, if you have it. The day is brisk, and the walk was longer than I expected." Christina took the chair offered with a minimum of fuss. She knew she'd been insulted at not being offered the best chair in the house, but she didn't care. She'd come for information and wouldn't leave until she had it.

Rather than disturb the cook, Mora measured tea from the tin and poured hot water from the fire over it. "I will assume from your entrance that you are not one to mince words, so I will return the favor. You had some purpose in seeking us out?"

"So many purposes I cannot begin to list them all, or even list them in order of importance," Christina admitted once the table was set. "Harry told me he remembers you as direct and trustworthy." Actually, Harry hadn't said any such thing, but Christina didn't have any compunction about twisting the truth to cover knowledge gained from reading auras.

Mora offered cream and sugar from chipped containers of once fine china, then poured the tea from a pot with a lid that didn't match. "His Grace barely knows I exist," Mora corrected. "I daresay it's Peter who told you that."

The woman certainly didn't intend to make this easy, Christina reflected, sipping her tea. "Harry has not lived at home much in more than a decade. His duty was to his government. He assumed his brother would inherit the estate."

Mora bent her head in acknowledgment of that truth but said nothing.

Gritting her teeth, Christina let her gaze wander around the kitchen. The wooden counter had been scrubbed to a gleam; every dish and pan had been neatly stored in its place. A vase of jonquils added a splash of color to a worn window ledge. Despite the care with which it had been tended, the kitchen reflected poverty. The pots were dented and blackened beyond repair, the china nicked and faded, the chairs so old they tilted on worn legs.

"What the late duke and his son did here does not reflect my husband's beliefs and behavior," Christina said. If no one would tell her what was wrong, then she would surmise it for herself.

"The late duke was maddened by grief, and as his heir, Lord Winchester coped as best as he could with the lot given him," Mora replied.

Check and checkmate. Christina studied the other woman's aura, but Mora seemed to be in perfect control of herself now. Christina could divine nothing but a curious streak of rose that she seldom found in anyone but her fair-haired family. Odd, but not outlandish. "Harry is doing all within his power to return the estate to profit. I would like to help him."

"How lovely," Mora murmured into her teacup, her gaze again hidden beneath dark lowered lashes.

"Dash it all!" Unable to contain her impatience any longer, Christina stood. "If you do not wish to help me or your neighbors, then send me to someone with more compassion than you have. I can see the poverty here, and I would see it corrected if I could, but I do not have magical solutions to problems I do not understand."

Mora rose with more grace and poise than Christina had ever possessed in her life. "It's a pity titles do not come with magical powers. I wish you well of your marriage. I bid you good day, Your Grace."

Beyond insulted by this regal dismissal, Christina glared at the other woman. "I do not give up, Miss Abbott. And right now I'm angry enough to believe that anyone who isn't helping me is against me. I suggest you give some thought as to whether you really wish to oppose me."

She'd never said anything so outrageous in her life, but she was beyond furious. She needed to find out more about this self-contained Mora Abbott.

Dejectedly walking from the village some hours later, Christina located a lovely streambed where she could cool her tired feet. She had many things to think about, more than her head could hold.

She had received no satisfaction from the women of the village. None were brave enough to talk with her directly. Most scurried away when she appeared. When she cornered a captive audience in the mercantile and spoke of how hardworking and brave Harry was, the customers nodded their heads and hastened to leave.

If no one would talk with her, how could she find out what was wrong? And something was definitely wrong if no one would talk to her. Or to Harry.

The stream beckoned. Perhaps the tree faeries would guide her. She took off her pattens, shoes, and stockings, pulled her skirt and petticoats up to her knees, and dipped her feet into the cool water.

The tree faeries tempted her with the sensuous rush

of liquid over her bare toes, the gentle whisper of spring leaves, and the sweet scent of violets—all reminding her of her duty to be Harry's wife, to offer him the comfort and support he deserved.

She had been a child to insist on love when what Harry needed most was a wife and helpmeet. How lonely he must be with no one to talk to! She wished she could give him the same kind of love and understanding her sisters shared with their husbands, but she shouldn't demand love if she didn't have it to return.

She wasn't at all certain that she knew how to love. She admired Harry. She enjoyed his company—when he wasn't being pigheaded. She would love to love him, if she only knew how. But if she couldn't give him love, she had to offer what she could.

She knew the one thing Harry really wanted was an heir, but she didn't think she could give him one.

The faeries whispered of rowans and ancient rites. The trees murmured, the water rippled, and her Malcolm nature stirred, responding with urges not easily denied. Her romantic nature longed for love. But she yearned to make Harry happy as well.

It was time for her to be a woman, to forgo the dreams of childhood and learn the mysteries of life. Perhaps then she would know how to help Harry.

And as a Malcolm, she had a reputation to uphold. Malcolm women *always* defended their husbands and supported their families. It was the reason they married well—because men knew their reputation.

Thus far, Harry had every right to accuse her of childish irresponsibility, even if he had nobly refrained from doing so. She had done little but follow her own inclinations.

She was *married*. That meant far more than the freedom to finally learn about the pleasures of the marriage bed. But the marriage bed might be the place for her to start.

And once she had learned what she could from Harry, she would find a means to converse with the tenants. Her gift had to have *some* purpose.

Harry found Christina sitting beside a stream, her bare feet dangling in the water. Reining in his gelding on the bridge, he admired the pastoral image of his wife in wool challis and apron, her golden hair partially tumbled from its pins, and her lovely limbs exposed to the sun.

"Need a ride?" he called.

Startled, she almost fell into the water. What the devil had she been thinking about so intensely that she hadn't heard him arrive? Harry swung down to join her.

"I'd enjoy a good gallop," she agreed, reaching for her stockings, "but I'm not precisely dressed for it."

He loved watching her dress but wished he could be undressing her instead. Diverting his thoughts from that direction, Harry studied her warily. After last night's revelation, he was surprised she wasn't hastening back to London. He'd kept a close watch on the road all morning just in case, but naturally, Christina never did as he expected.

"We can ride before breakfast tomorrow, if you'll still be here then. I haven't meant to neglect you."

He hated how stiff he sounded, but he wasn't entirely certain who he was anymore. The Harry who had courted Christina had been a man cocksure of his place in the world. The Harry who had married her had had his world shattered.

"Of course I'll be here." She sent him a puzzled look as she pulled on a shoe. "Did you think to send me elsewhere?"

Relieved that Christina was still Christina and the one certainty in his broken world, Harry knelt on the stream bank to help her buckle on her shoe and iron patten, resisting the desire to run his hand up under her skirt. "I thought you might run back to your father to tell him that you've been cheated. Unless the lawyers find a way out, I really do stand to lose the estate come fall."

"I am not very good at money matters, but my father and brother-in-law are. You could call on them." She wriggled on the other stocking.

Harry bit his lip while resisting helping her tug it up. He had to stand up and walk around to disguise his body's reaction to her innocent actions. "I'll keep that in mind. Have you heard from your sister yet? Will she be joining you here?"

"Haven't had time to hear. It's spring planting season, and Dunstan will be busy. It may be summer before they can come. But I'm hoping Ninian will send me some gardening advice." Buckling her other shoe, Christina fastened her patten and jumped up. "I have decided what I would really like is a small gathering of local people."

"Local people?" Harry swung around to stare. He,

of all people, knew that the guileless smile Christina bestowed upon him hid a mind that had leaped three steps ahead and into a different dimension. "What sort of gathering?" he demanded. "There isn't cash to fund musicians and an army of cooks and maids."

"A simple gathering. We could call it an open house. We'll throw open the doors to all who have been wanting to see what your father has done to your home. We'll have some punch and a few cakes and things that Cook can put together. And we'll invite the villagers and your tenants."

"Tenants?" Harry couldn't think of anyone in the aristocracy who entertained landless farmers. He didn't think they'd come. But he wasn't averse to asking them, he supposed. "What about our other neighbors?"

Christina waved her hat airily. "We'll invite everyone. I think it's time to discover who is friend and who is foe."

Ah, so she had discovered the animosity the entire populace had displayed toward him. Even Harry's working beside that farmer this morning hadn't loosened the man's tongue. It seemed damned odd that tenants wouldn't share their grievances. Maybe they were waiting for Jack to return.

Harry hoped Christina wouldn't be too disappointed if no one came to her party, but he couldn't deny her the opportunity to try. Human nature being what it was, curiosity might overrule animosity for an hour or two. "I suppose we could safely open the new wing. I'll help you however you like, but do not put too much hope in a large turnout."

Christina flung her arms around his neck and kissed his cheek soundly. "Thank you, Harry! And now, to celebrate, I think we should take a picnic to the ruins. I have plans, Harry."

She darted toward his horse before his blood could return to his head.

Sixteen

The early afternoon sun was remarkably warm for a spring day. Harry shrugged off his coat and threw it over a tree branch while he puzzled out Christina's intentions for this picnic.

She'd had the newly hired stable grooms carry a daybed from a back parlor up to the mosaic floor of the Roman ruins on the hill overlooking the house, in the shade of a copse of rowans. Then she had spread out an old comforter and some pillows next to the daybed and opened Cook's picnic basket containing a meal of cold chicken and ham, salads made from spring greens, apples, and freshly baked breads and cakes.

To her credit, she hadn't ordered the entire staff up here with crystal and silver to wait on them. He'd been to picnics where the guests had dined as if they were still in the dining parlor. Instead, she'd asked for simple foods they could mostly eat with their fingers. By themselves.

Studying the scene she'd set up, Harry hoped Christina's mind was on the same path as his, but he didn't count the likelihood as high. Christina's mind was a thing of wonder he might appreciate but would never understand. Or even want to try, given her propensity for talking to beings long dead.

Which made him wonder how many of those imaginary beings were cluttering up the clearing. The ghostly encounter with the chalice had left him with more questions than answers. He didn't see how even someone as imaginative as Christina could have dreamed up a hidden room and chalice. He still refused to believe in ghosts though. He preferred to think Christina possessed amazing instincts.

"Is this entertainment just for us, or did you think Lady Anne and Father Oswald needed airing?" he asked, not entirely jesting as he studied the upholstered seat set on the mosaic floor. He'd always loved that mosaic. He'd expected it to be covered in years' worth of leaves and dirt, but someone had kept it clean.

"I don't think they leave the house much," she said absently, removing bowls and plates from the baskets the staff had carried up. "I wouldn't trust General Rothbottom to stay where he belongs, but I'm hoping the rowans will discourage him."

"The rowans?" He had no inclination to inquire about General Rothbottom. The only General Rothbottom he knew about dated back to the fifteenth century. There was a portrait in the gallery of a bearded old rogue wearing a dashing feathered hat and a padded surcoat over a plated cuirass. If he remembered correctly, the general fought the French and brought the Winchesters a tidy sum of gold and the title of earl. So actually, he was Raleigh Rothbottom, Lord

Winchester, when he died. The general's son had taken the Winchester title for his name, for which Harry was eternally grateful.

"Rowans are sacred trees," Christina said to answer his earlier question. "There's a natural spring inside that circle where my ancestors would have worshipped the nature gods and goddesses. My grandmother used to tell us that faeries, and spirits waiting to be born, live inside rowan rings. I shouldn't think the general would appreciate their company. Judging from his rude behavior when I entered the castle, he seems a surly, unpleasant fellow." Settling her skirts on the blankets, she looked up expectantly at him.

Harry thought he might be gazing at one of those faerie sprites right now. His wife still wore her peasant-style wool gown that he knew was all the rage in London. The simplicity suited her well, and suited him even more. Except Christina had chosen not to wear hoops but a petticoat to prevent the hem from dragging. Instead of wearing an elaborate shift with lace at collar and cuff, she'd covered the low-necked laced stomacher with a bit of gauze that revealed more than it concealed. Seeing her golden hair caught in a ribbon and spilling over her breasts, he allowed his gaze to linger in the shadows between her ripe curves.

But this wasn't a bedroom, and he had to take his thoughts elsewhere.

Removing his vest and using it for a seat, he sat cross-legged on the blanket and leaned back against the daybed while Christina fixed a plate for him. "We could divert the spring and build a Roman bath on this spot," he said. "I'm sure there is one buried under this mound somewhere, but I haven't the time or resources to dig it up."

"Unless the spring is a hot one, you wouldn't have slaves to feed it fuel and pump the water," she reminded him.

"A good Roman bath had an aqueduct to provide the water, and a small one didn't require a lot of fuel." Ravenous for more than food, Harry tore off a bite of chicken and tried to think lofty thoughts while his wife leaned over and displayed her assets. He hoped the display was for his benefit, but she was reaching for the jam.

"Leila's farm near Bath has a hot spring," she said. "It's quite lovely. Perhaps we could run water into the castle grotto and heat it."

"I'm amazed my father hadn't done that already," he said dryly. "I don't think there will be more castle additions anytime soon."

"It might not cost much." She shrugged, and the kerchief at her throat slid down her shoulder a little, teasing him with a glimpse of creamy skin. "One of the advantages of having a large family is that there is usually someone among us who can do whatever one needs. One of my brothers-in-law, Ewen, is an inventor who does amazing things with dams and plumbing. But he's in Scotland right now."

"I've never had the benefit of a large family." Harry would like to be starting a family of his own right now, but he thought the setting a trifle inappropriate for an inexperienced bride. Maybe later this summer he could introduce her to the wonders of lovemaking in the outdoors.

Not that he'd ever had a lover who was much interested in lovemaking anywhere except in a bed with silk sheets. Now that his thoughts had traveled down this path, Harry wondered if Christina's lively imagination might take their bedplay to entertaining heights. Right now, he simply hoped she would welcome him into her bed tonight.

Was this her way of "getting acquainted" so that she might be reassured that he loved her adequately? He certainly hadn't proved it these last few nights. Since she hadn't run screaming back to London, perhaps she was offering him a second chance. He wished he knew what love looked like so he could show her. It might be the only gift he could afford.

"You have a large family through me now," she said simply, passing him a roll with strawberry jam. "They can be interfering nuisances, but they'll be there when you need them."

Given his experience with family, Harry thought aid unlikely. Since his mother's death, he'd more or less raised himself. Savoring the sweet strawberry, he didn't argue but leaned over to lick a dollop of jam from his wife's delectable lips.

He was certain he had something fascinating to say, but it flew straight out of his head the instant Christina slid her smooth palm over his rough cheek, held his mouth to hers, and slid her tongue between his lips.

Blindly setting aside his roll, Harry cupped Christina's face and held her steady as she explored his mouth. Her tongue tasted of jam and the rich wine he'd poured for her, setting off sensual explosions he couldn't resist. Catching her slender waist, he dragged her closer so he could sample her mouth as thoroughly as she had his.

When Harry's kiss deepened, Christina moaned low in her throat, and her body reacted in several regions at once. She decided his hand upon her face wasn't enough. He would need three or four hands for all the parts demanding his attention. Her breasts ached with the need for his caress. And in her lower abdomen, a pulse pounded that required some release she didn't know how to obtain. Clasping the back of his head, running her hand through his thick hair, she kissed him back and arched against his chest in hopes of relieving the pressure.

She had thought of this seduction as being about the estate and the dukedom and growing up to be the woman Harry needed. She hadn't understood until now that in granting Harry's wishes, she fulfilled her own desires as well.

He responded to her kiss with gratifying sureness. Releasing her cheek, he skimmed his hand downward, brushing a curl against her throat. His mouth traveled after his hand, nipping and kissing and awaking her skin so that she shivered all over. His hand slid lower, pushing aside her neckerchief, grazing her shoulder and the top of her breast, before he lowered his mouth there.

Harry's warm, moist breath against her flesh taught her what she was missing. Her clothing seemed cumbersome and an artificial hindrance. Fortunately for her, Harry grasped that better than she did. Discovering the ties fastening her bodice to her stomacher, he loosed them, and her breasts spilled free of her stays.

She thought she heard him murmur in surprise and pleasure, but she was too lost to sensation to care for anything except his next caress. Harry in just shirtsleeves and breeches was a dream come true. Running her fingers down his neck, pushing aside his loosened cravat, she encouraged him to do more than look.

Harry scarcely needed encouragement. To her bliss, he slid his hand beneath her bodice to cup her breast, and his thumb performed miracles with the aching tip. Christina moaned again as the tight knot in her lower parts opened, releasing a flood of moisture. Instinctively, she knew the time had arrived to prove she could be his wife, even if she did not know precisely how to go about it.

Harry showed her the way. Following his actions, she unknotted his cravat, unlaced his shirt, and ran her hands beneath his linen to rub the warm, muscular planes of his chest. Harry rewarded her by kissing her breast and teasing the crest with his tongue until she thought she might have swooned. She didn't know how else she ended in Harry's arms and on the daybed like a sacrifice upon a marriage altar.

And a very willing sacrifice she was. Opening her eyes, she saw the blue of sky above. The leaves of the rowans whispered over her head, and the breath of a spring breeze blowing across her bare breasts felt very right. When Harry kneeled on the bed and leaned over her, she smiled dreamily at his studious expression, and his eyes narrowed in that half-lidded look that inspired delighted shudders.

"Do you read minds?" he inquired, returning his kiss to her cheek and temple, removing the ribbon from her hair so it spilled across the pillows.

"No, just auras," she murmured, not caring what he meant so long as his talented fingers continued their performance upon her clothing and person. She was completely bare from the waist up, and his leg was planted firmly between her knees, even though her skirt and petticoat hampered the act she knew would follow.

"Then I must have a very legible aura." Not explaining, he splayed his broad hand across her bare back, lifting her so he might remove her arms from the sleeves of her gown. Free, Christina slid her hands around his shoulders and dragged his head down for a kiss.

His tongue invaded and conquered and taught her who was master here, and she loved it all, knowing the time would come when he would teach her enough so they could play on an equal field. For now, she satisfied herself with pushing Harry's shirt off his shoulders so she could explore the powerful surge of his muscles as he held himself above her.

"If we go much further, I will not be able to stop, Christina," he said hoarsely against her ear while cupping and caressing her breast. "I would not frighten or embarrass you by taking you here like a serving wench. Tell me no now if that is your wish."

"Ninian said I would know when the time is right and the spirit is willing. That time is now, Harry. I would give you the heir you want."

Whether he understood or not, when she offered

him her body, she offered her future. There could be no going back to their carefree days after this moment. No matter what happened, they would be irrevocably tied.

Tugging free the hem of his shirt, Christina pulled it from his waistband while surreptitiously examining the bulge in his breeches. Her curiosity often got her into trouble, but her knowledgeable sisters had assured her she would enjoy this act that would permanently bind her to her husband.

She didn't know if she loved Harry as her sisters loved their husbands, but she knew she adored him as she admired no other man. She laughed in delight when he ripped his shirt off and flung it to the ground. My, he was a sight to behold—a golden warrior looming over her, prepared to claim what was rightfully his. She was glad she'd chosen this setting for seduction. Harry was a Roman god more powerful than any carved in stone.

Studying her face and finding no fear, he boldly lifted her and, while holding her gaze with his, peeled her skirt and petticoat out from under her.

Lying naked except for garters and stockings beneath her half-dressed husband, Christina felt astonishingly powerful. And perhaps just a little vulnerable. He kneeled above her, holding her thighs parted, while his gaze devoured her. His delight and the breeze caressed her skin more subtly than a physical touch. Had it been anyone but Harry . . .

Straightening, Harry began unfastening the buttons of his breeches placket. Sunlight caressed his golden shoulders and glinted off the fine hairs spread across his muscular chest and running in a ribbon down his middle, to the place where his hand worked the buttons. Forgetting to study Harry's aura or expression, Christina watched in fascination as he shoved his breeches down his hips, revealing the enormity of what he concealed behind the fabric.

Apparently reading her concern, he sprawled beside her, kissing her ear, toying with her breast, and whispering sweet words her heart needed.

"You are so beautiful. You take my breath away," he said as he stole *her* breath by stroking his fingers through the liquid warmth between her thighs. "I want to give you birdsong and sunshine and whatever your heart desires forever."

As if in response to his wish, a robin sang from a branch above them. Christina didn't know if she believed him, but she knew what her body preferred at this moment. Biting back a cry of desire, she arched her hips to drive Harry's marauding fingers deeper.

"You are a goddess of nature like Diana. Let me worship you." His fingers retreated, coaxing gently instead of relieving the maddening tension.

Before Christina could box his ears for his frustrating dalliance, Harry propped his hands on either side of her head and leaned over to suckle her breast. She did cry out then, cried and writhed and ached for that which was within her reach and yet withheld from her.

Her hips rose and fell in time with the tug of Harry's mouth and the desire flooding her womb. Just when she thought she must surely burst with the need swelling inside her, Harry dipped his head lower and lapped his tongue where his fingers had plied earlier.

Christina screamed and surrendered to the tides washing over her, lifting and taking and coming apart beneath this simplest of conquests.

Before the last wave engulfed her, Harry slid his body over hers, brushed her breasts with his chest, and whispered meaningless words against her ear. The tension began to build all over again as he parted her legs, and she felt the hard heat of his maleness where his gentle caress had been earlier.

He eased inside, giving her a moment to adjust. She didn't want a moment. Grabbing the sinewy arms straining on either side of her, Christina lifted her hips into his, glorying in the stabbing pain as he broke through her innocence, making her his wife at last.

Lost to the sensation of Harry filling the narrow passage of her maidenhood, she surrendered any conscious thought and became a true creature of nature, acting out of instinct, love, and the need for the intimacy this act forced upon them. She accepted his thrusts and returned them with fervency. When he rested to give her ease, she spread kisses across his jaw, dug her fingers into his shoulders, and raised her hips for more.

Unable to resist, Harry moved with increasing power, driving her to a frenzy of need all over again. Crying out, she clung to him and flew free.

Her response produced a roar of release from Harry. As his seed spilled into her, Christina opened to the spirits hiding in the rowans, letting them enter as they would, becoming one with the earth and air and with her husband, whose body held her close and shuddered with the spasms of life-giving release.

Seventeen

Conscious of his heavy weight crushing Christina beneath him, Harry rolled to one side. Christina rolled with him. Her firm breasts pressed against his chest, stirring the blood in his loins. Vaguely, he wondered if it would be monstrous to take her again. He couldn't remember the last time he'd felt so good. If ever. His hand slid of its own accord to her slender waist and curvaceous hip, pulling her into him.

"How many times do you think we should do this before you have your heir, Harry?" she murmured, nuzzling his neck with kisses.

"As many times as we can manage." To hell with heirs. He just wanted her body under him again, to experience the miracle of her instinctive responses. He'd never taken a virgin before. She'd been tight and eager, and he felt as if he'd just been given a precious essence to cherish forever. The emotion of the experience had disoriented him, and his mind still wasn't focusing right.

After the magic moments with which she'd just gifted him, he wanted to be the romantic hero she longed for, but all he could think to ask was "Are you cold? Should I take you to the house?"

"And shock Lady Anne?" she murmured with what he hoped was a giggle. "Can we do it again here?"

Exulting in her answer, forgetting all his other concerns, Harry covered her mouth with his and let his kisses answer for him.

She was every bit as warm and pliant as the first time. He loved the tiny moans she made in her throat and the way she threw her head back and arched her hips demandingly. He even loved the way she grabbed him in frustration if he didn't proceed at the pace she thought she desired.

He knew what she needed better than she did right now. He worked her slowly, bringing her back to the peaks of earlier, not wanting her to be disappointed in any way. She was weeping in frustration and whipping her lovely hair back and forth by the time he entered her the second time. His bride was an enchantress, a seductive siren, and a woman with all the wiles of nature. It was a joy and triumph to claim her.

The hills echoed with her cries as he drove her high and higher, and he responded to her music with more enthusiasm and desire than he could remember ever experiencing. With total loss of control, he tumbled her over the precipice with shattering thrusts. He'd never so lost himself as to forget his partner, but Christina had the power to twist his head around.

Collapsing back on the daybed, he lifted her head to his shoulder and curled her beneath his arm to keep her warm. Her hair spilled across his chest and her breasts, but he could still admire the way her nipples grew taut at the slightest breeze.

"Can we do this even when I'm big and round?"

she murmured against his neck, shooting a thrilling shiver through his skin. "I hated to ask my sisters that."

Harry chuckled. "Most ladies chase men away once they're breeding. I'm willing to experiment if you are. But I don't recommend our outdoor boudoir for expectant ladies."

"Hmpf." She snuggled her nose against his throat. "You'd rather do it with Lady Anne and Father Oswald watching? I'll have to forbid them access to our chamber. Although now that Father Oswald has his chalice, he probably won't come around much."

"Once I tear down the Abomination, maybe they'll go back to their graves where they belong. They deserve a good long rest," he said from the comfort of satiation.

He knew he'd said the wrong thing the instant Christina shot from his arms as if stung by a nest of hornets. The cold of her departure doused his languor.

"Tear it down? You cannot! The house is their *home*. How can you possibly tear it down?"

Harry blinked in bewilderment, uncertain how to react to the Valkyrie raging above him. A very naked Valkyrie. "The castle and manor are falling down, Christina. I can't afford to shore them up."

"You don't know that they're falling down." She leaped up and raced about the clearing, gathering her clothes.

If he lived to be ten thousand he'd never forget the sight of his wife flitting about the woods in the sunshine as natural as the day she was born. She looked more forest sprite than duchess, but it was definitely the duchess who was flinging his clothes at his head. A buckle on his breeches clipped him on the nose before he grabbed the offending garment and jammed his legs into it.

"The bloody parapet fell and killed my father and brother," he countered. "The lintel nearly killed you. I've called for engineers, but I'm not a total fool. The buildings are centuries old and falling down. I can't afford to maintain them."

"You have no idea how many spirits inhabit those buildings!" she insisted. "Where would they go?" She struggled with the hooks of her stomacher, hiding the ripeness of her splendid figure. He'd always thought her slender and hadn't expected the lovely bosom filling her bodice to be more than a woman's artifice. Now that he knew what she hid behind her men's shirts and simple shifts . . .

Dragging his breeches up, Harry wanted to growl, but she'd successfully drained him of anything remotely resembling anger. "I refuse to pander to your imaginary characters. I'll grant that you see things others don't, but I'll not build houses for ghosts."

"What about Lady Anne's spinning wheel?" she demanded. "She uses it all the time—I can hear it. And Father Oswald showed you the chalice. How can you drive him out of his beloved chapel after all these years? Your father restored that room for a reason."

"They're dead people, Christina! Dead, dead, *dead,* buried in their graves where worms have long since eaten them. If the engineer says the buildings are safe, I'll leave them alone. That's the most I can promise." He pulled on his shirt and tucked the hem into his breeches. "Unless, of course, your friendly spirits want to uncover more buried treasure like the chalice so I can pay the damnable mortgage."

"You can't sell the chalice," she said in horror, her hands freezing on the hooks of her bodice.

"I don't *want* to sell the chalice." Amazed that they agreed on one thing, Harry crossed the clearing to pull her stomacher into place. "But if I must choose between a chalice and my land, I will choose my land. Don't use this as an excuse to pull away from me, Christina. I need your support, not your tears."

As if in answer, a hot tear fell upon his head while he tied the last lace. Scalded, Harry jerked his head up, but Christina scrubbed at her eyes and met his gaze as boldly as any man.

"It's my duty as a Malcolm and a wife to support you, Harry. And I will, wholeheartedly." Her lower lip trembled but she stood magnificently straight, her hair blowing in the breeze around her. "Just don't expect me to do it according to your terms."

Relieved in ways he didn't understand since they were still at odds, Harry laughed at her defiant stance. "I never expect you to do as expected."

She nodded, satisfied. "Just so we understand each other."

Wrapping his arm around her waist for the reassurance that he wouldn't have to fight the battle for her bed all over again, Harry hugged her close. "We will never understand each other. That's part of your charm. Tell me why you think my father restored a chapel for a ghost. Did he see them, too?"

"I can't say, but the pages in the ledgers that describe the Elizabethan manor have been clearly marked, and the chapel description is precise. Over the centuries, people change the way they live, boarding up doors and taking out walls and such. Maybe all he was trying to do was put them back the way they once were. The new part of the manor that he built does not seem to be occupied by any spirits that I've noticed."

Oddly relieved to think his father's madness may have only been a means of burying his grief by recreating the home of his ancestors, however badly he'd done it, Harry reluctantly steered Christina from the magical grove. "I could only wish he hadn't bankrupted us in the process. I don't think the ghosts are properly appreciative."

"It's possible they are but have no means of expressing it." Lifting the bulk of her skirt over her arm, Christina followed his stride with ease. "I can't imagine many people see them, and even I have difficulty communicating with them. Being a spirit must be very lonely."

Feeling better than he had since his father's death, Harry laughed out loud at her observation. "If all you have to tend is ghosts, I must see about providing you with a more productive pastime."

He enjoyed her fancies, but he had no desire to learn *why* she thought the spirits hung about. He feared that if she told him, he'd have to do something about it, and he really needed to deal with his live tenants first. The remembrance of how he'd been treated by ungrateful farmers darkened his mood, but he did his best not to let Christina know.

"Oh, I have plenty to keep me busy," she announced. "I have a party to plan, and we can expect my family soon enough. And I suppose children will happen eventually."

Her casual mention of children so startled Harry that he stumbled over a tree root. *He would have to start planning for children.*

He couldn't return to his carefree London life. That was over.

Mentally adjusting to a realization that was long past due, he decided he wouldn't miss politics. He might miss London, but right now, he was more interested in the new experience of his wife and the possibility of children.

Out of the corner of his eye he watched Christina striding blithely down the hill and tried to imagine her round with his child. He couldn't do it. He wasn't an imaginative man.

But they'd just committed an act that could have created a child already. They had done nothing to prevent a child from happening. And Malcolms were very fertile.

He had to save the estate for his children.

Even though the burden on his shoulders grew heavier, Harry walked with a lighter step toward the sprawling palace he called home.

Watching Harry ride off to his duties, more aware than ever of the fine-honed integrity of the man shouldering responsibilities for which he'd never been trained, Christina was determined to be the helpmeet he needed. She couldn't let him tear down his home.

Besides, she didn't think Harry *wanted* to destroy his home. He loved old things. He just considered tearing down the castle another of his duties, the kind that made him miserable.

So she had to set her mind to saving Harry and the estate and the village. It was growing into quite a challenge. She thought she knew how to accomplish it, though, if all went well. And if the ghosts would cooperate.

She looked for Meg first, to discuss the idea of holding a party for the entire village. As Harry had ordered, she and Peter had returned to their rooms in the manor. Finding Meg sipping tea in the new salon while frowning over the household books, Christina dropped into a lovely gold silk chair and explained her plan for gathering the local people. She didn't think she could easily explain the rest of her plan, since sending invitations to ghosts wasn't in any etiquette book she knew. But reading auras wasn't enough. She hoped the ghosts could help her interpret the auras of her guests.

"A party?" Meg asked doubtfully. "Didn't you say no one is talking to Harry? Will anyone come?"

"What if we say it is an open house? I still cannot fathom why anyone would blame Harry for the problems that are so clearly not his fault."

"It is easier to blame someone they don't know, I suppose." Meg wrinkled her forehead prettily and gave the subject some thought. "Perhaps everyone thinks he went off to London and forgot about them."

Concluding Meg was a little naïve or not telling everything if she thought the villagers were angry because Harry went away, Christina held her tongue. "Could you make a list of neighbors to invite?"

Meg practically bounced in anticipation. "Why don't you write your family as well? The promise of having your aristocratic family there will give the neighbors even more incentive to attend."

Given her family's meddling ways, Christina didn't think that quite so fine an idea, but it wouldn't hurt to make Meg happy after all she'd done to help out.

In the interest of determining what rooms might be available should any of her family accept, she set out to explore the possibilities.

She'd already ordered the cleaning staff to remove the funeral wreaths from the statuary as well as open and air the chambers Harry had approved. They had hired a handyman to begin sealing leaks and repairing damage caused by rodents. With a good, stiff cleaning the family floor of the old manor would be almost respectable.

She'd located but hadn't opened a locked suite she assumed had once belonged to Harry's mother. Under her orders, the hired handyman had pried off the bolts on the duchess's chamber, but the doors had remained stubbornly locked. She'd have to ask the housekeeper for a key.

A disorderly suite the next door down had been buried in building plans and sketches and more old ledgers. She assumed it must have belonged to the late duke. She'd checked with Harry earlier, and he'd seemed relieved that she was willing to tackle opening those chambers, as well as his brother's, assuming they were structurally sound since they'd been in frequent use. She didn't think Harry was prepared to occupy them, but if they were to have guests, they would need the space.

Except to check on the servants' quarters, she hadn't dared consider the upstairs nursery floor. Perhaps she ought to investigate that section more thoroughly, but she'd just learned the joys of marriage and wasn't ready to contemplate the results.

She was still a bit sore from Harry's enthusiastic lovemaking, but every step she took reminded her of the beauty of their intimacy. As she went in search of the housekeeper to unlock the duchess's suite, she wondered if Harry would come to her bed again this evening.

Just thinking of what they might do tonight had her flushed with desire by the time she'd located Mrs. Hoskins and her key ring and dragged her up to the locked chamber. How did people live with this constant urge to couple? She'd thought that once she'd satisfied the need, it would go away. Instead, now that she knew Harry's seductive talents, she wanted more.

Lost in dreams of what she would wear tonight to entice him, which of her mother's candles she would burn, and which sweet words she hoped he would say, she wasn't totally prepared for the locked door to swing open.

"Sweet blessed Jesus," the housekeeper murmured as they were hit with a blast of icy air.

Glancing over Mrs. Hoskins's shoulder, Christina inhaled sharply.

The locked room was neat as a pin, far neater than any previous they'd encountered. On the vanity was a vase containing a single yellow rose—as fresh as if it had been plucked that morning, even though the room had supposedly been locked for years.

But the inexplicable rose wasn't the reason for Christina's shock. Stepping past the housekeeper, she stared in astonishment at the mirror above the vanity.

A dashing courtier in the chin-length bobbed hair, cultured goatee, and feathered cap of the fifteenth century stared defiantly from within the mirror. Until his square-jawed face realigned into a scowl, she almost believed a portrait had replaced the mirror. His resemblance to Harry was so striking that she nearly held out her hand to him. The image rapidly began to fade—but not before the likeness pointed toward a dark shadow in the background.

Christina strained to recognize the silhouette sitting in what appeared to be a chair at a desk, but the man was only an indistinct form—too thin to be Harry but not readily recognizable as anyone else.

"What are you trying to tell me?" she demanded of the mirror, but by then the glass merely reflected her own image.

"Your Grace?" the housekeeper inquired.

"Did you not see it?" she demanded, although a moment later she wished she could take back the words. Of course the housekeeper hadn't seen it.

"The rose, Your Grace? Strange, isn't it? Do you think His Grace may have put it there in honor of his mother? The room is as cold as the outer rings of hell. I'll have someone lay a fire and dry it out."

"Yes, of course." Backing away from the mirror, Christina let the housekeeper rattle on of airing and fires and damp. Harry hadn't placed that rose there.

Harry hadn't cleaned this room. And that hadn't been Harry playacting in a fifteenth-century courtier's costume.

That had been General Rothbottom. She had *seen* a ghost. Not just an aura. A ghost, with clothes and everything. Only once before in her life had she seen a fully formed apparition—and that had been her aunt Iona warning her that her life was in danger. Her heart beat a little faster in fear. What could he be warning her of?

In the stiff gallery portrait, she hadn't noticed the general's resemblance to Harry, but she'd seen the image move in the mirror. He scowled like Harry did. Had he once laughed as Harry did?

What had he been trying to tell her?

Something unpleasant, she was certain. Aunt Iona had spoken. Why hadn't the general? Did the presence of someone else lessen his ability to speak? Or her ability to hear?

She blinked and frowned. Whatever was happening to her? Her gift was changing . . . broadening.

Not knowing whether to be excited or frightened, or simply gratified that her Malcolm gift was maturing, she hastened back to the archive room to discover what she could about the general. She was imaginative. She could speculate that the spirits were placing roses in gratitude to Harry's mother for improving their home, but she couldn't speculate on who the shadow in the background was. The old duke?

She really needed to *talk* to the castle's inhabitants if she meant to discover the source of Harry's problems with the tenants. Might the general speak if she found him alone? She found the ledger from the fifteeth century and perused the crumbling pages carefully.

The meticulous old script seemed to be that of a clerk who carefully recorded every basket of apples and every acre of grain, but she could find no mention of the castle's inhabitants. Scanning the entries, she located the record of the purchase of a new chest and bed for the general's—by then, the earl's—bride, then entries for the expenses for improvement of the keep.

Apparently the notes from the general's era had encouraged later generations to continue relating the house's history. Though the initial entries were scanty, succeeding entries had spilled over into numerous volumes, each increasingly detailed.

Deciding she did not dare ignore the general's warning any longer, Christina abandoned the ledgers. She must try to talk to him in person. If Harry or his house were in some sort of danger, she must do everything within her ability to protect it. If the first Lord Winchester had something to say that was important enough for him to materialize in so dramatic a fashion, she must seek him out. Heedless of Harry's warnings, she hurried downstairs and through the drawing room toward the castle keep that the first earl had evidently expanded for his bride.

She remembered clearly the ghostly laughter on another occasion when she strayed near here. If it had been the general laughing at her, surely he had the power of speech. Whether or not a fifteenth-century earl would deign to speak to a mere woman was another question entirely.

Although she had found doors on all floors between the new manor and the old one, so far she had found only one entrance into the castle. In turning the Elizabethan attics into servants' rooms, she'd seen a cluster of rooms at the end of the hallway indicating that someone lived there. Judging from the muddy boots and male clutter in the chambers, she assumed it must be the missing steward. When asked, Harry had said Jack kept rooms in the house.

It did not seem likely that there would be an entrance into the castle from private rooms, so she had not intruded on the steward's privacy to search for one. She had never gone out on the dangerous parapets to look for a connection on the roof either, although she'd seen stairs that might take her up there.

She had to admit that Harry was right about one thing. The architecture of his home was a trifle strange.

Reaching the first floor and racing through the drawing room and gallery, she recognized the instant she crossed the threshold between the manor and the keep.

If General Rothbottom was a fifteenth-century earl, his ghost was more likely to linger here than anywhere.

Taking a deep breath, she boldly entered the great hall of the keep.

An odd sensation stole over her as she tiptoed across the wide planks of the cavernous chamber. Daylight still poured through the long narrow windows high on one wall. Her lantern illuminated the path directly in front of her, but the far wall and paneled ceiling were hidden in shadows. Perhaps it was simply a fear of the unknown that stirred an excess of sensitivity in her, as if her sight and hearing were more acute.

A creak caused her to hesitate uncertainly.

Straightening her shoulders, she marched on. Old houses creaked. She knew that well enough. But the oppressive stillness crept along her skin. Shouldn't there be birdsong or wind whistling through the rafters? She had the urge to shout just to hear the sound of life. The place was silent as a tomb.

How would she find the general in here? Did she dare go above?

Was that a rattle? She swung around but saw nothing.

She tilted her head back to scan the upper story. Heavy chandeliers hung from the center of the high, arched ceiling. The one directly over her head swung ponderously in some air current from a broken window or rotten roof. The chain holding it in place creaked and groaned from the weight. That was all.

She'd clambered through graveyards and talked to *ghosts*, for pity's sake. She shouldn't be in the least squeamish about air currents and squeaks. Well, maybe squeaks if they sounded at all ratlike. She had an aversion to furry things that streaked across her feet without warning.

To avoid any such encounter, she stood in the empty center of the chamber and stomped her feet as hard as she could. That should send them scattering into the walls.

The chain creaked again, and a rustle in the rafters almost sent her fleeing.

It belatedly occurred to her that she normally trespassed in the keep in accompaniment with a friendly spirit, but this time she was all alone. Foolish of her to worry about that now. The floor seemed safe enough. Actually, she thought great halls usually had stone or dirt floors, so the boards had most likely been added when the manor was built. They should be solid. Although she supposed if there were dungeons underneath . . .

No, that was in the tower. Different fortification entirely.

She heard no rodent rustlings, just the creak of the roof or floor and the odd swaying of the chandelier. The uneasy stirring in her midsection was most likely hunger.

Telling herself that finding General Rothbottom shouldn't be too difficult, she edged across the towering chamber, testing the floor as she went.

A low moan raised the hackles on her neck.

A sudden draft of chilly air raised goosebumps on her arms.

A loud crash similar to that of chains echoed through the empty hall. The iron wheel of the chandelier overhead creaked.

Deciding it might be better to come another day, Christina turned around to seek the safety of the known.

Only to be halted by the sight of the general in tunic, hose, and feathered cap, holding up a gloved hand in warning.

An instant later, the heavy chandelier gave a rusty sigh and plummeted toward her.

Eighteen

Harry wasn't in a state conducive to logical thought as he rode through the village toward home. Eager to return to Christina and anticipating a firelight dinner with longing gazes and seductive kisses after a day of dealing with taciturn tenants, he wondered if his bride would be agreeable to more love-making so soon after their lusty luncheon. He wondered where she might be right now and if she would be eager to see him.

He needed all the cheerful thoughts he could summon. He'd just paid the estate's bank debt with the last of Christina's dowry. That left him with no cash to buy seeds to plant the fallow fields unless he borrowed it. It would take only one small disaster to topple his precarious house of cards and render him unable to pay Carthage's installment with profits from rent and crops in the fall. He wasn't a gambler by nature. He hated risk.

For cash to tide them over until fall, he'd had to write to his solicitor and ask him to rent out the London town house for the season. He didn't know how to tell Christina that they wouldn't be returning to the city anytime soon.

But his bride's enthusiastic lovemaking had lightened his stormy mood and given him hope for a brighter day. He'd decided he wanted his sons to romp through the Roman ruins as he had. An adult might love the intellectual stimulation of London, but children belonged in the country.

Riding through the village, he tried to concentrate on that happy thought so he wouldn't terrify Christina into running away from him. She seemed to be sensitive to his darker moods, so he would do his best to relieve her of the burden of his anger and frustration.

The sight of an imposingly large stranger leaning broad shoulders against the tavern wall halted his eager progress.

Wearing a gentleman's coat without the accompaniment of wig or hat, the giant seemed occupied in talking to a tall, slender man in equally unfashionable garb. The instant the slender man scratched his head with a pencil, Harry recognized him as Robert Morton, an old school chum and the engineer he'd hired, and his mood plummeted. Christina had made clear her opinion of his tentative plan to tear down the castle. Rob would be an unpleasant reminder of their differences.

Harry couldn't place the brawny, black-haired stranger, although there was something familiar about him. Since both men looked up at once, he didn't have the leisure to study the situation. He swung down from Caesar and tipped his hat to the engineer.

"I didn't expect your arrival so soon, Rob. Glad you could come down."

"It's a pleasure to serve you, Your Grace." Morton

bowed formally, if a trifle awkwardly. He'd never quite conquered his height and lankiness.

Harry cuffed his shoulder. "I'm still Harry. After sharing the same swill at school for years, we ought to be brothers under the skin." He offered his hand to Rob while keeping a close watch on the giant, who was in turn watching him. The newcomer didn't straighten from his careless pose or behave as if he was at all impressed by Harry's title.

Harry hadn't decided if that was a good or bad thing when Morton said, "Your wife's cousin here has been apprising me of your happy state, Harry. I congratulate you on your recent marriage. Are you acquainted with Mr. Dougal, or shall I make the presentation?"

Racking his brain for a Dougal on Christina's family tree, Harry was fairly certain he hadn't met the gentleman at their hasty wedding. Swarthy, with eyes as dark as his hair and a proud jut of nose, her so-called cousin looked more gypsy than gentleman. But when he shoved away from the wall to tower above them, he resembled a king more royal than any from the House of Hanover.

"We've not the pleasure," the stranger rumbled from deep in his chest. "Aidan Dougal, at your service, Your Grace. More a cousin-in-law than cousin to your wife. I hear you have a medieval chalice for sale."

Harry felt his eyebrows skid skyward before he brought them under control. "Since we just found it, I had not mentioned that to anyone."

"You've married a Malcolm. You need not mention it for it to be known. If I am unwanted, you have only to say the word, and I will take myself off."

Harry had his doubts about that. Aidan Dougal did not appear to be the kind of man who walked away easily.

But thinking Christina might be so delighted to see family that she would excuse him the engineer, Harry nodded his acceptance. "I cannot say that I'm ready to part with the relic, but Christina will welcome a guest. If you have knowledge of medieval artifacts, we can examine the chalice together. Did you gentlemen ride in or take the coach?"

"We've stabled our horses," Morton replied. "Are you sure we would not impose by appearing without warning?"

"No, no, come along. We're early yet for dinner. We can find suitable rooms and give you time to wash up, although I must warn you the accommodations are far less than I would wish—which is the reason you're here, Morton."

"Ah, well, the good scent of country air will make it all worthwhile. I've heard much of your father's construction. I'm looking forward to seeing it."

Morton kept up a pleasant dialogue as they rode the final mile to Sommersville. Eager to rejoin Christina, Harry responded absently at best. With the noncommittal expression of a judge, Aidan Dougal rode his big black stallion in silence. Had Harry been less wrapped up in thoughts of his wife, he might have pondered the man's impassivity, but as it was, he accepted Dougal as another Malcolm—or was it Ives?—eccentric.

In anticipation of seeing Christina again, he spurred his mount into a gallop by the time the mansion rose up behind the curtain of trees. It wasn't yet dusk, but close enough that lights flickered behind several of the windows, and outdoors.

Puzzled over that, Harry flew into the yard at a reckless pace, bringing Caesar to a rearing halt when Meg raced toward him.

"Harry, have you seen Christina? Is she with you?" She threw a glance past him to the two men riding at a more sedate pace up the drive. Disappointment warred with interest in her expression before she turned back to Harry. "I thought perhaps she'd gone into the village."

Harry was already off his horse and running for the manor where a footman held the door for him. The Elizabethan manor. The one that had already dropped a lintel on her. "When did you see her last?" he demanded, trying to sound authoritative and in control when his heart had sunk to his stomach and fear dulled his brains.

"Hours and hours ago." Meg ran to keep up with him. "I went into town to speak with Mora, and Mrs. Abbott came back with me to discuss the party, and Christina said she had plans . . ."

Harry scarce heard past "hours." Forgetting his guests, he grabbed a lantern from the footman. "Where have you looked?" He didn't wait for an answer but strode down the main hall expecting everyone to follow.

"The maids have searched the new wing, Your Grace," the footman answered, catching his breath as he caught up with Harry's long strides. "Me and Miss

Winchester been looking upstairs and down in here. The grooms ain't seen Her Grace and her horse is in its stall."

"I'll start in the attics," a deep voice thundered from behind them. "She has a partiality for ghosts in attics."

Relieved that someone understood, Harry turned to acknowledge Aidan Dougal's offer. "Up those stairs, then. I'd advise taking a left at the top and using the back stairs in the first chamber on the right to find the attics. You'll need light in the stairs. They're dark even at noon."

"I'll help. Where should I go?" Morton accepted a candle from a maid who came running down a corridor with a handful of them. It was only April, and clouds were rolling in from the coast. The meager light from the windows would fade soon.

"If you can judge the safety of the stairs as you go, take the tower steps down to the dungeons. Meg can show you the door. Has anyone searched the gardens?" The awful memory of Christina falling into the pond rose in his mind's eye, and Harry nearly staggered under the pain of it. If he lost Christina to this damned house, he'd personally set fire to the monstrosity.

"The grooms have. I can send them back again and tell them to search farther afield," Meg offered.

"To the Roman ruins, please. After you take Rob to the tower door, stay in the foyer and keep us all apprised of what each finds." Without more ado, Harry dashed into the drawing room on his left—in the direction of the derelict castle. He'd forbidden the servants to traverse the old floors down here. He couldn't ask them to join him now.

If he wasn't so terrified, he could work himself up to a really fine rage. He'd *told* her these floors were treacherous. She *knew* the old parapets had killed his family. How could she defy him like this?

What would he do if he lost her?

That painful question crawled around and around in his head like some maggot gone mad, rendering him incapable of further thought. He tried hoping she'd just gone to visit with a tenant or that she was out gathering posies in the wood, and he would soon hear cries of welcome. But even her cousin had acknowledged the unlikelihood of that.

"Christina!" Harry shouted now that he was out of range of the others and could unleash some of his panic. He threw open door after door on the ground floor of the manor and was startled by some of the changes he discovered within once familiar chambers.

His mother's downstairs sitting room remained just as she'd left it, with her embroidery unfinished on its stand. But his father's old library now resembled a storeroom of stuffed and mounted animal heads, with a few ugly spears and crossbows thrown in for good measure.

Christina wasn't in any of the rooms he searched.

He shouted her name again, only to receive echoes in return. As he approached the doors connecting the manor to the old castle, his heart pounded loud enough to hear. Surely she hadn't entered the castle. His brother and father had fallen from the parapet of the front tower located between these two buildings. He'd had the entrance boarded up.

A resounding clangor echoing out of nowhere caused him to leap two feet into the air. The metallic clamor echoed so obnoxiously that he couldn't immediately discern its direction or the difference between its reverberations and the terrified pounding of his heart. What the devil could make a noise like that aside from a battle between several suits of armor and the bells of St. Paul's?

He raised the lantern to look around, and the light bounced off a spear similar to the ones in the library. It lay on the gallery floor, pointing in the direction of the great hall ballroom. He didn't think the thing could have caused that racket. He glanced at the walls to see from where it might have fallen, but without windows, it was too dark to see. Thinking a weapon probably wasn't useful if Christina had fallen through the floor, he grabbed it anyway.

"Christina!" he shouted again, praying he was coming closer. Apart from last night, he hadn't been in the castle in ages. How large could it be? Could she hear him?

He heard a loud thump in the rooms above, and he halted, trying to remember the location of the nearest staircase. A muffled male curse followed, and he remembered Christina's cousin. Aidan would be searching up there and had no doubt come up against one of the many architectural oddities. He should have warned the man about the windowless room with the swinging door.

Ahead of Harry, the elaborately carved wooden

doors to the ballroom gaped open, a certain sign that his orders had been disobeyed. Hurrying forward, he almost stumbled at the sound of a weak cry. Heart pounding, he shouted, "Christina!"

He stood still, waiting for the echoes of his shout to die down. The cry he'd heard had been muffled and didn't seem to come from the echoing vastness of the great hall. When he heard no further response, he held up his lantern—and nearly fell to his knees.

One of the massive chandeliers lay in the middle of the ballroom floor in a shattered heap of iron. If Christina had been anywhere near it—

Harry bellowed Christina's name loud enough to shake the rafters. Dust trickled from overhead as he raced to the chandelier, set down his lantern, and braced his legs and arms to lift the heavy wheel.

The moan again. But not here. Releasing the iron, he swung around, trying to pinpoint the sound. Nothing. He passed the light back and forth over the chandelier. No bright swath of color indicated Christina's presence. But it had fallen. She might have been under it. She wasn't there now.

"Christina, damn you, do you want me to die of fright? Where are you?" he yelled fruitlessly at the rafters.

"I don't know precisely" came the reasonable—if muffled—reply.

Wanting to lie down and roll on the floor with relief and laughter at this commonsensical end to his harrowing fear, and equally desiring his hands around a pretty neck so he could shake some sense into his adventuresome bride, Harry heroically did neither. He raised his lantern to scan the beams around the outer reaches of the room.

"Keep talking. Perhaps I can find your direction. Was that you moaning a moment ago or have you captured a ghost?"

"I may have cursed a time or two," she admitted, her voice sounding weak and hollow from some distance on his right. "I think I may have broken something."

"Besides the chandelier?" His heart knotted up his throat until he could barely speak, but he managed the jest for her sake. Advancing in the direction of her voice, swinging the lantern back and forth, he tried to stay calm. This was Christina, after all. She'd fallen out of more trees than he could count and walked away unscathed. "Broken what?" he asked when she did not instantly reply.

"My leg?" she said doubtfully.

He tripped over an old crossbow that had no reason to be in a ballroom. Did he mistake or was it pointing at the far wall? He would become as imaginative as Christina at this rate. He could almost think her ghosts were pointing the way. "Don't move. I'll find you. Are you bleeding badly?"

"No, I don't think so. It may be my arm. It hurts. I can't move. Do you have a candle, Harry? It's awfully dark in here."

He could hear her scrambling about, moving as he'd just told her not to do. "Sit still, damn it! Yes, I have a candle. Can you see the light from it yet?"

"I think so. That's why I asked. I think I see the door now. It's a very tiny door. How strange."

He would tie her to the bed, he mused. Post guards at the doors and windows. Maybe in the attic as well, so she didn't hack her way through the ceiling. He didn't think he could live through this stomach-knotting terror again. A life without Christina in it was too bleak to contemplate. Although, it would certainly be less harrowing. "Did you fall through the floor?"

He scanned the wide plank floor but couldn't see any gaping holes. The light caught on the shaft of a discarded arrow. What the devil had she been doing in here? Target practice? The arrowhead pointed at a carved window seat where there was no window.

"No, I don't think so," she said thoughtfully. "The chandelier crashed and I fell, but I don't think the floor gave way."

"What do you mean, you don't think? Wouldn't you know if you fell into the cellar?" He studied the window seat. She'd said she saw a tiny door. It didn't make sense. Why would she put herself in a box?

But he could hear her quite distinctly from here.

"I think I may have . . . fainted," she said with such a tone of disgust that Harry almost smiled—until he realized what it would have taken to cause his intrepid bride to faint.

Setting the lantern down, he sprawled on the floor to examine the elaborate carvings on the seat. The box below it was wide and deep enough for him to crawl into. "Can you see the light now?"

"Yes, it's quite distinct. Right about here." A wooden knock sounded from behind the carvings.

A key dropped in front of his nose, as if from thin air.

"I do not believe in ghosts," he muttered, picking up the tarnished bit of metal and squinting at the box. She must have knocked the key loose from its hole.

That begged the question of how she could have crawled behind a locked keyhole. Locating a darker depth to one of the carved patterns, Harry stuck the key at it. "Can you hear that?"

"I hear something scraping. I can hear you well, Harry. Where am I?"

He tried to chuckle at this reversal of his question. "I think you may have locked yourself in a window seat. Take your time coming up with an explanation. I can't find the keyhole."

"A window seat? Under a window?" She pounded on the door again. "Ouch."

"Stop that. Yes, a seat under a window, except there's no window. Just a niche." Perhaps he should ram his spear through the niche wall. That had worked well in the dungeon. He shoved the key at another hole.

This time, it clicked.

Christina pounded, and the carved side of the box divided into two small doors that swung open, revealing a billow of blue silk and white lace and Christina's pale face.

"Sweet heaven," Harry murmured, reaching to caress her cheek to be sure she was real and alive.

"I'm not entirely certain I can get up from here, Harry," she warned in a whisper that almost sounded like a sob.

"No, sweetheart, don't move an inch. Let me see what you've done to yourself." Gently, he located her arm and drew his hand over her full sleeve, finding the swollen place she complained of.

Running footsteps pounded down the hall outside. More lights danced across the aging plank floor.

Harry didn't know how they'd been found so soon, but he was grateful for the company. "Fetch a physician," he shouted without turning to see who had arrived.

"If I'd known that's what it would take to hold her still, I would have locked her in a trunk sooner," a deep male voice said dryly.

"Aidan?" Christina squeaked.

"Aye, and from the way the duke is clinging to your silly hand instead of wringing your neck as you deserve, it seems you have found the perfect husband. I congratulate you both."

By this time Harry had worked his way through Christina's skirts to her legs, but he had to tug her from the cramped space before he could adequately examine them for broken bones. Unappreciative of his guest's repartee, he threw Dougal a black look over his shoulder. "A physician. Meg will know."

"Aye, and Ninian will, too. Prepare yourself." With that enigmatic message, the giant sauntered out, covering the distance in lazy strides in the same time another man could match only at a run.

"Aidan means trouble, Harry," Christina whispered.

Not giving a damn about anything except having her back, Harry lifted her into his lap, wincing at her gasp of pain. He cradled her against his chest, stroking her face, trying to soothe her and banish the remaining panic. He was so grateful she was alive that she could have told him the mountains had crumbled and he would have rejoiced. "It's good to know you don't have a corner on the trouble market, sweetheart. Can you straighten your legs?"

Her skirts rustled, and he could feel her flinch.

"The right one hurts. My knee hit the floor pretty hard. Maybe it's just a bruise."

"Just in case, I won't move you until the doctor says it's safe. I don't suppose you remember crawling into that box, do you?" Harry turned to look from the fallen chandelier to the window seat and judged the distance to be a painful one if she'd truly broken her leg.

"I'm not very fond of boxes, Harry. I think General Rothbottom put me there to protect me from falling chandeliers."

He sighed, held her tighter, and wondered why it hadn't occurred to him to marry a normal female, one who fainted when she fell, cried when she got hurt, and didn't go exploring where she didn't belong.

"I'll have to thank him someday," he said dryly, before finding her lips and kissing both their fears away.

Nineteen

Lying on their bed, Christina tried hard not to wince when the physician pressed her swollen wrist. Harry looked as if he might draw a sword and decapitate the next person who hurt her. Hair mussed and hanging over his rumpled jabot, he paced back and forth, keeping an eagle eye on the physician. She thought Harry looked like a gallant knight of old, but she was in too much pain to tell him so.

She clenched her teeth, and Harry was there instantly, hovering over her, glaring at the physician.

"Harry, I won't die of a sprained wrist or knee. Stand back, do, before poor Dr. Hormsby has an apoplexy."

Looking exceedingly grim, Harry stepped back. Christina set her mind to admiring his chiseled jaw and the loose strand of hair brushing his collar rather than on her pain. She had wished to make Harry happy again, but she had succeeded in just the opposite.

"Take her word for it, Your Grace," Aidan's dry voice said from the doorway. "She'll be bouncing off your walls again in a day or two. Be glad that she's stationary for whatever time you're granted."

"If you wish to be useful, Harry," she countered in

her best duchess voice, "you may send that irritating creature away. Whyever are you here anyway, Mr. Dougal?" She wasn't entirely certain if she was glad or wary of his presence. Aidan was even more annoying than her aunt Stella, turning up when he shouldn't, but he could also be a harbinger of her family's arrival. Perhaps her cousin Ninian was already on her way with her healing potions.

Harry cast mistrustful glances at Aidan, the doctor, and anyone else who invaded their chamber. His aura had lost much of its color, but the jagged streaks of black and white battling for dominance fascinated her. In Harry's case, black didn't mean bad so much as anger and melancholy, rather like a thundercloud. His need to protect warred with his masculine instincts to strike out at whoever had harmed her, except he had no idea who it might be, which tied his hands and frustrated him.

Harry didn't artlessly demand an explanation of Aidan's presence as she had, but he stopped pacing long enough to pour a glass of brandy and regard his guest expectantly over the goblet's brim.

Aidan shrugged his big shoulders. "Your sister Felicity and her inventive husband have turned my home into an experimental laboratory, and I couldnae stand the noise a moment longer."

"You could throw them out or tell them to stop if you did not like what they were doing," Christina scoffed, knowing Felicity was too gentle a soul to do anything anyone didn't like, and that Ewen was working on so many scientific projects that he could easily shift his attention from one to another.

"Ach, well, the heat from their new device is warming my home," Aidan conceded. "And should I ever find a wife, it would be pleasant to give her a warm abode."

The physician stepped back from the bed to rummage about in his black bag, interrupting this discussion. "Her Grace must stay off her limb until the swelling is down, and you must not use the damaged wrist until it has healed. If you like, I can put it in a sling so you cannot move it, and I'll give you something for the pain."

"I don't suppose you could give orders to have her tied to the bed," Harry asked darkly, taking a deep draft of his brandy.

"Harry!" Christina attempted to sit up, cringed at the pain shooting up her leg, and pushed the pillow up behind her so she could recline more comfortably. "That's not very noble of you. A hero should stay by my side, gazing deeply into my eyes while asking what he can do to ease my suffering."

Aidan snorted loudly. "Your very noble husband has demonstrated every aspect of a hero by not throttling you as you deserve. Be grateful."

Christina thought Harry's familiar laughter tugged at his lips, but he hid it behind his brandy glass. Had she felt stronger, she would have flung her pillows at both of them.

Feeling unwarrantedly cheerful at the hint of Harry's good humor, she settled back against the pillows and plotted her next step. Telling him about the general in the mirror was probably not the best way of improving his humor. It had only got her into more trouble and delivered a serious setback to her plan to find the source of Harry's problem with the tenants. How could she have a party when she could barely walk?

She waved away the physician's offer of laudanum. "I have no trouble sleeping. I will be fine in the morning. I'm quite ravenous. I don't suppose dinner will be ready soon?"

"I'll see to it at once. Gentlemen . . ." Harry gestured for the departure of the physician and Aidan. At the same time, he sent Matilda running in search of nourishment and to inform the household that all was well.

Once he and Christina were alone, he turned back to her, and all laughter fled his face. She mourned the loss of her carefree friend, but she cherished the powerful Harry who had rescued her. He'd carried her down what seemed like miles of corridor as if she were no burden at all, not once knocking her injured limbs into the many obstructions. He'd murmured reassuring solicitudes, hugged her close, and made her feel wonderful instead of scolding her, as most people would have done.

Now that she'd been found well and only slightly incapacitated, she suspected he was about to ring a peal over her, and she braced herself.

"Your cousin has come to ask about the chalice," Harry said calmly enough, but he didn't take a seat or hold her hand or kiss her.

Christina wriggled for a comfortable position, but her discomfort had more to do with Harry's tone than her position. She thought he was hurting, too, and she was the cause. She didn't know how to correct that.

"He's not my cousin," she responded curtly when what she really wanted to say was that she had been trying to help. "He's a troublesome Ives." Then to be perfectly correct, she added, "Although, he does have an odd rose color in his aura that I've mostly seen only in Malcolms."

"I will need to sell the chalice to pay for the demolition of the castle," Harry continued, ignoring her circumlocutions. "I thought perhaps you would prefer that the relic went to family."

"Tear down the castle? With proceeds from Father Oswald's chalice? Harry, no, you cannot do that! All hell will break loose. I know it!" She wanted to fling herself into his arms and kiss him into compliance, but just moving her knee shot pain up her leg. She beat the bed in frustration with her uninjured hand. "I know the ghosts are trying to help, but we're not understanding what they're telling us. I won't go in there again, I promise, but please, don't tear it down."

"Robert Morton has arrived to inspect the keep, but chandeliers do not fall from ceilings unless there is good reason. The castle is unsound and a danger to you and our children," he said with unarguable firmness. "I would be a murderer if I allowed that ruin to kill anyone else."

At his mention of "their children," Christina knew all was lost. Harry's aura took on that implacable protective glow she could not fight. All the natural world would consider his actions reasonable. She was the only one who fought from a position of the supernatural. She couldn't win.

"Now I see why it is very impractical to be a Malcolm," she said angrily, turning her back on him and burying her face in the pillow. "I wish we really could conjure spells." She wished she knew how she'd conjured that vision in the mirror. It would be helpful if she could speak to the general that way.

"It's not any easier being a duke," Harry returned gruffly. "Perhaps some small portion of the castle can be saved for your spirits to inhabit, but I must give more concern to the people who live here."

When she did not answer, he walked away.

She *hated* that he was right. But she also hated that she'd spent her entire life trying to communicate with the spirits and now that she'd finally established a connection, Harry meant to take it away.

Well, not all of it, precisely. The realization melted a portion of her heart. How many husbands would offer to preserve a portion of *anything* for the sake of his wife's ghosts? Obviously Harry was a reasonable man. She would just have to find a way to extend his reason to preserving the entire castle.

If only she could prove to him that Lady Anne and the general and Father Oswald were useful, perhaps Harry would not be so quick to tear down what he did not understand.

Besides, as far as she was aware, Aidan couldn't afford to buy a medieval jeweled chalice any more than she could.

*　　*　　*

Harry wished Jack were here. He needed someone more knowledgeable than he was to start searching the sprawling mansion and castle for whoever had sought to harm Christina. She didn't sleepwalk. She had been put, unconscious, in that box by someone who possessed a key. Despite his wife's protests otherwise, he did not believe ghosts held keys. He could not fathom why anyone would want to harm her, but nothing else made sense.

And if he could not make sense of it or find the person who meant to harm her, he would have to send her back to London. With all his heart and soul, he didn't want to do that. To prevent it, he would have to ask for help. He hated asking for help, but he was prepared to get down on his knees and crawl if it would keep Christina safe.

After seeing their guests amicably settled with brandy and port in the study after dinner, Harry poured a glass of brandy for himself and paced in front of the fire. "I have a problem, gentlemen."

Aidan and Robert quieted, waiting expectantly. Harry knew little of Christina's cousin-in-law, but if he were anything like his Ives relations, he was a man to be counted on. Aidan had carried out his earlier search with dispatch and arrived to help with amazing alacrity when Christina was found. And he was a stranger to Sommersville so he could not be suspected of causing any of the incidents.

"It is possible the chandelier fell accidentally," Harry said, "but I want you, Rob, to inspect it thoroughly to be certain the fall wasn't deliberate."

Robert gasped in astonishment. Aidan merely shot

him a severe look and sipped his brandy without comment.

Harry continued. "Christina claims a ghost stuffed her in that cabinet to protect her from falling chandeliers. I think it far more likely that human hands turned the key and locked her in. I want to search the castle."

He did not know why he hadn't thought of it sooner, but if his father truly had gone around the bend, he could have squirreled cash away in the castle, and someone else might know of it. A hidden treasure would be motive enough for someone to frighten away adventurous intruders such as Christina.

"Do you have men you can trust to help us?" Aidan asked in a matter-of-fact tone that said he'd already surmised there was more trouble here than anyone had let on.

"No," Harry said flatly. "For all I know, the servants may have murdered my father and brother. Or it may just be the castle falling down. I cannot even say what we should look for. I only know I won't sleep until we've searched every cranny."

"I took a quick look at the foundation while I was in the dungeon," Robert said. "There has been considerable settling in the towers. Vibrations of any sort might cause bolts to slip or stones to fall. Before any search can be instituted, I think I'd better mark the unsafe areas."

Taking a seat, Harry listened, and together they began to sketch a strategy. He might be frustrated at not acting as quickly as he wished, but at least he'd have a plan of action.

Later, after he'd done all that he could do, he hurried back upstairs to Christina. Not knowing how else to protect her, he must keep her within the shelter of his company at all times.

That gave him excuse enough not to leave her side at night, even though he feared making love to her until after her injuries had healed. Their energetic romp at luncheon gave fair warning that neither of them were inclined toward docility in the bed. Just thinking of how Christina had responded to his slightest touch heated his blood. He hungered to repeat the experience, but he was a grown man, not a heedless juvenile. He could wait until she was better.

He entered their chamber quietly. A fire still flickered in the grate, but she'd blown out her bedside candle. He could see the golden glow of her hair spread across the pillows, and he wanted nothing more than to climb in beside her and hold her tight. She was the one good, steady thing in his life right now, and he desperately wished to keep her.

He lived one hell of a life if he could consider *Christina* the only stability in it.

Smiling wryly, he brushed a gold tendril from her forehead, but she didn't stir. Perhaps she'd finally given in and drunk the laudanum. He hated that she was in pain, but at least he'd know where she was for a few days so he could do what he had to do.

He supposed he'd have to wait and see whether they had a marriage left if he gave the orders decreeing the castle's destruction.

That didn't mean they couldn't sleep in the same bed tonight. After their lovemaking that day, he felt that she was a precious part of him. He needed his arms around her. She'd have to lock him out before he'd give up that right.

"Why do you always keep your room so cold?" Meg complained, entering Christina's bedchamber the next morning, unaware of Lady Anne's aura hovering in the background. At Christina's shrug, Meg continued with her real purpose. "We are receiving notes of sympathy from everyone in the neighborhood," she declared, handing over the morning post.

"We are?" With interest, Christina flipped through the correspondence from the vicar's wife, the squire, and other people she had not yet met. After confronting Mora, she had never thought to seek out the vicar's wife. And she'd been told the squire was out of town . . .

Apparently not all the neighbors refused to speak with her.

Perhaps she had made a mistake in attempting to talk with only the villagers. Could the people of society tell her why Harry's tenants didn't respect him? It didn't seem likely. She stared at the bland notes and pondered. "I suppose we'll have to postpone the open house now, but do you think we might invite the neighbors to visit?" she inquired.

She'd learned Lady Anne's ways enough to read the ghost's nod of approval at her suggestion. She didn't mind the cold surrounding her friendly spirits. It was good to know that *someone* approved of her, even if it must be from a different spiritual plane.

Harry had been so angry with her that he hadn't

made love to her last night. Or this morning, even though she'd wanted to. He'd removed himself from the bed the instant she'd woken and had barely spoken to her except to order her to stay put so she didn't hurt herself again.

Setting her chin stubbornly, she refused to think about that or she'd turn into a watering pot. No matter what her husband thought of her, she could help him, if he'd let her. She could read auras and tell when people were lying or concealing something. If she enlisted Lady Anne and Father Oswald in the task, they might help her interpret what she saw. She might not be able to hold a party, but looking at the notes, she enlarged a nugget of an idea. "Perhaps I could establish calling hours."

"I thought you said your family might arrive?" Meg replied. "I can't think they would want to be bothered visiting with the likes of the vicar. He is in his dotage."

Lady Anne was laughing. Delighted that she could understand Harry's ancestor so well, Christina held her ground. Once her family heard of the goings on, they'd be here whether she liked it or not. "My family is quite able to entertain themselves."

"Besides, your family will most likely *be* the entertainment," said a mocking voice from the doorway.

"Mr. Dougal!" Not entirely displeased at his appearance since sitting still was tedious and gentle Meg much too easily alarmed, Christina sat up straighter. "You might have sent up a maid to ask if I was respectable."

"And how is the poor maid to be a judge of that? Besides, they are all in a tizzy over the visit of some female bearing scented lotions or some such." He nodded a greeting at Meg.

"Mora!" Meg exclaimed. "She sells herbal bath powders and soaps that smell marvelous. Christina, do you have enough paper and ink? I'll leave you to your replies. Peter is home and can deliver them a little later. Come along, Mr. Dougal. I'll introduce you to the vicar's daughter."

"Call me Aidan, please. We are all family of sorts." He cast a glance back at Christina. "I'll send up Harry. He was most adamant that you not be left alone."

"Harry is worse than my father. I can come to no harm when I cannot move from the wretched bed. I only wish I could witness your meeting with Mora. I have a feeling the two of you will devour each other alive."

"Christina!" Shocked, Meg hesitated in the doorway. "Are you certain you're feeling well? Mora is the quietest, most timid person I know. She's completely harmless. And Mr. Dougal has been all that is polite."

"Forgive her, for she knows not what she speaks," Christina said to Aidan, who hid a smirk at her sarcasm. So, maybe the big brute wasn't entirely insensitive to his effect on the world around him. "I'm fine, Meg. Perhaps Mora and I simply started off wrong."

"I'm certain that is it. She will have brought a tisane to make you feel better. You will see."

Meg had as little insight into human nature as Harry, Christina reflected while Meg left and Aidan remained. They both thought everyone in the world was as good-natured as they were. Despite the odd flecks of gray in Meg's aura that implied she held back some resentment or other negative emotion, she had been nothing but sweet and charming. She ought to have a good husband to love her.

Christina eyed Aidan's expression and dismissed the match instantly.

"Sounds as if this Mora is as much witch as any Malcolm," he said before removing his shoulder from the door frame in preparation for departure, although she was certain he wouldn't be heading for the women in the kitchen.

"We're not witches," Christina corrected. "But from what I've seen of her, Mora could very well be. If she's making potions out of herbs, perhaps you ought to go downstairs and guard the house against evil charms."

He chuckled deep in his throat and cast her an approving glance. "You may have the common sense of a rabbit, but I'll grant you're a perceptive witch. Harry will be up to see you directly, so don't stir from that bed."

Before she could return the insult or tell him to bring her hairbrush or her maid so she would look presentable for Harry, he was gone.

"Well, I suppose I could take that as a compliment," she said to Lady Anne. Even in this light, she could still discern her transparent form as well as her aura. Pages of a ledger idly drifted in a seeming draft, but she could tell the lady occupied her time in glancing through the descriptions of past fetes.

At Christina's comment, the ledger flattened, knocking the pen from its place across it. Two splats of ink fell out, marring the crumbling paper.

"Oh, bother. I didn't mean to ruin the old book." Christina leaned over to blot the spill, but the two words accented by the drops caught her attention— *a wizard*.

A wizard? She read the rest of the line, which merely declared some Henry was a wizard at playing the lute. Innocent enough. Perfectly coincidental. Just because she was talking to a ghost about Aidan at the time the ink spilled didn't mean a thing.

She sought Lady Anne's aura, but she was demurely hovering in a corner, admiring the scenery outside the window.

"I don't think Aidan Dougal is a wizard at playing the flute," she informed the apparition, testing to see if the spilled ink might have been deliberate.

Perhaps she imagined it, but she thought she heard the faint sound of a woman's merry laugh.

She wished Lady Anne were alive. She could really use an understanding friend right now, preferably one who could communicate more effectively than with spilled ink.

Twenty

Christina's family began arriving two days later. The first Harry knew of it, he was in his study, polishing the chalice while waiting for Robert to finish the final inspection of the castle floors. He doubted that his engineer could prevent dangerous intruders from hiding over there, but an army might. He was prepared to summon an army the instant Robert said it was safe.

A cold draft blew on the back of his neck as he held up the now gleaming chalice for Aidan to admire. "It is a magnificent artifact. I think the stones are genuine. I'm amazed Cromwell's men did not melt it down for the gold and sell the gems."

"Perhaps it wasn't the Roundheads who hid it in that chamber," Aidan speculated. "It is more likely that a priest or a member of the family sealed it up in there to preserve it."

"And died before uncovering it again?" Harry squirmed uncomfortably in his chair, remembering Christina's talk of the ghost of Father Oswald. Could the man have died protecting his church?

Harry determinedly turned his mind to more practical matters, like the value of the chalice should he be forced to sell it. Before he could even broach the prospect, he heard the rattle of carriages and glanced out the window to see who had arrived.

Aidan was out of his chair and aiming for the door before Harry could identify the crest on the side of the lead carriage. "Christina's family is here," Aidan announced as he made his escape. "You might consider an extended vacation to Scotland. They'll natter you to death before you know it."

Harry watched in amazement as the carriages spilled silks and laces, children and servants, and a cadre of tall, black-haired young men, the latter of which headed straight for the castle walls.

"Perhaps country life has been rough on you, but you've been good for Harry." Ninian, the Countess of Ives and Wystan, examined Christina's injured knee in the relative privacy of the bedchamber. Outside the door, voices carried up and down the old hall while rooms and family and servants were sorted out.

Christina was glad Ninian had accompanied her mother. Ninian had a soul far older than any of the cousins, and a healing touch they relied on. Cousin Lucinda had also come along, retreating from some fresh gossip caused by her painting. Together they would make jolly company.

But the noise in the hall outside warned that the marchioness was in full mother-hen mode. Christina assumed that her mother was trailing scarves and ribbons upstairs and down, commanding carpenters and servants into converting the best bedchambers into suitable guest rooms.

If it made her mother happy and kept her from interfering in more important concerns, Christina wasn't averse to letting her turn the entire manor upside down.

Trapped in bed by her injured knee, she was determined to help Harry no matter whose aid she had to enlist. Right now, Ninian and Lucinda were available and of far more use than noncommunicative ghosts.

She had hoped to speak privately with Harry about her concerns, but these last nights, he hadn't come to her bed until after she had fallen asleep, and he was up before she woke. She supposed he was being considerate of her injuries, but she very much wished to experience his lovemaking again so she knew it hadn't been a fantasy. And she definitely wished to speak with the wretched man. He was becoming as uncommunicative as the general.

She was also terrified that he was proceeding with his plans to tear down the castle now that his engineer had arrived, and she wasn't able to stop him.

"Harry was quite morose at your wedding," Ninian continued, "and I feared for your happiness, but I see now that it was only mourning for his father and brother and not the wedding troubling him."

Like most Malcolms, Ninian was as fair and blue eyed as Christina, but there the resemblance ended. Her older cousin possessed the pretty curls and the petite, well-rounded figure that Christina never would. Ninian not only more closely resembled Hermione than Christina; she emanated the marchioness's maternal benevolence as well.

"He has been saddled with a terrible burden and

hasn't truly had time to grieve," Christina agreed. "And I am not the most useful of helpmeets."

Ninian laughed. "Harry is quite responsible enough for the two of you. Your role is to lighten his burden. How does your wrist feel?"

"The swelling has gone down, but Harry fears I will overexert myself."

Ninian unwrapped the bandage. "Does this hurt?" She squeezed gently and turned the wrist back and forth.

Ninian's touch exuded soothing heat, and Christina's whole arm felt stronger at once. "It feels lovely. I wish I had your gift for healing. It is a much more useful gift than my own."

"Every gift has its price. My gift costs me the ability to tolerate crowds. With too many people around me, I'm overwhelmed. Gifted artists are said to be condemned to poverty. Gifted mathematicians are condemned to obscurity and madness or, worse yet, to teaching schoolboys." She laughed at Christina's raised eyebrow. "Well, I have been listening to my husband and his brothers complain about being underappreciated, so I thought I might include them as well."

"I do not know how you keep up with all those rough-and-tumble Ives. It is all I can do to concentrate on Harry. I don't think I was meant for motherhood," Christina added, voicing one of her many fears.

"I am more sister than mother to them, and you do sisterhood very well," Ninian said complacently. "You will be the kind of mother who loves to romp with her children, and they will adore you."

Gratified that her perceptive cousin thought she wouldn't be a dreadful mother, Christina tried not to overthink the matter. After the experience in the rowan grove, she could very well have conceived Harry's child already. Malcolms were always fertile. The thought would petrify her had she time to consider it.

They both looked up at a knock on the door. Lucinda stuck her fair head around the edge. "May I come in? I think I have just terrified Mr. Dougal into retreating to the castle."

Ninian laughed. "It is not you in particular but Malcolms in general who keep Aidan at bay. We hold the fascination of fire for the gentleman, pretty but dangerous."

Lucinda popped around the door and took a seat in a corner with her sketch pad in hand. "Then I shall just stay out of his sight, shall I? What are you two conspiring? I don't need any gift to know you're up to something."

"I don't suppose you can draw ghosts?" Christina asked with interest.

"No, I don't suppose I can. Do you mean you have ghosts?"

"We do. And I wish to have them help me discover the reason Harry's tenants aren't speaking to him. I have notified our neighbors that I will be taking afternoon calls starting tomorrow. Would you be interested in helping?"

Ninian's eyes widened, and sweeping her skirts back, she took a seat. "Tell me all about it."

Lucinda merely nodded and listened, her fingers

flying over her sketch pad without thought as Christina spoke.

The next afternoon, at the designated calling hour, Christina selected a book from the small bookcase of leather-bound volumes beside her while she waited in the parlor for her first visitors. At the sound of footsteps on the stairs, she set the book aside to arrange herself. Propping her injured leg on an ottoman, she spread her skirts out in an elegant blue waterfall.

Although she had no idea whether or not they paid attention, she concentrated hard on calling her familiar ghosts. She had enlisted the aid of Rob Morton in persuading Harry that the drawing room in the old manor was soundly constructed, and far easier to reach than having Harry carry her through the entire house to the new wing. The once elegant room had faded with time, but she hoped at least Lady Anne would accompany her down here.

She realized that unless she knew people well, her ability to read their auras was unreliable. She needed aid in interpreting what she saw. If only her ghosts could talk . . .

As it was, she needed real live people to explain what was wrong with Harry's tenants, and that's what she meant to do today, if she had to hit her guests over the head to achieve it. She preferred to hope her family's gifts might help, although without her sisters Felicity or Leila here, she was dubious of her chances.

Lucinda's gift of second sight disguised in her art wasn't much help, since it took far too long to produce a painting, and one very seldom understood the message in it even when it was done. Ninian's gift for sensing emotion might be of some use, except Ninian seldom betrayed what she sensed. She had promised to tell Christina if she intuited any danger though.

To Christina's relief, Lady Anne materialized with the sound of the first horses riding up the drive.

"Harry said to keep an eye on you," Ninian said serenely, sweeping into the room shortly after the ghost's appearance. "There's a spirit in here now, isn't there? I can feel the chill and sense her life essence but cannot see her."

Sometimes Ninian could be quite impressive, despite her deceptively cherubic appearance, Christina reflected. "Lady Anne," she explained. "According to the family ledgers, she was a spinster aunt of an earlier Winchester and helped design the gardens in the courtyard of the Tudor manor. She has just curtsied to you, although whether in mockery or respect is up to my interpretation."

Ninian raised her rounded blond eyebrows in surprise. "My, you have made splendid progress. Marriage suits you. Grandmother once told me that some of us don't come into our full gifts until we marry, although she did not explain if it was the act of joining with our husbands or the results that might influence us."

"The results?" Realizing what the inevitable result of lovemaking might be, Christina blushed. "Oh. Well, that's possible. It was a rowan grove where Harry and I . . ."

Ninian waved away her explanation. "If you made

love in a rowan grove, it is very likely that the spirit of one of our ancestors is already growing within you. In that case, pregnancy could quite certainly aid your abilities. My gift grew much stronger while I was carrying, especially when I carried a boy. A rowan grove, Christina?" She shook her head in astonishment.

Christina tried to put two and two together. She had been taught rowan groves were sacred and that faeries resided there, although, since they weren't very distinct, she seldom noticed them. She'd made love with Harry beneath the rowans. She'd felt . . . And then she'd seen the general in the mirror . . .

Ninian was saying she became pregnant the first time they made love, and that the child she carried increased the power of her gift, and that's why she'd actually seen and heard the general. Was Ninian saying she carried a boy? Christina's heart caught and fluttered at the possibility, and her hand strayed to her lower abdomen. Could it be?

The probability was much too difficult to puzzle out, and she refused to raise anyone's hopes. She'd rather experiment with her new abilities and see what happened. Time would tell about the rest. Lucinda's arrival, sketch pad in hand, and carriages drawing up outside put an end to all speculation.

The sound of men huffing and puffing outside the salon warned that the rest of her experiment was underway. With Ninian and Lucinda to oversee, she wasn't indulging in anything overtly dangerous, she hoped. She watched as two footmen carried in the mirror from the vanity in the late duchess's bedroom. She had no idea if this would work, but she wanted as many aspects of this day in her favor as she could contrive.

"Turn it where I can see it, please," she requested as the men arranged the mirror on a long mahogany table beneath the windows. "Now pull the drapery closed so the sun doesn't shine so strongly in here."

"You could be playing with fire," Ninian murmured as the footman complied. "Perhaps I should fetch the duke."

"No," Christina whispered. "Harry would have an apoplexy if he knew I was about to summon ghosts in front of his guests. They're not dangerous, I promise." Not physically dangerous anyway. What they might do to her reputation remained to be seen. The gossip about a mad duchess who thought she saw ghosts would carry straight to London.

The mirror gleamed dully even with the sunlight banished, but no magical image appeared. Nervously, Christina ordered candles lit. She could hear the occupants of the carriage speaking among themselves outside the window.

She had stationed a footman at the door, but she knew Harry would have seen the arrival of their guests from his study. She hoped he was too busy to join them. While Robert was cordoning off the unsafe sections of the castle, Harry and Aidan had been poring over the estate books from the last decade. Talks of turnips and bank loans made their dinner conversations exceedingly dull. It seemed Mr. Dougal was far more of a practical, logical Ives than she'd first thought.

Moments later, she heard men greeting one another in the foyer. To Christina's delight and dismay, her husband's voice welcomed them. She longed to have Harry by her side for this visitation, but he was bound to interfere with any experiment she might try. Harry as her husband was far more protective than Harry as her betrothed.

He entered with three gentlemen she did not recognize. He glanced at the drawn draperies and mirror with puzzlement but did not remark upon them.

"Christina, Lady Ives, Lady Lucinda, let me introduce our neighbors, Squire Chumley and his son, Basil." Harry indicated a stout older man in clubbed wig and a younger gentleman of about Harry's age wearing a sour expression.

The squire seemed genuinely happy to meet her, and Christina greeted him as graciously as she'd been taught. "Squire Chumley, I had heard that you were in London. It's so good to meet you at last." She watched the older man's aura glow brighter with pleasure. Nothing dark there, nothing hidden or filled with guilt that she could see.

The squire stepped aside so his son might make his bow. In a brown velvet coat that had seen better days, Basil Chumley swept his hat over his chest and bent his knee to make a formal leg.

Ninian and Lucinda nodded their greetings. At Christina's side, Lady Anne fluttered in dismay. Despite Basil Chumley's grandiose gesture, Christina read anger in him.

"Mr. Chumley, it's a pleasure," Christina purred,

casting a glance from Harry to his neighbor. She had never met the Chumleys in society, but Meg had told her that their estates bordered Harry's.

She had heard the squire had left his son to oversee the spring planting while he spent the spring with his family in London for his daughter's season. Now that she could see Basil and Harry were of an age, Christina thought they would have talked with each other. But not once had Harry mentioned doing so. How very odd.

Basil did not possess a handsome visage, but Christina thought it was an honest one. She didn't like the darkened colors of his aura and glanced to Lady Anne for confirmation. Christina held her breath until her ghostly companion pointed to a title on the bookshelf: *A Yorkshire Gentleman.*

She did not think Basil was from Yorkshire, but she understood the lady to agree that he was a gentleman. Not a villain. That was disappointingly insufficient information.

"And lastly," Harry continued his introductions, "Mr. Aloysius Carthage, a landowner in the neighborhood."

Carthage had sent a syrupy note of sympathy upon Christina's mishap, and Meg had explained that he was relatively new to the area. Christina wasn't familiar with his name, and she could see that he wasn't the type of man to frequent aristocratic society. She narrowed her eyes and studied him.

A rotund man in garishly adorned gold waistcoat, lavish lace, and black frock coat, wearing his gray wig bagged and tied with a ribbon, he stepped forward to make a creaking bow. "Your Grace, I am so sorry to hear of your injuries. These old houses can be terribly dangerous."

Christina noticed Harry bristling with outrage. His stiffening posture distracted her from the merchant's aura, but she hadn't caught anything that struck her as dangerous.

"Nonsense, Mr. Carthage," she said firmly. "Houses that have withstood the centuries are far less dangerous than the shabby constructions we fling up today. I just happen to be a little too reckless upon occasion."

The merchant's aura flared red at that, and she knew she'd hit a sore spot. Interesting.

Harry, on the other hand, hid a surprised laugh behind a cough. Good. She glanced to Lady Anne, who merely shook her ghostly head in doubt.

At the sound of the marchioness coming down the stairs, Harry turned to welcome her. Christina knew his warmth toward her mother was genuine. Her husband might be annoyed at her family's interference, but he enjoyed their company.

She had plotted this moment with her mother earlier. If Harry chose to join them—as he had—she needed someone to lure him out of the drawing room so she might talk with his neighbors privately.

She had never put her gift to such uses before. Combined with the family ghosts, these next hours could be an enlightening experience, or a disaster beyond even her ability to imagine.

Twenty-one

Surrounded by Christina's charming, gregarious family, Harry allowed himself to be diverted from his anger and frustration at the arrival of his ex-friend. Chumley hadn't said anything directly insulting, after all.

Harry winced inwardly as Basil's challenge rose from the murky depths of his memory to haunt him: *A thousand pounds and my Roman coins against yours that she'll make you the laughingstock of all London by this time next year.* That had been a drunken wager if ever there was one. He should have just plowed his fist into Basil's jaw and put an end to it.

And Carthage was just being his unctuous self. Harry had almost laughed aloud when Christina pinned the merchant's intentions within a minute of meeting him. His wife was a dangerously perceptive woman, but then, he'd known that for a long time.

A woman as perceptive as Christina had chosen him, above all others. He would bask in that recognition if he didn't suspect that she had chosen him because he would let her do what she wanted.

Harry had known his wife's family since birth, knew their various eccentricities, and often admired their odd means of accomplishing tasks normally reserved for trained diplomats or scientific experts. He also knew when they were up to something. The demure expressions of Christina's cousins didn't fool him for an instant.

"Thank you for greeting my guests, Harry, but you may go back to work now," Christina whispered after he'd seated the marchioness, who was looking about her with overly eager interest. "I am surrounded by family and friends and can come to no harm ensconced in my favorite chair." Looking lovely but brimming with mischief, she flattered him with fluttering eyelashes and a seductive smile.

Now he *knew* something was afoot. He bent to kiss the golden hair she'd elaborately pinned in fashionable curls. "You are my work, my love. I am quite prepared to spend the day by your side, seeing to your every need."

Harry could tell his vow had her seething with frustration, but she also shot him an appreciative glance that bubbled his blood. He hadn't wanted to slow her recovery by requesting lovemaking, but if she was ripe for mischief, he could find productive uses for her energy. Anticipating the night to come eased his irritation at Chumley and Carthage.

Harry thought she would throw a book at him, and he couldn't fight back a grin at her threatening expression. When she saw he teased, she tugged his jabot until he bent his head down to her.

She pecked his cheek, shooting a thrill right up his spine.

"Your charm is more annoying than the Dreadful

Dougal's insolence, my dearest duke. You may send all the guardian angels you wish to watch over me, and they will find me right here, behaving properly. Now go. You know you want to."

"I know you're up to something, my darling beloved," Harry murmured into Christina's ear.

She batted her eyelashes prettily and kissed his cheek. "I always am unless I'm sleeping, my sweet," she responded in kind.

"And if you do not behave," he countered, "I'll tickle you into helplessness tonight. Your entire family will hear your shouts."

Her eyes widened at the image of her family hearing what they did in bed. As a blush colored her cheeks, Harry kissed her forehead.

The vicar and his wife and daughter arrived, postponing Harry's departure. Servants rolled in carts of coffee, tea, and pastries. The women fell to chattering easily, enjoying themselves in the marchioness's ebullient company, and perhaps somewhat under the influence of her candles emitting scents of harmony, flickering near the mirror.

Love and joy swelled Christina's heart at the gentle cooperation of all her family and their faith in her abilities. Somehow, she had to make use of them to find out what she wanted to know, but how could she do this in front of Harry? She sent her mother a warning look, but the marchioness was deep in conversation about knitting and refused to glance up. She was supposed to send Harry out of the room, not encourage him to stay.

This was impossible. The men were standing stiffly, sipping their coffee, barely speaking. She had to do *something*.

She stared at the mirror, willing the general to appear, to give her some sign, some indication of what to do next. She saw only the reflection of the darkened room.

"Ask the dolts flat out who they think drained the coffers," a rude voice said bluntly in her ear.

Blinking, not realizing she'd closed her eyes, Christina stared at the mirror. The general still wasn't there, but out of the corner of her eye, she saw an apparition leaning over her chair, watching the guests shrewdly. So startled at his vivid image that she almost yelped, she bit her tongue instead. He turned his head slightly to observe her with a wry gleam in his—one—eye. Today he wore a patch over the other. She hadn't seen *that* in the portrait gallery.

He was supposed to stay in the mirror. He wasn't supposed to arrive until after Harry left. He was *talking*. So much for thinking she had any control over his behavior.

She ought to be shaking in her seat, but she was too stunned. No one else seemed to notice his presence, although several of the women adjusted their wraps about their shoulders.

She didn't know how long the general would—or could—linger. If she was to accomplish anything, it must be now, with Harry still in the room. That made her more nervous than the general, who watched the room's inhabitants with displeasure.

Knowing she had to do something but not knowing what, Christina tapped her raised teacup and brought the room to order.

Harry raised his eyebrows at her interruption, but he made no objection. Instead, he leaned his broad shoulders against the doorjamb, crossed his arms over his elegant coat, and waited expectantly.

She couldn't do this with Harry watching!

She had no choice. The general was breathing down her neck.

She'd never made a speech in her life, but for Harry she had to enter a wider world. Sucking in a lungful of air, she said the first thing that came to mind. "Reverend and Mrs. Abbott, ladies, gentlemen, I'm so happy that you could all be here." Uncertainly, she sought the next sentence. "This is my home now, and I should like to think we can all be friends."

Setting her cup down, she gazed over her guests. Basil scowled as he whispered to Carthage. The vicar's wife smiled pleasantly, and Mora watched with curiosity. Harry looked mildly amused.

To her startlement, the general's colorful aura popped up behind Basil. "This one's about to spit, lass," the apparition murmured. "Let's see you pry the venom out of him."

Christina watched in amazement as the general faded. She had never . . . She couldn't believe . . .

How did one "pry venom" out of anyone?

Shaking her head clear, she turned her gaze fully on the man whose aura reflected his anger. Taking a deep breath, she dived into the unknown.

"I'm of the belief that talking about problems is the

first step to solving them. I understand the tenants are not speaking to my husband, and I would like to know why. Mr. Chumley, I believe you know something of this. Would you care to explain?"

There, she'd done it. Listened to a ghost and risked the entire county thinking her mad. She hoped she'd fooled her guests into believing her knowledge was the wisdom of a duchess and her appalling bluntness the privilege of aristocracy.

Harry pushed off the wall and grimly shoved his way toward her, but rising from her seat by the fire, Christina's mother placed a hand on his arm, forcing him to halt out of respect for her.

Basil stepped back in surprise. A chilly wind rustled the draperies immediately behind him. He jumped, shivered, and glanced over his shoulder, but the guests had shifted away from him, and he could blame no one for the cold draft down his neck.

"I have no idea of what you speak," he said with a scowl.

Well, she couldn't hold a gun to his head. Or even a ghost, apparently. The general had vanished. She would have to appeal to his neighbors.

Christina turned to the vicar and his wife. "I suspect the estate hasn't paid its debts recently, and that is at the bottom of the problem, but surely everyone understands that the duke has just stepped into his position. Wouldn't it profit everyone to sit down and discuss what must be done?"

Harry gently removed the marchioness from his arm, but Ninian stepped into his path, holding him back with a warning finger to her lips. Christina tried not to watch. She had two ghosts in here somewhere and needed her wits about her.

Lady Anne hovered near the bookcase, trying to point out a word on one of the volumes, but in the dim light, Christina could only read the gold leaf lettering that mentioned *rents*. With a flash of insight and growing confidence, she realized that she could do this. She could combine her gifts with her own knowledge and establish communication between people and the spirit world.

She just hoped no one realized that she could communicate with spirits, or they'd be asking her to talk to their late auntie Jane or uncle Bob.

"Did I hear someone mention rents?" she asked coyly.

"They're not fair!" Basil shouted and looked surprised as he did. As he ought, since the general had reappeared to envelop his throat with an icy hand.

Forgetting his manners, Harry shoved past Ninian, his expression a study in thunderclouds. Just as quickly, the general disappeared again, leaving Christina with a room full of consternation and shocked expressions.

"The tenants are starving their children to feed the duke's filthy habits!" Basil continued belligerently now that everyone was already staring at him.

Stunned, Harry halted. His face whitened when none of his neighbors leaped to defend him. He stood taller than everyone here and could see their faces clearly, as Christina could not from her chair. She relinquished the safety of her seat to limp up beside him and take his arm. He tried to shake her off as he had the rest of her family, but she clasped him firmly.

She'd provided the catalyst for this disclosure. She'd

never meant to hurt Harry by doing so. The least she could do was stand by his side and take the blows with him. She'd interfered enough. The floor was his now.

"What filthy habits?" he asked incredulously. "I grew up here. We used to play together. Did I have filthy habits then? And if the rents are unfair, why hasn't anyone talked to me about them? Or to Jack? Or to my father before then? We're not ogres."

"The rents went up regardless of how people talked," the vicar interceded. "It can't go on much longer. The village is fair starving."

"Because of you, lad," the squire said. Nodding unhappily at Christina, he added, "Excuse us talking of this in your drawing room." He turned squarely toward Harry. "As you can see from what's around you, your father just scraped by, trying to keep you out of trouble all these years. I believe your gambling ways disturbed him more than we can say."

"Gambling?" So astonished he could only gape, Harry wrapped his arm around Christina's shoulders to prove he hadn't slipped into another world. "You think I *gambled* away the estate's wealth?"

"We all heard about it," Basil sneered. "You've run with a wild crowd for years. Your father hasn't been right since you left for London."

Murderous rage filled him. Even Christina's reassuring squeeze couldn't control it. Not bothering to question her motive for instigating this, Harry concentrated on the one gentleman in the room who had treated him with contempt, a man the villagers trusted, a man who had tested him with a stupid wager rather than ask him for the truth.

Harry released his interfering wife to confront Basil. "What lies have you told them?" he demanded. "What the *devil* did you think you could accomplish by spreading such slander?"

Refusing to be intimidated, Basil shoved his coat-tails behind him and glared back. "Lies? The truth is right here before our eyes—the estate prospers, but the profits disappear like smoke over water. Your father reduced his staff, turning off people who relied on the estate for income, while you lived the grand life up in London. This is a very colorful show your witchy wife has produced—"

At this insult to Christina, weeks of frustration exploded in Harry. His fist connected soundly with Basil's jaw before anyone could halt him. The vicar's wife screamed, the guests stepped back, and Basil staggered. Stunned by his own violence, Harry regretted his reaction at once.

Undeterred by his ex-friend's powerful title, Basil aimed a punch at Harry's embroidered vest. Harry sidestepped, swung again, and sent his neighbor sprawling across the carpet. It was not the thing a duke should do, but by Jove, it felt *right*.

Before Harry could grab Basil by the back of his coat and heave him out the door, the portrait of the late duke over the fireplace leaped from the wall, bounced off the mantel, and crashed to the marble hearth. Harry stopped to stare. There wasn't a soul on that side of the room who could have disturbed it.

The vicar's wife screamed again.

Even Basil propped himself up on one elbow to stare at the fallen frame.

"General Rothbottom is not amused by your antics, gentlemen," Christina said calmly from somewhere behind Harry.

He swung around, but she was doing nothing more than standing there, surrounded by her family, who watched with interest.

"General Rothbottom may go back to the grave where he belongs," Harry roared, insensibly he knew, but he couldn't help it. His wife was making a fool of herself and him and the whole damned town just when he was getting to the source of his problems.

He was accustomed to Malcolm antics. He wasn't accustomed to having them used on *him*. How the devil had she made the portrait fall?

Christina shrugged. "The general is a bit of a poltergeist, I believe. He's well beyond my control. I suspect he thinks it would be more sensible to ask Mr. Chumley why he's spreading lies than to beat him into a pulp."

The murmur among his guests was growing into a low roar that Harry could hear over the clamor in his head. He'd poured his lifetime's savings and Christina's dowry into this blasted estate, spent his children's future, was in debt beyond his ability to comprehend, and now he must listen to his reputation being unfairly maligned because *ghosts* wished to hear the lies?

"I've always wanted to own a haunted house, Your Grace." Carthage's voice rang out. "Why not sell it to me?"

Harry saw Christina whirl toward the merchant. Seeing a glint in her eye that boded ill, Harry hurriedly wrapped his arm around her waist to prevent her from charging forward on her lame leg.

"Not one word, Christina," he warned in a whisper only she could hear. Ignoring Carthage and his taunt, Harry said out loud, to distract their frightened, angry audience, "You've tired yourself, my dear. You shouldn't be submitted to such unpleasant turmoil." He turned to their guests. "If you will excuse us, the duchess needs to rest."

She opened her mouth, then shut it abruptly as she glanced up at him. Good. Apparently the glint in his eye was more frightening than hers.

As he hoped, his guests eagerly made their excuses, their curiosity diverted by his concern for Christina as she limped out under his guidance.

Leading her back to a small sitting room, he caught her when she stumbled. This time, he picked her up and carried her, slamming the door behind them with his boot heel. He deposited her on the settee and stepped back to glare down at her without any idea of what he would say.

"Don't talk to me, Harry," Christina commanded. "If you sell the house to Carthage, I shall never forgive you."

He stalked to the window to gather his thoughts and dilute his anger. Outside, his guests were climbing into carriages and calling for horses. Harry didn't know why the portrait had fallen. Wind currents. Drafts. Settling foundations. Christina's rage. Anything was possible.

For a moment, Carthage's offer to take his supposedly haunted house off his hands had been tempting. He didn't know how Christina had read his mind. She was entirely too observant for his own good. But why should he stay where people he'd known all his life believed he would lose fortunes gambling?

The thought of losing Christina if he went bankrupt was enough to convince him that selling was an option.

As if she guessed his thoughts, Christina left her seat to limp up and down the carpet. Watching her had him longing for an entire decanter of brandy. She was his future, the sunshine he depended on, but she had a way of casting shadows that required all his strength to dispel.

Would the marchioness believe his neighbors and report to Christina's father that he gambled to excess? Lady Hampton could surely see that his home was no place for their daughter.

If he thought selling the land and returning to solvency would keep the marquess from hauling his daughter home, he was ready to seriously consider it. But Christina was making it plain that if he sold the estate, he would lose her as well. He was caught between a rock and a hard place, and he would end up crushed no matter what choice he made.

"If you should so much as say a word to that dreadful man about selling your home, I shall never speak with you again," Christina announced.

"Fine, then. I won't talk to you," he retorted. "Maybe we both talk too much and act too little anyway. I'm off to beat some sense into Chumley." Swinging on his heel, he stalked out, wincing as something breakable smashed against the wall after him.

Musing on how men preferred smashing faces and women preferred vases, Harry went after Basil. His former friend had taunted him for a reason. He had to know more than he was imparting. Unlike Christina with her subtle antics, Harry preferred direct confrontation.

"Running, Basil?" he called loudly as the Chumleys prepared to mount their horses.

Basil removed his boot from the stirrup and turned. He had a split lip that had stopped bleeding but had swollen to generous proportions. That didn't stop his insults. "Do you hide your bride out here so she can't turn you into the laughingstock of London, Harry? Afraid to lose our wager?"

Harry took a deep breath to quell his flaring temper. "Give over, Chumley," he said. "I've held the title for little more than a month. I'd have to finance an army to cheat anyone as quickly as you claim. If you think that by insulting my wife you'll save your coin collection, I'll forget our wager, but quit throwing charges with no substance."

"Without substance?" Basil asked incredulously. "Did you think I idled away my brief time in London? I wouldn't believe the rumors without proof, so I set out to verify them. Just as you accepted my wager, you've accepted others. Your name is on all the betting books and known in every gambling house in town. Does your wife know you've spent her entire dowry already?"

Harry didn't have to explain to the likes of a troublemaker such as Basil, but he wouldn't have his name slandered in front of people he respected. He turned to the squire and vicar. "Yes, over the years, I have visited every coffeehouse, club, and honest gambling establishment in town. I make wagers and gamble because that is what society does. I have also visited most of the homes of society, attended their balls and soirees, and regularly appeared in Parliament to vote on affairs of state. That was my *duty*—to work with people who can support my bills, wherever I might find them. I have never, at any time, lost any money other than my own. I would like to know who claims I have bankrupted the estate with my work."

The squire looked taken aback by this direct command and didn't answer immediately. Basil had no such compunction. "I heard it right here, down at the tavern in the center of your family's holdings, where every word uttered in your ducal palace is carried."

"A man cannot prove himself against gossip except by his actions," Harry countered. "I am willing to sit down with every single tenant and come to a fair assessment of the value of their farms. Together we'll decide upon a fair rent, if they will give me the opportunity."

"Fool others, if you will," Basil shouted, "but by throwing away your money in London instead of paying what you owe here, you've beggared us all." He swung up on his horse and rode off, leaving his father behind.

A friend with no loyalty was no loss, Harry decided, but he regretted the sour taste the confrontation left in everyone's mouths. He would have to figure out how much the estate owed Basil and his father. If Peter was right and Basil hadn't the wherewithal to marry the woman he loved because the estate's debt had impoverished him, Harry could understand his old friend's enmity.

He glanced toward the squire and the vicar, the two most influential men in the village after him.

The vicar stepped forward to pat Harry's shoulder and offer a hand. "I believe you have a good heart, Your Grace. The deaths of your family must be a source of great grief to you. I'm certain everyone will understand and give you time to turn things around. Give my regards to your lovely wife. I hope she will be on her feet again shortly."

After what Harry had just said to Christina, she would more likely be packing her bags and fleeing with her family.

He had to get back to her immediately.

Twenty-two

Surely Harry didn't mean to sell the castle to that nasty Carthage. He wouldn't do that to her. Not the Harry she knew. Or did she know him at all these days? His aura had been exceedingly black when he'd stomped out.

Waving away assistance, Christina limped upstairs to their chamber.

Maybe if she lay down for a while, she'd discover a new solution. She had hoped she could help Harry uncover the root of the estate's dilemma so he wouldn't worry so much about the castle crumbling around them, but she'd only stirred up more trouble for everyone concerned. Harry, *gambling*? Someone had their wits to let if they believed that.

Despite her supernatural help, she wasn't a very useful creature after all. All rural society would probably shun him now that they'd seen the ghosts at work. She'd made things worse instead of better. A *haunted house,* indeed. Harry simply couldn't sell to that dreadful man.

Lying down on their marital bed, she stared at the canopy, blinking back tears. She had so much wanted

Harry's *love*. She didn't want to be just another plague in his life.

My darling beloved . . . Harry had called her that. Had he meant it, or had he just been trying to silence her? He'd very nearly succeeded. If she wasn't so well acquainted with the society they moved in and their insincere endearments, she might have swooned at his feet. Should he ever say such a thing to her and mean it—

Out of the corner of her eye, she caught the flicker of blue that she recognized as Lady Anne. She wanted to close her eyes and make the apparition go away.

The rainbow of blues flitted frantically back and forth between the bed and the wardrobe where Matilda had stored Christina's gowns. Was that fear in the lady's aura? What did a ghost have to fear?

Her knee throbbed, and she didn't want to get up to see what a ghost wanted. She supposed there must be something in the wardrobe. A rat? Let it stay in there. She hadn't the energy to chase it.

The wardrobe. Slowly sitting up, remembering the hidden stairs she had found in the room next door, Christina stared at the massive walnut armoire only a few feet away. Lady Anne wouldn't warn her of rats in an armoire. Were there more stairs? Another room?

Before she could rise, the wardrobe shuddered, creaked, and began to topple—directly toward the bed where Christina lay!

She rolled off the bed, hitting the floor with a bone-jamming thud a moment before the armoire crashed into the bed. She gazed in disbelief as the elaborate cabinet crushed the feather mattress and shattered the bed beneath it. Had she truly been sleeping, had Lady Anne not warned her, she would be flattened right now.

Holding her hand to her chest and gulping air, Christina attempted to calm her nerves. Shaken, she wasn't at all certain she was ready to accept what had just happened. Her family must have all retreated to the nursery not to have heard the crash.

She pulled herself up by a chair. Standing there, swaying with fright, she gathered her strength and pondered what she should do next. The bed was demolished. She could have been under the wardrobe. That was one more incident than she could accept. Taking a deep breath for courage, she limped down the corridor in desperate search of answers.

In the late duchess's bedchamber, she stared at the blank mirror the footmen had returned to the vanity, but the general didn't materialize to answer her horrified questions.

Until she was certain it wasn't her imagination playing tricks with her, she was reluctant to admit to another mishap or state her fears aloud. Harry might send her directly to London and sell the house by nightfall.

Limping to the window, she drew the draperies closed to eliminate sunlight and prayed for the general to appear. She needed sound advice or the castle would be lost, along with all hope of future happiness with Harry.

She lit candles and stared at her reflection in the mirror. She supposed, under the circumstances, that she was fortunate she hadn't been reduced to a ghostly aura herself.

She had so many questions to ask and no one to ask them of. Why did some spirits linger on this earthly plane and others pass on to their just rewards? What did the general want? Father Oswald had apparently clung to his home until the chalice was uncovered. She hadn't seen much of him lately. Would he leave now if he thought the chalice safe, or haunt the place forever if Harry sold the goblet? She thought the shy priest might be far happier if he went wherever spirits were supposed to go.

Why could she see and hear the general and not the others? Was he so mortally bound to the earth that he could not depart? He probably hadn't been a very nice man in his lifetime. Most of the nobility didn't gain land and titles by being noble.

Then there were the less spiritual questions. Why would people think Harry had gambled away the estate's fortunes? Who had stuffed her into the ballroom window seat? Was the castle really falling down or was someone playing tricks to force Harry to sell?

And most terrifying of all: Had the deaths of Harry's father and brother really been accidents?

Caught up in her reverie, she didn't acknowledge Harry's entrance until strong, reassuring—and bruised—hands wrapped around her waist. Gratefully, Christina leaned into her husband's embrace. He had come back to her. He didn't hate her.

"I thought I might find you here when I saw the candlelight," he said, brushing his chin against her hair and clasping her tightly. "I wanted to thank you."

"For what?" she asked in genuine puzzlement. "For making you so angry that you hit a friend? I wanted to make you happy, not blacken your aura worse. I wanted to answer questions, not raise more."

He bent to kiss her cheek. "Chumley isn't a friend if he can't come to me and ask questions openly and believe my answers. But people are talking to me now that the complaint is out in the open, and that will help me get to the bottom of this inexplicable mess. I have ordered my tenants up here on the morrow so I might interview them about the rents."

She sighed at the pleasure of Harry's kiss and warm embrace, knowing they wouldn't last. They were doomed to be at odds, it seemed, no matter how hard she tried to fix things. Harry would always have to do what was right for the earth-bound matters around him, while she had to listen to a spirit world he couldn't comprehend. Not that she was doing very well at interpreting that world either. "I don't think the tenants will help solve the problem," she said.

"You don't think I can talk to farmers?" he asked, sounding insulted. "Or that I'll understand about rents and acres?"

"I think you could talk to kings or kittens if you put your mind to it. I don't doubt your abilities at all. I just don't believe rents are the solution."

He raised a hand higher along her boned bodice, stroking beneath her breasts and pressing kisses to her ear. Christina wanted what he offered, longed for it. Perhaps she should just keep her mouth shut and say nothing. Maybe a bed was the answer for everything. Maybe she should close her eyes to auras and forget she'd ever seen them.

"Your ghosts have better ideas?" Amusement tinted Harry's voice.

And maybe her noble husband needed to learn a lesson or two before they shared a bed again—provided they had a bed to go to. Christina shot him a look of irritation over her shoulder. "The general helped me to ask the right questions today. Don't laugh at him."

"I'm willing to admit that a plummeting painting is an excellent means of emptying a room, and that however you did it, you asked the right questions of the right people."

"I suppose I am fortunate that you do not call me mad," she agreed with a sigh. One of the many reasons she adored Harry, she had to remember.

"No madder than my father," he teased, locating the closure of her gown and unfastening the hooks at the neckline.

His fingers skimmed the upper curves of her breasts, and Christina shivered in anticipation. It had been days since he had brought her such pleasure. She'd not had nearly enough. But she couldn't concentrate on lovemaking when she was still shaking with fear.

"I wonder how many people who see or hear or think things differently are called insane?" she asked quietly.

"It may depend on how they present themselves," he admitted, halting his depredations to watch her reflection, "but I do not want to talk about these things now. We have a house full of guests and I must return to work soon. But tonight—are you well enough to share your bed with me?" He slid his hands from her breasts and tugged her bodice closed.

She lifted her gaze to his in the mirror and almost swallowed her breath at the intensity of Harry's longing she saw reflected there. They had just reached the crux of the matter. "I think we will have to find a new bed, Harry," she said, waiting to see if he would break her heart.

Startled, he stopped refastening her bodice. "Is there something wrong with the old one?"

"The wardrobe fell on it."

"The wardrobe—" Staring at her face in the mirror, understanding at once, Harry left her to dash down the hall to the room they shared.

That evening, Harry stormed up and down the front salon of the new wing, wearing a path in the expensive rug beneath his feet. "Take her home with you!" he demanded of those guests currently occupying the room. "Carry her out of here to somewhere safe."

He had given up trying to keep up with Christina's family. The younger Ives boys had apparently taken residence in the castle with Rob, but they knew when to appear for meals. Aidan came and went at will. The marchioness and Lady Ives dashed back and forth to the nursery to calls he didn't hear. And Christina's quiet cousin disappeared for hours with her chalks and pencils.

The only person he kept in his sight was Christina. She sat in her favorite chair, rubbing her newly unbandaged wrist and not looking at him.

"Christina is welcome to come with any of us, whenever she likes," her cousin Ninian replied in her soft voice.

She didn't bother adding, "We won't kidnap her for you." They'd already made that clear.

"Can't you see she's at risk here?" Harry demanded, staring them down. He wouldn't admit aloud that he feared more than the house was at fault. They'd start fearing for *his* sanity as well. "If a wardrobe can just fall over like that, then no place in the manor is safe! I've rented out the London house or I'd send her there."

"I wouldn't go in any case," Christina reminded him in a perfectly normal voice, without a hint of anger or stubbornness or irrationality.

Harry dug his hand into his hair. He'd be bald before this was over. "Then stay in this wing and don't venture elsewhere again," he yelled. "I'll have walls put up in the new ballroom, and we'll carry all the beds over here. You could stay with Meg and Peter until the work is done. I've already told them to pack up and go home."

"I'm not certain that would be very useful, Harry." Looking thoughtful, his wife tugged on a loosened curl.

"Why?" Harry demanded. "You want chandeliers and wardrobes to drop on their heads?"

"She's saying the accidents only happen to her." Sitting in front of the fireplace with her knitting, the marchioness pointed out the obvious. "You have servants and guests running up and down the manor halls night and day. Aidan and your engineer friend have been living in the castle without incident. Lintels, chandeliers, and wardrobes haven't dropped on anyone else."

He was struck dumb by their logic. It was bad enough thinking his house contained a villain. To believe the villain wished to kill his wife . . . "If accidents only happen to Christina, that is all the more reason why you should take her away from here!" he shouted.

"I won't go," Christina repeated, wiggling her foot on the ottoman. "I believe the ghosts are the only way to discover what is happening, and I'm the only one who can see them."

Rendered speechless by her foolish obstinacy, he stalked up and down the room and shouted obscenities inside his head.

"I take back everything I ever thought about Harry's amiability," Ninian said to the room at large.

"He does seem to be growing into his ducal authority, doesn't he?" Lucinda replied, as if there were no further need of explanation.

"I could burn a few candles of peace," Hermione added, spreading out the shapeless shawl she worked on. "A duke in turmoil is dangerous. He might think more clearly if he calms down."

"Billiards, Duke?" Aidan asked wryly from his position against the mantel. "They'll have you spitted, basted, and broiled before you know it unless you escape soon."

"Will you all just leave me alone and start nattering

at Christina?" Harry roared. "I'm fine. If it's Christina the house or the ghosts or whatnot are dropping things on, take her away with you!"

Standing, Aidan crossed his massive arms over his shabby coat and set his feet apart in a belligerent stance. "This argument goes nowhere. Rob has cordoned off the unsafe areas of the castle. I say we hunt ghosts."

For the first time that evening, Christina looked up with eagerness. "Do you think we might?"

"You will not set foot in that ruin!" Halting in front of her chair, Harry imitated Aidan's stance and blocked her escape. "I have the staff setting up a bed in the upstairs card parlor for you so you needn't go near the old manor."

She beamed at him. "Thank you for knowing I would stay, Harry. I've always said you are a very smart man. If you won't let me seek out the general, perhaps you could set your engineer to looking for ways a real person might crumble parapets, overset wardrobes, and drop chandeliers."

Harry set aside his brandy and turned to take the full brunt of the blow her family would deal him after Christina's revelation.

If Harry had any instinct for people at all, he'd say thunderheads had just formed and were rapidly spreading to cover the ceiling. The women had a way of expressing their mood without a word.

He'd been so intent on connecting the accidents to the missing money, he hadn't considered that they weren't accidents and someone meant to harm Christina.

It made more sense than ghosts, but not by much.

If anything, they ought to be out to kill him . . . or his family.

A gaping hole developed in his midsection as logic leaped three steps forward, and he recalled her mention of parapets. "Are you saying that my father's and Edward's deaths may not have been accidental?" he asked, surprised to hear the wrath in his voice.

Christina reached up to touch his arm, and sincerity softened her response. "I cannot say, Harry. I simply don't think a house has the ability to target one particular person as it has targeted me. The general showed me a shadow of a man sitting at a desk. I think that means something."

Carthage! Did the damned merchant want the estate badly enough to kill for it? Appalled at thinking anyone would murder for land, Harry staggered beneath the enormity of the possibility before realizing he'd just accepted Christina's ghostly vision without question. He must be as mad as the rest of her family.

Or so desperate for explanations he didn't care if they made sense.

"Do you think we have enough people for a manhunt, Harry?" Christina asked. "This is a very large place."

"Not tonight, love," Harry said wearily. "It's late and we're likely to lose any evidence and half our party in the dark. I've already organized a search for tomorrow. If anyone is hiding there, we should be able to drive them out."

The room fell ominously silent. Harry glanced around and discovered everyone watching him with various degrees of wariness and anticipation. What the devil did they expect of him? He was a duke, not a magician.

Christina stood up and bit back a wince when she came down the wrong way on her injured leg. Instantly Harry grasped her waist to hold her weight off her knee. She leaned on him as he needed her to do right now. He had to believe he was in charge here despite all evidence to the contrary.

"You must consider that it's someone who lives here, Harry," she said. "It would seem very odd for a stranger to live in hiding."

The impact of that possibility nearly crushed him. Would someone he knew hate him so much that they would take away all that he held dear in the world? What could he have possibly done to justify that?

"I prefer to believe the house is at fault," he said stiffly, leading her across the long floor to the doorway Aidan still blocked. "And that accidents happen." Sadly, he knew better. When accidents began to pile up into unbelievable coincidences, he could no longer delude himself.

"You are certain you don't mind if we take a look around?" Aidan asked, stepping aside to let them pass.

In resignation, Harry shook his head. "No, I would appreciate it if you stayed and searched the Abomination from top to bottom as we planned."

Christina was silent as Harry led her upstairs to the card parlor in the new wing where the staff had efficiently moved their belongings. She smiled at the Elizabethan bed—sans draperies—with which he'd chosen to replace their broken one.

"It is a very grand bed, Harry." She admired the towering mahogany head and footboards and the carved cherubs and apples and fig leaves of the wooden canopy. "However did they move it so quickly?"

"Rob showed them how to dismantle it, and Aidan and the boys carried the heavier bits."

She could tell he was disturbed by her theory and his own conclusions, but beneath his anger and sorrow remained the underlying regard and reliability that she loved in Harry.

She loved him.

Looking at him with eyes opened by wonder, Christina absorbed the impact of discovery. In the light of the candle, his hair gleamed a golden-brown. A lock had fallen loose over the sharp jut of his cheekbone, and his wonderfully honest eyes were hidden in shadow, but Harry's aura glowed with integrity. She knew he would stand by her and protect her until his last dying breath, and that devotion awed and humbled her.

"Don't ever give up on me, Harry," she whispered, wrapping her arms around his neck and standing on her toes to touch her lips to his. "I really do mean to make you the happiest man on earth."

If he was surprised or flattered or grateful, she couldn't tell. She closed her eyes so she might derive the greatest pleasure from the exquisite hunger of his kiss.

His tongue offered promises his words did not, and she believed them, because this was Harry, her chosen.

Beneath his skilled fingers, her gown and petticoat slid to the floor, but she scarcely noticed their absence. She pushed at Harry's coat and vest and untied his cravat to reach the warm flesh and muscle of his chest. The pounding of his heart beneath her fingers fed the rhythm of her own.

"You are the one treasure in my life, Christina," he murmured, unpinning her hair until it fell loosely over her bare shoulders. "I couldn't bear to lose you. Please, let me take care of you."

"I don't think it's possible to watch over me night and day, Harry." She pulled the shirt from his breeches so she could slide her hands up his hard abdomen and chest, testing the flexibility of the muscles there, loving his response to her touch. "I am not a child in need of advice and watchful eyes. Accept that I'm responsible for my own fate, just as your father and brother were. You cannot save the world."

"Let me believe I can save my small corner of the world or I'll go mad." Lifting her, he carried her to the bed, laying her down so he could remove her slippers and stockings and rub his hands up her calves to her garters. "Without Jack here to guide me, I am feeling singularly useless as an estate steward. Let me be your lover and protector."

"My gallant prince," she agreed, reaching to pull him down to her, reveling in his hard body as he half covered her. "For tonight, we are safe in our ivory tower."

"Without ghosts," he added half jestingly as he bent to take her breast in his mouth.

"No ghosts," she promised knowing her friendly

spirits preferred the old manor. "This bower is all ours without a wicked witch in sight."

"Or even a meddling one to hear us." With that, Harry suckled her aching nipple until she screamed with pleasure.

He made her scream several times that night. Since they possessed the only habitable bedchamber in the new wing, there was no one about to hear her cries. She loved having Harry to herself.

Twenty-three

The next morning, forced by her promises to Harry not to leave the safety of her family while he interviewed the tenants and the rest of the company searched the castle, Christina sat on the floor of the nursery with her four-year-old nephew Alan, helping him hide miniature dragons and faeries amid the flowing draperies. She felt frivolous sitting here while the men ransacked the castle looking for someone they would never find without her help.

As if sensing Christina's frustration, Ninian intruded upon her thoughts. "Drogo arrived a little while ago. I believe he is helping Harry go over the ledgers while they talk with his tenants. Perhaps he can find the discrepancies. Drogo is very good with money." Ninian bounced her infant daughter, Margiad, on her knee. "Your duke seems to be quite relentless in his search for the source of the estate problems."

"I'm glad he has Drogo, but that is no reason not to let me help, too. I'm sure the general could tell me who is responsible for the accidents if I could just be allowed to seek him."

"Your general has had any number of opportunities to tell you more and has refrained from doing so. It's very possible he isn't even aware of the danger. He may only see the world through your eyes."

Struck by her cousin's insight, Christina considered that possibility, then shook her head. "No, the general seems to be abrupt and disagreeable, but I think he protects his home. He'll know if there's a danger here."

"Then he should have told you so. It is most ungentlemanly to test you this way." In a swirl of petticoats and a flutter of scarves and shawls, Hermione swept into the room. "I have no patience with uncommunicative men, even dead ones. You really cannot stay here, dear, if there is some danger."

Christina snorted inelegantly but merely pushed Alan's toy duck in his direction. Its flapping wooden beak rattled loudly enough to express her opinion and provoked the boy's laughter.

"Is it not odd that we have all discovered the depths of our abilities while living in the country?" Christina had thought about this ever since she'd first seen the general. She'd never had a ghost attempt to communicate with her in London. Now she even had one who could *speak*.

And they wouldn't let her talk with him.

"I think it may be that the city with all the people about is too distracting," Lucinda said, looking up from her sketching.

"Or you found your focus in your husband," Ninian pointed out. "Grandmother taught me how to use my gifts when I lived in the country, but once I married and moved to London with Drogo, I learned far more of their use because I had a husband and child who needed the very best I could give. Although," she added to be honest, "my gifts tend to be useless in the city where there are too many confusing distractions."

Amazed by these admissions, Christina settled her nephew on her lap to read him a book, but her mind raced along the more important subject.

She was a Malcolm. She had to explore the extent of her gifts and use them as they were meant to be used. To love Harry as he deserved, she would have to disobey him. She would be no wife at all if she didn't do all she could to save Harry's home.

After kissing Alan's fair curls, Christina set him back on the floor. She was no longer a child to be protected. She was a woman now, capable of making her own decisions. It was time to be the wife and helpmeet Harry deserved. She would be careful and not take any risks if they could be prevented, but she intended to find Harry's foe.

Christina was certain General Rothbottom lurked in his castle home, dropping panels and swords on all the Ives and Harry's engineer friend scouring the nooks and crannies for a villain. Undoubtedly, the abandoned castle was the most likely hiding place.

But the shadow the general had shown her wasn't necessarily in the castle. Someone needed to search the old manor with its odd stairs in wardrobes and windows that opened onto nothing.

She had told her family that she had to use the necessary. She'd avoided her maid by darting into an unoccupied bedroom. Now that she had reached the darkened chamber that had belonged to the late duchess, she studied the mirror where she'd seen the general before.

This time, he was waiting for her, lurking in the shadows behind the glass. He must have been quite a dandy in his day, as well as a pirate and a scoundrel. Wearing a felt hat with curling ostrich plumes brushing the rich velvet of his tunic, the general scowled at Christina from the reflective glass.

"If the caperwits you've sent to disturb me would use their noggins for something besides battering rams, they'd realize the villain and the money are together," the general said with undisguised irritation. "You would think my noble descendant would notice his cousins dress more richly than he does."

"You think Harry's cousins stole from him?" she asked incredulously. "I cannot believe that." She hadn't seen thievery in their auras. Or even real guilt. Their auras weren't perfect, but an evil as large as the general hinted at should be more obvious. Perhaps knowing people as well as she did could be beneficial in dealing with capricious spirits if they were inclined to make sweeping generalizations and petty insults— just like real people.

"They are puling milksops like the rest of his family," the general said dismissively. "Blood weakens to water over the generations. If your duke can't figure out what's right in front of his nose, he deserves to lose it all."

The apparition in the mirror began to fade, and Christina panicked. "Don't go yet! What about Harry's father? How did he die?"

But the general was gone. She didn't know whether

he came and went deliberately, or if he had only enough energy to appear for short periods of time.

She turned to catch Lady Anne's aura hovering in a corner, twisting her hands together. "Do you know where the villain hides?" Christina asked.

She thought the lady shook her head, but she disappeared so rapidly that Christina couldn't be certain whether she meant that negatively or if she was just warning her not to find out.

The general had confirmed the house contained a villain. Now she had to use her talent for exploration to find out who and where.

Heart thumping erratically at knowing she was on the track of something beyond her experience, she longed to race off to the castle to search. But she no longer had to work alone. She had Harry to help her. Even if he didn't believe in ghosts, he believed in *her*. She cherished the knowledge that a man as smart and worldly as her husband believed in someone whom all society thought a loose screw.

She discovered Harry in his father's study with Ninian's husband—Drogo, the Earl of Ives. The tall, black-haired earl was an imposing man of many accomplishments, but even he wore an expression of puzzlement as they pored over musty accounting ledgers. A tenant waited in front of the desk, worrying at the felt brim of his hat.

She hated to disturb them, but this matter was too urgent to wait. "Harry, I must speak with you. It's quite important."

He looked a little distracted when he glanced up, but the warmth of his smile reflected the intimacies they had shared the previous night. Her heart found reassurance in that smile. They were too much man and wife for him to ignore her plea.

"Could it not wait a moment?" he suggested. "We've just discovered an important discrepancy, and I'd like to track it down before I lose my train of thought."

But the general's warning could not wait. She hesitated, and Drogo politely removed himself from the desk so she might lean over to whisper in Harry's ear. "General Rothbottom says Meg and Peter dress too richly. He says blood weakens to water over the generations, and that the money and the villain are together. What can he possibly mean?"

Looking tired but very dignified behind his broad desk with its ducal seal, Harry shook his head. "I cannot begin to imagine what he means. Peter is searching the castle with the others, but I believe Meg is in the kitchen overseeing the menu for our guests. Why don't you speak with her? I'm just beginning to grasp the rent problem, and I have men waiting on me."

This wasn't at all as she'd planned it. The general's information was *important*. Desperately, Christina tried again. "The general is *right*. Meg even makes me look a positive frump. *They* are not bankrupt. What can that possibly mean?" she murmured as quietly as she could.

"That they wisely invested our grandfather's funds?" Harry asked. "That Jack is a better provider than my father? Please, Christina, we can discuss this later. It's not proper to air the family linen in public."

With his hair neatly clubbed, his jabot white and

starched, and a noble expression of disapproval written across his jaw, Harry portrayed the image of the stern duke he must be to rule an estate as large as this one. Even his aura bristled with responsibility. His firmness would have deterred people far stronger than she.

Diverted by his mention of Meg and Peter's father, Christina refused to bow before his authority. "Do you know when your steward will return?"

Harry tapped his quill against the ledger. "I've sent for Jack, but he's in the wilds of Scotland and my message may not reach him for days yet. It could be another week before he can travel the length of England to return. If the general is concerned about my cousins' clothing allowance, we can ask about it when Jack comes home."

Angry at Harry's dismissal, hurt that he was more concerned with what these men thought than the warning she had brought him, Christina plastered a smile across her face and performed her best curtsy. "Of course, dear. How foolish of me to interrupt. Excuse me, gentlemen, I must go stir some soup."

She dashed out, leaving Harry to face the curious stares of his guests. He shifted uncomfortably in his chair, fighting back his need to race after his wayward wife. Stir some soup! Christina had never stirred a soup in her life. She had just flung a challenge at him, and now that he was finally getting to the root of his problems, he wasn't in a position to pick it up.

"Now, gentlemen, where were we?" he asked. "I'm showing that Jack has recorded receiving the rents for the Bryant farm last October in the amount of fifteen pounds, three shillings, the same as was paid every year for the last ten, if I do not mistake. I cannot locate any further payment or sign of an increase in last year's books. Do you say my father raised the payment and did not record it?"

"I paid that sum in October to Mr. Winchester and placed the same amount on that very desk for the duke in March," Bryant declared angrily. "Just as I have for these five years past. I've been taking odd jobs to make that double payment. It's hard to pay rent before the spring planting."

Uneasiness stirred in Harry's midsection, but he couldn't let the others see it. Instead, he jotted a note on a paper he kept at hand as if he merely recorded an error. Bryant wasn't the first man this morning to claim he'd paid twice the rent showing in the books.

He knew his father hadn't been quite sane. But his father had never been a cheat.

And as far as Harry was aware, his brother had been not only sane but too blunt to be anything except honest. Still, if Edward had discovered their father was collecting cash payments that their steward didn't know about, might he keep the cash? That was a good possibility. Edward wouldn't know how to hide cash in the books, and he wasn't likely to argue with their father's actions, but he would do what he could to repay their debts. But then why was the estate still in debt, especially since the income had doubled?

"Did my father by any chance give you a receipt?" Harry asked in desperation.

"He gave all of us receipts, written in his own hand. If we bring them to you, will you believe us?" the farmer demanded.

"I will have to." Could his father have handed out receipts without actually having received the cash and the tenants were taking advantage of Harry's ignorance? Or his father's insanity? He despised that thought. "If you have written receipts, I will record them in the books as payment in advance for the next years'."

Which would mean he would have no rent income this fall, when Carthage expected the balance of his debt. The harvest wouldn't touch a sum that size. A chill shivered down Harry's spine.

He watched in despair as Drogo led the tenant out of the study, leaving Harry to return to his books alone.

He had a vague recollection of his father sitting behind this desk, collecting the tenant rent, talking of crops and families, and depositing the receipts in a cash box for Jack to record later. It was a comfortable memory, not one fraught with deceit.

Perhaps he'd better have a word with his cousins after all. Could his father have been passing the cash box on to Meg or Peter, and they failed to tell Jack about it? Aside from his brother's possible involvement, that was the only other reason Harry could see that the money hadn't been recorded. The books proved Jack was meticulous in his record keeping.

But record keepers had been known to keep more than one set of records . . .

Jack? No! Harry shook his head. It made no sense.

Jack was loyal. He'd kept the income-producing part of the estate running efficiently. He'd come to Harry with the financial problem as soon as he could legally do so.

Perhaps Peter had thought the money was part of their allowance. That might make sense.

Now that Christina had planted the maggot of his cousins' income in his mind, he couldn't let it go. Peter was probably in line to the dukedom, though their relationship was a distant one. Could there be some resentment there?

And what could that have to do with Christina's accidents?

He looked up at a knock on his door. Rob stood there holding what appeared to be the written report on his findings about the castle.

Behind him stood Basil Chumley accompanied by London's biggest gossip, Freddie, Viscount Sinclair. Harry had a feeling Basil had come to throw the gauntlet down on their wager before witnesses.

"Meg, can we send for Peter? I would really like to speak with both of you together." Nervously, Christina paced the archive room where she'd led Harry's cousin so they might speak in privacy. Aware that she had casually relegated the running of the household to the petite woman who was watching her with curiosity, she didn't know how to regain the role of duchess.

"Peter's off in the castle with everyone else. I can send a maid."

That could take hours since the maids had been

ordered not to set foot in the castle and would have to wait for a footman to come out. Christina would prefer to act quickly before anyone else was hurt.

"Perhaps you know the answer without my sending for Peter," she suggested.

Meg looked interested. "If it's about the estate, I'm the one who is here most often. Peter has always felt unneeded and spends much of his time in Brighton."

Christina didn't wish to pursue that avenue at the moment, but she didn't know how to ask the right questions. Lady Anne and Father Oswald had deserted her. The general wasn't here, and neither was his mirror. She stopped pacing to open a journal on the desk. Brushing her fingers across the neat penmanship, she forced her thoughts to focus on what was important.

Watching Meg's aura for signs of guilt, she formed her words carefully. "Harry might lose Sommersville if he cannot figure out where his father's money has gone. Carthage will tear down the house to build homes for rich merchants. That will mean turning off all the tenants and their families who have lived here for generations."

Meg frowned. "At one time, I heard Edward discuss selling off the land. He said it would provide income for everyone and better housing. He said Mr. Carthage had grand plans for a new village designed by some famous architect. It sounded quite lovely," she said with a trace of wistfulness.

Christina had heard about other rich men who'd moved villages and created pretty new towns, but she knew nothing about architects and estates. Perhaps if she meant to be Harry's duchess, she should try to learn more.

She resisted telling Meg that selling the land to a man like Carthage would not guarantee fairy-tale endings. Instead, she concentrated on the interesting colors in Meg's aura when she spoke of Edward. Rather than letting her thoughts flit about like one of the ghosts, she needed to focus on what was being said. "I know little about Harry's brother. I don't think I ever met him. He must have been a very patient man to endure his father's eccentricities and keep the estate running so well."

Meg beamed as if she herself had been heaped with praise. "He was a *wonderful* man." Her lower lip quivered as she continued. "I miss him so. He carried such a heavy burden, and he never complained."

That stirred some of the darker colors Christina had noted in Meg's aura. Harry's cousin genuinely mourned Edward. "Was he resentful that Harry could go off to London while he had to stay here to watch over their father?" Christina asked.

Meg considered the question, then shook her coiffed curls. "Edward was much like me. He didn't care for the city. He liked his hounds and horses, and rural company suited him. I don't think he worried too much about his father's eccentricities. The way he talked, I thought there was always sufficient income to cover the duke's building plans."

Christina blinked in surprise. "Edward didn't know they were bankrupt?"

Meg looked shocked. "If he did, he didn't mention it to me. I knew the village had fared badly these past few years, so I always tried to purchase what I needed locally to help out, but I hadn't realized the estate was the cause."

Harry's cousin seemed genuinely puzzled. And maybe just a little bit thickheaded. That wasn't a nice thing to think of a lady who managed a household this large with efficiency. That observation opened Christina's eyes.

"You know a great deal more about running a duke's household than I do. Why did the late duke not let you tend to affairs here? It's almost as if you've been trained to handle them."

Meg burst into tears.

Christina's first thought was to flee to her mother for help. She didn't know how to handle the tears of near strangers.

But she couldn't abandon poor Meg. Awkwardly, she hugged her new friend and let her weep on her shoulder until Meg had control of her sobs. Then she offered her lace-edged handkerchief to dry Meg's tears. "I'm sorry. I didn't mean to hurt your feelings. I don't know where I'd be without your help."

Meg shook her head and blew her nose. "It's all right." Her voice was muffled by the linen. She wiped her eyes with the back of her hand. "My mother trained me to be a duchess. I know we have no title or wealth, but living close to the big house, we couldn't resist dreaming."

Of course. Had Christina not been so self-involved, she would have seen that at once. "You and your mother ran the household after the duchess died, didn't you? And you and Edward . . ."

Meg nodded into the handkerchief. "We always thought we would marry. But the duke wouldn't allow it. He and Edward had words, and Edward told me he owned nothing of his own, so he couldn't afford to disobey his father, that we would have to wait until he brought his father around. And now it's too late! I should have made him happy while he lived," she wailed, falling into another fit of uncontrollable weeping.

Or if Edward knew of their financial plight, he may have thought it his duty to marry wealth, Christina thought with a touch of unaccustomed cynicism. Perhaps he hadn't signed the entail because he didn't want his own sons to be bound by the same constraints.

Although there were a dozen more questions she would like to ask, she sympathetically sent Meg to a family parlor to recover herself. After ordering tea and biscuits sent up, Christina chewed her lip and tried to fit together these new puzzle pieces.

She flipped the pages of the household ledger before her, noting the last entries were from years ago, in a feminine script that was most likely Meg's. Had that entry been the day Edward and the duke had words? It was obvious Meg hadn't been allowed to run the household for years, or it would never have deteriorated to the state she and Harry had found it in.

Meg couldn't be responsible for draining the family

coffers. Harry's cousin wasn't clever enough, she hadn't had access in years, and she loved the place.

Peter was seldom here. He didn't have the opportunity either, did he?

Meg and Peter's father had more opportunity to steal than anyone else except the old duke and his son. Did he also have motive?

Harry had said it could be weeks before Jack returned.

The general had said the villain and the money were together. In Scotland? She wished Harry had listened to her.

Perhaps it was time to explore the steward's rooms in the manor portion of the house. It was located in the servants' attics and shouldn't be as dangerous as the castle.

First, though, she would tell Harry what she had learned. Perhaps he wouldn't be too busy to listen now.

Twenty-four

"Harry! I am so glad I found you." Christina raced down the corridor from the kitchen stairs to the foyer, looking like a pink confection in her taffeta skirt and ruffled petticoat. "I have just been speaking with Meg and did you know—"

"Christina," Harry said in a warning tone. "You've met Basil Chumley and his friend, Freddie, Viscount Sinclair?"

His wife's blond prettiness did not lend itself well to black looks, but Harry read her disapproval easily enough. To his relief, instead of arguing, Christina offered her hand to the viscount in an almost regal gesture that impressed Harry, if not his foolish guests.

"So good to see you again, Freddie. Basil." She nodded loftily. "I trust you have brought all the latest tattle from London?"

That was a barbed dart. That Freddie had come all the way to Sussex meant he'd heard something so ripe that he couldn't resist, even if he must endure rustic discomforts to do so. And Basil could be the only source of the gossip.

"Freddie will be staying elsewhere since our accommodations are so sparse," Harry murmured.

He admired the way the morning sunshine poured through the skylights onto Christina's golden hair. Her translucent features glowed as if a candle flame burned behind them. He liked to imagine her eyes lit more warmly when she gazed upon him. He could tell she had something important to say, but he preferred hearing it in the privacy of their chamber, where he could soften any blows with kisses.

He knew their guests were hoping to hear outrageous nonsense from his duchess. Harry was amazed her family hadn't come down to entertain them with their eccentricities.

"Could we not find room for your friend in the castle?" Christina asked with a purr and a provocative flutter of eyelashes.

Harry bit back a grin at her deviousness. She was telling him she didn't mind if the old towers dropped stones on Freddie. He longed to make her laugh and her eyes dance with approval. His marriage would be a delightful one if he could always give Christina what she wanted.

But he'd encouraged her when he hadn't understood the danger of her fantasies. He could no longer hide behind the veil of ignorance. Their future relied on his making the right decision about the castle and the chalice, whether she approved or not.

"Rob was just here," he told her. "He doesn't recommend housing guests in the castle until repairs are made. He has given me an estimate of the costs of saving that section." Harry did his best to hide his bitterness. Had he any funds at all, he might have saved the relic. But he couldn't risk lives. Even if they uncovered the villain, the castle was in a poor state of repair. It had to come down before it fell on someone. Or he had to sell it.

Perceptive as she was, Christina instantly understood what he hadn't said, and her eyes flashed with fury, even as she pleaded with him. "Don't tear it down, Harry!" she whispered.

It tore at Harry's heart to deny her anything, but the image of Christina lying crumpled underneath the weight of an iron chandelier steeled his courage. "Let us discuss it later," he suggested.

He knew their guests watched them avidly. Rather than provide their entertainment, Harry caught Christina's elbow and led her in the direction of the kitchen from whence she'd come. "Tell Meg we'll have another two guests for dinner, would you, please?"

"Tell her yourself, Harry." She jerked her arm free of his hold. "If you cannot believe in me, then you do not need me to help you. I will not stay where I am neither wanted nor needed."

She stalked up the stairs, head high, billowing skirts swaying. Harry watched her go, struggling to keep from following her. The pink taffeta confection flounced around the corner and was gone from his sight.

It hadn't escaped his notice that she'd worn her finest day gown—for him. He knew that because he knew her so well, just as he knew her mind would always wander down whimsical paths. She'd worn the gown because of what they had done last night. Because in Christina's romantic mind, lovemaking meant love.

And maybe it did, Harry admitted. Maybe this desperate desire to chase after her and make her look at him with adoration was love. Certainly her vow to leave him was crushing his heart. If he could protect her only by sending her home to her parents, he may as well let her go now, before her father claimed her. It was simpler this way. She was young. She'd recover.

He might not.

He wanted to shout after her that he desperately wanted and needed her, but dukes didn't make fools of themselves before all the world. He'd always been the unflappable courtier, the cool diplomat who laughed off the fears of others. Now he had to be the duke to whom others looked for authority.

He clung to that image when all else around him crumbled. If Christina left him, his pride might be all he had left.

"You're in danger of losing your wager to Chumley, old boy," Freddie called out behind him. "Your duchess is undoubtedly beautiful, but wisdom may be beyond her reach."

Torn in two by his need to run after Christina and his need to maintain his dignity, Harry swung around to confront his guests. "I'll thank you to keep civil tongues in your heads and treat my wife with the respect she deserves."

He winced at the sound of crashing glass and Christina's shriek of fury from above.

He had to believe she wouldn't leave him just yet. He'd give orders to not let any of the horses out of the stable until he could talk with her.

*   *   *

"Harry cannot love you the way he ought if he can even *think* of selling his home," Lucinda declared from the corner of the upstairs family parlor where they had congregated so as not to disturb the naps of the nursery inhabitants.

"We will take you back with us. That will teach him a lesson." With her toe, the marchioness delicately shoved aside the broken brandy snifter Christina had tossed across the room when she'd first entered.

"Harry loves me." Christina said, but she had no real assurance of any such thing. She might *believe* Harry loved her, but he'd never said as much. "I simply must prove to him that I am right and he is wrong in this."

"Christina, dear, you mustn't do something that will bring you to harm." Hermione hid her alarm well, but she edged closer to the door to prevent any precipitous exit. "If there really is a villain lurking in the shadows, there is no sense in tempting him. Wait until the men have chased him away."

"The villain has had every opportunity to leave already," Christina argued. "If he has not, then there is a reason, and I must find it. I need one of you to speak with Meg. I cannot keep her calm as you might. She has more to tell. I know she does."

"Let's call her up here, shall we?" Ninian said calmly. "She seems glad of our company. We'll try some chamomile tea. It's efficacious for nerves."

"Thank you," Christina said gratefully. "I'll send Matilda to find her. And Harry's manservant, Luke, can fetch Peter. He must have *some* knowledge of what has happened here these last few years."

Before her family could gauge the danger of letting her leave the room, Christina escaped.

She was close to tears, but she would rather act than give in.

After sending Matilda and Luke to run her errands, Christina set off in the direction of the weapon-filled library. She wanted a sword she could carry when she went in search of their resident villain.

"The women are holding a conclave upstairs, and I've been summoned." Peter grabbed the brandy decanter and poured a swallow into a glass, throwing it back quickly as if he had just announced his death sentence.

Harry lifted a disapproving eyebrow but privately admitted his cousin had a right to be wary of an assembly of Malcolms. He didn't think he wanted to be present, not after Christina had stormed off to unburden her grievances to them.

"They'll probably only fling you into their cauldron with an eye of newt to see if they can make something useful of you," Basil Chumley drawled from his lounging position beside the fire.

Harry's comrades had moved into the billiard room where they could make themselves comfortable. For the first time since he'd arrived in Sommersville, he didn't miss his London library and coin collection and his club of city acquaintances. That life seemed empty in the face of what he could accomplish if he could turn the estate around. He needed to get rid of his guests and return to work, but that would be rude as well as undiplomatic. While he had the man here, he needed to uncover Basil's motives for telling all the world that he had ruined the estate by gambling.

"I wish the ladies well of their effort," Harry said in his best nonchalant manner. "No one else has ever succeeded in making anything useful of Peter."

"What would you have me do?" Peter protested. "Court a countess? It's not as if I have any land or home to offer."

"You've a pretty sister you neglect by leaving her to languish in rural society," Aidan said, entering the room with the unexpectedness of an invading army, accompanied by a cadre of Ives, all of them except Drogo covered in dirt from their explorations of the castle. The earl remained immaculate but frowning as he studied the room's inhabitants.

Behind them a maid appeared with a tray of coffee and pastries. The search party had apparently decided not to continue on empty stomachs. With a bouncing curtsy, the maid departed, leaving them to serve themselves.

Amazed at the new efficiency of his household, Harry didn't mind the arrival of Christina's relations. They were men of ideas and action. Perhaps in his diplomatic days he had cultivated the wrong sorts of friends, although admittedly, except for Drogo, the Ives men weren't much at politics.

"Marry Meg off, then," Harry offered, pouring a cup of coffee. Remembering Christina's warning, he probed a little. "I imagine Grandfather left her a comfortable dowry."

"We live on your generosity, Harry," Peter corrected. "The little bit we inherited was wasted on Meg's one season in society."

Having just poured coffee from the urn on the tray, Harry halted in surprise, his cup in midair, at this new piece of information. "I have looked. There's no entry in the books for your—"

The ornate coffee urn levitated before his nose, interrupting his objection.

All conversation froze. Instead of tipping over, the pot drifted closer to Harry.

Drogo stepped forward, his brow wrinkled in puzzlement as he studied the floating urn. "There must be a string—"

The spout of the large urn turned in the earl's direction. Instead of halting his approach, Drogo reached for a poker to swat it.

Before anyone else could react, the pot sped across the room as if flung in a ghostly fit and smashed against the stuffed head of a stag that Harry had always thought particularly ugly.

The stag head tilted, then slid down the wall with an echoing thud. Chumley jumped from the chair next to it.

Coffee spewed against the paneling, splashed the billiard felt, and dribbled to the floor. A steady *drip-drip* fell into the conversational silence.

"I say, Harry," Freddie finally said, nudging the fallen stag head with the toe of his boot. "That's quite a spectacular trick. How is it done?"

The last time Harry had seen it done, Christina had been in the room, and the display hadn't been quite as—angry. What had she called the general? A poltergeist? A ghost that wreaks havoc.

Two of the younger Ives brothers picked up the urn to examine it.

Harry's gut experienced a painful grip as he accepted the realization that they wouldn't find any strings attached, that there was no possible *physical* explanation for what they had all seen.

His house was haunted.

He'd dismissed Christina's imagination as fanciful. If she believed she spoke with spirits, he had no problem with that at all. If she wanted to impress people with plummeting paintings, he considered it an amusing trick. He knew she had inexplicable instincts that had led them to the chalice, and that she understood things beyond his comprehension, but then, many women understood things he didn't.

But Christina wasn't in the room to explain the flying coffee.

"It's all parlor tricks," Chumley declared, dabbing at his coat with his handkerchief. "Harry would do anything to protect his wife and win our bet by making fools of us."

"Right-o," Harry agreed sarcastically. "Whole room is rigged for your entertainment." What else could he say? My wife drives ghosts insane? He really would be the laughingstock of all London.

At his denial, billiard balls began circling the table, slowly at first, then gaining speed and bouncing against the table's edge until they flew off in all directions. Chumley dodged two; Aidan leaped to catch another. The room's other inhabitants ducked and dodged the rest, until only the eight ball remained. Everyone turned to stare as it rose and hovered, quivering dangerously. Without further warning, it flew across the room as if heaved by an invisible hand, smacking Harry right between the eyes.

He staggered, almost folding to his knees until he caught a chair back. He didn't need to be hit on the head with a billiard ball to know something was desperately wrong. Before Harry could utter the cry on his tongue, a statue in the corridor outside toppled and smashed a window.

Christina's poltergeist was on a rampage, and knowing his wife's propensities, there could only be one reason why.

To hell with the dignity of a duke. Shouting *"Chris-tiii-nnnn-a!"* with all the urgency and terror of a trapped man screaming *fire!*, Harry lunged for the door.

As if to confirm his worst fear, Meg rushed into the room. "Harry," she called, "Christina has disappeared."

With every man in the room already staring at him as if he were crazed, Harry held his bruised brow, grabbed a blunderbuss off the wall, and pointed past Meg to the draperies blowing sideways over the gallery windows. "Follow General Rothbottom!"

Twenty-five

H arry ignored the pounding pain beneath the goose egg purpling his brow as he ran down the corridor. There had been far too many other incidents for him to doubt that Christina had run off into danger and her ghostly companion had come to warn him.

Some other time he'd ponder how insane his reaction appeared to others. Right now, terror clutched his lungs so tightly that he feared he would quit breathing before he found Christina.

He should have *known* she wouldn't obey his order. He must have maggots for brains to believe she understood his concern. What the hell had she done? His imagination wasn't large enough to encompass all the possibilities.

Had she gone searching for her mysterious villain?

Of course she had. He would have pounded his head against the wall at his stupidity, but the general had already taken care of that.

A maid stepping out of the dining parlor screamed as an oil painting of a fox hunt fell off the wall and tumbled down the main staircase, galvanizing Harry into running faster. The ghost's angry urgency grabbed him by the throat and wouldn't let loose.

Taking the stairs two at a time, he reached the upper hall and searched for the general's path.

A wall sconce rocked and toppled from its hook in the direction of the family rooms in the old manor. Harry turned down that hall, keeping an eye out for any movement.

Ahead of him, the general was apparently running out of steam. A heavy statue rocked in its niche but didn't topple. Still, the motion told Harry which way to turn when he reached the maze of corridors in the manor. He began praying the general had enough tenacity to get him to Christina.

Behind him, he could hear the heavy footsteps of a herd of Ives. He was glad someone had understood his orders, but if there truly was a villain in the house and he had Christina, it wouldn't be safe for her if they all came upon the scoundrel at once.

Harry halted, swung around, and held up his hand. Big broad men carrying weapons they'd snatched from their surroundings skidded to a stop on the hall carpet. Aidan apparently thought his fists were sufficient. Drogo carried a heavy, nail-studded Bible. Behind them, the younger brothers wielded lamps and pokers.

Peter followed uncertainly, his hands empty, his gaze questioning.

Basil and Freddie were nowhere to be seen. If he were really lucky, they'd be rolling on the floor in laughter at their practical joke.

If only this were a practical joke. But Harry knew better.

Down the corridor behind him, a door crashed impatiently. This definitely wasn't a joke.

"Block every exit," he commanded his small army. "If someone means harm to Christina, we cannot let him take her out of here."

None of them questioned his sanity, or even how he had come to the conclusion that Christina was in danger. Good thing, because he couldn't have answered them if they had.

As eldest, the Earl of Ives and Wystan turned to interpret Harry's commands to his family, ordering each of them to a specific door. One by one, they took off running to their assignments. To Harry's relief, Peter was sent down to look after his sister. Harry didn't know if he should trust his cousins, given Christina's questions.

Only Drogo remained behind, probably due to a flurry of feminine voices drifting down the corridor behind Harry. His stomach lurched in hope, and he swung around to search the trio of Malcolm women forming in the hall. Christina's tall form did not appear among them.

Another statue crashed farther into the interior.

Harry saw the fear in the ladies' eyes. They knew what was amiss. "When did you see Christina last?" he demanded of them.

"A half hour or so ago," Ninian replied. "She went to send servants for Meg and Peter. Meg arrived. Peter didn't."

"Peter came to us first," Harry said. "We just sent him back to Meg." Harry wanted to race after the path of destruction, but he needed as thorough a grasp of the situation as possible. "Did Christina say anything before she left?"

"Not a thing she hasn't already told you." Lucinda held her aunt's shoulder, preventing Hermione from dashing down the hallway in the same direction as Harry wished to go. "Tell us what we must do."

"Arm the servants," he ordered curtly. "Position them in every corridor throughout the house, including the castle. The walls have held this long; they'll hold a while longer. We simply need to prevent anyone from leaving until we find Christina. Then I suggest you go to the nursery and keep watch over the little ones."

Again, no questions, no laughter. The three women consulted among themselves, discussing the most expedient means of carrying out his orders.

Not one of them doubted that he was the best man to give those orders. Harry wished he had their confidence in his abilities, but he didn't have time for doubts. Another door crashed in the direction of the castle.

Refusing to imagine what harm Christina could come to in his home, Harry met Drogo's solemn gaze. "There are three ways into the castle from the interior," he said. "Downstairs, through the old ballroom. Upstairs, through the tower door in the attic. And on the roof." That is, if his father had not boarded up doors or built a dovecote in front of them or a chimney in the stairway. He hadn't spent much time exploring the old manor since his return, and Rob's report only covered the castle.

"I can hear the general taking the stairs up," Harry continued. He didn't add "to the ramparts," where his father and brother had died. Fear clutched his heart at the thought that Christina might be up there. "Someone must guard the bottom of the stairs by the ballroom."

"I know where to find them," Drogo said. "Be careful. A great many people are depending on you." Bowing to the ladies, the lofty earl took long strides toward the wide marble stairs down to the foyer and the corridor that would ultimately lead him to the downstairs door to the castle tower.

"We cannot sense her presence," Christina's mother murmured worriedly. "We had no idea—"

A painting spun impatiently on the wall.

Harry nodded his understanding of the marchioness's concerns, although he really didn't have a clue as to what she meant. He just knew that Christina was silent and the house was not. "I'll find her. I fear for any villain who dares cross her."

Despite their worried frowns, all three women nodded agreement. "I cannot think she can come to harm from ghosts," Ninian offered.

From what Christina had said to him, he didn't think it was a ghost they should fear. Should he have placed a guard on Meg and Peter?

Hurrying down the hall to the attic stairs, Harry found his mind racing with doubts, recriminations, and regrets.

He hated to think his childhood companions could wish to hurt his wife. What could it gain them? Perhaps if they killed *him,* Peter might stand somewhere in line to the succession, but his cousin had never showed much interest in titles or estates.

Still, Peter had sounded a trifle bitter earlier. He

really should have taken more time to talk to the people around him, Harry told himself, but he had been anxious to lay to rest the problem of the estate debts.

Eager to prove his competence, just as Christina had been doing.

He should have listened more carefully, encouraged her instead of putting her off. Why hadn't he learned the first time? Once he'd told her about his debt, she'd produced a solution. Perhaps if he'd confided his worries to her more, they wouldn't be at odds now. She would have come to him—

She had come to him. And he'd turned her away. He'd traded her trust in favor of his dignity. He deserved to have a lintel dropped on *his* head. He fought a shudder of fear.

If he could just find her safe, he'd never dismiss her whimsies again. It wasn't his duty to *protect* her but to *listen* to her—as an equal, not as a child to be coddled.

With the urgent feeling that he'd lost the most valuable treasure in his possession, Harry reached the attic. Taking old corridors he'd once known by heart, he ran past newly refurbished servants' rooms, down empty halls not yet touched by mop or duster. Then, turning toward the castle tower, he hit a blank wall.

He stared in confusion at the wall with a neat niche and a bust of Caesar in it. This wasn't right. He'd lived here all his childhood, and he *knew* the door to the tower should be right here.

Why the devil hadn't he explored this blasted ruin more thoroughly after he'd returned?

Because he couldn't bear to see the evidence of his father's insanity.

The hall had fallen quiet. Not a statue rocked; not a painting spun. The silence was positively eerie. Almost expectant. Had he imagined the havoc? Had he lost his mind and Christina was sitting in their chamber, laughing to herself at his foolishness?

No. Without giving it another thought, Harry gripped the blunderbuss by its barrel and pounded the heavy stock into the plaster blocking his path.

"Harry, have you gone mad, boy?"

So startled that he dropped the weapon, Harry stared as Jack appeared in the doorway to his right. Or Jack's apparition. Short, wiry, and balding—it looked like Jack. He blinked to clear his eyes and be certain he wasn't dreaming. "When did you return?" he demanded.

"Last night," the older man said in puzzlement, looking at the plaster dust on the floor. "I meant to come to you straightaway this morning, but I over-slept."

Jack lived down the lane in the dower house with Meg and Peter, but he also kept rooms in the manor house. Harry remembered Christina mentioning her explorations of the attic and finding the steward's room. He hadn't paid attention, per usual.

He'd better start paying closer attention—if he could just find her.

But he was stymied. Christina couldn't walk through walls any more than he could. The general had led him up here, he was certain of it.

Surely she hadn't gone out on the ramparts . . . The possibility made him dizzy with fear.

"Have you seen Christina?" Harry asked, still staring over Jack's shoulder as if she might be hiding under a bed.

"Have you lost the gel already? That's not like you, lad. What makes you think she's missing?"

Once, he might have believed she could be out playing in the pond, planting fish in the potatoes, or picnicking in the ruins. Christina had a habit of disappearing. But the visceral fear tearing at his guts told him this wasn't one of those times.

Behind Jack, a brass candlestick flung itself against a wardrobe in a resounding crash and splinter of wood.

A wardrobe, like the one with the hidden stairs to the solar. With mad certainty, Harry knew what his father had done. He'd created secret doors and passages where there had been none, so that he could hide from the ghosts or his enemies or his memories. The manor was riddled with places where a man could stay concealed.

With crystal clarity, Harry understood that only one man had stayed hidden these past weeks.

As Jack began to turn to investigate the source of the crash, Harry murmured an apology beneath his breath and smashed his fist into his steward's jaw.

Jack staggered, looked at Harry incredulously, and just as he raised his fists to strike back, Harry plowed his other fist into Jack's soft belly. The older man crumpled with an "oomph," and Harry stepped over him.

"Christina!" he shouted, tearing open the wardrobe door, seeing only Jack's coats hanging there. He ripped at them, flinging the garments to the floor.

Did he imagine it, or did he hear a faint cry? "Christina, if you're in there, I'll find you if I have to tear the place down with my bare hands," he shouted.

A jeweled dagger abruptly flew over his shoulder into the wood of the wardrobe. Hearing Jack still groaning on the floor, Harry knew the steward hadn't thrown it. "Thanks, old man," he shouted at the air, using the knife's point to pry at the back panels of the closet. "If you'll help me find her, I'll take better care of my treasure this time."

Maybe he imagined the puff of cold laughter on his nape. Maybe Christina had taught him that the world was full of mysteries and that he couldn't see beyond the nose on his face unless he opened his mind. He needed centuries of Christina's company to find out. He wanted to spend his life and all eternity learning from her laughter and her keen sight.

Behind him, Jack groaned. Harry dug harder at the paneling, prying at a crack. "Christina! Tell me you're all right!"

"To the left a little, Harry," her voice whispered through the wood. "I can see the knife tip. I think there's a lock. If I had a candle, I could probably spring it."

He almost choked on the relief swelling his throat. "Stand back," he warned. "I'm coming through."

To hell with locks and knives and cracks. Dropping the knife and keeping his balance by gripping the wardrobe sides, Harry rammed his booted foot through the center of the wardrobe's back panel. The wood cracked, crumpled, and gave way.

"That is the most beautiful boot I have ever seen, Harry," Christina said faintly. "May I see it again?"

Laughing until tears stung his eyes, Harry gladly kicked in the entire panel, giving her many opportunities to admire his boot as he unleashed his fury on the prison that held his beautiful, courageous, totally sane wife.

When the last sheet of paneling gave way, releasing a blast of icy air, he stepped through the wardrobe and into the large hole behind it. He tugged his disheveled wife into his arms, sweeping her off her feet so he could hold her tight and never let her go.

"I have never been so glad to hear you laugh at me in all my entire life," she whispered into his coat collar, wrapping her arms around his neck and holding on. "I didn't think you'd ever find me, and I would be dusty bones haunting the house forever."

"Do not *ever* plant that image in my head again," Harry said firmly. "I will have nightmares enough as it is." Carrying her, he stepped back through the wardrobe into the room.

Now that she could see again, Christina lifted her face from his collar to kiss his cheek. A hard object nudged her dangling foot, and she stopped to search for the cause. "What's that beneath your coat, Harry?" She tilted her head to stare quizzically at the jeweled scabbard she remembered from the general's portrait. It now hung beneath Harry's elegant coattails.

"My coat?"

A smatter of clapping from the corridor distracted them. From her secure position in Harry's strong arms, Christina peered over his shoulder.

Aidan and Drogo were hauling a wiry, balding man off the floor by his collar. Behind them, filling the corridor, must have stood half the household and their guests.

Embarrassed, Christina ducked her head back into Harry's collar. All of London would hear of this escapade. She was used to being a laughingstock, but Harry would hate it above everything. "I'm sorry, Harry," she whispered.

"About what? About being the most perceptive, most courageous, most beautiful woman in the world?" Striding toward the doorway, Harry faced their audience boldly. "Haul Jack downstairs. I'll question him later. Ladies, if you would be so kind as to see to my wife's comfort, I'll take her to our chamber."

"Harry, put me down." Christina kicked her feet in an attempt to free herself from his grasp. "I want to hear this, too."

"You'll have ghosts destroying what remains of the house," he protested. "I'd rather see you safe and happy than stir the general to arms again."

"You saw the general?" Pleased as punch, she quit kicking and let him carry her down the stairs. "Are you planning on doing something that will make him angry? If so, I wish to hear it."

"Christina—" he said warningly. Then, wincing at his tone, he abruptly shut up and gently set her on her feet. Surprised, she looked up to meet his eyes.

They blazed with an emotion she'd never seen before, and his aura glowed golden instead of just yellow. Her breath caught, and she prayed she wasn't reading what she wanted to see but what Harry really felt.

Recognizing the interest of all the people crowding the corridor, she resigned herself to waiting for the answer.

Harry offered his arm. "If you think you are well enough to come down to the drawing room, may I escort you?" he asked politely.

He had listened to her! Harry hadn't laughed or scolded or ignored her wishes. He'd *listened* and was treating her as if she were as smart and knowledgeable as he was. It was a miracle.

"My gown is ruined, but I am very well indeed," she informed him in her most courteous tones. "I told you I would fare better in breeches."

He laughed joyously and hugged her. "I shall call my tailor in the morning to design breeches for a duchess."

Ignoring the shock and laughter following his announcement, Harry let her lead the way, oblivious to the dashing sword protruding from beneath his coat.

Twenty-six

"Papa, we did not know you were home!" Arriving in the manor's drawing room after everyone else, Meg rushed into her father's arms. "Oh, whatever happened to your poor face?" She touched his bleeding lip, then looked around for an explanation.

Christina squeezed Harry's arm before setting him free to do his duty. While he strode over to his cousins, she whispered to her family, who immediately set about clearing the room of the audience gathered there. It would serve Harry's scoundrel friends right to get their gossip secondhand.

While everyone else was efficiently ushered out, Hermione remained behind to cluck over Christina, forcing her to take a chair by the fire while a maid ran off to fetch tea and coffee. Drogo stayed as well, whether to lend support to another peer of the realm, as friend and family, or simply as a representative of the law, was impossible to tell from his impassive expression. The Earl of Ives and Wystan was not a demonstrative man.

Harry *was* a demonstrative man, fortunately for Christina, even though he tried hard not to be. She must teach him that even dukes were allowed to laugh, especially her duke.

She admired the sword at Harry's side as he confronted his steward. She took the jeweled scabbard as a sign that the general approved of his heir. Gentlemen generally carried light rapiers these days, but the medieval sword had *presence*. Harry appeared as if he could lop off a head with a single stroke.

"Do you wish to explain to me, Jack, or shall I turn you over to the earl and the court so you may testify in public?" he asked coldly.

Both Meg and Peter stared at him, but Harry remained implacable, crossing his arms and confronting his steward as if he were judge and jury. As he was, Christina supposed. She would simply have to get used to the idea that her husband was a powerful duke, not the laughing courtier of her youth.

It was her duty to lighten some of his burden, but she didn't think he needed her interference just yet. She was learning to think of others before she acted. If she wished to be given the freedom of a duchess, she must accept the responsibility that went with it, as Harry was doing.

"I'm only helping you, lad, as I helped your father afore you," Jack replied mildly to Harry's accusatory tone. "We didn't always see eye to eye, but we worked things out, and the estate prospered. I can teach you the same as I taught him."

"The estate hasn't prospered," Harry pointed out. "We're in debt far beyond our means."

"Well, that's where you're wrong, you see. Might I

have some water? It's been uncomfortable living up there without none knowing."

Meg turned to the tea tray to pour water for her father, and Christina studied the steward's aura. It wasn't healthy at all. Wisps of black curled through layers of brown without a single positive color shining through. They were not necessarily colors of evil, but those of a very confused and discouraged man with tendencies toward negative attitudes. It was the aura of a man who never laughed.

And the aura was wispy, as if it were damaged or not quite complete. Puzzling over that, she almost missed the next part of the discussion.

"Your father wasn't quite right in his brainbox and needed looking after," Jack began. "Your brother was the one I trained to oversee the land, just as he ought, and he did a fine job of it. He would have carried on my teaching proudly, made a good husband for my Meg, raised good boys to keep the place into the next century."

Christina watched as Meg blushed and handed a glass of water to her father. So it wasn't just Meg's idle dream when she'd said she and Edward had talked of marriage.

"If Edward was doing so damned fine a job, why didn't he pay his debts?" Harry had apparently reached the limit of his patience. His question emerged as a low roar.

"Edward didn't know nothing about the books. *I* didn't pay the debts, lad," Jack said, unfazed by the roar. "Couldn't let your father ruin the place, you see.

Only way to stop him was to persuade everyone to cut off his credit. So I entered the expenses, didn't pay them, and moved the money elsewhere."

That almost made sense, except Jack's aura was wavering more than before. "You were saving the money for Edward and Meg, weren't you?" Christina asked.

The old man glanced at her guiltily, then looked away. "The old duke, he didn't look at the books any. What he collected, I didn't write down but tucked in a nest-egg. After the duchess found those old journals describing how the rooms used to look, she wanted him to fix things so they were grand again. When she died, he vowed he'd carry out her wishes, but he went about it strange and the money went fast. Then he started into building hiding places so no one could find him."

"Edward said there at the last, he thought his father believed he was talking to the spirit of your mother," Meg whispered. "I couldn't tell you that, Harry."

The story almost made a certain lopsided sense, except a few vital pieces were still missing, Christina realized. She waited, and Harry pounced on the first of the holes, just as she'd known he would.

"Edward didn't sign the entailment." Harry kept his voice below a roar this time, but he still wasn't happy. He paced up and down between Jack and the exit. Drogo leaned patiently against the doorjamb. Jack couldn't escape past the two of them. "A man who wishes to be duke and loves the land does not mortgage his future to merchants and give up the protection of entailments."

"Edward didn't *understand*," Jack complained. "I

told him not to worry, that I was taking care of things, but he kept looking at the village and the tenant houses and muttering that he couldn't repair them in a thousand years. He even sold the silver to pay off some of the debts. The boy had no head for numbers, and he didn't believe me, when I said we'd be fine. I couldn't tell him about the money, you see."

Jack was becoming more disturbed as he spoke, his story a little less clear. Meg patted his arm and urged him toward a chair. Peter merely stood back and watched, his head pivoting to keep everyone in sight. He was frowning, and Christina could see a shade of doubt rising around him.

"Did you tell Edward not to sign the entailment?" Harry looked confused, as he had every right to be.

"No, of course not," Jack protested. "This would all be Meg's someday. And my son would take my place when the time came. I had it all planned. But the boy kept putting off signing the papers, listening to Carthage's grand ideas, not trusting me to save the place like I told him."

Peter's eyebrows shot up, but his lips tightened, and he said nothing. Christina couldn't see any guilt in him. She turned back to Jack, who was growing increasingly nervous.

Harry rubbed an ugly purple bruise on his brow and frowned. "Just tell me how Carthage ended up with a mortgage on our inheritance."

"I didn't know at the time, but when everyone cut off his credit, your father started borrowing from Carthage. It musta been Carthage what had that mortgage paper drawn up after Edward talked to him about selling. It was all his fault that this happened." Agitated, Jack started to stand, but Peter caught his father's shoulder and held him in place. Jack glanced briefly at his son, then let his gaze wander the room as if trying to remember where he was.

That's when Christina began to understand, and her heart tore in sorrow. Standing, she limped over to Harry and leaned her head against his shoulder. His arm circled her waist and held her close. She sighed in gratification that he could still be aware of her even in the face of these devastating discoveries.

"You found out about the mortgage and had to get rid of the duke before he ruined all your plans, didn't you?" she asked quietly, as if agreeing his decision was the only one that could have been made.

Jack glanced up eagerly, saw her, and looked away again. "The duke was all the time walking up on them parapets, even in storms. Mad as a hatter, talking to your mother as if she were there. It was bound to happen, sooner or later."

"You just arranged for it sooner," she agreed gently. "Did you know Edward hadn't signed the entailment?"

"He signed it! I saw it. I witnessed it, made certain of it myself so there'd be no mistake. But he and the old duke argued that night, and the next morning they were both gone and no one knew where the paper was. I been looking for it. It's bound to be about somewhere." Jack looked hopeful.

Christina remembered the appalling disarray of the rooms when she'd first arrived. She'd thought the chaos a result of neglect. It could just as easily have been a result of Jack's search. Only the duchess's locked and bolted room had remained untouched . . .

Jack began to speak before she could carry that thought further.

"With all these people here, you could have a regular treasure hunt for them papers. That would put a stop to Carthage . . ." The steward's voice meandered off again as his gaze fell on Christina.

Everyone in the room was watching her. Harry's grip on her tightened, but he didn't interfere. She could see the grief in his aura, the dawn of comprehension, and she wanted to comfort him. He hadn't grasped it all yet, as she had. After all, he hadn't been the one Jack had locked in a crumbling tower.

She should never have confronted the old man by herself, but she hadn't known he was there. She'd only meant to search his room, look for clues, look for the door connecting to the castle that should have been at the end of the hall. But he'd stepped out of the wardrobe while she was looking around, and she'd been so startled that she'd allowed him to take the weapon she carried. She'd screamed, but she was too far away for anyone to hear.

For a thin man, Harry's steward was strong. He'd tripped her, caught her arm when she stumbled on her weak leg, and shoved her backward into the gaping hole he'd stepped out of. She'd hit her head falling down the stairs, so it had taken her a little while to realize the full extent of her peril.

He would have left her in that locked tower, the one whose normal entrance the old duke had boarded off because it was unsafe. The wooden stairs had given way every time she'd tried to climb them. Only hearing Harry's voice had supplied the daring to try one more time, to locate the sound treads and put her weight on them.

She might have died. As the duke had—by tumbling from the top of the tower accessed from the closet of Jack's room.

"I take it words were said the night before the duke died that revealed the extent of your duplicity?" she asked without the same gentleness of earlier. "Did the duke learn you weren't banking the rents you had him collect? Or was it Edward who figured it out?"

"Edward looked up to me!" Jack cried. "I was more father to him than the old man ever was. I never meant anything to happen to the boy. He wasn't supposed to be up there. He never went out on those parapets. Only a madman would."

"As you did," Christina continued for him. "You went out on the parapet and loosened the stones, didn't you, knowing the duke was the only man to walk there? It was the only way, actually. If the duke and his son began comparing notes, they'd figure out what you'd done. You couldn't afford to have Edward turn against you. The duke was a bitter, crazy old man and didn't trust you anymore. He was expendable."

"He wouldn't let Edward marry my Meg!" Jack shouted. "She'd ruined her life for his son, and he didn't think she was good enough! Called her stupid and not fit to be a duchess. My Meg! Just because she didn't look like the late duchess, didn't hold her chin up high enough and lord it over people, she wasn't fit? *He* was making a mockery of the name and title, and he thought my *Meg* wasn't fit to be a duchess?"

Meg was crying quietly, Peter holding her shoulders and casting a helpless look to Christina and Harry. They hadn't known of their father's treachery. She was certain of it. She shivered, and Harry hugged her tighter.

"Edward followed his father out on the parapets that morning to apologize for the argument, I imagine," Christina murmured to Harry.

"I want to think they were friends at the end," Harry murmured back. "I want to believe they're happy with my mother now."

"I haven't seen their spirits here," she reminded him. "If they were unhappy, if they had tales they wanted told, I think they would have stayed. Or come back. They're at peace, trusting you to take care of everything."

She thought she felt Harry shake with an unleashed sob and wished they could be alone so she could comfort him properly, but they weren't done yet. He needed to know everything.

Drogo summarized concisely from his place in the shadowed doorway. "In effect, you're saying you stole the estate money, arranged for the parapet to fall and kill the duke, so the heir could marry your daughter?"

"Only Edward died, too," Christina reminded him. "And the entailment agreement couldn't be found. Carthage wanted a huge sum of money or the estate, and Harry was already betrothed to me, with no interest in Meg. Jack and his family would be left with nothing if he returned the estate money he'd stolen."

"Which is why he persuaded me to marry you for your dowry," Harry added. "So I could pay off Carthage, and he could keep the embezzled funds. I knew even my father couldn't spend everything we earned. Where did you hide the money, Jack?"

"It belongs to Meg and Peter," Jack said. "She's supposed to be the duchess, and my son's supposed to take care of things here, just as we have for centuries. Just as they would have once Harry had time to see things as he should."

"So you tried to kill me, too," Christina finished his incomplete statement. "You wanted Meg to be duchess after I was gone, but I wouldn't die."

A ripple of shock traveled the room, but she continued relentlessly. "The lintel?" she asked.

Jack shrugged and stared at the rug. "It were loose anyways. I only hit it with one of them long swords from above and it fell. You didn't need to be wandering about the house while I looked for the entailment. Figured Harry would keep you back."

"And the laughter and the panels falling in the castle?"

"I didn't laugh," he said indignantly, looking up. "I took the lugs off the chandeliers maybe, but you was the one to stomp about where you shouldn't."

She could see the muddle of his aura, understood he was striving for some form of truth, but he'd made excuses for so long, he didn't know right from wrong. "Who stashed me in the window seat?"

Jack looked truly puzzled now. "You stashed yourself, didn't you? You wasn't there when I went down to see if you was dead. I saw the chandelier fall, but it musta missed. Just like the wardrobe. You have the lives of a cat."

Anger and disbelief hissed through the room. Christina didn't need to see anyone's face but Harry's. She turned her gaze to him, saw the realization and rage in his eyes, and clutched his hand tighter. She smiled, letting him see the love she hadn't spoken.

"Jack lost touch with reality," she told him gently. Now that her curiosity was satisfied, she didn't care about the "accidents." Harry's problem with the estate remained paramount. "Your father may have been grief stricken and hiding it behind erratic behavior, but he had sufficient grasp of the truth to suspect Jack's treachery. I think your father deliberately hid the entailment papers. The duke may have feared Edward was working with Jack against him. We may never know for certain what went through his mind that night. But I think he acted rationally. Jack didn't."

"Are you telling us that this sniveling churl tried to kill you," an unexpected but familiar voice said. "But we should forgive him because he's off his nob?"

At this rudeness, Christina glanced toward the doorway where Drogo had stepped aside to let in his obnoxious cousin Aidan. She had known the Dreadful Dougal hadn't shown up here to buy a chalice. He always appeared when there was trouble. She didn't believe in coincidence. He had no reason to be here unless he possessed a gift of sight more dangerous than her aunt Stella's.

The possibility that someone other than a Malcolm possessed their unusual gifts might have shaken her at some other time, but right now she dismissed Aidan to turn her attention entirely on Harry.

"I think the exertion of 'saving' the estate from the old duke," she said, "and the resultant guilt from hiding the money, unbalanced Jack. If he were in his right mind, he couldn't possibly believe that killing me would induce Harry to marry Meg. Jack's aura is pockmarked. He's not a well man."

"Harry," Peter said warningly, "he's our father. He's served the estate all his life. Don't do anything in the heat of the moment."

Broken, his eyes blank as he retreated into his own private world, Jack sat slumped in his chair, clinging to Meg's hand. "She's a witch," he muttered, shaking his head. "I married the poor lad to a witch. She don't stay where she's put. She comes back to life. It ain't right."

Harry clenched his jaw and closed his eyes, shutting out the sight of the man he'd once loved dearly. But he couldn't close his ears.

Jack had almost killed Christina. He'd dropped chandeliers and wardrobes on her. If she hadn't believed in ghosts—if they hadn't looked after her . . . He shuddered at the consequences. Yet if anyone could read his thoughts, they'd call him as insane as Jack.

The fact remained that Jack had killed the duke and Edward—the latter unintentionally, which had probably been the final blow that had driven him over the edge. The web Jack had begun to weave when he'd hid the first coin had tangled and wrapped him in its tentacles as thoroughly as his victims.

Jack had killed a duke and a marquess. He would hang if turned over to the authorities, even if Christina's "accidents" weren't mentioned.

The Bible said to turn the other cheek, and let no man throw stones unless he was without sin. Harry figured he sure the hell wasn't without sin. He held a man's life in his hands, but grief and not revenge racked him. He'd already lost two members of his family. Jack would make a third.

Dukes might be a mere two steps below God, but he didn't want to take on God's tasks today.

Crushing Christina against his chest, knowing her mind without a word being said, Harry opened his eyes to meet the pleading gaze of Meg and the fearful one of Peter. He'd grown up with them. They were all the family he had left.

The enormity of the job of managing the estate without Jack's knowledge might have knocked him to his knees, but now that he knew his father hadn't been completely mad and his brother hadn't attempted to cheat his heirs of their entitlement, he was willing to shoulder the task they'd left unfinished.

"If we can find where your father hid the money, we should be able to pay off the outstanding debts," he told his cousins. "I doubt there will be cash enough to continue paying whatever allowance your father was giving you from the stolen funds, though. Meg, I'll be happy to have you stay on here and help Christina, if you wish, and when I'm able, I'll sponsor another season in London for you. Peter, I'm going to need your expertise. If your father really has trained you, I'll need you to step into his place."

"He wouldn't let me near the books or make any decisions, but I've watched him since I was a lad, and I've learned," Peter said slowly, studying Harry but not yet agreeing. "What will you do with him?"

His cousin's cooperation might very well depend on Harry's next decision, but he had already made up his mind and wouldn't be swayed. "When I was sponsoring legislation for the insane, I visited various institutions around London. I know of one that is costly, but they'll take care of him. You may visit. We just can't ever trust him to leave. If he does, he would have to stand trial. Do you understand that?"

Meg fell to her knees and sobbed, laying her head in her father's lap. Jack stroked her hair and said nothing, as if he hadn't understood a word.

Peter stepped forward and offered his hand. "Thank you, *Your Grace*," he said with pride.

For the first time, Harry felt like a duke.

A giggle bubbled out of the woman he still held against his chest. He cocked his head to look down at his wife, who tilted her head just enough to give him a wide smile.

"You're golden again, Harry. Don't let the dark come back. The general's sword looks very dashing on you. The jewels are the color of your aura."

With a wife like Christina at his side, he would more than survive. She would remind him every day of the joy of living, and be the helpmeet he needed, even if not in quite the usual manner.

With a sigh of acceptance at her seemingly mad words, Harry turned to the mirror over the fireplace. It wasn't the bearded general reflected there but himself, wearing a flamboyant scabbard of colored stones beneath his tailored blue velvet coat. So much for ducal dignity.

He couldn't help it. He laughed with joy.

Twenty-seven

"Is there enough, Harry?" Christina asked anxiously later that evening as her husband returned from searching Jack's chambers.

"He had enough gold hoarded to pay Carthage, and if the receipts Drogo found are any indication, there's more in the Bank of London in Jack's name to pay off everyone else. My father's construction really did eat into the estate's profit, if that's all Jack could save over several years of doubling the rents. And hiding the money instead of investing it cut the income considerably. I think he meant well—at first."

"Do you think Jack's the one who told the tenants that your gambling was the reason your father doubled the rents?"

"He didn't think I would be coming back to find out, so, yes, that makes sense. I haven't been home much since school. People are more likely to believe those they know than a distant stranger. I just wish Basil had thought to write me rather than believing Jack. But then, it never occurred to me to write to him to see how things were."

Dusty from the search for the money, Harry collapsed into a chair by the fire in their makeshift bedchamber and ran his hand over his tangled hair. "Is that a bath waiting for me?" he asked hopefully, seeing the tub behind the dressing screen.

"It is, my lord and master," she said teasingly. "My hero deserves the best of everything. Supper will be ready when you're refreshed."

He grinned. Harry actually grinned. Christina's heart swelled with pride at bringing back her laughing courtier. Other parts of her had decidedly less noble reactions. Her Harry was a handsome man; and his aura danced with lust as well as all the other positive colors she had always associated with him. Overcome with unexpected nervousness, she glanced down at her velvet robe, smoothing the rich gold cloth in place.

"And where are the general and his companions this evening?" Sprawled in the chair, his long legs filling the floor, Harry twisted his neck upward to unfasten his jabot.

It was such a relief to hear Harry speak of her ghosts as if they were as real to him as to her. A man with an open mind was a wonder to behold, and he was all hers. She wanted to dance with delight and take him on a brownie hunt.

"It is hard to say," she admitted. "They don't exist in the world as we know it, I believe. They tend to react to disturbances." She'd thought about it a lot. She still wasn't certain what made her ghostly friends come and go, but she was beginning to see patterns.

"And you make a delightful disturbance," he agreed, hitting upon one of her observations without prompting. Shirt loosened, he pried off his shoes with his toes and let them clatter to the floor.

"I suppose if Felicity's husband were here, he'd talk about magnetic vibrations or electric distortions or some such disturbing the atmosphere. I prefer to think they simply come when I need them."

Christina tried not to watch Harry disrobe with too much interest, but she couldn't help herself. She very much needed him right now. It had been a trying day. Even a good long soak in the tub hadn't rid her of the terror of that crumbling tower and skittering rats and spiders. She tugged the belt of her robe tighter.

"Easier just to say you attract trouble," Harry said with a laugh, apparently unperturbed by the notion of ghosts appearing at her behest. "Will you miss them if things become boring around here?"

She thought he studied her a little apprehensively at this question, and she hastened to lay his doubts to rest. "It is very nice to know that spirits might come to my aid when called upon, sort of like having guardian angels looking after me. Although I think Father Oswald is very attached to the chalice and will not come out much anymore. But I am far more interested in helping you if you will let me, Harry. I think mortal companions suit me better."

He relaxed, lounging in his chair as he regarded her with lascivious interest. "Undoubtedly, it would be in everyone's best interests if I keep you happy and satisfied."

She perked right up at that. "Oh, certainly, that is the best solution. How might we start? By your promising not to tear down the castle?"

Pure laughter rumbled from Harry's very attractive chest, and Christina admired the way his muscles played as he stripped off his shirt. She wanted to stroke the downy hair on that sculpted perfection, but she thought she ought to stay out of his reach for a little while longer. The purple swelling on his head had lessened, but he no doubt needed to soak away the hurts of this day as much as she had.

"Rob Morton has offered his services in stabilizing the castle, until opportunities for paying employment come his way. He thinks it will add to his prestige to have worked for a duke. But we will not be using the castle any time soon," he warned.

"This is very generous of you, Harry. I'm glad you see that the castle wasn't at fault." Gathering up the train of her robe so she did not trip, Christina nodded in understanding and headed for the door. "I must tell Matilda and Luke. Did you realize that they are very much of an age and inclination?"

"Christina!" Harry shouted in alarm. "Where the devil are you going?"

"Not far. I shall be right back, I promise." She said it as earnestly as she knew how so as not to disturb him too greatly.

"Why must you go at all?" he demanded. "Why do Matilda and Luke need to be told?"

"Harry," she sighed in disappointment, "use your imagination. You do not really think I would let you tear down the general's home, do you?"

She was gone before Harry could fasten his breeches. Debating whether or not to race after her, he glanced at the inviting bathwater, decided he'd prefer not to use his newly discovered imagination in this case, and continued to undress.

Easing into the scented water, he closed his eyes and smiled in contentment. Life wasn't perfect. Challenges still lay ahead, but they no longer seemed insurmountable. He could keep the estate.

And he could keep Christina. That alone made life worth living. He could expect arguments and laughter, worry and surprise, but he'd never wanted life to be a smooth road. He liked the adventure of the unknown.

He more than liked Christina. He loved her. He wanted her to love him back. He wanted to keep the admiration sparkling in her eyes and to know her feelings went deeper than admiration. She was such a fey spirit; how could an unimaginative duke hope to claim her heart?

He was still a diplomat, trained in obtaining what he wanted through negotiation. He simply needed to determine what Christina wanted most.

Replaying their conversation, he sought clues to her heart. She had called him her lord and master and offered him a bath. But he didn't want to be her lord and master. He wanted to be her husband. And maybe her hero. He had rather enjoyed the awe in her eyes when she'd called him that.

Remembering how she'd curled up in his arms after he'd rescued her, kissed his cheek, and held him as if he were the conquering knight saving the damsel from distress, he struggled with a sudden surge of lust. If she wanted a romantic hero, he very definitely wanted to be one.

She'd told him to use his imagination. Until Christina had come along, he hadn't believed he'd possessed such a thing. The world as he'd known it had been fairly cut and dried. But Christina had opened his eyes to possibilities he'd been unaware of—stimulating possibilities.

Harry drifted into a half sleep while thinking of brownies and faeries and lovemaking beneath the trees. By the time the water grew cool, he knew what he wanted to do. He wanted to do it so much that he could scarcely climb out of the bath as a result of the stimulation. It might be more helpful if he stayed in the water until it turned icy, but he was too eager to put his plan into action.

Toweling briskly, willing his arousal to go half limp, he pulled on his dressing gown and rapped for his manservant.

Luke arrived looking less than his usual impeccable self and smelling vaguely of a woman's scent. Remembering Christina's hint that Luke and Matilda were of a similar age and intent, he eyed his valet surreptitiously but saw no sign that he'd lost his head. Yet.

Harry gave his instructions and waited for Luke to leave.

Instead, he lingered. "Your Grace, Mr. Chumley and his friend have departed."

"Excellent. They can declare my wits to let before all London, and I need never behave normally again." Harry toweled his hair dry, his thoughts far from his ex-friends. If he thought about them at all, it would be to wish Christina's brothers-in-law had dipped them down a chimney and sent them on their way covered in soot. It must be great fun to be an Ives and not be expected to behave as the rest of the world.

He was beginning to see the advantage of not resting on his dignity.

"Mr. Chumley left a wedding gift in lieu of the wager you won."

Harry peered quizzically from beneath his towel to stare at his poker-faced servant. He appreciated Basil's apology, by way of declaring that he had won the wager, but he was suspicious of his motive. "What's the gift?"

Luke's lips twitched, very much as if he wished to smile. "A coin collection, Your Grace. I'm not certain the duchess will understand."

He probably shouldn't accept it since he had an entire Roman fortress to call home, but it was a handsome apology. He would have to see that the estate's debt to Basil was one of the first paid. "The duchess understands far more than we wish to know, Luke," Harry said. "Just assume she knows everything and don't bother to keep secrets from her. Some ghost or another is bound to tell her anyway." Rather pleased with that observation, Harry waited for Luke to depart. He wanted to be ready for Christina when she returned. "You are dismissed for the evening. I daresay Matilda will enjoy that."

"Yes, Your Grace." With a definite smile in his voice, Luke backed out of the room.

Satisfied that her family and the servants would not carry out the small insurrection they'd planned at her behest to save the castle if Harry had chosen to be unreasonable, Christina turned her steps toward the card room in the new manor that had become their bedchamber.

A footman halted her at the foot of the stairs, handing her a folded message on a silver tray. In a hurry to return to Harry, she almost didn't read it, but the servant stepped in front of her, blocking her path.

With a sigh of impatience, she held up her candle and scanned the carefully inscribed invitation. She smiled when she realized it was from Harry. "Now? He wants me to meet him in the garden at night?"

Whatever on earth could he be up to? Curious, she followed the footman through the halls to the back of the old manor and a passage of doors set with colorful stained glass windows. She supposed the windows had been taken from an old chapel at some time, but she hadn't researched them yet.

She stepped out into the warm air of the walled garden—Warm air?

She glanced around, discovering a stone fireplace ahead, alive with a roaring fire, built into the garden wall. How delightful! She may have noticed it in passing but had never thought to put it to use. Lifting her gold robe, she followed a flagstone path marked by faerie lights—her mother's votive candles, she suspected. Just breathing the delightful air reminded her of what she and Harry had done beneath the rowans, and she shivered with delicious anticipation.

The hearth stepped down to a secluded terrace surrounded by tall yews illuminated by blazing torches. As she passed the evergreens, a flock of doves flew into the moonlight, startling her. She gazed upon their graceful forms flashing silver against the sky, and her heart skipped a merry beat. Harry had said Malcolm weddings belonged outside where doves flew free.

Catching her breath, she stepped out onto the terrace. Buckets of flowering spring branches decorated the outdoor chamber. The subtle fragrances combined with the candles in such a way that she thought she could stand here forever, absorbing the wonder of this fairyland.

That's when a violin began to play.

Surprised beyond all comprehension, she froze where she stood. Ghosts didn't play violins, did they?

"Don't stop now," a familiar warm voice said from a shadowed entrance between the yews. "Supper is waiting."

Harry stepped into their private garden, a casually elegant Harry in evening clothes, with his hair neatly clubbed—the Harry she'd seen in London for years, mostly at a distance except on those rare occasions when he'd condescended to dance with her. Her romantic heart sighed in admiration.

He held out his gloved hand, and in awe, she accepted it, searching his eyes for answers to questions she didn't know how to form.

"You look exquisite this evening, my love," he murmured. "I would always see you with your hair down if I could."

She reached to touch the tangle of tresses that she had loosely pinned up after she'd bathed. The pins had slipped, and strands tumbled all about her throat. "Are you quite all right, Harry?" she asked quizzically. "I'm a mess, as usual."

"You are absolutely perfect, as usual. I believe you once requested courtship. Would you care to dance first, or dine?"

Courtship. She had requested that Harry court her.

She had wanted Harry to believe in her. She had wanted romance and *love*. Was it possible . . . ?

He led her to a cleared area near the supper table. The general's sword at his hip dipped as he bowed formally in the steps of the dance. He looked beyond dashing and elegant, a duke beyond measure.

Christina bit her lip, curtsied in her flowing robe, and pointed her toe in the first steps of the dance the violin played.

Harry twirled her around as if this were the most elegant ballroom in all London and she the finest princess in the land. Firelight played off his hair and heated his gaze. He never looked beyond her but knew her every movement before she made it.

"Harry, why?" she whispered as they clasped arms in an allemande.

"To see if brownies dance?" he teased. "Are there any about?"

"Do you believe in brownies?" she asked, hope rising so rapidly she might drown beneath the flood.

"I believe in you," he said with such sincerity and intensity that she would have stumbled to a halt had Harry not wrapped his powerful arm around her waist.

He would believe in brownies if she did. He knew she talked to ghosts. He *understood*!

He believed in her!

Then he swept her off her feet in a step no dancing master had taught him, and she ended up crushed against his chest, laughing. "Harry! What on earth are you doing?"

"Exploring possibilities, my dear. We would not wish to become a dull old married couple mired in routine, would we?" He bent to place a kiss on her ear, then her cheek.

His breath warmed her skin, and his embrace heated all else. "I wouldn't mind being a dull old married couple if it means there's a bed about, Harry," she murmured provocatively. It wasn't something she might have ever said before, but tonight anything seemed possible.

"Did you think that I would forget that essential detail? You must think me a crass, unimaginative husband." He stepped back and swirled her in time to the music. Her robe flared open, and she came to rest before a corner of the terrace concealed by the bouquets of spring flowers. The daybed they'd first made love on awaited, lit by firelight, surrounded by candles and lilacs in a magical faerie bower all their own. Behind the bed, a tree shaded the bower, blocking all sight of the towering mansion beyond.

"Oh, Harry, it's a rowan! Do you think there might be faeries about?" Captivated, she glanced high into the branches, searching for brownies and elves or any other life-forms amid the leaves.

"I hope they are discreet enough to disappear for the next few hours," he said with pure Harry dryness from behind her.

She swirled about again and flung her arms around his neck. "Harry, you are so . . . so . . ." She was so enthralled words failed her.

"Heroic?" he finished for her, bending to taste her earlobe.

"My hero's name is Harry Winchester, and he's quite the most exciting man I've ever known." She sighed in appreciation when he stepped back to admire her and ran his fingers from her nape down her spine. She could scarcely tear her gaze away from the splendor of his starched linen and the breadth of his shoulders beneath the emerald velvet of his coat.

"I did not wish you to think I lacked imagination," he said, studying her expression in the flickering light.

She could see the hunger in his eyes, and she did not think it was for the food on the table behind them. "For a duke, you show a great deal of creativity," she assured him. "I trust that will serve us well in the years ahead."

"I have a feeling the years ahead will take more than creativity," he concurred, but the twinkle remained in his eye.

Content that she had her very own Harry back, Christina abruptly clambered to a standing position in the center of the daybed. "But it will be worth the effort, don't you think?" She dropped the golden robe to her feet, revealing the gossamer-thin nightdress beneath. The daring neckline enhanced her bosom, and the tight, pointed bodice clung to her curves and fit low below her hips. This was the gown she'd chosen for her wedding night, one designed to resemble an Elizabethan gown she'd admired in an oil painting because it looked so romantic.

Harry must have thought so, too. He halted where he was to appreciate the effect, and she could see the light of approval in his eyes. Her heart pounded a little faster, and her bosom swelled.

"The only aura I see here tonight is yours, Harry, and it's so bright it puts the moon to shame."

At her words, his aura gleamed a glorious gold and purple, and with the prowling grace of a tiger, he climbed up to join her, halting so she could caress the pretty gold silk of his vest.

He placed a finger beneath her chin and lifted her gaze to his. "I have come to win the heart of the fair princess for she has stolen mine. If I promise to be very, very good, will you love me?"

"I have *always* loved you, Harry," she whispered, awestruck at his words and regal presence. He truly was the prince of her dreams. Here, in the privacy of their estate, she could see the real Harry, the loving, caring friend beneath the glitter of glory. In joy, she raised her arms and wrapped them around his neck. "I shall love you into eternity and beyond."

He clasped her close and sighed into her hair. "I never gave a thought to love or romance until you came long. They seemed silly things for bored ladies to simper over. But today . . . when I thought I'd lost you . . ." He shivered and rested his cheek against her head, stroking the curve of her spine with hands that needed to touch and hold. "I knew I'd never be alive again without you. If that is love, Christina, it's a terrifying, overwhelming, awe-inspiring thing. I don't ever want you out of my sight again."

She chuckled against his chest. "Oh, that will change, probably by morning when I've climbed a turret or fallen into the Roman bath in the rowan grove. I'll never make a proper duchess, you know, but I can promise to take someone with me when I go exploring so you need not worry ceaselessly about me. I want to help you, not drive you to madness."

"You help just by being you. I love you," he murmured, pressing kisses behind her ear. "And you're not to look for Roman baths without me." He tugged the sleeve of her gown off her shoulder and kissed her throat.

"That can be arranged," she assured him, thrilling to his words as much as his caresses. "Perhaps we could assign an hour a day just for the two of us to go adventuring. First thing in the morning, perhaps?"

"And noon," he suggested, lifting his head to gaze into her eyes before dipping to capture her mouth. "And suppertime," he murmured before pressing his kiss deeper.

"And now," she agreed, discovering the secret to unfastening a scabbard and divesting him of his weapon. "Can we do this standing up?" she inquired.

"Not without a wall." Laughing, he caught her waist and tumbled her down to billows of feathered batting. "But later we'll experiment. Imagine filling the Roman baths with warm water and us."

"You will have a great many heirs to support if we continue making love beneath rowans," she warned, slipping her arms from the gown so Harry could slide the bodice down.

He lifted his head away from the path his kisses were taking to stare down at her. "I will?"

She smiled enigmatically. "Ninian says the faeries hide our sons beneath the rowans."

"Explain that to me in the morning," he advised. "I have a princess who needs rescuing in my arms right now."

He lowered his mouth to her breast, and Christina cried out with sensual delight.

Epilogue

In the morning, Christina led a search of the late duchess's chamber. The mirror remained empty, the yellow rose had disappeared, but all else was exactly as the last duke had left it, including the hidden drawer in the vanity and the passage through the wardrobe that Jack hadn't discovered.

Nothing and no one could explain the yellow rose. Christina liked to believe that the shade of the old duke had placed it there to lead her to this hiding place.

Inside the drawer was a vellum letter sealed with the Sommersville crest and franked with a ducal signature.

Wrapped inside was the entailment agreement, a letter ceding the care of estate monies and land to Edward, and a note from the late duke:

> *My sons, my heart is with your mother. I have recently recognized how badly I have failed you. Edward will be a far better steward of the title and estate than I. Harry, I hope you will stand in support of his choices as I have not.*
>
> *Should anything happen to me before I rid the*

*estate of the pestilence that has befallen it, know
that I am proud of both of you, and that your
mother and I are happy together again.*

Christina held her noble husband while he wept for
the first time since he'd received word of his family's
deaths.

"Love hurts," she murmured, "but it also heals,
Harry. Perhaps we ought to go to Father Oswald's
chapel and light a candle to your father and your
brother. And then," she added with a hint of mischief,
"we can go to the rowan grove and I'll show you how
my ancestors offered gratitude."

Through his tears, he laughed and hugged her.
"And after we thank the trees, we can thank the
stars?"

"Oh, very good, Harry." She beamed up at him.
"Just think of how many things we can be thankful
for, and how many ways we have to show it."

Elliot couldn't remember traveling with a woman for
pleasure. He'd certainly never driven down a country
road in a pink Cadillac with a sexy pixie bouncing
on the seat, singing "I Am Woman" at the top of
her lungs.

Today, she wore a faded blue halter top and black
hip-hugger jeans revealing a curving waist and flat
belly. She didn't look a day older than sixteen unless
he happened to catch her eyes. Now he knew why
they reminded him of crystal balls—they held age-old
wisdom and a world of woe.

Her offer to sacrifice her trip for his sake had
knocked him flat. How many other people in the
world would have understood his anguish enough to
give up their own pleasure for him?

He longed to make her laugh so she wouldn't regret

her offer, and to erase the pain behind the unblinking crystal of her eyes.

He swerved off the road into a gas station. "We need gas. You didn't tell me that driving Route 66 instead of the toll road would mean we wouldn't have service stations."

"This is a service station. It just hasn't been torn down and replaced with plastic." She leaped out of the car the instant he turned off the ignition. "I'm going to see if they have ice cream bars."

"Try not to incite any riots while you're at it." He might as well have talked to the Caddy. Alys raced off, hair and breasts bouncing, to the admiration of every male in sight.

From the collection of Harleys at the side of the station, Elliot figured there were plenty of males inside enjoying the view. It was ridiculous to worry about a twenty-seven-year-old woman who should know how to take care of herself.

A woman who had never been outside of the state of Missouri and looked as if she were sixteen might not be quite as experienced as she ought to be.

It took forever to fill the huge Caddy tank, and Alys hadn't returned by the time the nozzle clicked off. In keeping with the sixties traditions of the old road, the ancient gas pump didn't have credit card capability. He had to go inside to pay. Route 66 might have been America's Main Street half a century ago, but it looked to him as if the rest of the country had picked up and moved to the suburbs in the decades since.

Idly wondering how many people drove off without

paying, Elliot entered through the fly-specked glass door into smoke-filled air barely stirred by the wooden ceiling fan. The only man in the place seemed to be the attendant leaning on the counter, watching out the side window. Elliot followed the clerk's gaze, and his heart sank.

He could barely discern Alys's sleek hair over the heads of a dozen burly bikers sporting tattoos and heavy leather. He could see the end of a rotten picnic table and figured she was sitting cross-legged on the table top, eating her ice cream bar. The bikers were shouting and jeering, but Elliot couldn't catch more than glimpses of a blue halter and bouncing hair past broad shoulders and beer bellies.

Slapping two twenties on the counter, Elliot loped out the side door. He wanted to curse fool women and innocent pixies and the laws of the universe, but his brain was too paralyzed for words. He wasn't a coward. He knew he had the strength for a good fight if necessary. But a dozen men . . . ? Think, Roth. Tell them their bikes were on fire? Did motorcycles burn?

Heart pounding, Elliot elbowed his way through the crowd, hoping he could just lift Alys off the table and carry her out. The men crowding the table glanced at his face and eased from his path, apparently recognizing murderous rage when they saw it. He'd wager his next royalty check that Alys wouldn't.

A sharp cry sounding like *Aii-e-e-e* followed by a loud crack stood his hair on end. The bikers at the front of the crowd roared in approval. With one last vigorous elbow punch, Elliot shoved to the front—just in time to watch Alys split a board in half with the side of her hand. She offered the two halves to a bearded old guy with a graying ponytail.

Seeing Elliot arrive, she grinned and leaped to the ground. "The ice cream was messy," she explained.

Stunned enough for that almost to make sense, Elliot staggered beneath a pounding blow to his back.

"Don't need to tote hardware with an old lady like her along, right, son?"

Tote hardware? Mental images of tire jacks leaped to mind, but Elliot had his arm firmly around Alys's shoulders now, all but shoving her toward the car, and he didn't care what the hell they were talking about.

"We'll see you later!" one of the bikers behind them yelled.

Alys waved. "Put some lotion on your nose or it's gonna fall off!"

Elliot winced but when no one came after them with that tire jack, he opened the Caddy door and without finesse shoved her inside.

Alys didn't appear fazed. She sang along with the radio, something about rolling down the river and toot, toot. Somehow, that seemed fitting.

"You can break boards?" he finally asked, deciding that was a neutral subject and didn't involve yelling his head off.

"They have a karate class at Mame's school. If I'm going to be a woman alone, I thought self-defense classes were called for. Control of one's life promotes positive energy."

He didn't care. He shouldn't care. It was none of

his business. She was her own person and not his responsibility.

The refrain sounded hollow, even to him. "Karate does not work on men wearing heavy leather," he all but growled. "If you make it a habit to entertain bikers, you'll need a better weapon than karate."

He caught her surprise without even looking.

"Were you *worried* about me?"

"You were surrounded by a dozen men and it didn't even occur to you that it might be dangerous?" Okay, he was shouting. *Chill, Elliot.*

"I have lived the last few years in terror," she announced coolly. "I'm not doing that to myself anymore. *No fear* is my motto these days."

"No brains," he muttered, clutching the wheel. "You won't survive long that way."

"Then I'll have enjoyed what's left of my life," she said, staring ahead out the windshield.

Hobbling on the spare, they found a tire store when they reached Oklahoma City. The clerk took one look at the pink Caddy's enormous whitewalls and cackled. "Those are special order, man. I can have 'em tomorrow, or maybe next day. Ain't seen them beauties in a long, long time."

Looking grim, Elliot jammed his hands in his pockets. "We'll get back to you then. Thanks."

Alys trotted out of the store on his heels. "Is the small tire safe?"

"Yeah, but it's probably tearing up the transmission and brakes and wreaking havoc on the other three tires. Let's just hope Mame comes to her senses before tonight."

Alys was ambivalent about that, but she didn't mention it aloud.

Elliot drove down to the next exit, circled the block, and parked the car near the historic district of the stockyards.

"Writing books is out too, huh?" Picking up on her earlier topic of careers, she climbed out beneath his withering look. "There ought to be some *fun* job I can do."

"Like sing in a rock and roll band? You're showing your age again. C'mon, this way." He led her down the main street of the district.

Passing a western-wear store sporting ten-gallon hats in the window, Alys tried to picture Elliot in cowboy boots and a Stetson and liked the idea so well, she grabbed his elbow and steered him inside. "You have to play the part right. You're not even wearing *jeans*. What kind of cowboy are you?"

"A comfortable one? What am I doing in the old west, anyway?" Entering the enormous old building with its warped pine floors and battered wood counters, he stared around at saddles on the wall, cubbyholes filled with jeans, and an entire corner devoted to felt cowboy hats.

"Just exploring, of course. Hats, first. We can't walk around in the sun without hats." She pounced on a small black hat with delight, balancing it on the back of her head and heading for a mirror.

"It seems to me black would be hot in the sun," he commented, looking in the mirror over her shoulder.

He stood so close, she could feel the heat rolling

off of him in waves. "Black matches my jeans," she said firmly. "You can buy a white one."

"I'm not wearing a cowboy hat," he protested. "I'd look like an idiot."

"Wearing that knit shirt, you would. But try a hat with one of these western shirts." She pulled a red and black number off the rack, complete with ivory snap buttons on the cuffs.

Not satisfied with just a shirt, she waltzed down the crowded aisles, gathering the necessary elements for her latest fantasy, and Elliot cringed. On a slow weekday, the cowboy-hatted clerks were more than happy to assist, and she soon had a wizened old man dancing to her tune. Before Elliot could explain that he was only humoring an idiot, the old man ushered him into the dressing room with jeans and shirts, and when he came out, the clerk was holding up boots for his approval.

"James Garner!" Alys cried, eyeing the cream-colored shirt with a top-stitched yoke that he'd chosen as the least horrifying of the lot. "You need a fancy western vest and you could look like a gambler instead of a cowboy."

"I don't want to look like a gambler *or* a cowboy." But Alys looked at him as if he were James Garner and Clint Eastwood rolled into one, and with resignation, Elliot tried on a pair of brown stitched boots.

They were remarkably comfortable. Standing, testing the heels and toes, wearing the faded jeans she'd chosen, tucking his fingers into the belt loops in imitation of some old cowboy movie he must have seen, he *felt* like a cowboy. He even gave in and let Alys pound a flattish brown Stetson on his head. He hated his curly hair anyway. Might as well cover it up. At least the hat wasn't one of those ten-foot-tall jobs, or one with a turquoise and silver headband like the one she was trying on.

She looked cute with the broad brim shading her light eyes. She tilted it at a rakish angle, and his heart picked up a beat. She still wore her faded blue halter and black jeans, but the black hat with its sparkly headband suited her.

He was disappointed when she hung it back on its hook and turned to smile in approval at him.

"Perfect. Now we can go riding in the canyon tomorrow, and you'll look as if you belong there."

She spun around to investigate a rack of leather belts, leaving him reeling in her wake. Riding in the canyon? Horseback? Tomorrow? He hadn't even planned how to get through today. He had deadlines to meet, work to finish. He hadn't planned on a roller-coaster ride with a lunatic in a pink Cadillac from which there didn't seem to be any getting off.

When she handed him the hand-tooled belt she'd chosen, Elliot refused to put it on. "Does this mean you packed riding clothes?"

She blinked in surprise. "I'm wearing jeans. I have a baseball cap to shade my eyes. And a scarf for my neck!" She beamed as if she'd told him she had silver and gold.

Elliot caught her shoulder before she could spin away again. "The hat you had on looked good. Get that, and I'll agree to wear the rest of this ridiculous gear."

"Do you have any idea how much this stuff costs?" she asked in incredulity. "You don't have to buy any of it. I just wanted to see how you looked in it. Cool, isn't it?"

She darted off, leaving Elliot to stare at the startled clerk who'd overhead. She just wanted to see how he *looked* in it? No way. He wasn't buying that for an instant. Women did not simply look at clothes and walk away. He might be out of touch, but he wasn't comatose.

"I'll take these," he told the clerk, who looked more than relieved. "And add the hat she was looking at."

Elliot caught up with Alys in the bolero tie section. There wasn't any way she was getting him into one of those string nooses, but that wasn't on his mind when he caught her shoulder again.

"Boots," he ordered, steering her toward the shoe department. "If I'm wearing them, you're wearing them."

"My suitcases are already too heavy," she argued, resisting his push.

"Boots." He sat her down in the women's boot department and gestured at the clerk following him around. "Black ones. With some kind of silver things on them to go with the hat."

"They cost hundreds of dollars," she whispered. "I had no idea they cost so much. Let's get out of here before they start toting up all this stuff."

"Clothes cost money. These jeans were cheap. A hundred bucks for a hat is no big deal. When was the last time you looked at prices?"

At her wounded look, it dawned on him. Maybe he

ought to just go bang his head against the plate glass window a few times. *Dumb, Elliot.* Her husband had died after years of illness. She had no job. She'd sold her damned *house.* Mame had been paying her way. He'd been hanging around with the comfortable crowd too long.

"I'll write it off as research," he said with an edge of desperation. "I can probably get a show out of it, and a chapter in the next book."

"Yeah, how to shop your way to fitness in two easy days," she scoffed.

She started to rise, but he stood in front of her chair, blocking her egress as the short clerk tottered over bearing a swaying tower of boot boxes.

"Out of my way, Elliot," she said between clenched teeth. "You forget, I know karate and a few other more useful martial arts."

"It won't kill you to try the boots on." He refused to budge.

"I can break bones in your foot," she warned.

"Not while I'm wearing cowboy boots," he taunted.

Grasping his shirt front, she planted her feet on his booted toes, and he rocked backward—into the clerk with the tower of boxes.

Hats and boxes and boots flew everywhere, bouncing off narrow shelves of more boxes and toppling the stacks.

Wrapping his arm around Alys's waist, Elliot hauled her off her feet, but he couldn't swivel fast enough to catch anything.

Hanging on to Alys, gazing at the chaos they'd created together, he had the amazing urge to laugh out loud, only he figured he'd end up rolling on the floor with some of the loose hats if he really let go. He set her down.

Alys dropped to her knees to scramble after boots and boxes while the clerk insisted it was no problem at all. She was trembling and didn't quite know why.

Elliot had held her as if he'd done it all his life, as if she belonged in his arms, as if they fitted together like two pieces of a puzzle. It had seemed so natural, it had scared her half to death.

Hiding her flushed cheeks, she dug under a chair for a runaway boot. Broad hands captured her waist and hauled her upright.

He was doing it again. She stared up into Elliot's short-lashed dark eyes and caught her breath. His gaze dipped when she filled her lungs, reminding her that she was wearing a halter with nothing under it. The smolder developing in his eyes warned he'd noticed.

"We'll buy them all if you don't sit down and try them on," he growled.

She sat. She wanted to argue. She wanted to wriggle away just to assert her rights. But he'd been cooperative with all her whims until now, and she kind of liked the way he'd just asserted *his* rights.

"Remember, I know karate," she reminded him as Elliot pointed out a pair of boots to the clerk.

"You can break boards. Can you hit a moving target?" He lifted his expressive dark eyebrows.

The boots he'd chosen for her had gorgeous stitching all across the toe, a dainty silver and turquoise chain at the ankle, and heels that would really let her look him in the eye. They fit her feet as if they'd been tailored for her. Sighing with regret, Alys stood. Well, she could almost look him in the eye. Her nose reached his chin.

"Want to find out if I can hit a moving target?" she asked.

In answer, he leaned over and kissed her.